PAPER DREAMS

Phyllis J. Burton

Copyright © 2011 Phyllis J. Burton

The moral right of the author has been asserted.

Apart from any fair dealing for the purposes of research or private study, or criticism or review, as permitted under the Copyright, Designs and Patents Act 1988, this publication may only be reproduced, stored or transmitted, in any form or by any means, with the prior permission in writing of the publishers, or in the case of reprographic reproduction in accordance with the terms of licences issued by the Copyright Licensing Agency. Enquiries concerning reproduction outside those terms should be sent to the publishers.

Matador
9 Priory Business Park,
Wistow Road,
Kibworth Beauchamp
Leicester LE8 0RX, UK
Tel: (+44) 116 279 2299
Fax: (+44) 116 279 2277
Email: books@troubador.co.uk
Web: www.troubador.co.uk/matador

ISBN 978 1848767 898

British Library Cataloguing in Publication Data.
A catalogue record for this book is available from the British Library.

Typeset in 11pt Stempel Garamond by Troubador Publishing Ltd, Leicester, UK

Matador is an imprint of Troubador Publishing Ltd

Printed and bound in the UK by TJ International, Padstow, Cornwall

This book is dedicated to my family, especially my husband Jim, who has given me much love and support during the writing of this novel, and my daughter Julia for her copy-editing expertise.

ACKNOWLEDGEMENTS

I acknowledge with thanks, the assistance of Trevor Burton (no relation) with various legal points during the writing of this novel.

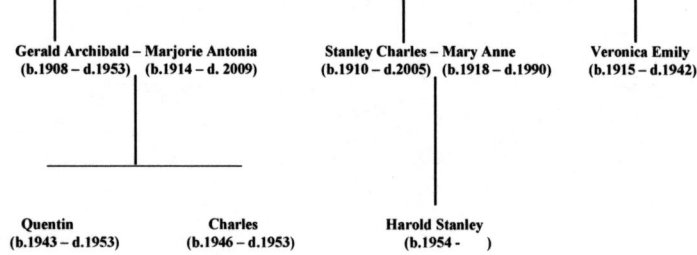

PAPER DREAMS

THE PROLOGUE

September 1952

What is life? A frenzy.
*What is life? An illusion, a **shadow**, a fiction*
And the greatest good is of slight worth
As all life is a dream
And dreams are dreams…
(Pedro Calderon de la Barca – 1600-1681)

* * *

Gerald Hapsworth-Cole's heart lurched as the huge ship's siren reminded him that Amy's departure was imminent. 'How can I let her go?' he asked himself. But deep down, he knew that there was nothing he could do or say that would make her change her mind, but he had to try. Feeling frantic, he reached out to embrace the woman standing by his side.

'Amy, my dearest Amy, what am I going to do now? I love you so much and I just can't envisage a life without you.'

'Gerald honey, it's no use, can't you see? I have to go home to Vancouver. We've been over everything again and again. What choice do we have?'

He looked blankly at her, momentarily lost for words. The inevitability of it all made him feel impotent. He searched her face for hope, but there was none, except for the gathering of tears in the corners of her eyes that threatened to engulf her.

Amy Butler was making the ultimate sacrifice for the sake of his family.

A lump appeared in his throat making it difficult for him to speak. 'My darling Amy,' he said in sheer desperation, 'I can't...I just can't believe what I've...I've done to you and how can I possibly let you go now?' He hadn't felt quite so emotional since the day his father had died and coupled with the fact that she now looked more beautiful than ever, made the moment of her departure even more poignant. She looked pale and fragile, just like a porcelain doll and he tightened his grip on her.

'My dearest, you must know that we really have no choice,' she said as unrestrained tears now rolled down her cheeks. 'Just think what would happen if your wife and sons found out about us: it would destroy them all. You must see that it is all...so impossible. I will def...'

A loudspeaker cruelly interrupted their final moments together and obliterated what she was saying. The preparations for the huge liner to get under way had been completed. There was an air of excited tension as people began to walk up the ramp and on to the ship that would be taking them across the Atlantic and away from their families and friends.

'Honey, I'll be waving my yellow handkerchief so look out for it and I promise that I will write to you as soon as I reach home.'

'But Amy, it's not too late to work something out.'

'No Gerald, there really is nothing else we can do, can't you see? I have to go. Goodbye my dearest,' she said kissing him on the lips. 'Always remember, even in your deepest and darkest moments, that I love you and that will be the link between us.'

She broke away from him...and was gone.

Gerald was left with an empty void between his arms, loving Amy, wanting her, his whole being crying out for her. He had to stop himself from running after her, but even as his heart cried out in pain, he knew that he had to let her go. He watched her in sorrowful silence as she ran up the gangway before disappearing from his view. After what seemed an age, the huge liner pulled away from the quayside. Panic began to overtake him as he frantically searched for Amy amongst the passengers leaning over the ship's railings. Then he saw her. She was waving her yellow handkerchief and he waved back putting on a brave face, but inside his heart was breaking. He watched the vessel as it gradually pointed itself in the direction of the open sea. "Come back…come back…please come back," he wailed inwardly but he knew it was useless: his beloved Amy had gone.

He continued to watch as the ship grew smaller and smaller until finally he saw a faint plume of smoke drifting into the sky, before the ship disappeared over the horizon.

He looked upwards. The sky was leaden and everything and everyone around him seemed as miserable as he was. The puddles under his feet were a testament to the fact that it had been raining hard for some time and he hadn't even noticed. He pulled up his coat collar and shoved his hands into his pockets. His heart sank. Lying at the bottom of one of them was a small box containing his farewell present for her. It was a diamond solitaire ring and a symbol of his enduring love for her. How could he have forgotten to give it to her, he asked himself? With a huge sigh, he pulled his sodden grey trilby hat further down on to his head, turned and walked sadly back to his car.

* * *

February 2009

The following extract appeared in the obituary column of THE EPTON HERALD on the 29th February 2009:

"**MARJORIE ANN HAPSWORTH-COLE** (nee **Bettisford**) died recently, aged 95. She was the widow of **Captain Gerald James Hapsworth-Cole, RN,** who, along with his two young sons, died in 1953 under mysterious circumstances. Their bodies were never found. Captain Hapsworth-Cole had been a distinguished sailor who fought in the Second World War, was decorated for outstanding bravery and mentioned in despatches on two separate occasions.

Marjorie Bettisford, a well known debutante and an heiress in her own right, was the only daughter of a wealthy industrialist and following her marriage to Captain Hapsworth-Cole, had lived in Epton Hall, the family's large ancestral home in Sussex. There has been a Hapsworth-Cole family member living in Epton Hall for many generations.

Because Mrs. Hapsworth-Cole died intestate, a search is being carried out for any surviving family members who, it is understood, will probably inherit the house and the estate."

* * *

EPTON HALL (2009)

A tall dark stranger entered the old house in silence, not quite believing how easy it was to gain entry. He looked around with quiet satisfaction, and a smile gradually suffused his severe features. He had waited so many years for this moment.

His father, Stanley, had been quite happy to forget his origins, but he had not…

* * *

PART I

Chapter One

Katie

March 2009

'Simon, speak to me please.' Katie Nicholson walked out of the Brighton cinema complex on the arm of her fiancé, Simon Brand. She looked up at him. His face seemed to be set in stone and she shivered. It was a cold, clear, frosty night and she drew closer to him, but he immediately pulled away again. A feeling of fear passed through her.

Katie had noticed that Simon's behaviour towards her had been decidedly odd. What was happening to them? He'd practically ignored her throughout the whole evening. What had she done? What had she said?

'Wow, that film was great wasn't it?' she said, trying to elicit some sort of a reaction. 'I nearly jumped out of my skin when that lorry exploded.' Simon didn't answer and looked the other way. A worried frown spread over her face, because even though it had been an enjoyable and absorbing film, a little worm of worry and doubt had begun to wriggle in the darker recesses of her mind. She'd spent the evening snuggled up against him, but he'd seemed to be distant, distracted and had fidgeted throughout the two-hour long film. 'Simon, didn't you enjoy the film? After all you were the one who wanted to come to see it.'

Simon's reply was non-committal. 'It was OK.'

Katie was an attractive, fun-loving, vivacious 25 year old, but this evening any thoughts of frivolity had been completely blown away. They drove the 20 miles to her home in Anston in complete and devastating silence. The air felt thick and heavy in the confines of Simon's small car, despite the fact that the temperature outside was extremely cold even for a March evening and frost glistened on every surface. At any other time, she would have commented on how beautiful everything looked.

Simon pulled up outside Lilac Cottage and switched off the car's engine. His whole body seemed tense. It was now late evening, but there was enough light from a nearby street light for Katie to see the look on his face when he turned towards her. He looked scared, terrified even. What on earth was going on, she wondered? Was he ill, or had he lost his job? Or was he…?

A sudden thought had made her heart thump. Was he going off her? Had he found someone else? Had he…? Katie's fears tumbled over one another in an effort to be aired. She'd noticed that he'd been breathing heavily and that now he seemed a little out of breath.

'Katie?' he at last managed to say.

'Yes?'

'I…Oh shit. I don't know how to say this.'

'Come on out with it, Simon' she prompted. 'Something's on your mind, you've hardly said a word this evening. What's up? We don't have any secrets from one another, do we?'

'I…I er…'

'Well, do we?' she replied feeling irritated. 'There's something bothering you that's for sure.'

'But…'

'Simon, please tell me what's wrong: you're worrying me.'

'You won't like it.'

'Let me be the judge of that. It can't be that bad surely?'

'Can't it?'

Katie was beginning to lose patience. 'Oh for god's sake, Simon, get to the point will you. We haven't got all night.'

'Katie…I'm…I'm sorry, but there's only one way of telling you this. Sally Longman and I have been seeing one another for some time,' he finally blurted out.

She wasn't quite sure whether she'd heard Simon properly. 'What did you just say?'

Simon groaned and sighed heavily. 'Sally Longman and I have been seeing one another for some time,' he repeated.

'You and Sally have what?' For a moment, Katie was rendered speechless. She felt a huge black cloud beginning to hover ominously over her head. Finally, she managed to speak: 'Simon, how could you...I...' Despite her shock and rising anger, she couldn't help noticing that her fiancé seemed relieved that the words had at last been said.

'Sally and I love one another you see and...'

'But I don't understand.' She felt her whole world crumbling around her. She closed her eyes in the hope that what was happening was not real and that it would go away. 'Surely you can't be...'

'Katie, I'm sorry to be so brutal.'

'You...you love one another? Great.' A feeling of utter devastation took control of her and it felt like a knife had just pierced her insides, as intense angry pain shot throughout her body. 'You and Sally? You bastard.'

'I...I moved in with her yesterday.' He grimaced and looked away.

'Yesterday, but you told me that you were going ...' Katie felt strangely light-headed and sat in her seat quite unable to think of anything more to say. Eventually, her pain reached boiling point. She could feel her hands beginning to tingle as she gripped the sides of her seat. She couldn't believe what she was hearing: she wanted to hit him. 'What about me Simon? You...you,' she screamed. 'You bastard,' she repeated almost choking on the words. The angry, bitter words seemed to echo around the car and Simon flinched as the tirade continued. 'How dare you? How dare you just sit there and tell me what you and Sally, who...who is supposed to be my best friend, have been doing behind my back? How could you? Didn't you even consider my feelings?'

'I'm sorry, Katie. I…we…we're both really sorry.'

'You're both sorry? Is that all you can say?' she scoffed, her face contorted with a mixture of disappointment, anger and grief - grief for the love she'd thought that Simon had for her and grief for what the future would hold without him.

There was now a yawning black hole in her life.

'I knew how you would take it, but there was no other way of telling you.' Simon looked downwards.

'You can say that again,' Katie retorted. 'I can't believe what I'm hearing. You and my so-called friend Sally, have been…have been…'

'I'm afraid it just sort of happened. We didn't mean to hurt you. I don't know what else I can say, except…'

'What?' she snapped.

'Sally is pregnant,' he replied in a quiet ashamed voice. Simon's courage began to lose momentum and then appeared to desert him altogether. His long, lean features looked even more lugubrious than usual. He sat next to her looking small, silent and crestfallen.

Katie didn't respond again for several panic-stricken moments, whilst her bruised mind tried to work out the implications of what Simon had just told her. Her heart, which had been beating wildly, now seemed to have turned to stone. The silence around them seemed to go on forever. She couldn't think straight, but finally, managed to utter a few strangled words.

'So, Sally is going to have…a baby?'

'Yes.'

'How long has this been going on?' she demanded to know. Simon didn't answer. 'Am I not allowed to know then? After all you owe me that much.' There was still no answer. 'Simon, I thought that **we** were going to get married and I...' Her body seemed to crumple and she continued to whisper in a quiet and strained voice. 'I thought you loved me, Simon. How wrong could I be?' Katie's world was crashing all around her and once again she closed her eyes in an effort to make it all go away. She wanted to scream, but fierce pride prevented her from doing so. She only knew that she had to make a dignified exit and so she opened the car door and with her legs trembling uncontrollably, she turned towards him.

'Cheers Simon. Sally is welcome to you and I hope that you'll both be very happy in your own misery.' She knew that what she'd just said didn't make any sense, but somehow with angry distraught tears streaming down her face, Katie climbed out of the car. She stood on the narrow stone pathway, not quite sure what to do next. Finally with her head held high, she walked through the open gates of Lilac Cottage.

She didn't look back.

Simon sighed, before driving away and out of her life.

Katie was surprised to see that her landlady, Brenda Bellingham, was waiting in the hall to greet her.

'Hello love. I heard the car. Did you enjoy the film?' Brenda stopped in her tracks when she noticed her distress. 'Whatever's wrong? You look dreadful. Look, let me get you a cup of tea or something.'

'No thank you Brenda, it would probably choke me.' Katie stood in front of her feeling confused and helpless, her shoulders heaving with pent-up emotion. Brenda put her arms round her.

'Oh Katie love. Come on, tell me what's happened.'

'It's Simon.'

'What about Simon?' Alarm sprang into Brenda's eyes. 'You haven't had an accident or anything, have you?'

'No, nothing like that.'

'He hasn't hurt you, has he?'

'No, not physically, but he...he...,' she hesitated and then answered vehemently. 'Yes, he has hurt me, Brenda.' Katie stared into the distance for a while and then finally burst into tears. 'He's just told me that he's moved in with Sally Longman, an old friend of mine,' she managed to say between shuddering sobs. 'And he's been seeing her for some time.'

'He's actually gone to live with her?'

'Yes, he said that he'd moved into her flat yesterday.'

'Yesterday! Oh Katie.' Brenda was clearly shaken and her soft brown eyes showed deep concern.

'Yes and there's something else too. Sally is going to have a baby.'

'A baby! Oh my goodness, it gets worse. I don't quite know what to say to make you feel any better love.'

'There's nothing to say is there. What am I going to do, Brenda? I can't believe that they could have done such a thing to me, or that I didn't realise what was going on right underneath my nose,' she said with a loud sniff.

Brenda cuddled her again. 'I'm so sorry, Katie. Look come on into my sitting room and you can tell me all about it, but...only if you want to of course. I will get you that drink you look as though you need one.'

Later that night, she found it impossible to get to sleep. Constant visions of Simon's face swam before her closed eyes and jumbled thoughts tortured her as she remembered the happy times that they'd spent together. She remembered too her long and happy friendship with Sally. Why, they had even started school together! They had shared all the things that little girls are supposed to share, like dressing dolls and attending birthday parties. And later, side by side they had taken their first exciting steps as teenagers and had been able to swap the most intimate details of their first fumbling kisses with two young and spotty boys. She sighed as she recalled the endless excited discussions about what clothes and make-up they should both wear. And now, her best friend Sally had chosen the ultimate insult and had stolen Simon from her. What had made Sally behave in such a way? This surely meant that you never really knew a person at all and when were the words "loyalty" and "trustworthiness" thrown so casually out of the window?

What was she going to do now? Why had this all happened? She had felt secure in his love for her and had mentally started preparing for their future together, but now her life was in ruins. When had it all started to go wrong?

Even though it was painful, Katie's mind took her back to her friend Claire Banham's birthday party two years' earlier. It was there that she had first met Simon Brand. Even though they had little in common it hadn't seemed to matter much, because Simon was fun to be with. He'd introduced her to a new crowd and they all enjoyed going to concerts and parties. She had felt a little out of her depth at times, but her life was at least exciting and happy and as the weeks and months had passed by, her feelings for him had deepened. They would often spend weekends together in his flat. It was small, but warm and cosy and Katie had never felt more loved and happy.

During one such weekend, he had taken her out for a meal in Brighton. She remembered that it had been a warm, balmy evening. They had been completely absorbed with one another as they'd sauntered hand in hand to their favourite restaurant. Simon had chosen a table well away from the other diners and the candlelight had flickered and danced between them, creating an ambience of timeless romance. She remembered that he'd grabbed hold of her hand and given her that certain half smile which always made her feel all tingly inside.

'Katie?' he'd whispered.

'Yes Simon?'

'Why don't we get married next year? I'll be earning more money then. What do you think?'

'Yes, yes, Simon,' she'd replied, her eyes twinkling with love and happiness.

Now as she lay curled up in her bed, she wondered how it could all be over. But she knew that it was and the word "traitor" suddenly screamed into her mind as she recalled how she'd been taken in by his words of love. Even the engagement ring that Simon had promised to give her had never materialised. He's probably given it to Sally by now, she thought as she sobbed into her pillow.

Katie found it impossible to stop thinking and close her mind. What was she to do? She'd even told friends that she was going to marry Simon. What would she say to them? She was on a roller coaster ride from which there was no escape. Her overactive imagination began to play cruel games with her, as first Sally's happy face and then Simon's taunted her as she pictured them living together in their new home with a new baby. She tried to stop these pictures, but instead cruel and soul-wrenching snippets of conversations took over as she rehearsed what she was going to say to all her friends. She had even thought about asking her cousin Helen to be a bridesmaid at her wedding. A cry of anguish escaped from her lips and she pounded her pillow in anger. All Katie could think about was this great big black hole into which she was now plunging and she had absolutely no idea how she could extricate herself.

Life ahead seemed bleaker than ever.

* * * * * *

Chapter Two

Katie woke the following morning feeling dreadful and no clearer in her mind about what she would do in the future. She felt that there seemed no reason at all why she should even get out of bed and the inevitability of her future life stretched out in front of her. Friends probably wouldn't invite her anywhere now, instead Simon and Sally would be the favoured ones, she thought in abject misery.

She tried to work out in her mind whether there'd been any clues about her so-called friends' relationship and she'd been too much in love with Simon to take notice of them. Up until last night he'd seemed quite normal. He'd been his usual happy and talkative self, but perhaps on reflection, just a little too much almost as if he'd been putting on an act.

Her mind then turned to Sally. They had been drinking in the local pub a few evenings before and Sally had joined them for the latter part of the evening. Katie remembered that Sally had sat down next to Simon and had seemed to focus a lot of her attention on him. When he had walked to the bar to get some more drinks, she had leaned towards her with a conspiratorial look on her face.

'And how are you two getting on together?' she'd asked.

'Oh Sally,' she remembered replying with great enthusiasm. 'I can't believe how happy I feel at the moment. Simon is so…'

'What? Passionate, loving, considerate and attentive?'

'Yes, all those things and more.'

'Wow,' she'd replied with a sly smile and then quickly changing the subject, 'Have you seen Emma and Charles recently by any chance? A certain knowing little bird told me that they were moving in together again.' Before Katie could reply, Simon had returned with their drinks and the opportunity to discuss this juicy piece of gossip had dissipated.

She hadn't thought any more about their brief conversation, but on reflection it was almost as if Sally had been trying to tell her something. Their long friendship had come to an abrupt end and feelings of hatred for Sally now threatened to engulf her. She wasn't a vindictive person by nature and knew that forgiveness was always one of the things that her parents had taught her, but right now that was not possible and she doubted whether it ever would be.

Eventually, Katie crawled out of bed and after smoothing her tear-stained pillow, pulled the duvet up as she did every morning. She dragged the curtains open and the sunshine glared at her and she pulled them back again. Getting ready for work was going to be difficult, she told herself as she went over to her small dressing table and sat down on the pretty kidney-shaped stool. She peered at herself in the mirror. She had an attractive oval-shaped face with high cheekbones. Her large blue, deeply set eyes were red-rimmed and puffy, and stared back at her, but no amount of carefully applied make-up could make her look or feel any better. After having a shower she sorted out some clothes to wear. 'What does it matter what I look like anyway,' she cried. 'Simon only has eyes for Sally now.'

She stood up and pulled at the zip of her black skirt, but it refused to budge. She tugged at it savagely and the small metal tag came off in her hands, breaking one of her fingernails in the process. 'Oh hell, I don't need this - I'm going to be really late for work.'

After rummaging through her wardrobe, she found another short skirt which was a little creased, but she put it on and tucked her blouse into the waistband. She had a trim, neat figure and the length of her skirt emphasised her legs, which were long and slim. Katie tore a bright green plastic hairbrush aggressively through her long hair and gazed at herself in the mirror again. Her unhappy face creased and once more tears began to pour down her cheeks.

'Why on earth didn't I realise what was going on?' she wailed. 'Was I the only one who didn't know that they were an item?'

Katie slammed the brush down on her dressing table and absent-mindedly tucked her hair firmly behind her ears. Through her tears, she'd become aware that her friend Sally's betrayal was hurting her every bit as much as Simon's and to make matters worse, her pride was badly dented. She gave a deep sigh. What was going on? Nothing seemed to be going right for her and even her car was playing up. Yet again, it was languishing in the local garage and she was reduced to cycling to work. At least I'll be in favour with the carbon footprint people, Katie thought idly.

She took a deep breath and shrugged her shoulders, trying to reduce the tension and anger she could feel building up inside her. She didn't want to cry any more, after all, it wouldn't achieve anything she told herself stoically. Simon had gone from her life and that was it. He would now be spending the rest of his life with Sally and not her. But her tears refused to go away and were threatening to spill over and engulf her, just like a wall of water being held back by a dam which was starting to crumble. She tried to pull herself together and began to apply some more eye make-up to try to hide the fact that she had been crying most of the night. A quick cup of coffee revived her spirits, but she had no time for anything else.

Katie was on the verge of leaving Lilac Cottage when she heard the phone ringing. She remembered that Brenda had left home early. Should she answer it? No, she decided, I'm late enough as it is and she closed the front door behind her. But it wasn't long before her conscience began to bother her.

An insistent little voice inside her head nagged at her. 'It could be something important. It could even be Simon, saying that it had all been a mistake?' Forlorn hope began to rise within her and she reopened the door and hurried to the phone.

'Hello, Katie Nicholson speaking.'

'Hi, it's me. How are you?' Helen was her cousin and was prone to doing things on the spur of the moment. She had an engaging personality that went with her voice.

'Helen, it's lovely to hear from you. I'm well thank you.' Katie tried to hide her disappointment that it wasn't Simon.

'I've been trying to get you on your mobile for ages. You do still have one, don't you?'

'Yes, but it's just like everything else in my life at the moment. It doesn't work any more and I keep meaning to get a new one.'

'Oh, I'm sorry.'

'I was just about to go to work. You've only just caught me.'

'Good. I was just wondering if you would like to come down to Penzance this weekend? It's the bank holiday of course. I'm not doing anything much and we haven't seen one another for ages. And what's more, according to the weatherman the dreaded rain will be in your part of the country not here in Cornwall. So come and enjoy the sunshine.'

'Yes, that would be great, thanks Helen,' she replied. Katie was trying to keep her voice light and happy, but she knew she was failing miserably.

'Is everything OK, Katie? You sound a little down this morning. Are you having problems with that man of yours?'

'Yes, well you could say that.'

'Come on, out with it?'

'Helen, I'm sorry, but I can't talk about it now. I'm going to be late getting to the shop because my car is sitting in the local garage and I'm using my bike.'

'Katie, it's high time that you bought yourself a new one. It isn't as if you can't afford it, is it?'

'No, you're right of course, but I am fond of that car. I'd feel like a traitor if I sold it. Anyway, I'll explain everything when I see you. I must dash otherwise my boss, Brian will kill me.'

'Well…if you're sure?'

'Yes Helen, I'm sure. I'll catch the usual early train on Saturday morning. Could you meet me at Penzance station, please?'

'Of course. Are you quite sure you're OK?' she insisted.

'I'm fine really. It'll be great. I'm looking forward to it.'

'So am I. See you then. Bye.'

Minutes later, Katie was pedalling up the long winding hill that led into the centre of the village. She puffed as the steep gradient began to sap her energy. Finally she pulled over to the kerb, got off her bicycle and walked the rest of the way to the top. Once there she paused for a while to get her breath back.

The sun was trying its hardest to warm up a rather cold, late March morning. Her spirits lifted only briefly when she heard the argumentative sound of several birds twittering away in the bushes. Katie had always loved springtime, but this morning there was only one thing on her mind.

Simon and Sally's betrayal!

She had to keep reminding herself that a long weekend spent with Helen would help her to relax and help her to forget what had happened. But Simon's parting words were still echoing in her mind.

'Sally and I love one another. I'm sorry…I didn't mean to hurt you…I didn't mean to hurt you.'

'Why, why?' she asked herself over and over again. 'What did I say, what did I do wrong?' Finally she climbed back on to her bicycle and continued on her way. As she pedalled along, her past life dominated her thoughts. She knew that such deep introspection was fruitless, but she couldn't help herself.

Katie had spent most of her life with her parents in their comfortable little terraced house on the outskirts of Brighton. Although small, it had been the centre of all their lives. She had been an only child and her earliest memories had been full of happiness and plenty. Her parents had always showered her with endless love and affection and she had lots of friends and had never felt lonely. Consequently she had grown up to become an attractive girl with an optimistic view of life, but she did have a tendency to daydream. Indeed, she had often found herself getting into trouble with her parents and her teachers at school. One teacher in particular, used to throw small pieces of chalk at her whenever she appeared to be inattentive.

He had always said the same thing to her.

'Katie Nicholson, will you please stop dreaming and concentrate child. You will never learn anything unless you do, believe me.'

However, despite her teacher's dire warnings, Katie managed to obtain three good 'A' level results. Once she had left sixth form college, she toyed with the idea of going to university, but none of the courses offered interested her. She had always loved anything to do with books and her determination to become a librarian had sent her scurrying off to find a job in the main library in Brighton. She had enjoyed those first few years after leaving college. She had made lots of new friends who, like her, enjoyed books and music. She was a good squash player and often played with Sally Longman…

Dark thoughts once more entered Katie's mind, but being the stoic she was, she brushed them all away. She remembered that the coach at the local club had recognised her talent for the game and had tried to persuade her to take it further. She had toyed with the idea for a while, but she was far too busy having a good time to spend all her time practising squash.

Just after her twenty-first birthday, calamity had struck. Her father died after suffering a massive heart attack. Katie's mother, a frail sweet person who had idolised her husband, found it almost impossible to get over his untimely death. Despite the love of her family, she just seemed to wither away like a flower that lacked the necessary sustenance to keep it alive. In a frighteningly short period of time she became morose and disinterested in herself and her surroundings. She died from pneumonia at the early age of 46. Katie was of course, totally grief-stricken and a few weeks after her mother's funeral she decided to move away from Brighton. She needed to escape from the memories of her shattered life and the echoing sadness of the family home.

She managed to sell the family home quite quickly and deposited the money in a building society until she could make up her mind what to do with it. Having so much money meant that Katie would never want for anything, but she knew that she would rather have her parents still alive and happy. She shared a flat with a couple of girlfriends, but she was never happy there. Living in Brighton was like a magnet to all their friends and Katie had felt smothered by people and endless parties: there was never any peace and quiet and that was what she longed for more than anything now.

Soon afterwards, a friend had told her about a flat that had just become available in the small village of Anston, about twenty miles away from Brighton and she went to see it the following day. She knew that if she liked it, she would still be near enough to see her friends when she wanted to.

It was on the first floor of Lilac Cottage, a quaint, but charming old half-timbered house on the outskirts of the village. Right from the start Katie had loved it and although it was small, she felt at home. The rooms all had sloping ceilings and pretty little dormer windows with leaded lights and she recalled the fact that she couldn't wait to move in.

She had particularly loved the garden and her first view of it had been from the room which was to become her bedroom. The garden was crammed full of plants and flowers and was well tended. At the bottom of the lawn, an ancient apple tree stood amongst some flowering shrubs, its old and gnarled branches dipping into a little meandering stream. Katie had been quite sure that she could be happy in this delightful place and she remembered walking downstairs to speak to the owner and being assailed by a black Labrador dog. He had bounded up to her wagging his tail furiously and holding a tatty old blanket in his mouth.

'Oh you do look silly.' She had laughed and patted him affectionately on the head. Mrs. Bellingham had heard her coming downstairs, because she too had been waiting for her in the hallway.

'Well, do you like the flat? I always think they are such lovely bright rooms.'

'I love it, Mrs. Bellingham,' Katie answered with genuine enthusiasm. 'I've decided to take it, if that's OK with you?'

'Of course it is my dear,' she replied with a beaming smile. 'Oh, I'm so pleased. I'm really looking forward to having some company again as it gets a bit lonely here sometimes. My name's Brenda by the way. Mrs. Bellingham sounds a bit stuffy, doesn't it? Anyway, come on into my sitting room and we can sort a few things out.'

'Thank you Brenda,' Katie had replied whilst stroking the dog's silken ears.

'And I see you've met Albert. He's lovely, but not much of a conversationalist I'm afraid.'

Brenda Bellingham was a middle-aged divorcee with a kind expressive face that matched her disposition exactly. She was stocky, dependable and had a wonderful sense of humour. Brenda could often be seen walking around the village of Anston with Albert trotting along at her heels. She liked to wear tweed skirts and comfortable brogue shoes and always wore an old and battered pork-pie hat, whatever the weather. As a freelance journalist, she spent a lot of her time hunched over her ancient typewriter and although she'd purchased a computer a few months earlier, she had so far failed to understand any of its little intricacies. 'You can't teach an old dog new tricks, you know,' she'd later told Katie. The new machine still sat in the corner of her study, unused and still encased in its original box.

Brenda loved her home with its well-manicured thatched roof and 'Olde Father Tyme' weather vane perching precariously on its highest gable. Over the last eighteen months or so, some of her more lucrative writing assignments had dwindled away, but that hadn't stopped the bills from appearing on her doormat with monotonous regularity. So, Brenda had decided to let the top part of Lilac Cottage.

Katie moved in a week later. Right from the start she'd known that the cottage's peaceful ambience was just the thing to help her get over the deaths of both her parents. She grew to love the village of Anston too. It nestled in amongst the green, rolling Sussex hills and Katie never tired of the sight of the picturesque cottages and the little church with its crooked spire. It was called St. Saviours and it seemed, like the trees and fields that surrounded it, as if it had always been part of the pastoral landscape.

Once Katie had settled down in the flat, she had set about the task of finding herself a job and scanned the advertisements in the Epton Herald. Eventually, she managed to find one that interested her. The owner of The Good Book Shop in Anston, Brian Ainsley, was looking for a new Assistant Librarian. The advertisement stipulated that 'only someone with a real passion for books, old and new, need apply.'

Later, she was telling Brenda about it and she was surprised to see her landlady's face lighting up with pleasure. 'Brian is a dear friend of mine, Katie. You couldn't work for a better person, believe me.'

She couldn't believe her luck and wrote to him requesting an interview.

Brian Ainsley had been immediately impressed with her, because he offered her the job on the spot and she'd started work in the shop the following week. Katie enjoyed herself immensely and with Brenda and Brian's help, she was able to put her grief to the back of her mind.

Now as she approached the centre of Anston, her spirits were at their lowest ebb. Once again tears ran down her face. Simon and Sally were getting married…Simon didn't love her any more. These same words went over and over in her mind. How could I have been so stupid as to think that Simon was as committed to the relationship as I was, she asked herself? And why is it that every time I have a chance of happiness, something always comes along to spoil it?

※ ※ ※ ※ ※ ※

Chapter Three

Katie arrived at the bookshop feeling harassed, exhausted, and 25 minutes late. She placed her bicycle against the wall in the narrow passageway that separated The Good Book Shop from the village bakery, secured the padlock and stood outside for a few moments to calm down. She felt that she couldn't allow her problems with Simon to affect her work, because it wouldn't be fair to Brian.

Heavy rain had fallen during the night and the dark passageway smelled of a mixture of dampness, freshly baked bread and another more unpleasant odour that she couldn't quite identify. She wrinkled her nose in disgust and rushed around the corner of the building. Katie was a punctual person and hated being late anywhere. An ancient black bell jangled noisily as she walked through the doorway of the shop and accentuated her late arrival.

The ground floor area of the shop was divided into two sections. The front section was always dedicated to the display of new books. There was row upon row of books of every description, large and small, thick and thin, hardback and paperback and each section was marked by a bright blue notice with white lettering, proclaiming the various categories for sale. These ranged from cookery, to the world's religions, psychology to gardening in the non-fiction section and a comprehensive array of fiction.

Although she liked the new books, the ones she really preferred were kept at the back of the shop. This was where Brian kept his treasured second-hand collection and she walked through the narrow archway that separated the two areas. During the occasional quieter moments, Katie liked nothing better than to browse through these old books, some of which had been well cared for and cherished and others had been mistreated by their previous owners. She always felt sad that they now all sat neglected and squeezed in amongst their neighbours.

Brian Ainsley was nowhere to be seen.

There were several old books piled haphazardly on his desk. Katie felt mystified. Brian was a neat and methodical person and always kept the downstairs areas of the shop, tidy and uncluttered. What on earth was he doing, she wondered?

'Hi Brian, it's me, Katie. Where are you?' There was no reply. A musty, dusty smell permeated throughout the shop and a slight haze of dust motes appeared to hover just above her head and could be seen moving around in the shaft of sunlight coming through the only window at the side of the entrance door. Strange thumping and scraping noises could be heard. Then she understood. Brian was upstairs where he kept some of his stock and various other things that were not needed in the shop. She climbed the first couple of metal steps which spiralled upwards above her.

'Hello Brian, it's...' She stopped speaking as a cloud of dust came from the doorway above her and she sneezed hard just as a friendly, bearded face appeared around the door.

'Hello love, I'll be down in a minute.' Brian Ainsley disappeared again.

Katie dusted herself down, and idly picked up a book and flicked through it. It was an old nineteenth century gardening book. Its pages were yellowed with age, but the illustrations were all beautifully drawn, which gave the book added value when compared to the photographs used in more modern books.

More rumbling noises could be heard above her head and Katie smiled despite the way she was feeling.

Brian suddenly emerged from the upstairs room and startled her. His hair was in complete disarray and his usually clean clothes were now in need of a good brush. He sneezed hard.

'Oh excuse me,' he wheezed, taking out a dark blue polka-dot handkerchief from his top pocket, before sneezing hard again.

'Bless you,' Katie said with a weary smile.

'Thanks,' Brian replied. 'I thought that I might be able to find some more room up there for some of the older stock. There's an unbelievable amount of rubbish up there and all covered with a large amount of dust.' He sneezed again and wiped a smudge from the end of his nose whilst looking at her keenly. 'Are you feeling OK this morning? You don't look your usual bright happy self.'

'I didn't sleep well last night, that's all.'

Brian was 55 years old, tall, bearded and thick-set. She thought that he'd probably been quite handsome in his younger days. Even though his hair was now getting a little thin on top he always combed a few straggly, greying and wayward strands across the top of his head. But his face was unlined and this tended to make him look quite youthful.

Katie's landlady, Brenda had known Brian for several years and on occasions, they went out together. Katie harboured a secret wish that they would get together, but so far any attempts at matchmaking had not borne any fruit.

'I'm sorry I was a bit late this morning Brian, only I had a phone call just as I was leaving home.'

'That's not a problem, Katie. As you can see, we are quiet at the moment.'

Katie looked at the pile of books. 'What about all this?'

'Well, it would be useful if you could sort them out and make a note of their condition, subject, author, you know the sort of thing, you've done it before and there's a load more in that old tea chest over there.' Brian was silent for a moment whilst stroking his beard.

'Do you want me to find room for them on the shelves afterwards?' Katie said with a worried frown. 'I can't think where they will all go.'

'No. They'll have to go back to the old house after they've been catalogued.'

'Old house? Which old house?'

'Epton Hall,' Brian replied in a matter-of-fact fashion, almost as if she should have known. 'It's empty now, of course. Haven't you heard all the talk and gossip that's been going around the village about it all? I'm sure that most of it isn't true.'

'No I haven't,' she said feeling intrigued. She shivered. 'Epton Hall…even the name makes it sound creepy. It's bound to harbour ghosts and dusty old furniture.'

'You could be right there,' he said with a twinkle in his eyes. 'Well you've missed a treat and no mistake. The old house and its occupants, has been shrouded in mystery and controversy for years.'

'Mystery?' Katie's eyes lit up.

'It's a mystery because nobody knew exactly what happened at the time, because the family kept it all very quiet. In those days, money and influence went a long way. Of course you could do that sort of thing then, but not now with our scandal obsessed media. The paparazzi would have been all over the place.'

'What sort of thing, Brian? Don't keep me in suspense.'

Brian moved a few books from the edge of the desk and sat down. 'Well all the speculation seems to centre around the year 1953 which is long before your time of course and practically mine as well come to that.' He threw back his head and laughed. 'Anyway, Epton Hall was a beautiful ancestral-type house and had been in the Hapsworth-Cole family's hands for several generations. Captain Gerald and Mrs. Marjorie Hapsworth-Cole and their two young sons lived there in some luxury.'

'And...?'

'Well that's it, nobody knows. All we do know is that Gerald and the two boys just simply disappeared.'

'But...but how can people just disappear?'

'Well there was a school of thought at the time that he took the children abroad somewhere and even that Marjorie Hapsworth-Cole had been involved in some sort of skulduggery. There was also talk of a sailing tragedy, but as I said, it was all covered up.' Brian tapped his nose. 'Conspiracy was heaped upon conspiracy and according to Anthony Robson, a local historian, speculation almost reached fever pitch.'

'People don't just disappear without trace, do they? And surely, the police must have been involved.'

'Yes of course, but you must remember that newspapers back in 1953 kept very much to information that could be confirmed, rather than the speculation and comment that we get today. In those days, it would have been easy to keep unpleasant things away from the media. Anyway as in most things, over time speculation lessened and people just moved on to other things I suppose. But it didn't alter the fact that Gerald Hapsworth-Cole and the two boys were still missing and as time went by, were presumed to be dead.'

'But that's awful, Brian. Someone must know what happened to them, surely?'

'Anthony Robson told me that there'd been talk of opening the case up again.'

'What happened to his wife, Marjorie Hapsworth-Cole then?'

'Therein lies the rub.' Brian said mysteriously, tugging at his beard. 'The poor woman died from a stroke three weeks ago. Er...there's a bit about her in the obituary column this week. She was quite a character apparently. She was well into her nineties and was a bit of a recluse too.' Brian stopped speaking, shook his head and picked up one of the books from the table, '…and she collected hundreds of books.'

'That's so sad, Brian.'

'Yes. We've been asked to catalogue the whole library. The collection is huge and I brought a few of them back here with me. Do you know Epton Hall?'

'No, I've never even heard of it.'

'It's a rambling old mansion between here and Epton and quietly sitting in the middle of hundreds of acres of prime Sussex countryside.' Brian paused. 'Katie? I've been thinking. If I do all the books that I've brought back with me, perhaps you would like to catalogue the rest back at the house? You could learn all about its history. It is quite fascinating. There doesn't really seem much point in bringing any more of the books here. What do you think?'

'Yes, I'd love to, but…'

'Just look at this one?' Brian interrupted. 'It's exquisite, well bound and illustrated.' He appeared to forget her existence as he handled the book and his eyes softened as he turned the pages.

'What will happen to all the books after we've catalogued them?' she asked.

'I beg your pardon, what did you say?'

'I wanted to know what was going to happen to the books afterwards?' Katie said, trying to gain his attention.

Brian often seemed to live in a world of his own. His wife Louise had died a few years earlier. He had grieved for her openly for about two years and had carried on grieving inwardly ever since. Books were now the most important things in his life. His eyes opened wide. 'Well presumably they'll all end up in book shops or the auction rooms again.'

'And what will happen to the old house?'

'Well, there's a mystery all round. They haven't been able to find a will, which complicates matters. According to the housekeeper, Nancy Brown, Marjorie Hapsworth-Cole had no relatives left alive, but Gerald had a younger brother, Stanley and a sister, but she unfortunately died during the Second World War. There was a lot of bad blood between the brothers – arguments over money, you know the sort of thing. Oh, I don't know, money always brings out the worst in people.' Brian was now in full flow and enjoying himself. 'Of course, after the deaths of her employer, Nancy Brown contacted the family solicitors in Epton. They are now in the process of trying to trace the brother and he must be pretty long in the tooth now too.'

'Wow. Is the estate worth a lot of money then?'

'Yes, I should say so, with property prices as they are nowadays, although a proper valuation hasn't yet been carried out. Anyway, now that you know a little more about it, are you still keen to do the cataloguing for me at the house?'

'You know me, Brian, I like a challenge, and I would love to. When would you like me to start?'

'Today, if you wouldn't mind. Can you make your own way there?'

'My car is in the local garage at the moment. There's another problem with the engine and I'm having to cycle everywhere again.'

'That's a shame. It's time you traded it in for a new one, Katie. And don't forget the Government Scrappage Scheme,' he added as an afterthought.

'Yes, Brian. I'm beginning to think you're right, but I suppose the exercise is doing me good. How do I get there?'

'It's about halfway between Anston and Epton. Go to the end of the High Street and take the first turning off to the left, signposted to Epton. You'll come to a little 'T' junction after about a quarter of a mile. Turn right on to the Epton Road and the entrance is about half a mile along on the left – just after a neglected duck pond. You can't miss it. There's a long drive up to the house, and do watch out for the potholes.'

'Potholes! It doesn't say much for the house. I'll make a start right away shall I?'

'Yes, if you wouldn't mind. Good,' Brian said finally, without looking up.

Katie smiled: Brian had a familiar faraway look in his eyes as he perused the old book that he held in his large, gentle hands.

* * * * * *

Chapter Four

Following Brian's directions, Katie set off for Epton Hall. All the branches of the trees, the bushes and the grass verges were laid low with the vestiges of the overnight rain. It had settled like a fine mist on everything in its path and tiny droplets of moisture clung tenaciously to the branches, making them look like strings of miniature transparent pearls. They sparkled and glinted in the sun's rays lending an air of quiet and ethereal beauty to the surrounding countryside. She slowed down so that she could have a closer look. She noticed that even the tiniest spiders' webs were transformed into jewels of such exquisite beauty that she could only stare at them in wonderment. 'I'd never have noticed this if I'd been driving my car. People miss so much nowadays in their hurry to reach their destinations,' she whispered to herself.

Soon Katie arrived at the duck pond. Brian had been right she thought, because it had been neglected. She pulled over to the side of the lane, dismounted and placed her bicycle up on to the grass verge. She spent the next few minutes staring down into the weed-choked water. A sudden splash of colour underneath the weeds attracted her attention – a goldfish was struggling to reach a small area of clear water and was followed by a second much smaller fish. She found a dilapidated old wooden seat which overlooked the pond and sat down for a while. The slight warmth from the early spring sunshine began to enervate her flagging spirits and as she sat there, Katie was reminded of the old poem "What is this life, if full of care, we have no time to stand and stare…", and as she tried to remember the rest of it, a sudden loud quacking noise disturbed her thoughts.

A Mallard drake appeared out of nowhere and skidded across the dwindling area of open water. It flapped its wings and feet untidily in a frantic effort to slow down. She couldn't help smiling as it fought to straighten itself before settling down onto the surface of the pond, before gliding towards the opposite bank. The sun glinted on the blue-green feathers on its head and back as it set about searching for its mate and some food amongst the reeds.

Despite the beauty of her surroundings, her tortured mind inevitably strayed back to the way Simon had treated her. She was haunted by the memory of the time that he'd put his arms around her, kissed her and whispered the words 'I love you, Katie,' in her ear.

She sat up straight.

'I must stop feeling so sorry for myself all the time she told herself. 'It's a good job that I found out what he was really like before I committed myself any further to him: huh, so much for his love and his promises!' The only thing that she could do now was to put Simon well and truly in the past where he belonged. 'I don't need him in my life any more,' she said placing her hands on her hips and still bristling with indignation.

The noise of the arrival of several more ducks to the pond reminded Katie of her task. She stood up, retrieved her bicycle and walked the remaining one hundred yards or so to the huge gateway entrance to Epton Hall.

The once imposing but now rusting gates, with their enormous ornate hinges, creaked and scraped noisily when she pushed her way through. It all seemed dreadfully creepy and menacing and a frisson of fear crept over her. The tall brick pillars that supported the gates looked unstable and the ancient mortar was beginning to crumble in places. Several types of weed and brambles had grown up around the entrance, making the whole area seem neglected and untidy. Katie looked upwards to see a pair of magnificent, but dirty, bronze eagles with outstretched wings, proudly perching on the old pillars. How long had they been protecting the house, she wondered?

The driveway curved away into the distance. She mounted her bicycle and set off for the house. She found the going quite difficult, because there were several deep holes in the old tarmac. Her progress was further hampered by small branches which had fallen from the tall thin Poplar trees that lined up like sentries along the route, so she decided to walk.

Everything around Katie now provided her with the perfect ingredients for a daydream and she allowed her imagination to run riot. Because she had been an only child, she had often let her mind drift in this way. In her mind's eye, she pictured herself being driven along in a coach pulled by four snow-white horses, each prancing and cantering towards the house. She imagined that she was wearing a magnificent crinoline dress, the bodice of which was studded with gems and pearls. The skirt ballooning in front of her was made of yards of scalloped lace interspersed with small pink bows. Katie's golden hair was piled high upon her head and small neat ringlets swayed from side to side with the rocking movement of the coach. She was going to a ball…

She conjured up two liverymen and they sat with straight backs on top of the carriage, each wearing scarlet uniforms with white edgings and black tricorn hats on top of their powdered wigs. Even the horses seemed real to her and their hooves made a rhythmical clip-clopping sound as they sped along the driveway…

Katie's mind was brought back to stark reality, when having negotiated a bend in the drive, she saw Epton Hall for the first time. She took a sharp and involuntary intake of breath. The Hall stood ostentatiously amongst the neglected and overgrown gardens and a few wisps of morning mist gave it a mysterious aura. The house was enormous and had obviously been added to over the centuries, leaving it over-large and sprawling, but despite this, she became transfixed by its air of long forgotten grandeur. She dismounted from her bicycle and stood for a moment looking upwards.

In its turn, the old house appeared to stare back at her. Its cold, austere windows were like so many sad unseeing eyes. Two huge chimneys reared upwards on each wing of the building and everywhere exuded a feeling of neglect and decay. She placed her bicycle up against a wall and stepped gingerly over some debris which had fallen from the crenulated ramparts and parapets that she could see above her. Several pigeons flew over her head and called suspiciously to one another when she approached the main door to the house. They had been startled and frightened by her sudden appearance. But just as quickly, they resettled themselves amongst all the little nooks and crannies of the old house, pushing and shoving one another in order to get to their original and favoured perches.

Feeling nervous and a little frightened of this old austere house, Katie walked up the old granite steps which led to the huge pillared doorway and knocked on the door. She waited for a few moments before knocking again. There was no reply. Where was the housekeeper Nancy Brown, she wondered? She reached into her pocket and withdrew the key Brian had given her, placed it into the enlarged and worn keyhole and turned it. The lock was a little stiff, but it gave a loud click and the door creaked and scraped as she pushed it open.

She stopped short when she entered the enormous hallway and looked upwards. The ceiling was high, rib-vaulted and quite breathtakingly beautiful. Despite this, Katie shivered. She stood still and listened for a while. It was quiet and spooky, apart from the ticking of a large ancient Grandfather clock, which was standing up against the wooden panelling near the grand staircase. The emptiness of the house surprised and alarmed her and the hairs on the back of her neck felt uncomfortably erect as she walked across the hall. Her footsteps echoed on the marble floor, making her feel that someone was following her. She nearly jumped out of her skin, when a figure loomed up in front of her...but she soon realised that it was only a full set of armour standing to attention in the gloom created by the old staircase. By now she was feeling uneasy.

'Is anybody here?' she cried out. 'Hello. Is anyone here?' The sound of her voice reverberated upwards and seemed to bounce back at her from the ceiling way above her head. How I wish I hadn't agreed to do this, Katie thought as she looked around her. There were several ancient wooden display cases dotted around the walls, each containing coins and butterflies and a collection of naval memorabilia but their ordinariness did nothing to allay her fears.

On the opposite side of the hall, she noticed that one of the wooden panelled doors was slightly ajar and she walked towards it. The door had huge hinges which sprawled across its surface like black metal fingers. She pushed it open and peered inside. It was the library. She heaved a huge sigh of relief and walked into the room, closing the door behind her. She leant back against it and closed her eyes. She took a good deep breath in an effort to quieten the loud and rapid beating of her heart. The door was thick and made of age-blackened oak and she locked it with the aid of a wooden wedge which hung from the door on a leather thong. Even though she was scared, she remembered an old saying of her grandfather's. 'It's cold, so put the wood in the hole...' She had often wondered what he'd meant, but now she understood and smiled.

The library was about thirty foot square and it too had a high rib-vaulted ceiling. Three of the walls were fitted with shelves and crammed full with books of all shapes, colours and sizes. The remaining wall, which included the door, exhibited several expensive-looking paintings and portraits. The gaps between the tops of the bookshelves and the start of the ceiling were filled with ornate Romanesque shaped urns, interspersed with models of old sailing ships in dusty wooden display cases.

There were three Gothic laucet windows, which overlooked the drive and the front gardens. They contained fragments of what she thought were the original stained glass. It all reminded her of a building she had visited in Reims in France with her parents. The windows there had been similar to these and had the same transcendental quality and emphasis on light. Katie felt another pang of grief. Her father had been an architect and had always taken great pride in showing off his knowledge to his family.

A small area of shelving was empty of books. She could see lines of dust on the shelves showing precisely where the books had stood for so long. Just to one side, were some large packing cases and a small drum table which Brian had used over the weekend. Katie recognised Brian's copper-plate handwriting on a pad on the table. She smiled, Brian was a methodical person. He had already discarded several tatty and dilapidated books and magazines, many of which didn't have covers or had pages mutilated or missing. She now felt a lot more relaxed: Brian had unwittingly managed to allay some of her fears with his usual efficiency. Ah well, I must get on, she told herself. She pulled the dust cover away from a chair and set about the enormous task ahead of her.

She worked hard for about an hour until the dust made her feel thirsty. She decided to leave the library and try to find the kitchen. She walked into the hall, but this time she was determined to view her surroundings.

Immediately opposite the front door, the ornately carved staircase rose and curved away upwards and out of sight. She noted that the balustrade was now scuffed and old, but it was enough to set her wayward and romantic imagination off again. She stared at the staircase and soon imagined herself being rapidly transported backwards in time – back to the moment in history that had always fascinated her...

A ball was being given in Katie's honour and her eyes sparkled with the magnificence of the scene laid out before her. Beautiful crystal chandeliers hung from the ceiling, reflecting one hundred-fold, the many candles which lit up the fairytale imaginary scene. There were baskets and vases everywhere which were crammed full with flowers and she could almost smell the heady intoxicating perfume they exuded. Women with elaborate crinoline dresses, appeared to float down the stairs, the hems of their dresses making a slight rustling sound as they descended. Each woman's hair was expertly coiffured and dotted with jewels and real flowers and they drew expensive looking fans across their heavily made-up faces in a feigned effort to conceal their mock coquettishness.

The women were all being received at the foot of the stairs by their equally well-dressed and bewigged menfolk as they bent elegantly dressed knees in deep bows and patronising sweeps of their arms. The lace cuffs of their sleeves just grazed the floor as they looked up with feigned expressions of love. To complete the picture, footmen with white powdered wigs and haughty expressions on their faces, weaved in and out of the assembled throng, handing round glasses of wine and delicious looking canapés, all displayed and served from ornate Georgian silver trays. The sound of a string quartet playing a Mozart minuet appeared to drift into the hall through one of the open doorways. Katie could hear the excited chatter of happy people having the time of their lives.

Just then everyone seemed to stop what they were doing. They turned and walked towards her, their arms outstretched in friendly greeting. She smiled, inclined her head and gave a deep curtsy…

A loud noise startled Katie and her vision evaporated.

The heavy front door of Epton Hall opened and an elderly woman walked in. Katie was left in mid-curtsy and felt rather foolish and embarrassed.

'Hello Miss Nicholson. I see you managed to find us then.' The woman looked flustered and slightly out of breath. 'I'm Nancy Brown and I'm sorry that I wasn't here to meet you.' Much to her relief, the woman didn't appear to have noticed what she'd been doing.

'Yes, hello,' Katie replied.

'Good. When Mr. Ainsley said you'd be coming this morning, I did wonder whether you would be able to find the house on your own.' She was short and quite plump and wore her long grey hair pulled back into an old-fashioned bun. The lenses of her glasses were thick and gave her an owlish appearance.

'Yes, thank you,' she replied, 'I found it quite easily. My name is Katie by the way.'

The woman took off her hat and coat and placed them on the large, dark oak refectory table just to the left of the stairway.

'I'm pleased to meet you,' she said, walking over to where Katie was standing. 'I've been working in this old house now for so many years that I've lost count. I was a mere slip of a girl when I first came here, so there's not much I don't know about the old place.' They shook hands.

'It's a marvellous old building isn't it, if not a little scary,' Katie blurted out, 'and it's such a pity that parts of it have been allowed to fall into such disrepair.' As soon as she had said these words she regretted them and her hands flew up to her mouth: she knew that she was being insensitive.

'There used to be lots of staff here in them old days,' Nancy replied ruefully. 'There's only been me for some years now and I just couldn't be expected to do it all.'

Katie now felt even worse. 'I'm sorry, I didn't mean...'

'I know you didn't m'dear – but mark my words, there've been some in the village who've criticised me for it I can tell you.'

'I've already made a start on the books,' Katie replied, trying to change the subject, '...and I was just looking for the kitchen. I'm so thirsty, it must be all the dust I suppose.'

'Oh, I'm so sorry that I didn't get here earlier to show you around and make you feel at home, only me husband had to go to see the doctor this morning and I really needed to be there with him, you see.' Nancy walked towards a door to the right of the refectory table which led through to a small dark corridor. 'Come in to the kitchen, it's just through here and I'll make you a nice cuppa.' Katie followed her.

Now that Nancy Brown was in the house to keep her company, Epton Hall seemed to lose some of its mystique and emptiness, despite Katie's Walter Mitty-ish daydreams. The kitchen itself was light, cheerful and altogether quite different from the rest of the house and she could see a small, cosy sitting room through a narrow doorway. Nancy opened a drawer and took out a pink housecoat which she quickly put on. She filled an electric kettle, and set out two cups and saucers and a plate of biscuits on to the well-scrubbed wooden kitchen table. Soon they were chatting as if they had known one another for years.

Katie soon discovered that Nancy was a mine of information. Her knowledge of the history of the Hall seemed infinite and before very long, she even began to like the rambling old building.

'Mrs. Hapsworth-Cole was a wonderful but lonely person,' Nancy said draining her teacup. 'She went to lots and lots of book auctions and never came away empty handed, bless 'er. She had such a troubled and unhappy life, that I suppose books became her whole life and who could blame her?' Nancy stopped speaking and pushed her glasses back up her nose. 'I imagine that when she was thinking about books, she could forget all her troubles. But it's a funny thing you know dear, Mrs. Hapsworth-Cole hardly read at all. She was always complaining about her glasses being wrong, or something.' Nancy walked over to an old Welsh dresser, opened a drawer and took out a photograph. She handed it to her. 'This was Mrs. Hapsworth-Cole and I think it was taken at about the time Mr. Gerald and the two boys disappeared. Oh she was beautiful, wasn't she?'

'Yes, she was.' A strikingly handsome woman with her hair piled high on the top of her head, stared back at her. Marjorie Hapsworth-Cole was tall and slim with an upright, aristocratic bearing. In fact, she looked positively regal. But it was the haunting sadness of her eyes which affected Katie the most. She was smiling at the camera, but her eyes seemed to betray her feelings. She was like me, unhappy, she thought.

As their conversation continued, she began to feel real sorrow for Mrs. Hapsworth-Cole. Even though she had never met her, she could imagine her sitting alone in this vast house surrounded by hundreds and hundreds of books. How lonely she must have been. It was obvious that Nancy had loved her and had tried to make her final years at Epton Hall as happy and as comfortable as possible.

Nancy fell silent again and seemed to be staring into space. Suddenly she sat upright and smoothed her hair and Katie couldn't help noticing that her hands were shaking. 'Mrs. Hapsworth-Cole was so good to me and never really treated me like a servant,' Nancy said looking down into her empty teacup. 'She was such a lovely, old lady and she could trace her own family back several centuries, you know. There's an old saying, "breeding will out" and it was so true in her case.' she added with a loud sigh. 'But just like all good things it had to come to an end sometime. I believe that Mrs. Hapsworth-Cole was the last of the line, so to speak.' She looked away.

'It must have been quite a shock for you when she died.'

'Yes, it was.' Nancy's eyes narrowed and then glazed over with tears as she spoke. 'They're trying to trace Mr. Gerald's brother, Stanley, as he's the next in line to inherit the estate and…and I really can't see that he should inherit all this.' Nancy's face expressed the anguish she felt over the way people had treated her employer and she spread her hands out in a gesture of hopelessness. 'He certainly knew nothing of the terrible heartache she suffered during those long, lonely years. He made no contact with her at all and it was little wonder that she turned to books for help. But then if Mr. Stanley doesn't have the house and all the money, who will? I suppose if they don't find any long lost relatives, the government will pocket it all! Oh I don't know all those wasted unhappy years.' Nancy shook her head sadly and began to clear the table. 'Oh I'm sorry, listen to me going on. Would you like another cup of tea, m'dear?'

'Yes please. I hardly tasted the last one, I was so thirsty.'

'Now, tell me about yourself? Are you enjoying sorting out the old library? There are a lot of books, that's for sure.'

'I'll let you know when I've finished whenever that will be,' Katie said smiling at her.

'Well, what do you do when you're not working then? Have you got a boyfriend? A pretty girl like you must have dozens.'

Katie's heart sank and she looked downwards. 'Well I…'

'Oh dear, did I say something wrong? I'm so sorry.'

'No, it's nothing really, I…'

'Would you like to tell me about it? You know the old saying, "a trouble shared" and all that.'

To her surprise, she found herself telling Nancy everything – she was such a good listener. When she had finished, Nancy patted her hand. 'It sounds to me as if you're well rid of him. You mark my words, they'll be queuing up you'll see.'

'Thank you and I know you are right, but I thought that my

life was going to be spent with Simon – I'd made plans you see and it's difficult to clear all that out of my mind – but when I think of how they have both treated me…and all those lies…'

'Lies…lies! I know all about those,' Nancy said quietly to herself, before standing up and putting her arms around Katie's shoulders. Large tears were starting to roll down her face. 'Now my girl,' she said, 'You're not going to waste any more of your time and energy on two people who have wronged you. Forget them and look forward, not backwards. Do you promise me?'

Katie blew her nose on a piece of kitchen roll and tried to smile. 'Yes Nancy, I will. Neither of them is worth worrying about. Well I must be getting on with my work, or Mr. Ainsley will wonder what I've been doing with myself all day,' she said standing up. 'Thank you for the tea and the chat.'

'You're very welcome m'dear. It makes a nice change to have someone to chat to. It can get a bit lonely here sometimes.'

She eventually found her way back to the library and was soon immersed in the enormous task ahead of her. But at the end of the day, it seemed that she had only just begun to scratch the surface – the rows of books seemed to go on forever. However, she persevered and by five o'clock on Friday evening, she had begun to feel that she was making good progress. She packed everything away and covered the furniture with the dust sheets.

Before leaving the house, she made her way to the study to telephone Brian to tell him about the progress she had made. Brian complimented her saying, 'I'm grateful for all your hard work Katie. God only knows how I'd have found the time to do it all myself.'

'It's not the best job in the world, Brian, but at least it's the weekend at last. By the way, I'm going down to Penzance in Cornwall in the morning by train and I won't be back until Tuesday morning. My cousin Helen will be quite a contrast to all those old dusty books, I can tell you.'

'Wow, that's quite a journey and I imagine that you'll have an early start. Well have a good time and don't do anything I wouldn't do, will you?' Brian quipped.

'I'll try not to. Bye and have a good weekend yourself. Are you seeing Brenda during the holiday?'

'Probably, I'm sure that she will organize something for us to do.'

'Well, then, the same applies to you then, doesn't it? Bye.' Before she replaced the receiver, she could hear the happy sound of Brian's laughter. It was good to hear him sounding so positive about his life.

Despite this happy exchange, Katie's enthusiasm for her task at Epton Hall was waning. The spectre of the old house's treasure trove of books hung over her head like an omnipresent huge black cloud. Even the thought of Simon's betrayal had been forced to the back of her mind. There had been no time at all during the week to prepare for her weekend away and a pile of washing and ironing was waiting for her at Lilac Cottage.

She mounted her bicycle and rode away from the house. Just as she approached the first sharp bend in the driveway, she stopped and turned round. She saw Nancy Brown standing in the doorway, waving goodbye to her. She seemed such a small figure up against the forbidding exterior of the old house. Katie couldn't help wondering what it would have been like to have worked in the house during those troubled times. She recalled the look on Nancy's face as she'd talked about the family and her heart went out to her.

* * *

Nancy Brown watched Katie as she disappeared round the bend in the driveway and gave a huge sigh. She had only known her for a few days, but in that time she had grown fond of her. She was such a nice girl, Nancy told herself, lovely manners too and it was such a pity about all her problems. She shivered as a cold breeze suddenly shook the shrubs at the side of the old steps and she hurried indoors. She still had a lot to do before she went home. Once she was back in the kitchen she felt strangely subdued.

Nancy had spent a lot of time during the past few days talking to Katie about Mrs. Hapsworth-Cole and the family. Since her employer's death, she'd barely had time to dwell on it, or to grieve for that matter. Now, as she sat silently at the old kitchen table with a cup clasped in her hands, she allowed herself to give full vent to her bottled up emotions.

'Oh dear, my poor old lady,' she said as she sobbed. Her former employer had just seemed to go through the motions of living. Nancy just couldn't imagine what she had gone through and it was truly amazing that despite everything, she still managed to retain full control of her mind: a lesser person would have gone to pieces. Whenever Nancy found the time to remember those early years, she always ended up feeling depressed and angry, so she allowed the memories to fade. The little snippets of information that she had gained at that awful time, and the intercepted letters which were carefully hidden at the back of a cupboard in her house, would have to remain as her dark secret and if necessary she would take their whereabouts to the grave. Nothing would be gained by letting the world know about the Hapsworth-Coles' private lives. She couldn't bear the thought of it all being sifted through now, when as far as she knew the principal players were all dead. Nancy rose stiffly from her chair and walked out of the room.

※ ※ ※ ※ ※ ※

Chapter Five

Early on Saturday morning, Katie was trying to look out of the grimy train windows but the countryside flashed by in a blur - the incessant rain drops were streaking sideways across the window in a never-ending stream. She soon gave up and snuggled down further into her seat and concentrated on reading her magazine. Katie was enjoying her enforced inactivity and felt relieved to be on her way to Penzance at last. It had all been such a rush and with a hard week's cataloguing now behind her, she started to relax and the memory of that lonely old deserted house began to diminish. She listened to the steady rhythm of the train as it ate up the miles on its long journey to Cornwall.

Katie could hardly wait to see her cousin again. Helen was five years older than her and still single, but she was quite certain that she would be snapped up sooner or later. Helen possessed a puckish sense of fun and had a truly expert way of playing the field as far as men were concerned. One of these days, she thought with a silent chuckle, Helen will say yes to some handsome hunk.

A negative thought suddenly crossed Katie's mind and she closed her eyes in consternation. Helen was bound to talk about Simon, and what would she say when she learned about the callous way he had treated her? Helen hadn't liked him right from the start and she felt miserable all over again: love was blind after all and Helen had been proved right.

There was a loud noise and the interconnecting door from the next carriage opened.

'Can you get your tickets ready for inspection please,' an

officious voice intoned. The next thing Katie knew, a ticket inspector was peering down at her with an imperious sneer. Feeling flummoxed, she quickly rummaged in her purse and was filled with momentary panic when she couldn't find it. 'You do have a ticket, don't you?' he asked.

'Yes, yes of course I do, only I can't remember where it is,' she said turning to her travel bag.

'Excuse me miss, but I'm a very busy man. I don't have all day.'

'Please hold on a moment while I look for it.' Her bag had several different compartments and as she searched for her ticket, she was aware of the ticket inspector's impatience. Then her heart sank; the ticket wasn't there.

'Well if you haven't got a ticket, then I'm afraid that I'll have to ask you to pay for your fare right now and you are lucky that I don't fine you on the spot!' The man seemed to be enjoying himself. 'You young people think that you can get away with murder nowadays. When I was young, we used to have respect for the law, but you lot...' He stood there with his stubby pencil poised. 'Where are you going?'

Katie thought that he looked like a hawk standing eagerly over its prey. Then she remembered that she had put the ticket in her jacket pocket which was now folded neatly in the luggage rack above her head. 'Excuse me,' she said trying to gain some equilibrium. She stood up and took down her jacket. To her utmost relief, she found the ticket and handed it to him.

Looks of suspicion and disappointment merged as they passed over his aquiline features. 'Thank you,' he said and without apologising he walked on to the next compartment.

With that particular panic over, Katie tried to relax again. She stretched out her legs to make herself more comfortable. The swaying movement of the train gradually exerted a soporific effect on her and she was soon lulled into sleep…

She found herself in a huge cavernous room. She was surrounded by bookshelves and cupboards and they all appeared to be leaning towards her. Books hung at crazy angles and some were even suspended in thin air, whilst others littered the floor. Confused thoughts of fear and an overwhelming sense of hopelessness, invaded her mind. Misty overwhelming shadows floated around her…and feelings of dread enveloped her. What was going on? She felt compelled to place the books back on to the shelves. And just like an automaton, Katie circled the room, but as fast as she picked them up, more fell silently around her. Nightmarish ghostly pieces of paper and parts of books swirled around her head. She raised both arms in front of her face to protect herself…

A peculiar noise made her turn around in alarm. A man appeared in a doorway, which had loomed out of nowhere, and without any warning he threw something at her. Books…more books rained down upon her as a hideous smile spread across his frightening face. His demonic eyes burned into hers and Katie felt real terror. She struggled and fought to protect herself from this onslaught as her whole world became a storm…a total blizzard of small pieces of paper. She could no longer see anything, but she could feel…evil…and menace.

She awoke with a jolt. She was sweating profusely and for a moment she felt disorientated, until she remembered where she was. It was only a dream, she told herself…only a paper dream. But why on earth should she have had a dream like that? It was probably a direct result of working in Epton Hall all week, she concluded.

Katie had the compartment to herself so no one was aware of her fear, but because it was open-plan she could hear sounds of voices and movement further up the carriage. Still feeling shaken and thirsty, she walked through into the Buffet Car, but much to her relief, she saw that there were few people around. She was not in the mood to do battle with other thirsty passengers and after ordering a cup of tea and a biscuit, she made her way to a table. Her dream had really scared her, but with each mouthful of the soothing liquid, she began to feel a little better. But, she was convinced that she would never be able to forget the awful face that had reared up in front of her: the man's eyes had been filled with abject hatred.

The rest of the journey to Cornwall passed by without further incident and when to her relief, the train pulled into Penzance station, she lifted her weekend bag down from the rack, opened the door and alighted from the train. She walked through into the large cavernous area containing the Ticket Office and saw Helen standing in the main doorway, waving excitedly at her. They hugged one another.

'Hi,' Katie said, smiling at her.

'Hello love and how are you?'

'I'm OK thanks. And you?'

'I'm fine. Oh, it's wonderful to see you again,' Helen said holding her at arm's length. 'Actually, you look a little peaky: have you had a bad journey?'

'Not exactly, but I have had quite a week and it's really great to be here.'

'Good. Anyway, I've got simply loads to tell you. Come on, the car's just outside.' She grabbed Katie's bag and almost dragged her through the door. Katie smiled when she saw Helen's old dark green Morris Minor: it was parked in front of a 'NO PARKING' notice! She knew from previous visits to Penzance that the station was adjacent to the largest car park in the town. No wonder she was in a hurry to get back to the car, Katie thought to herself and they were fortunate that there were no officious traffic wardens lurking in the shadows either. She couldn't help thinking about the rather nasty ticket inspector on the train. Thank goodness she had managed to find her ticket.

Katie took a good deep breath of fresh seaside air. She could see lots of boats on the harbour side and in the water, and seagulls swooped overhead calling to one another in their raucous voices. She was glad to be here.

Once they were both safely in the car, she looked at her cousin. 'I mean to enjoy myself here, Helen. I haven't been having a good time lately. In fact at the moment, life sucks.'

'Well, you did sound a bit down when I spoke to you. Do you want to talk about it?'

Katie looked down into her lap. 'I…I was upset yes. Simon, he…'

Helen's face expressed disapproval. 'What's Simon done now?'

'He's been seeing my friend Sally Longman behind my back, and…'

'He's been what? Oh the little shit!' Helen looked really upset. 'Sorry Katie, I didn't mean to swear, but I never did think that he was right for you. I rest my case.'

'He told me last week. He said that they loved one another and that they'd just moved in together and…they were going to get married soon.' She closed her eyes – the pain had begun all over again.

'Katie, I'm so sorry, but I do think that you're well rid of him. Anyone who could do something like that is not worth knowing believe me, and with your friend too. I remember meeting her once and she seemed quite a nice person to me, but it just shows you, first impressions are not always what they seem. I know what I would have said to both of them,' Helen said vehemently.

'That's what I keep telling myself, but it's not easy. For the past year, he's been my world. Now, there's nothing.'

Helen gave a long sigh. 'I don't know what to say, Katie love. I never thought that the day would come when I'd be at a loss for words.' Helen drove in silence for a while and when they had to wait for some traffic lights, she placed a caring hand on her shoulder. 'Look, what's done is done. Simon has gone from your life now. I always felt that you deserved better and he had shifty eyes and you were opposites and…'

'I know that now Helen. He's about as sensitive as a brick wall and uncaring and he…he had a cavalier outlook on everything.'

'So it's just as well that he's now with Sally Longman. They'll be a good match.'

'Yes, but…' Katie's face began to crumple. 'There's something I haven't told you, Helen.'

'Do you mean there's more?'

'Yes. Sally is pregnant and…'

'Pregnant! It gets worse. The bastard! How could he have treated you like this?'

'I keep asking myself that question, but so far I haven't come up with any answers.' Katie closed her eyes hoping that the pain would go away.

'I just don't get it.' Helen was silent for a few moments. 'Oh love, listen to me ranting on. I'm sorry, you're here to enjoy yourself and that's what you're going to do. So let's change the subject, shall we? How's your job going?'

She told her about the huge cataloguing job at Epton Hall and described her first impressions of the old house.

'It sounds just like a set for a Hollywood movie,' Helen replied with a wry smile.

'Honestly Helen, I never imagined ever working in a place like that. Sometimes it seemed really spooky and I wondered if it was haunted. But I must admit that it had a romantic ambience. I could just imagine what it would have been like to have lived there in the past.' Katie's face developed a far away expression.

'Go on, dream on,' her cousin prompted.

'Well, I began to feel sorry for the house at the end of the week: all that history and now it's just sitting in acres and acres of gorgeous countryside and mouldering away. I've a feeling that unless someone takes an interest in it soon, there'll be nothing left.'

'Well now you're here, you can forget all about that big old house, books and Simon Brand. Come on, we must get home. I'm simply dying for a cup of coffee and I expect you are too.'

Helen's home was aptly named 'Cliff Cottage' and had been built about 250 years earlier out of hard Cornish granite, with a steely-grey slate roof. The cottage had been fashioned in such a way that it could withstand the rigours of the often inclement Cornish weather – a constant battering from slanting rain and often horrendously strong winds. It perched on the edge of a cliff overlooking a small cove just a few miles from Penzance.

When Helen had first bought the cottage she had decided to learn about its long and varied history. She'd managed to find a book in the local library and spent hours leafing through its pages. She learned that Cliff Cottage had once been used as a base for smuggling. Many years earlier, so called 'free traders' would bring their contraband goods ashore in the dead of night: the goods were then sold to inns and wine merchants throughout the area. Brandy was particularly popular and it was reputed to have been sold for about five shillings a gallon. Much to the authorities' frustration in the area, the free traders' fast ships always seemed to outrun the slower craft of the Revenue Officers and many a fortune had been made and lost during those exciting times.

Steep, oddly shaped granite steps ran down from the cottage to the rocky cove below. The pounding of many feet over the centuries and the even heavier pounding of enormous waves, had smoothed and moulded each step into a different shape and added to the mystery surrounding the area.

During Katie's first visit to the cottage about five years' earlier, she had spent a few idle moments daydreaming. She had imagined groups of swarthy sweaty men, wearing earrings and brightly coloured 'kerchiefs' around their heads. She pictured them climbing the rough granite steps, stumbling and staggering under their heavy loads which they carried aloft on their straining shoulders and it was of course always in the dead of night!

That first night, she dreamt that a ship had been wrecked in the cove almost in front of the cottage. "Wreckers" had appeared from nowhere and plundered the stricken ship, quickly spiriting the cargo away and leaving the ship and the crew to flounder in the heavy seas. Katie had woken with a start only to find that the window had been forced open by a strong gust of wind. It was swinging backwards and forwards, creaking alarmingly and she had raced to the window to close it. Since then, she had tried to keep a tighter rein on her imagination when she was staying there.

Helen was a successful artist and had converted one of the two bedrooms into a studio. And so when anyone came to stay they had to sleep in the small cosy living room. In common with all the rooms, it had a low ceiling and twisted old oak beams, which added to its mystique. Her artistic nature had taken charge when she'd first moved in and the result was a charming mixture of the old and the new. Some of her paintings were quite surrealistic in design. They depicted images of heavy seas, screaming winds and tossing ships. It was obvious to her, that Helen had spent a lot of time staring out of the small mullioned windows.

When they pulled up outside the cottage, a passing heavy hail shower decided to hover over the area. Laughing noisily, they climbed out of the car and raced towards the front door. The shower was short-lived however and by the time they were inside the cottage, the rain had stopped.

Helen rubbed her hands together. 'Do you know it's amazing how a shower of rain manages to lower the temperature,' she said. 'I'll put the kettle on and perhaps you could rekindle the fire.'

'Yes, of course,' Katie replied, '…but where…'

'You'll find some wood in the wooden box in the corner near the bookcase.'

'OK I've found it.'

Quite soon the flames began to lick up the chimney and Katie flopped into an armchair whilst Helen busied herself in the kitchen adjacent to the living room. Katie could see her moving around.

'Don't you ever get lonely here, Helen?'

'No. I can honestly say that I don't. I need peace and quiet in order to paint – this place is my inspiration. If I ever need people, I have my mobile and several good friends who understand my desire to be alone sometimes.'

'Is there anyone special at the moment? You told me some time ago about Roger Martin. He sounded rather nice.'

'No,' Helen replied firmly, walking back into the room with a tray containing two mugs, a steaming cafétiere and several chocolate biscuits on a plate. 'We both decided that things wouldn't work out between us. He wanted me to go up to London to live with him. I said no, of course. Well, you know me, Katie. He really wasn't one for the quiet, rural life. Then there was Roger Claydon.'

'Another friend called Roger? And what was he like then?'

'He was almost too much the other way. Do you know he actually wanted to move in here with me? He came on strongly one night and I had a job pushing him away. I knew that all he really wanted to do was to run my life for me and I wasn't having any of that, so I sent him packing. He was one of those men who ran straight to the bedroom, never mind the steaming cups of coffee lying on the table. Oh, I suppose I've been independent far too long.' Helen laughed and her brown eyes lit up with mischief. 'Besides I'm having far too much fun sampling all the pebbles on the beach at the moment, Roger or no Roger.'

'Oh Helen, thank you. You're just what I needed,' she said laughing happily. 'Somehow you've managed to put everything into perspective for me.'

Although Katie and Helen were related on her father's side, there was little family resemblance between them. Helen was tall, dark and slim and not really a great beauty. She always considered her face to be far too long and angular. But whatever Helen appeared to lack in beauty, she certainly made up for in sex appeal – she was popular with all her male friends.

She stretched her long legs languidly over the arms of the settee. 'I'm sorry Katie love. Here I am, jabbering on about my love life. Perhaps what happened between you and Simon was for the best? After all you could have married the guy and then found out that he didn't really love you. You're much better off now, you must admit.'

'Yes, I know you're right, Helen, you always have been and I didn't listen to you. It's times like this that you really find out who your friends are.'

'Yes, I know what you mean.' Helen stood up. 'Do have one of those chocolate biscuits, I know they're your favourites. Would you like some more coffee?'

'Yes please.'

Helen poured out another two cups from the pot. 'Well what shall we do after coffee?' she said picking up a hair band from a nearby table and deftly fashioning her long hair into a ponytail. 'We could go for a walk along the cliffs, or go into Penzance or Newlyn for a while?'

'Newlyn would be great.'

'Good. I was hoping that you would say that. We could meet

up with some of my friends,' Helen retorted with a twinkle in her eye.

A strong south-easterly wind was blowing when they left the cottage, but at least it was dry and the sun was now shining. They made straight for Helen's favourite pub. Katie already knew some of Helen's more colourful friends from her previous visits, several of them, like Helen, were artists and seemed to be drawn to the Cornish coastline like moths to a flame.

It was early evening and Katie began to unwind and even managed to forget Simon, but only for a while. One friend in particular, a young man called Stuart Wells, flirted outrageously with her and even offered to take her out for a meal.

'I've a feeling that I'm going to feel hungry quite soon,' he whispered in her ear. 'There's a little restaurant down the road. Would you like to keep me company? I mean, the two of us.'

'Thank you Stuart, but I've come down to spend the weekend with Helen and I can hardly leave her in the lurch can I?'

'I don't mind, really I don't,' Helen said. Katie couldn't help noticing the surreptitious looks which were being exchanged between her cousin and Stuart.

'Thank you for asking me, but after such a long journey,' she found herself saying, 'I'm tired and I've had a hell of a week, so I'm sorry, but the answer is no I'm afraid.'

Stuart smiled politely, got up and walked over to the bar. Helen turned to her cousin. 'You could have gone you know,' she whispered.

'Helen, I came down to see you. It doesn't seem right for me to go out without you.'

'But I wouldn't have minded. Your happiness is important to me. I don't have too many relatives around that I can cosset. Stuart is such a poppet. As a matter of fact, he's moving to a new job with a firm in Lewes in a few days' time. That's quite near you, isn't it?' Her eyebrows arched.

Katie felt as if she was being manoeuvred somehow: Helen was matchmaking outrageously. 'Yes,' she said.

'He's a newly qualified Accountant. He's also…'

'Helen,' she interrupted with a deep sigh, her blue eyes brimming over with tears. 'I can't get involved with anyone else at the moment. The only thing I need now, is space. I don't want to upset Stuart and he seems a lovely guy, but…perhaps you could tell him my reasons for not wanting to go out this evening, please? I'm sure he'll understand.' She took a sip of her drink and looked away.

It was only then that Helen realised just how much Simon's rejection had hurt and upset Katie and her heart went out to her. Even though she'd insisted that she was over Simon, her sagging shoulders and tearful face told her such a different story. She saw Stuart standing alone at the bar and went over to join him.

'Helen, what's up with Katie?' he said, trying to catch the barman's eye. 'I've never been rejected quite so comprehensively before. Am I using the wrong aftershave or something?' The barman came over and Stuart turned to her. 'Would you like another drink?'

'Yes, I'll have a Gin and Tonic please.'

'Right, one G and T and I'll have another pint of Tinners please, Henry.' Henry moved out of earshot in order to mix the drinks. Stuart shrugged his shoulders in resignation. 'I thought she looked a bit unhappy that's all.'

'It's not really surprising. Her fiancé dumped her for her best friend. How's that for starters?'

'Oh sh…I mean I'm sorry, I didn't realise. Trust me to put my large size 10 feet in it. Do you think it would be worth trying again? Perhaps she'd like to cry on my shoulder?' Stuart asked with a hopeful gleam in his eye. 'For starters, I'll buy her another drink. What does she like?'

'Gin and Tonic, with lemon but no ice.'

Stuart called out to the barman, 'Can you make that two G and Ts then Henry please, only one with lemon and no ice, OK?'

'Coming up.'

Helen placed a restraining hand on Stuart's arm. 'A word of advice, Stuart: it's early days yet. Take it nice and slowly.'

'OK if that's what you think. I will.'

Helen looked at Stuart for a moment and then smiled. Her eyes filled with devilment. 'But on the other hand, I don't think there is any harm in trying, do you?' Stuart winked at her and handed her a drink. She lifted up her glass. 'Thanks Stuart, cheers. Oh by the way, Katie only lives a few miles from Lewes, if you're interested. I'll give you her address and phone number.'

'Yes. Cool. You never know,' he said chuckling into his beer. Helen wrote the number down on an old till receipt and handed it to Stuart. He placed it in his pocket and they both sauntered nonchalantly back to where Katie was sitting.

As the evening wore on, Katie began to relax and enjoy herself more and more. She found Helen's friends to be stimulating company and ended up discussing art as if she was an expert, instead of a complete layman. They spent some time walking around Newlyn harbour and looking at all the boats. They marvelled at the way all the herring gulls swooped on to one fishing boat in particular as it came in to discharge its cargo: some of the catch was placed into crates on the quayside and the rest were unceremoniously dumped back into the sea. Helen explained the reasons why they had to throw some of the fish back. 'I hate to see that,' she said. 'EU fishing quotas must never be exceeded and in addition, if some of them are too small, back into the sea they go. But by then they are dead of course. Crazy isn't it?'

'Yes, you can say that again,' she replied pulling a face. 'Those poor fish.'

'Hey you girls,' Stuart said rubbing his hands together. 'Talking of fish...I'm feeling quite hungry. Anyone for dinner, only there's a quaint little restaurant round the corner. Come on.'

Throughout the evening, Katie realised that she'd hardly thought about Simon at all and had even managed to become quite friendly with Stuart. And later as she lay on the bed settee in Helen's living room, she smiled when she recalled the look of disappointment on Stuart's face, when the two girls had decided to call it a night. Despite everything she had enjoyed Stuart Wells' company. He was quite good looking. And she liked the way a dimple appeared on one side of his face when he smiled and the way that his eyes lit up when he looked at her. She sighed. When he spoke to her it was as if there was nobody else around. He seemed to concentrate totally on her. A tremor of excitement ran through her body. Perhaps there was life after Simon after all? Not every man was going to turn out to be like him and moping around certainly wasn't going to achieve anything, was it? In fact Simon could do what he wanted from now on and she didn't give a fig: Sally Longman was welcome to him.

Katie's time with Helen passed altogether too quickly and she soon found herself having to wave goodbye to her as she climbed into the waiting train. She waved and waved until she could no longer see Helen standing on the platform.

* * *

Stuart couldn't get Katie out of his mind.

After leaving the pub that night, he decided to go for a long walk before returning to his flat in the centre of Penzance. There was a distinct spring in his step as he walked around the town and harbour and didn't feel at all tired, in fact he felt elated. Was it fate that had brought this wonderful girl into his life? After all, he was going to be living just a few short miles away from her and he patted the pocket which contained her address and telephone number. He decided that when he was settled in Lewes, he would definitely call her. He smiled to himself when he remembered the way she'd kissed him on the cheek when they'd said goodbye.

He eventually returned to his flat feeling much more optimistic about his job change. Over recent weeks, he'd wondered whether he was doing the right thing by moving away from Cornwall and all his friends, but now that he'd met Katie everything seemed different somehow. His first priority would be to find himself somewhere to live in or around the Lewes area. He felt excited and exhilarated. In fact, his life now had a purpose.

Having gone over everything in his mind, he prepared for bed in the knowledge that his life could indeed be taking a turn for the better.

* * * * * *

Chapter Six

First thing on Tuesday morning Katie called in at The Good Book Shop. She walked through into the small back room where she could hear Brian working. He turned round on hearing her footsteps.

'Ah Katie, hello. Good to see you back safe and sound. I hope the weather in Cornwall was better than it was here. It poured down most of Saturday and Sunday and as for yesterday, well, the least said.'

'I hardly had time to notice the weather, the time seemed to go so fast,' she replied pushing back a stray lock of blond hair from her eyes.

'Yes, it certainly did that. Brenda and I decided to attend the spring book fair in Epton yesterday, but I'm afraid that was a complete wash out too.' He looked at her keenly. 'But you obviously had a good time in Cornwall. You look a lot happier than you did the last time I saw you.'

'Yes, I had a great time and it was just what I needed. I was able to put part of my life back into perspective,' she said. 'I take it that you still want me to carry on cataloguing the books at the Hall?'

'Yes please, if you wouldn't mind.'

'It's dead boring, Brian.'

'I know and I'm sorry,' he replied, 'but there's still a lot more to do. The remaining books are all in the attic, though.'

Katie's face fell. 'The attic!' Cold shivers ran up and down her spine. Attics were always spooky places, she thought. How many times had she seen them depicted in films as dark, dusty, menacing places and full of old things that nobody wanted or needed any more.

'Look I can see that you don't much like the idea of working in the attic, but it is only for two or three more days. I've spent hours in the library and I've managed to clear all the books from the other rooms. There's only the attic left now. And guess what, I found some first editions tucked away in a cupboard in Mrs. Hapsworth-Cole's bedroom. Whoever inherits the Estate is certainly in for a surprise.'

Katie wished that she could find a first edition, or at least something to brighten up her boring and endless task and the thought of spending so much time in a dusty old attic either, didn't appeal to her in the slightest. Her frightening dream on the train had unnerved her. Now deep down, she was feeling less confident about Epton Hall altogether and her horror of the unknown was beginning to nibble away at her. There was nothing that she could actually put her finger on, but it was there as a vague and insidious fear. She shivered.

'Are you cold? I'll put the electric fire on for a while, shall I?'

'No Brian, I'm not really cold, I was just thinking about creepy attics that's all, but thank you.'

'Well, if you are really worried about it, then I'm not going to push you, but…' Brian was looking at her with an expectant look on his face. Katie knew that she would have to learn to control her fears. Having agreed to do the job in the first place, she felt that she couldn't refuse now. She squared her shoulders.

'OK Brian, of course I'll do it.'

'Right then, I'll give Nancy Brown a ring and tell her that you are on your way. He patted her hand. 'I do appreciate what you're doing and the sooner you start, the sooner it'll be finished. To be honest with you, I'll be glad to be rid of the worry of it all.'

'Yes, so will I Brian.'

On the way back from Cornwall, she had thought a lot about the cataloguing of Epton Hall's books and how mind-bogglingly boring it all was. On her return that evening she had asked Brenda if she could look at her computer. Katie was quite sure that if Brian could take an interest in it, she might be able to persuade him to do all his cataloguing work on a computer in future. 'Brian, before I go, have you ever looked at Brenda's computer? She never uses it you know.'

'Computers!' Brian laughed and leaned towards her. 'Katie, can you see me using a computer with these hands?' She looked at them and laughed too: they were rather large. Brian continued to smile however and his eyes started to twinkle. Katie recognised the signs. She had caught his interest.

'A modern computer could save us an enormous amount of time. It's too late to help us with the books at the old house, but if something similar was to crop up in the future perhaps...?'

'You may be right, Katie. I'll have to look into it.'

She was about to leave for the Hall, when she remembered the search for Stanley Hapsworth-Cole. 'Brian, did the solicitors manage to find out anything about Mrs. Hapsworth-Cole's brother-in-law?'

'Oh yes, I forgot to tell you. I spoke to Nancy about it on Saturday morning. Apparently, the solicitors told her that he died a couple of years ago. Nobody this end seemed to know anything about it.'

'How strange. Did he have any family?'

'Yes there's a son, Harold and he lives somewhere in Malta. They don't know exactly where. He tends to move around a bit.'

'So now they have to find him?'

'Yes. Harold Hapsworth-Cole stands to inherit a fortune. Nancy said that he didn't ever get on with his father and they hadn't seen or corresponded with one another for years. Ho hum, families are funny things aren't they,' he chortled.

Katie had just turned the corner which led to the Hall, when she saw Nancy Brown standing at the top of the steps. Nancy was a down to earth person and she always felt a lot calmer when she was around.

'Hello m'dear, back again eh?' Nancy said cheerfully in her gentle Sussex burr. 'You're a glutton for punishment and no mistake. Come on along inside and I'll make you a nice cup of tea before you start work.'

'Thank you Nancy. Yes, I was hoping that Brian would have finished it all by the time I got back from Cornwall, but it seems I still have to do all the books in the dreaded attic.' Katie sighed with heavy emphasis. They both laughed and walked through into the kitchen.

Two cups of tea later, Nancy rose from her seat.

'Come on, then,' she said. 'I'd better show you how to get up there. You'll never find it on your own.'

'Perhaps you'd better give me a map,' Katie said with an impish grin.

They walked up the broad carved staircase and she felt like she was travelling backwards in time. There were portraits and paintings of people long-since dead hanging on all the panelled walls. Their sorrowful and stern painted eyes appeared to follow them as they climbed upwards.

'I wonder who all these people were, Nancy? They all look so self-important and sombre.'

'Mrs. Hapsworth-Cole told me that they were all ancestors of the family on both sides – a regular rogues-gallery from what I can gather. She said that they were all a vain lot.'

'I wouldn't want them on my walls, would you?'

'Well to be honest, no. But I have got used to them over the years,' Nancy said as they progressed down a long, dark corridor with several doors and other corridors leading off on both sides. Katie found it all quite eerie and shivered involuntarily. They took a turning to the left and came to a second staircase. It was nowhere near as grand and imposing as the main one. It disappeared upwards and into the gloom. Nancy stopped. 'Oh dear, all these stairs and I'm not as young as I used to be.' She turned a light on, but the slight glimmer emanating from the bare bulb above their heads, did little to light their way. In fact, it only accentuated the length of the shadows that appeared to follow them as they climbed. Nancy put her hand in her overall's capacious pocket and handed her a torch. 'Here,' she said, 'you'd better have this m'dear, because the lights are not much use I'm afraid. And do be careful, the carpet is a little worn in places.'

'Nancy, I really do think that I'll need a map to get up here again. I can't understand why anyone should want to live in such a large house: there are so many rooms.'

'Well in them old days, most of them would have been used. A house like this needed a lot of looking after. Apart from the butler and the cook, there were umpteen kitchen maids and parlour maids, and they all needed somewhere to sleep.'

Another gloomy corridor greeted them at the top.

Finally they stopped in front of a heavy oak panelled door with pitted rusty hinges.

'Is this the attic?'

'Not quite dear.' Nancy took a large key out of her pocket and unlocked the door. She had to push it quite hard before it finally yielded with a loud creaking sound which continued to echo around them. Katie shivered again. This house certainly had the ability to frighten her.

'I must remember to bring an oil can with me the next time I come up,' Nancy said. 'These doors are hardly ever opened now.'

Another dimly lit steep flight of stairs rose up before them and they picked their way upwards. There was a sudden sharp turn to the right and they were confronted by yet another door. She noticed that there was already a key in the lock.

'Well this is it,' Nancy said with a flourish of her arm. They had arrived at the attic. 'I brought Mr. Ainsley up here on Saturday morning and we improved the lighting. You couldn't possibly have worked up here otherwise.' Nancy seemed a little out of breath. 'Come on in then.'

A loose floorboard creaked almost like a rifle shot as they crossed the threshold, making Katie jump. Her heart thumped.

'Oh Nancy, that frightened the life out of me.'

'It's been like that for many years m'dear.'

Katie was now quite sure that she wasn't going to like being up here. There was only one small bare bulb and it hung from the dusty and cobweb covered rafters, swaying slowly to and fro as it caught the draught from the open doorway.

'Well, what do you think?'

'One word: WOW!' she said as she wandered around the room. There was an all pervading, unpleasant musty smell of age and decay and it seemed airless. It was immediately apparent to Katie, that anything Marjorie Hapsworth-Cole hadn't wanted or needed had been stored up here. Katie had never seen so much clutter. There were boxes and carrier bags everywhere, their contents spewing untidily on to the surrounding floor space. Odd pieces of furniture which were stored in no particular order, made it difficult to move from one part of the attic to the other and all four corners of the room were shrouded in shadow. She shivered. It was so creepy and she was going to have to spend quite a lot of time here.

'What do you think of this then?' Nancy said pointing towards a spinning wheel which stood by an old chest of drawers.

Katie walked over to where Nancy was standing. 'Nancy, it's beautiful.' She ran her fingers over the old wheel and just like everything else in this room it was covered in dust and cobwebs. Childhood memories of the pantomime, Sleeping Beauty and the wicked stepmother, sprang into her mind. In a curious way, it suddenly helped her to gain a sense of proportion. It was just an old room, filled with books and furniture, she tried to tell herself.

To her delight she saw a rocking horse. She walked over and rocked it. It was very old and the paintwork was flaking off in places. Unfortunately, the real horse-hair mane was straggly and matted. Even so, she thought that it was one of the most beautiful things she had ever seen. She stared at it for a moment and felt sad. What a waste.

'Do you know m'dear, I'd have given anything to have had something like that when I was a kid,' Nancy said wistfully. Then some tears began to gather in her eyes and Katie wondered why? Memories were such personal things, so she felt that it would have been wrong to press her for an explanation.

'Perhaps the rocking horse will be able to go to a good home, now that everything is going to be sold. There must be a child somewhere who will love and treasure it.'

'Yes, m'dear, let's hope shall we?' Nancy said with a pronounced sniff.

There was little natural light in the room. The only source came from a small dormer window halfway along the wall. Someone had hung curtains there once, but now all that remained was a dusty looking curtain rail and a few rusting curtain rings. Katie walked over to the window. The panes of glass were really dirty. She rubbed hard in one place to see which area of the garden the attic overlooked, but it was no use she still couldn't see anything properly.

The tortuous route that they had taken to get up to the attic had made Katie lose her sense of direction, so she tried to open the window, but it was stuck fast. Undaunted, she took out her handkerchief and breathed on the glass. She had to rub quite hard but soon managed to clear an area large enough to see through.

The attic was situated at the back of the house. She could now see the grounds of Epton Hall spread out below her. She had been so busy during the days she had been working here, that she hadn't had time to look at the gardens. The window looked down on to the remains of what used to be a fountain. It was surrounded by little marble cherubs each blowing trumpets, but sadly some of them had either heads or limbs missing. Katie sighed as she gazed down on all that past glory and splendour.

'The gardens must have been so beautiful once, Nancy. Do you think that they will ever be the same again?'

'Ooh, I don't know about that. It would take several full time gardeners to keep it up to scratch and there's not many people nowadays who can afford that. Unless of course it was opened up to the public, you know like they do at Petworth Park, and other grand houses.'

'I'd loved to have seen it in the old days,' she said trying to picture it.

Nancy turned on the two table lamps. 'There you are. Now you will be able to see what you're doing.'

'Thank you Nancy, that's much better.' Now Katie could clearly see several old bookcases standing up against the far wall and they were crammed to overflowing with books, pamphlets and magazines. She also noticed the dusty piles of old pamphlets and papers which were cluttering up the floor. Her heart sank. She hadn't imagined that there could have been so much more to sift through.

'There's several days work up here,' she said in dismay.

'Yes m'dear. I thought you'd be pleased,' Nancy replied. 'Well I must get downstairs. I've got a lot of cupboards and things to clear out myself. The solicitors have managed to trace Mr. Hapsworth-Cole's nephew and he'll probably want to come and look at the house. He's coming all the way from Malta, by all accounts.'

'Yes, Brian told me about it this morning.'

'Anyway before I go dear, have you got one of those mobile phone things?'

'No, it stopped working last week – I've got to replace it.'

'Well, in that case, I must explain something to you. If you want anything whilst you're up here, you can use this, providing I'm still here of course.' Nancy walked over to the door and pointed towards a peculiarly shaped object on the end of a tube. It disappeared into the wall. 'It's an old speaking tube, just like the ones they used on board ships many years ago. I think it still works,' Nancy added. 'Old Admiral Archibald Hapsworth-Cole, Mrs. Hapsworth-Cole's father-in-law, used to spend a lot of time in this attic room, so I understand, especially after he retired from the Navy. The Admiral used to imagine that this room was on board one of 'is old ships.'

Despite her fears, Katie giggled. 'I never thought that I'd ever see one of these, let alone use one, Nancy.'

'Mrs. Hapsworth-Cole often used to talk about them old days when she was young.' She looked at Katie and added, 'and between you, me and the old gatepost, I've heard that the Admiral was a wee bit potty. Anyway m'dear, this thing comes right down into my kitchen, so should you need anything, just you lift up the tube and give it a big blow. Now, are you sure you'll be OK?'

'Yes Nancy, of course I will. Don't worry I've got a lot to do, so I'd better make a start.'

Katie gradually became accustomed to working in the untidy and cluttered attic, with all its dusty memorabilia and paraphernalia of ages past. At odd times when she needed a break from the tedium of cataloguing the endless supply of books and pamphlets, she would search amongst the boxes to see what she could find. She knew she had no right to do any such thing, but she was convinced that as she was only looking, no real harm would be done. In fact it helped her to come to terms with the hours that she had to spend in the room.

One particular item held a particular fascination for her. It was an ancient sea chest. It was made of oak and from the various dents and scratches on its surface it had been well used. It had old metal hinges and edges and at one time Katie supposed, it would all have been cleaned and polished with pride. The key was sitting in the lock and almost inviting a quick look. She stared at it for some time until her curiosity overcame her…and she turned the key.

Feeling slightly nervous, she raised the lid slowly and like everything else around her, it made a creaking sound. Inside she found a complete officer's dress uniform, still neatly pressed and placed between sheets of thin yellowing, tissue paper. There were several old sea charts and logs and she spent some time trying to imagine what it would have been like to undertake some of the journeys which had been plotted and charted with such care. She discovered an ancient telescope, some mouldy looking silver cutlery and an old cracked plate, all of which had seen long service.

Right at the bottom of the chest, Katie found a seaman's kit bag and a walking stick with an ornate silver handle. It had the initials A.H.C. intricately engraved on the top. Tucked away in a corner lay a shabby photograph album, containing faded sepia-coloured photographs of row upon row of unsmiling people all wearing old fashioned naval uniforms similar to the one she had just found. They were all sitting stiffly and staring straight ahead. She closed the album and replaced everything exactly the way she had found them. Finally she closed the lid and turned the key. She felt as if she had been prying on the owner's privacy, even though she knew that he must have been dead for many years.

After more than three days' hard work, Katie's task was nearly at an end. It was Friday afternoon and there was just one bookcase left and as usual, she took several books from the shelves and placed them on the side of the desk.

A curious scratching noise just above her head, made her jump and she accidentally knocked the pile of books with her elbow. They landed with a thud on the floor. Dust sprang outwards and upwards making her sneeze. Katie looked anxiously around to see what could possibly have made the noise. The noise had really spooked her and the hairs on the back of her neck and arms stood up on end. Stop it, she told herself, it's probably only a mouse.

She picked up the books which were lying on the floor and placed them back on the table. As she did so, she noticed what looked like a piece of paper sticking out from between the pages of one of them. It looked like an old envelope. And yet again, her curiosity got the better of her. Katie picked up the book and turned the pages until she found what she was looking for and as she prised the envelope from its hiding place, her heart began to beat faster.

It was addressed to Gerald Hapsworth-Cole, but she couldn't read the postmark. She turned it over and stared at it for a moment. What revelations did it contain? Nancy had hinted about various family disasters. Did she have any right to read the letter inside? 'No,' she told herself firmly and placed the letter on the table. But someone had gone to great lengths to hide it, so perhaps it contained something of importance she argued with her conscience.

Without thinking further, Katie picked up the envelope, withdrew the letter and began to read the words that were written so long ago…

※ ※ ※ ※ ※ ※

Chapter Seven

Gerald

May 1953

A strong gust of wind tore playfully through the bushes and trees, bending branches and dislodging a few tiny freshly-opened bright green leaves. They fluttered gently and inexorably to the ground, their short lives soon forgotten. Undaunted, the wind continued on its way, before expending its energy by hitting and rattling the windows of Epton Hall.

Captain Gerald Hapsworth-Cole, R.N. stood in front of the small attic window overlooking the grounds of his large rambling, ancestral home. He didn't notice the effects of the wind because he was far too preoccupied with his own problems. He felt wretched. He looked down at the well-read and crumpled letter he held in his hands.

'Amy…my darling Amy, I miss you so much,' he said, his brow wrinkling with the effort of trying to juggle the two halves of his complicated life together. 'How can I even begin to live without you?' He picked up the old briar pipe that his father had given him and the feel of the wood and its warmth comforted him. He placed the pipe between his lips and breathed in deeply like a drowning man taking his last desperate bid for life. The dying embers glowed in obedience, but offered him only momentary relief. He exhaled slowly and the blue smoke rose in front of his eyes obliterating reality.

In his mind's eye, Gerald could still see the tortured look on Amy's face when she had finally torn herself from his arms. And minutes later when he saw her, now a tiny figure, waving as the huge ship moved away from the crowded quay. He could still feel the dull ache that had suffused his body as if a part of his essential being, his very soul had been cruelly torn away and carelessly thrown to the wind.

He loved his wife Marjorie and his two young sons, Quentin and Charles, he told himself, but his love for Amy was quite different: it was intense and all-consuming. Marjorie on the other hand, was an excellent mother and organiser and ran Epton Hall with efficiency and great enthusiasm. She even found the time to sit on various local committees and eagerly supported her "good causes". But Gerald knew that the physical side of their marriage had become stale, unsatisfactory and…yes, he had to admit it, almost unnecessary. Their lives had become boring and predictable. It had all been his fault and guilt stared him in the face. He had let Marjorie down. She had trusted him implicitly and he had betrayed that trust. He now had to make quite sure that she never found out about his affair with Amy, he concluded. The whole thing had been madness in the extreme. It was out of character, stupid and cowardly. And yet…he knew that he loved Amy and that he was totally lost without her.

He slammed the pipe down on to the desk in front of him.

Dammit, he hadn't been able to think straight since the day that he'd first met her. Beautiful Amy…wonderful Amy. His mind savoured their moments together. He remembered her perfume and the smell of her hair – he smiled, it reminded him of a fresh spring morning. He recalled her contagious laughter and most of all, the look in her eyes when she had kissed him. His body tensed as he grabbed both sides of the small window frame, his knuckles showing a creamy-white colour under his skin.

'I've been such a fool. I'm 42 years of age for goodness sake. I should have had more sense,' he scolded himself in anger.

It was early summer and despite the wind, the gardens were

looking at their best. Everything was burgeoning with vibrant new life, but in his present mood Gerald could not appreciate it. In silent anguish he closed his eyes and tried to shut out the perfect scene that was laid out before him.

Instead, he allowed his mind to drift backwards to that fateful day eighteen months earlier, to the time when his life had been uncluttered and uncomplicated. His eyes misted over as he remembered...

It was just two weeks before Easter and there was a hint of snow in the freshening wind, which had thankfully blown away the early morning choking yellow fog. Londoners shivered, turned up the collars of their coats, and hurried to their destinations.

Gerald was attending a meeting with his friend and accountant, William Anderson in his office in Lincolns Inn Fields. They had been discussing the annual profit and loss account for the Epton Hall Estate.

'Well William, the figures look pretty good don't they?'

'Yes, and the same goes for this year as well, providing the economy remains stable,' he replied with a self-satisfied look on his face.

Gerald beamed with pride and pleasure. 'I can easily afford to buy the new combine harvester that has just come on the market and those new-fangled milking machines we were talking about.'

'Yes indeed. But don't go too mad.'

'Of course I won't. You know me, I have my sons' futures to think about remember. But in any case, I really must spend the money we put aside last year, on improvements to the estate employees' houses. I don't want any problems in that direction, as the Union people have already been on to me.'

'Shop Stewards!' William said, pulling a wry face. 'Who needs them? In that case, make that your first priority.' The antique clock on the mantelpiece struck eleven o'clock and he pressed a small button on the wall behind his desk. 'Gerald, before we go on, I was wondering if you'd noticed that I had a new secretary?'

'No I didn't. What happened to Alice? She's been with you for years.'

'Yes she has, but she decided to retire. She's gone to live in the country, somewhere in deepest Devon, I believe. I'm surprised that you didn't notice her replacement. Walking around with your head in the clouds as usual, eh? Her name is Amy Butler and she comes from Vancouver in Canada. She is extremely efficient and charming too. What more could a man wish for?' William's eyes sparkled from behind steel rimmed spectacles.

A few moments later, an elegant young woman walked into the office. She exuded a distinct air of sensual confidence and knew that she was beautiful.

'Yes, Mr. Anderson?' she asked.

'Can we have some coffee now, please Amy?'

'Yes, of course,' she replied picking up a pile of files from the desk. 'Oh yes, Mr. Goldman wishes to change his two o'clock meeting to half past two tomorrow. I told him that would be OK.' Gerald noted that her Canadian accent was clipped and cultured.

'Good, yes...thank you Amy.' He turned to Gerald. 'I'd like you to meet Amy.'

Gerald stood up. His heart suddenly thumped as he looked at her and for the first time in his life, he found himself stuttering. 'How do...how...do you do, Miss...Miss Butler?'

'Hi,' she replied, flashing a smile in his direction. 'Would you like cream and sugar in yours too?'

'Yes...yes please.' He couldn't stop looking at her.

The room seemed empty after she had left the office. Gerald felt confused. He couldn't remember having been affected by any woman like this before and his pulse continued to race. Not even Marjorie had ever made him feel this way. Amy returned a few minutes later carrying two steaming cups on a tray. Her huge dark deeply set brown eyes looked into his as she handed him his coffee. He felt as if he was drowning. Her long hair was glossy and smooth and swayed hypnotically from side to side as she turned her head. She wore a small neat sleeveless white blouse and a patterned blue circular skirt which swirled around enticingly as she moved around in her high-heeled peep-toed shoes. He caught a glimpse of a fashionably stiff white petticoat underneath her skirt when she left the room. He thought that she was exquisite.

The meeting finished at 12.30 p.m. Gerald stood up.

'Well that seems to be it, William. Thanks a million as usual. I don't know what I would do without you.'

'Gerald, I'm glad to be of help, after all what are friends for?' William walked round to the front of his desk. 'I almost forgot. How's Marjorie, she had a bout of that awful influenza that's been going around recently, didn't she?'

'Yes. Quite knocked her off her feet, poor old thing, but you know Marjorie, nothing ever gets her down for long. She's fighting fit again and organising everything down to the last detail as usual.'

'Good, glad to hear it. We must get together after Easter. The weather should be better by then. What do you think?'

'That sounds like a splendid idea. I'll give you a ring and we can organize something.'

On his way out, Gerald found himself stopping at Amy's desk. He hadn't been able to get her out of his mind. 'Hello again,' he said. 'Th...thanks for the delicious c...coffee.' He found himself stuttering for the second time that day.

'All part of the service.'

'I er...'

Amy smiled coquettishly up at him. 'Was there something else you wanted Mr....I mean Captain Hapsworth-Cole?'

'Please call me Gerald.'

'Gerald. Mmm...that's a nice name.'

'Thank you. I...I was wondering if you would do me the honour of having lunch with me?'

Amy's eyes opened wide with surprise. 'I...I don't really know that I should, but...'

'No buts. Please say that you will?'

She hesitated. 'Yes...yes I will. I'll be ready in two minutes.'

It was now a beautiful day, cold and crisp with a brilliantly blue sky. Gerald and Amy conversed easily as they walked through Lincoln's Inn Fields. The bare branches of the trees were thrown into stark relief by the late winter sunshine and a few birds sang heartily: Gerald felt happy to be alive. He took her to his favourite restaurant knowing that it was small, quiet and above all, discreet.

Throughout lunch it soon became apparent that a strong emotional bond was beginning to develop between them. Gerald tried hard to deny his feelings, but Amy seemed to have taken possession of his entire being and it was as if she was using a magnet to draw him ever closer to her. He realised that he had been staring at her, when she said, 'Gerald, is anything wrong? Have I a smudge on the end of my nose, or something?'

'Oh, I beg your pardon. What did you say?'

'I asked you if anything was wrong, only you've gone all quiet on me.'

'No...no...I'm sorry, I was just thinking that I had never seen anyone with such beautiful eyes before. They are like deep pools.'

Amy looked embarrassed and was silent for a few moments. Finally she spoke again. 'Gerald, you're married aren't you? William told me about your family.'

'Yes. Yes, I am married,' he replied. 'But the way I feel now...'

She reached across the table and placed two fingers against his lips. 'Shhh. Please don't say it.'

'Amy. Do you believe in…in love at first sight?'

'Gee, I don't really know. I…'

'I didn't, but I do now.'

'But you can't love me. What about your wife…your kids? This is crazy. We've only just met.'

'Amy, can you look me in the eye and tell me that you don't feel at least something for me?'

She was silent for a few moments. 'No, Gerald, I can't.' She looked away. He took hold of her hand and squeezed it.

After that day, they met regularly and Gerald was forced to make excuses for his more frequent trips up to London, which Marjorie always accepted without question. As time went by, he began to feel more and more guilty about seeing her, but his heart had taken over his ability to think straight. If he had been able to stop and take a good look at what he was doing, he would never have asked her out to lunch in the first place.

Amy had been renting a small, but comfortable flat in the Euston Road area and they spent precious and fleeting moments locked in one another's arms, neither knowing nor caring about the consequences of their actions. They were lost in a wilderness of love, passion and desperate longing from which there was no escape.

One grey and wet afternoon Gerald let himself into the flat. He felt pleased with himself. He had just bought Amy a present. It wasn't her birthday of course, but he felt that he needed to show her how much she meant to him. He patted his pocket to make sure that it was still there.

He placed his wet umbrella in the corner of the small lobby and looked at his reflection in the mirror. He ran his fingers through his thick hair and straightened the knot of his tie. A few stray hairs just above his ears were showing the first tentative signs of grey, but he was still a very attractive man. Hmm he thought, not bad for someone of my age. Life was being good to him and with a self-satisfied grin on his handsome face he walked into the living room. He could smell the delicious aroma of freshly ground coffee. Amy had already arrived.

She looked unusually pale as she walked towards him. She was wearing a red dress with a full wide belted skirt and with her hair tied in a ponytail, Gerald thought that she looked about seventeen. His heart thumped so loudly that he was sure that she would be able to hear it. He put his arms around her and kissed her with a passion that astounded him.

He knew that there was something wrong. Alarm bells jangled inside his head. Why hadn't Amy returned his kisses with her usual fervour?

Amy pulled away from him. 'Gerald, I have something important to say to you.' She sounded tense.

'Something important? My darling, there can be nothing more important than me making passionate love to you.'

'Please, don't, I mean not now.'

'Amy, what's wrong?'

'I'm afraid that I…'

'Come along? Don't let's waste time talking. I haven't seen you for a week.' He pulled the mournful face that usually made her laugh.

But this time she didn't. 'Gerald, please be serious for a moment. I love you with all my heart and you must know how much you mean to me.'

'Yes darling and I love you too.'

'And now that we've established that we both love one another, where does it leave us?'

'Amy, you're not making any sense.'

'I'm sorry, but I just can't stand this covert, deceitful

existence any longer. I feel so guilty all the time. It is obvious to me that you cannot make any further commitment to me and that you will never leave Marjorie. After all, why should you? I feel that there is no future for us.'

'What do you mean? I love you and you love me, isn't that enough?' The warning bells now began to clamour.

'No, I'm afraid that it isn't,' she replied as a single tear ran down her cheek, 'and that is why I have decided to go back home to Canada.' He looked at her. He could feel the blood draining away from his face. 'Gerald, are you listening to me? I said that I am going home to Vancouver.' She stepped backwards and turned away from him.

'But...but...I don't understand.' Total panic now took over Gerald's brain and the bells now tolled the death knell of his happiness. He grabbed her and swung her round so that she was facing him. 'My darling you can't go home, you can't leave me I won't let you, do you hear?'

'It's no use, Gerald. I've already booked my sea-passage back home. I'll be leaving on Thursday.' Tears had begun to form in the corners of her eyes as she looked up at him, then she looked downwards.

'But...but that's only four days away.' A feeling of utter devastation swept over him and it was his turn to look away.

'I'm sorry Gerald, but I can't go on like this any longer. I have to go for all our sakes, your wife and children's especially. I'm going to...' she hesitated and cleared her throat. 'I...I have of course already told William about my decision to leave and he quite understands.'

'But...but are you sure there is nothing more that I can say or do, to make you change your mind my darling girl?'

'No honey, I'm afraid there isn't.'

Four days later, Gerald stood stiffly beside Amy on the crowded quay not knowing what to say or do. Her parting words filled him with dismay and sadness.

'Honey, I have to go back to Canada. Neither of us has been thinking straight since we met. Supposing your wife was to find out about us?'

Gerald took a deep breath and squared his shoulders, but the words that he had been practising all day just would not come out. Instead, he put his arms around her.

'Amy, please don't go. What must I say that will make you change your mind? I need you, can't you see that?' he pleaded. He was shaking with emotion and frustration. 'Dammit woman, what am I going to do without you?'

'It's no use Gerald, why can't you accept the inevitable? But…but there is something else that I have to tell you before I go.' Deep pain showed in Amy's eyes.

'Yes,' he replied dully.

'Before I tell you, you must make me a promise that you will not try to make me change my mind. Do you make that promise?'

'Yes, my darling, I promise,' he said in a voice full of resignation. But…'

'No 'buts', please Gerald.' She pointed towards a seat on the quayside. 'Let's sit for a moment shall we?'

He shrugged his shoulders and walked slowly towards the seat. To be honest, he was quite grateful for the chance of sitting down as his legs were beginning to shake.

'I've been so happy during these past months and now I…I am…' she continued, her voice faltering.

'Amy, my darling, what is it?'

There was an agonising silence while the tears in her eyes suddenly spilled over and ran down her face. 'Gerald, I…I'm going to have a baby…our baby.'

Gerald felt completely and utterly stupefied. His broad shoulders sagged and he stood up feeling totally confused. He looked down on the woman he loved. 'A baby! But Amy...' He could feel a mixture of pain, regret and hopelessness rising up within him. 'Why the hell didn't you tell me before? You owe me that much at least,' he retorted in anger.

Amy stood up and kissed him, stunning him into silence. 'I didn't tell you because I knew what your reaction would be. Remember you promised not to try to make me change my mind, so please don't. I have already told my parents. They were shocked and hurt at first, but I think that they're getting used to the idea now and have promised to help me.' Her voice grew quieter and softer. 'The baby will probably be born at the end of April, or the beginning of May next year.'

Gerald felt that the bottom had fallen out of his life. Amy was expecting his child, so how could he just let her walk out of his life? 'Amy...Amy my dearest,' he implored, 'I know that I made a promise to you just now, but how can I let you go knowing that you are carrying my child?'

'Honey, you must know that our position is hopeless. At least this way I shall have something to cherish that belongs to both of us. I promise you that I will look after our child with love and understanding. If it is a boy, then I'm sure he will grow up to be a wonderful man just like his father. You'll be able to come over to see us, won't you?'

'You try stopping me. You can be sure that I'll find a way.'

'We can work something out between us, can't we? It will be something for us both to look forward to.' Amy smiled through a veil of tears and at that moment, Gerald knew that he would remember her smile for the rest of his days and her parting words, '...I love you, always remember that.'

And she was gone.

* * * * * *

Chapter Eight

The memories of their final parting were always uppermost in Gerald's mind, but none more so as he continued to stare out of the attic window. The look on her face when Amy had torn herself away from his arms and had run up the ramp on to the ship was forever etched upon his memory.

The time since she had returned to Canada had been sheer hell for him. They had exchanged letters and had spoken briefly on the telephone, but this had only created in him such an intense longing to see her, that he had derived little pleasure from it. Due to the huge distance separating them, Amy's voice was always disjointed and cold. Her latest letter informing him of his son James's birth, had at first made him feel ecstatic and then had sent his spirits spiralling downwards.

His home, Epton Hall, had belonged to the Hapsworth-Cole family for nearly 200 years. Its many windows looked out on to gardens which would have been the envy of anyone. The estate spread out endlessly before him. Manicured flowerbeds and box hedges gave way to fields and to the gently rolling hills in the distance. It all belonged to him and his family. He could see Bert, the head gardener striding across the lawn towards the walled kitchen garden. Marjorie had just been speaking to him about her plans for the summer. Gerald sighed. She had some grandiose idea about holding the local school's fete here at the Hall. He sighed again. Could he cope with marquees, hundreds of people and screaming children with their ice creams, the new noisy music – what was it called, Rock and Roll? And worst of all…candy floss: nasty sticky stuff. He knew that he would have to of course. He should at least try to pretend that everything was normal and that he was happy. But he knew that happiness was the last thing that he expected in his life now. His love for Amy was increasing day by day and now that they had a child...what was he going to do? Angry, desperate tears began to flow down his cheeks, which were furiously brushed aside.

In the middle of the main lawn, an ornate fountain tossed a plume of water several feet into the air and all around the base of the fountain six small chubby cherubs blew stone trumpets, each spouting yet more water. The cherubs' cheeks ballooned with the effort as the sun's rays played on the fountain and gave the impression of a sparkling, jewelled crown, but even the sight of all this beauty failed to lift his spirits.

He moved away from the window, sat down at his desk and reached for his pipe. This was the only thing that gave him any relief now. He lit it and sighed. The resultant blue smoke rolled and swirled around the room and was highlighted by the sun as it shafted obliquely in through the window.

The bright sunlight also shone directly into his eyes. Feeling irritated, he stood up and closed the curtains. He was in the middle of writing a difficult letter to Amy and it was imperative that he kept his thoughts clear and strong.

During his childhood, Gerald had spent many happy hours in this room, eagerly rummaging through his father's treasured possessions. The old sea chest had been his favourite. It contained so many treasures: old logbooks and photographs, a telescope, a cracked plate, knives, forks and even an old naval uniform. He had been allowed to play with all of them. He also recalled the times when his father had lifted him gently on to his knee and he'd listened wide-eyed and enthralled by all the countless stories he had related to him. Of course, all this was before his father had become vague and distant and had finally succumbed to acute confusion and insanity. After this unhappy time, his dear father had existed in a strange world seemingly only peopled by demons and his death had been a blessed release.

The intervening years had gone so swiftly by. Now it was 1953 and Great Britain and especially London, was preparing for the Coronation of Her Majesty, Queen Elizabeth II, following upon the sad death of her father, King George VI, the previous year. Elizabeth was young, beautiful and enthusiastic and was set to rule over a country which was changing rapidly. Almost every day, news of some new technological advance would hit the headlines of the newspapers. It was the beginning of an exciting era of that he was quite certain and totally different from the one his father would have known and Gerald could hardly believe that he had been dead for nearly 25 years.

Two letters lay on his desk. One was from Amy and the other, his half written reply. An envelope lay beside them and already addressed to her in Vancouver. Although he had a perfectly good, large, well-furnished study downstairs, he sometimes found the quietness of the attic helped him to concentrate and in any case, he could hardly write to Amy in full view of his family. Today, however, he was finding his reply to Amy almost impossible to complete.

He had just written the words, *"I too, lie awake at night pretending that I am lying beside you and often curse the size of the ocean that is separating us. My darling I..."* He picked up her letter and read it for the umpteenth time. 'Amy, my sweetest Amy,' he said in despair. He was deeply moved by her words, *"...we now have a son and I have named him, James Gerald Hapsworth-Cole Butler. I hope that you approve?"* Towards the end of the letter, Amy had added, *"I lie awake at night, pretending you are holding me in your arms".*

He picked up the copy of James' birth certificate, which she had enclosed with her letter. This was proof of his son's existence. He tried to picture his dear, sweet Amy with her laughing brown eyes and their newly born son, James. He rubbed his eyes wearily and wondered how his life could have become so complicated. He still loved Marjorie in his own way, didn't he? And surely it would break her heart if she ever discovered evidence of his infidelity? Nevertheless, he knew that he would somehow have to see Amy and the baby.

Why did they now live so far away?

He stared into space, hoping for inspiration. He owed it to Amy. His conscience was nagging him and telling him that he needed to reassure her that his love was as strong if not stronger, than before. But how could he reassure her and what could he say? He had always been a loving responsible father to Quentin and Charles, so didn't his new son, James deserve the same devotion? He thought long and hard, until his head began to ache. Finally he decided that he would make an appointment with his solicitor the following day. He would have to work out a way in which he could make secret provision for James in a will. He was aware that he should have sorted it out before now, because the estate and the house were worth an enormous amount of money and he owed it to his family to make sure that his affairs were in order.

All this mental torment was beginning to take its toll on Gerald emotionally. In quiet, lonely despair he held his head in his hands. The intolerable burden of his secret was becoming almost too much to bear. More silent tears squeezed between his eyelids and slid down his cheeks and again he rubbed them away savagely. Grown men don't cry, he told himself. He picked up his pen and began to write.

Suddenly he heard excited voices. Someone was coming up the stairs to the attic.

In sheer panic, he picked up both letters frantically wondering what he was going to do with them. His father's old bookcase stared up at him. Nobody ever looked at these old books, least of all Marjorie as she was always far too busy. Gerald pulled an old and dusty volume from the top shelf and shoved the letter and the birth certificate from Amy in between its yellowing pages. He placed it back on the shelf. He hurriedly withdrew another book from the bottom shelf this time and without stopping to think further, pushed his reply and the envelope inside. He replaced the book and heaved a sigh of relief.

Just in time, he noticed that the little black velvet box containing the ring he had intended giving to Amy, was sitting on the desk. He realised that it had been hidden by the letters, and he heaved a sigh of relief. He would often get it out of the box and just look at it, remembering and wishing… With a pounding heart, he placed it in his pocket.

Gerald stood up just as the attic door opened. His wife Marjorie entered followed closely by Quentin and Charles.

'Come on darling,' she said. 'Do you remember promising the boys that you would take them out on the boat this afternoon?'

'Yes, come on Dad. We're fed up with waiting,' Charles echoed, his young face screwed up with indignation.

Gerald hadn't realised how late it was and he felt ashamed. 'Why yes, of course. I've just finished. I'm sorry that it has taken so long, but I had one or two er…business letters to write this morning. I'm already dressed for the boat, so come on then downstairs all of you,' He herded them all through the door. Before turning off the light and closing the door, he stared anxiously back into the room, hoping that the letters would not be discovered. I will finish the letter tomorrow and then make an appointment to see my solicitor, he reminded himself. He followed his family downstairs.

Gerald, like his father and his father before him, had spent years in The Royal Navy and was an excellent seaman. He had purchased his boat about two years' earlier. The children wanted it to be called 'The Sea Witch' and during a family naming ceremony, Marjorie had stood just like royalty and had smashed a bottle of champagne over the stern of the boat.

'I name this ship, I mean boat, The Sea Witch,' she had shouted. 'And God bless all who sail in her.' The speech had been accompanied by hoots of laughter from Gerald and the two boys. It had been a truly happy occasion. The family had subsequently spent many happy and carefree days cruising on the Solent.

Gerald now tried to put the morning's traumas to the back of his mind. He was determined not to disappoint the boys. The morning had given the promise of a fine day, but the afternoon failed to live up to expectations. Dark threatening clouds hovered ominously on the horizon, but he had far too much on his mind to notice these warning signs. He felt that he needed the freedom of the open sea in order to clear his head and so he took The Sea Witch further out to sea than usual.

The squall seemed to come out of nowhere.

Within minutes the wind had whipped up the waves to frightening proportions. The small cruiser was buffeted cruelly by first one wave and then another. The low clouds made visibility difficult too. Gerald realised that in order to keep the boys safe, he would have to send them down below whilst he battled with the elements.

'Quentin, Charles,' he barked.

'Yes Dad,' they chorused.

'Get down below now. It's not safe for you up here and please close the hatch firmly, do you hear?'

'But Dad...we...' A wave of gigantic proportions suddenly proved a point by hitting the port side. The Sea Witch shuddered and rocked alarmingly.

'Do as I say immediately and get down below,' he yelled at the top of his voice. 'And make sure that you do shut that hatch properly.'

'Yes Dad,' Quentin said his voice filled with despondency. 'Come on Charlie. I hope you realise that we will be missing all the fun,' he aimed in his father's direction as they stumbled down the steep steps. Gerald's reply went sailing into the wind.

Now that the boys were down below, Gerald took stock of the situation. The wind's direction was unpredictable and the small boat was being tossed around like a cork. On top of that the unrelenting waves lashed and pounded the boat's sides, creating a sound like thunder and he wasn't sure how much more the boat could take. His puny efforts seemed futile and real fear took hold of him.

Fortunately the rapidly decreasing visibility gave him no inkling of the disaster that was about to befall them. The large merchant ship bore down upon the small craft without any warning. Gerald noticed it too late and in sheer desperation tried to steer the boat out of its path, but any manoeuvre proved to be hopeless. He had no time to panic or take further evasive action when suddenly the Sea Witch was hit amidships. There was a sickening thud, following by a tremendous crunching and tearing sound…

…and the little boat was sliced in two.

The last thing Gerald Hapsworth-Cole ever knew was the sight of part of the boat containing his two beloved young sons sliding irrevocably beneath the waves. Feelings of panic, regret, fear and sorrow swiftly overtook him as the remaining half of the Sea Witch reared up in front of him. A loose plank of decking hit him savagely on the side of the head…and he was plummeted into the cold, dark and unwelcoming waters of the English Channel.

All that now remained of the little boat was a rapidly increasing patch of oil, as it bubbled inexorably and ominously, up to the surface. The crew were totally unaware that they had hit anything and the huge merchant ship continued on its way.

* * * * * *

Chapter Nine

Katie

2009

Nothing could have prepared Katie for what the letter contained.

The ink had faded in places and several words were difficult to read. The letter was written from an address in Vancouver, British Columbia, Canada and was dated the 24th April 1953. It read:

"*My dearest, darling Gerald,*

Thank you for your most welcome letter, you have no idea how wonderful it is to hear from you again. Each time you write you seem further away from me.

Gerald, I have some exciting news for you. I am so happy: we now have a son and I have named him James Gerald Hapsworth-Cole Butler. I hope that you approve. He is a fine boy weighing in at 8 pounds 7 ozs. He was born yesterday and looks so much like you my darling…"

Katie could hardly believe what she was reading. Gerald Hapsworth-Cole had a son with a woman living in Vancouver. Questions began to form in her mind and her heart began to melt as she continued to read the letter.

"*He is so cute and adorable. How I wish things could have been different between us and that you could have been present at his birth. I miss and love you so very much and I know I will never be able to forget those precious moments we spent together. If only we could have remained together always, but it was not meant to be.*

I desperately want him to know about you and what a wonderfully kind person you are. My one hope is that even if we cannot be together, we will be able to meet sometimes. That way, James will be able to see what a fine, upstanding man you are. I also want him to know that it was my decision to come back to Canada and not yours.

I quite understand and accept the fact that your wife and sons hold the first place in your life, how could it be otherwise? But I do know that I do not want James to grow up thinking that you had deserted us."

Tears formed in Katie's eyes. She couldn't read any more. It was a love letter and as such was a personal and private thing. She hastily placed it back where it had lain for so many years, and started to sort through the rest of the books. But after a few minutes, her curiosity again got the better of her and she found herself picking up the book and reading the letter again.

She felt excited. The letter she was now holding in her hands could hold the key to whoever inherited the estate. Thank goodness she had found it as it could just as easily have been destroyed. But what had happened to Gerald and the two boys? Some sort of tragedy must have occurred, because nobody had ever come up with an explanation for their disappearance. Was there someone out there who knew what had happened and was too scared to say anything? She read on…

"My parents as always are very kind and supportive, so our son will have no financial or emotional problems. I lie awake at night, my darling, pretending that you are holding me in your arms. From your last letter, I know that you feel the same way. If only there was not such a large ocean separating us.

I will send you a photograph of James soon, but in the meantime, I am enclosing a copy of his birth certificate, and that way he will seem more real to you. Perhaps you can keep it somewhere safely?

I send you my deepest and enduring love, always. Your ever loving soulmate, Amy."

Hidden in between the first and second pages of the letter, Katie found the birth certificate and it was yellowed with age. A feeling of excited anticipation enveloped her. Yes, there it was in black and white. Gerald Hapsworth-Cole had an illegitimate son called James, living in Canada. She looked at the date of the letter. James would now be in his mid-fifties. Slowly the implications of the discovery of the letter and the birth certificate became clear to her. I wonder if Amy Butler is still alive and what about James, her son, where was he now? Was it possible that he could have a legitimate claim to the Epton Hall estate? If he did, Gerald Hapsworth-Cole's nephew Harold wouldn't be very happy about it and he had apparently already been traced and probably been told that he would inherit everything! 'Wow,' Katie called out. 'What a dilemma.' Her forehead creased with concentration.

Katie turned back to the letter in front of her. She felt so sad. Reading a letter like this one was bad enough, but the mystery about what had happened to Gerald and the two boys, now made it assume huge proportions in her mind. Had Amy Butler ever received a reply to the letter in front of her, or was Gerald's fate sealed before he had a chance to reply? Nobody would ever know the answer, unless of course, the Hapsworth-Cole Butlers could be traced. And more to the point, had Marjorie ever found out about her husband's affair with Amy? Surely Amy would have written to him again if she didn't get a reply and if she had written to Gerald again, perhaps Marjorie had opened the letters and then destroyed them and if she hadn't intercepted them, where were they?

Her mind was in a whirl. What had happened to the principal actors in this tragic drama of fifty odd years ago? But even her fertile imagination could not come up with the answers. Instead, there were even more questions and just like soldiers getting ready for battle, questions began to form in the back of her mind. Had Marjorie Hapsworth-Cole died still believing in the love she thought her husband had for her, or had she known about it and that was the reason why she had become such a recluse? Had she felt guilty about something? No, Katie told herself firmly, she would not even think about something like that, but... It was much more likely that the poor woman had taken her secret to the grave, being too ashamed to mention it to anyone.

Katie found the whole thing confusing and depressing. She was horrified at the thought of poor Amy living all those thousands of miles away, her heart broken because Gerald had stopped writing to her. She must have felt bitterly betrayed. Why, she had probably spent the rest of her life believing that he had deserted her. A feeling of sadness crept over her as she replaced the letter and the birth certificate in the envelope and then hurried downstairs to the study to call Brian to tell him about her discovery.

As Katie walked across the huge entrance hall, she failed to notice a tall shadowy figure silently melting away into the darkness created by the enormous staircase.

Brian Ainsley's voice came over clearly on the phone. 'Hello, The Good Book Shop, can I help you?'

'Brian, it's me, Katie. You'll never guess what I've just found.'

'Oh, that's easy,' he said. 'Another first edition, or a skeleton in one of the cupboards?' he quipped.

'Well I suppose it could be regarded as a kind of skeleton and it could prove to be important to whoever inherits Epton Hall.'

'Come on. Don't get all mysterious on me, Katie.'

'Well, I was just going through the last of the books in the attic, when I found an old letter.'

'A letter?' he repeated, sounding curious.

'Yes. It fell from one of the books.' And Brian...'
'Yes.'
'I had to read it, and...' she hesitated.
'Go on.'
'You know that everyone believes that Gerald Hapsworth-Cole's nephew Harold is now the only living relative.'
'Yes?'
'Well, the letter I found was addressed to Gerald and it contained information that could prove this to be untrue.'
'Good lord,' came back Brian's surprised response.
'The letter was from a woman called Amy Butler, who at the time was living in Vancouver in Canada and was dated the 3rd May 1953. It was a love letter, Brian, telling him that they had a son.'
'A son?' Brian was speechless.
'Yes, and she enclosed a copy of his birth certificate to prove it, and it named Gerald Hapsworth-Cole as the father!'

The shadowy figure now stood in the doorway of the study. He was staring at the back of Katie's head with a look of incredulity and horror on his face.

* * * * * *

Chapter Ten

The conversation Harold Hapsworth-Cole overheard made his blood run cold with anger. There couldn't possibly be such a letter. The girl was obviously wrong, how could there be another child? The whole thing was preposterous, he told himself. And yet, this young slip of a girl was standing there telling someone that another child did exist. Supposing this letter was genuine? Panic began to course throughout his body. Nothing could take his prize away from him, not after all the plans he had made for his future.

Harold owned and ran a small tourist boating company in Sliema, near Valetta, on the island of Malta. Over recent months, he'd been finding it difficult to make ends meet and now his business was in danger of folding altogether.

Two days' earlier he had been sitting in his hot stuffy office and trying to juggle the quarter's figures into some semblance of normality: nothing seemed to be making sense any more. He was holding his head in his hands in despair, when the telephone rang shrilly beside him.

'Mr. Harold Hapsworth-Cole?' a man's voice enquired.

'Yes, speaking.'

'Hello. My name is John Broadbent and I represent Messrs. Broadbent and Crombie, Solicitors in Epton, West Sussex in England. We have been acting for the Hapsworth-Cole family for many years.'

'Yes. I seem to recall the name of your firm. How can I help you?'

'Yes, well…I hope you can. Can you confirm that your father's name was Stanley Edward Hapsworth-Cole and that you are the nephew of Captain and Mrs. Gerald Hapsworth-Cole?'

'Yes I can. I have all the usual papers to prove who I am,' he replied haughtily. 'Why do you want to know?'

'Mr. Hapsworth-Cole, I am sorry to have to tell you, but your aunt has died, and as you are now as far as we can ascertain the only living relative, you could possibly have a legitimate claim for ownership of the Epton Hall estate.' Harold couldn't believe his ears as he had almost given up waiting for the old girl to go. Mr. Broadbent went on to explain in greater detail the circumstances of his aunt's death and how it affected him personally. His heartbeat rose and his eyes glistened, not because he was sorry to learn about Marjorie's death – he had rarely seen her or his uncle and cared little about what happened to them – but the thought of all that money made his brain reel.

'Are you still there, Mr. Hapsworth-Cole? I can quite understand that this news must have come as quite a shock to you.'

'Yes…yes, terrible news. Poor Aunt Marjorie. Yes, a great shock indeed. So where do we go from here?' He wanted to shout his joy from the rooftops, but knew that he had to keep his elation to himself on this occasion.

'We will of course need you to come over to England as soon as possible,' the solicitor continued. 'The fact that no will has yet been found will delay things slightly, and the usual exhaustive searches are being made by an extremely reputable company but from our own preliminary investigations, we do not foresee any other complications. You must of course bring your birth certificate etc. with you.'

'Yes, yes of course.' Harold felt stunned.

'Perhaps you would be so kind as to let me know when you will be coming back to England. In the meantime we would like to offer you our sincerest condolences.'

'Thank you, Mr. Broadbent,' he replied. 'I'm afraid that I am rather busy at the moment, but you can rest assured that I will keep you informed about everything. Goodbye.' Harold really didn't wish to continue speaking to this obsequious man any longer than he had to.

'I look forward to meeting you, Mr. Hapsworth-Cole. Goodbye.'

After replacing the receiver, Harold sat in his shabby untidy office contemplating the feeling of owning such a vast fortune. Over the past few months he'd grown tired of the constant heat, the lack of rain and the fact that his business was failing. He realised that this telephone call could be the answer to all his prayers. Yes, he thought trembling with excitement; I can buy myself a state of the art yacht. Not the kind of tatty boat in which I've ferried so many people around Valetta harbour for so many years, but a large luxury sea-going vessel. Perspiration began to trickle down his face and he brushed it away with a less than clean handkerchief. 'I could even employ a crew to sail it for me.' He laughed. It was a strange, hysterical laugh and it echoed around his empty office, like a demon trying to find its way out. His new-found feeling of power was intoxicating and he literally danced around his office. Afterwards he decided not to tell anyone about his imminent return to England. He laughed again - they would find out soon enough.

He managed to book himself on to the next available flight to Gatwick, England. He only had a few loose ends to tie up before his departure. Due to his boating company's deep financial problems, nobody was really interested in whether he was there or not and even most of his so-called friends had now disappeared. They weren't interested in someone on the way down, he thought bitterly. But I'll show them, I'll show all of them. He rubbed his hands together with glee.

In no time at all, he was on his way to Luqa Airport.

Once he was in England, Harold hired a car, and booked himself into a small private hotel before driving to Epton Hall. He wanted to look around the estate on his own and didn't want any nosy solicitors or estate agents getting in the way. Above all, he was pleased to be back home. The air felt clean and fresh and he could breathe more freely and it was good to see green fields and trees again. Yes, Harold decided, once the estate was his he would make England his permanent home and be the master of all he surveyed. His eyes lit up with pure avarice.

For the first time in many months he thought about his parents. He had always loved his mother. She stood out in his mind as a shining example of what he thought a woman should be like. Throughout his life, no single person had ever lived up to her ideal. But he'd never been close to his father, Stanley. Stanley had been a weak man and even though he had known that Epton Hall would someday be his if he lived long enough, it hadn't seemed to bother him. Harold on the other hand hadn't forgotten about it for an instant. After his father's death, thoughts of this vast fortune were seldom out of his mind.

Now, he was actually standing in Epton Hall and this slip of a girl was still speaking and he couldn't believe what he was hearing. The existence of this letter could conceivably bring his whole new world crashing around his ears.

His mood darkened.

'What do we do now?' the girl was saying. There was a pause. 'Perhaps we could take it to your solicitor friend, Penny Humberston, she'll know what to do with it.' Harold strained his ears to try to hear the other side of the conversation, but it was no use. The girl continued, 'and yes Brian, Gerald Hapsworth-Cole's nephew Harold is going to be really upset if this letter proves to be genuine: I think that he will have a fight on his hands.'

Harold could feel his ire rising...

'Yes, I'll bring the letter round to you this evening then, so that you can have a look at it. Bye.'

In an instant, Harold Hapsworth-Cole knew what he had to do. In his line of business, he was used to thinking on his feet. It was imperative that he got hold of this letter so that he could destroy it before anyone else could see it. He stared at the girl's back with such venom and hatred that it made him feel nauseous and had to grab hold of both door posts in order to steady himself.

* * *

A slight noise behind Katie made her jump. She turned round. A man was standing in the doorway staring at her. Who on earth was he and what was he doing there, she asked herself in a blind panic? She had a distinct feeling of déjà vu, but had no time to think about the reason why. The man was smiling at her as he walked into the room and a shiver ran down her spine.

'Oh my god, you frightened the life out of me.' Her heart was beating like a drum inside her chest and she felt slightly light-headed. 'What…what are you doing here and how did you get in?'

'My dear, I'm so sorry if I startled you. I came in through the front door. The key was in the lock.'

'In the lock? Oh dear…I…'

'Yes. Is it usually so easy for people to just wander in here?'

'Well no but… Nancy the housekeeper has just left.'

'I should have thought that a place like this would at the very least, have a burglar alarm system to deter intruders. Anyway, I feel that I should introduce myself. My name is Harold Hapsworth-Cole.' He held out his hand to her. 'And you are…?'

Katie was filled with panic and her legs began to tremble. Oh my god, Harold, she thought and what on earth do I do now? I can't let him see the letter until it's been examined by a solicitor. Stay calm Katie, stay calm, she told herself sternly.

'My name is Katie Nicholson and I work for the Good Book Shop in Anston. I understand that you have come all the way from Malta?'

'Yes, and it's good to be back home again.'

'I've been cataloguing all the books in the house. Mrs. Hapsworth-Cole spent most of the last forty years or so, attending auctions and buying vast numbers of them.'

'So I understand.' He smiled again. 'Marjorie was my aunt – by marriage of course. Oh it's all such a sad business.' His voice registered deep concern, but his blue eyes remained emotionless and cold.

Katie studied him. He had a long, narrow face and he was sweating profusely and constantly mopping his brow with a handkerchief. There was an overall air of unkemptness about him and his clothes, although clean, were creased and shabby. His dark, greying hair was over long and hung around his ears. Katie was not impressed. His skin looked sallow, probably because he had spent the last few years living in Malta. She decided that she didn't much like this man, or the way his mouth twisted with tension when he spoke and…she began to feel intensely threatened by him.

'In case you are wondering why I am here, I've come to look at the house,' he said glancing around the study. 'MY house now, I believe. Unfortunately, my father and I were never welcome here all the time that Aunt Marjorie was alive.'

'I wasn't expecting anyone to come here this afternoon,' Katie blurted out. 'Nancy always tells me if anyone is coming.'

'I'm so sorry,' he said, his face a frosty mask. 'I know I should have telephoned to let Mrs. Brown know, but there didn't seem enough time, so here I am.'

Katie clutched the letter a little more tightly in her hand. She didn't want to draw his attention to it, after all she wasn't sure how much he had heard or understood of her conversation with

Brian. He would hear about it soon enough from his solicitors.

Harold Hapsworth-Cole cleared his throat making her jump. 'I understand that you are now near to completing your task here?' She looked at him sharply. 'I'm sorry, but I couldn't help overhearing some of your conversation just now. Is there some sort of a problem?'

'No there isn't,' she replied. 'Well if you'll excuse me, I'll leave you to look around. I must get up to the attic and finish off the last of the books. Goodbye Mr. Hapsworth-Cole.'

'Yes Miss Nicholson. It's good to have met you and thank you for all your hard work. Goodbye.'

Katie couldn't wait to get away from this obnoxious man. Even though he had a cultured voice, she didn't like him. There was nothing that she could put her finger on, but he made her feel uncomfortable and she didn't relax again until she was back in the attic with the door closed firmly behind her. She couldn't help feeling perturbed as she looked around the old attic. Just how much had Harold heard of her conversation with Brian, she wondered? But at least he hadn't mentioned the letter. Her shoulders now began to ache due to the tension engendered by his sudden appearance. Throughout this time she had been holding the letter tightly in her hand and she placed it on the desk. She had tried not to become involved, but she'd really begun to care about what happened to the Hapsworth-Cole-Butler family. What if he…?

The loose floorboard outside the attic door suddenly creaked.

Katie froze. It creaked again. She stood up and walked towards the door now convinced that there was someone out there. Suddenly the door was flung open…and Harold Hapsworth-Cole walked in.

'I was just wondering if you were OK up here on your own and left to your own devices?' he said with a sadistic twist of his mouth. 'Only when you were downstairs just now you seemed a little…what shall I say…preoccupied. Was it to do with a letter…an important letter and something to do with me…perhaps?'

There was something about his eyes that terrified Katie, almost as if she'd seen them before and they seemed to be boring into her soul. She didn't know what to do or say, but she did stand her ground. 'No, the letter was not important,' she replied trying to appear nonchalant.

'But you told someone, Brian was it, that you had found a letter, didn't you?'

'Well yes, I did, but it had nothing to do with you, nothing at all.'

'But you told him that it **was** important.'

'Yes it is important, but it has nothing whatsoever to do with you as I have just said. So if you wouldn't mind I must finish what I was doing. Nancy Brown will be here any minute now expecting me to have finished. She needs to lock up you see?' She knew this to be untrue, but she didn't want Harold to know that of course.

'My dear Miss Nicholson,' he said, walking towards her threateningly. 'I would like to have that unimportant letter as I'm quite sure that it belongs to me.'

'No, you can't have it. It needs to be seen by a solicitor.'

'Supposing that I don't want it to be seen by anyone?'

'I'm sorry but…' Without meaning to, Katie turned and looked towards the desk where the letter could clearly be seen.

'Thank you Miss Nicholson, mine I believe.' She ran towards the desk in a blind panic and accidentally tripped on a piece of worn carpet. She could feel herself falling, but could do nothing about it: she caught her head on the corner of the desk…there was pain, regret and then a sudden blackness…

* * * * * *

Chapter Eleven

Harold Hapsworth-Cole looked down dispassionately at the young woman lying unconscious at his feet. He knelt down and placed his fingers on the pulse spot on her neck. He always prided himself on his knowledge of first aid and resuscitation techniques. She had an angry lump and a cut just above her temple. She was pale but her pulse was reasonably regular.

He stood up. 'Silly interfering little bitch – she'll live. Fancy getting herself all worked up about something which isn't her concern.' He looked around the large attic room and shook his head. What a mess he thought, but even as that thought was born, it was immediately replaced by one of joy. It was all going to be his. He looked down at the girl again. What happened to her was a complete accident and had nothing whatsoever to do with him. He had merely followed her upstairs, trying to think how he could get hold of the letter. The way it happened was perfect and he'd enjoyed seeing the look on her face as she'd raced to get to the letter before him.

On an impulse he picked up her handbag. It was lying beside her and was partially open. He looked inside. Harold felt no shame as he plundered and searched through Katie's possessions. He found her diary and thinking that it might prove to be of value to him, placed it in his pocket. Finally he picked up the letter and as he read the words that were written so many years ago, his pulse too began to race. Lying beside it he found the birth certificate and his blood began to boil. This James…this usurper…this unknown person would now stay unknown. He placed the letter and the birth certificate into the envelope, put it into his pocket and walked towards the open door. He turned round and looked back to where the Nicholson girl was lying on the floor. He felt absolutely nothing; no compassion, no guilt, no remorse, just an overwhelming feeling of self-satisfaction as he switched the light off and left the room.

Harold stood for a moment outside the attic uncertain what to do next. He came back into the room and saw that the key was still in the lock. He removed it, and as he did so, a smile spread over his face. He walked out again, closed the door and placed the key in the lock.

It made a harsh grating sound as he turned it.

Once he'd found his way downstairs, he located the mains electricity switch and turned it to the 'OFF' position. He now felt elated. He was in control of his life for the very first time. Before the girl had come downstairs to use the phone he'd taken a quick look in some of the downstairs rooms. In those few moments he had seen a couple of Lalique and Dresden pieces and he had even seen what he thought was a Turner on one of the walls. It was all going to be mine, he thought. He threw back his head and laughed as he left the house.

As he walked down the granite steps, he happened to notice a bicycle propped up against the side of the steps. 'Ah' he said. 'The noble Miss Nicholson's only mode of transport, I presume.' He trundled the bicycle across the driveway and hid it amongst some trees. 'No one must know that she is still here,' he told himself as he walked towards his hired car.

Harold was planning his next move as he drove away from Epton Hall. He drew his dark eyebrows together in intense concentration and gradually a plan began to form in his mind. He drove along several country lanes until he found a phone box and was relieved to find that it was empty and had not been vandalised. News of the loutish behaviour of some young people nowadays had managed to filter through to him in Malta.

He remembered that the Nicholson girl had promised to take the letter to some book shop or other that evening and he knew that he would have to cover his tracks there. Now what was the name of the shop? Harold's eyes jerked from side to side, as he tried to recall the name. His solicitor had mentioned it and he'd thought that it was rather understated at the time. Now then what was it? He remembered that the girl had mentioned it too.

'The diary of course!' he said out loud and savagely cuffing his forehead. With trembling hands, he took it out of his pocket and flicked through the pages. He found a list of phone numbers and addresses. Yes there it was, The Good Book Shop and the name of the owner Brian Ainsley was beside the entry. That was it! He felt exhilarated.

'It won't work…it won't work…' a voice repeated in the depths of his brain. Harold shook his head and tried to concentrate. Underneath this number was the name of 'Simon Brand' and as he flicked through the diary he noticed that the name came up quite often: a boyfriend perhaps? It was certainly worth a gamble.

He worked out what he was going to say and then dialled the number.

'Hello. The Good Book Shop, how can I help you?'

'I would like to speak to Mr. Brian Ainsley please.' Harold tried to make his voice sound as youthful as possible.

'Yes, speaking.'

'Hi Brian. I've got a message for you…'

A few minutes later Harold replaced the receiver. He felt pleased with the way the conversation had gone but as he walked back to his car he felt a strange thumping and drumming sensation in his ears. He felt light-headed and odd and he took out his handkerchief and mopped the perspiration which was beginning to run down his face and into his eyes. What on earth is the matter with me, he wondered?

His brain listened more and more to the voices he often heard in his head and these voices were in direct conflict with what he really wanted to do. He felt confused. Even now, the voices were increasing in intensity and were beginning to goad him.

'You don't think it will work, do you?' they taunted. 'You have to do something…the money is yours…yours…all yours.' Then just as quickly as they had started the voices became silent. Harold's relief was almost tangible.

He spent the next few moments trying to relax before starting the engine and turning the car in the direction of his hotel. He felt exhausted and desperately needed a good night's sleep.

He woke early feeling refreshed and with a clear head for a change. There were no little voices offering him advice. He had arranged for his breakfast to be delivered to his room and it arrived promptly at seven o'clock. The cold bacon and congealed fried egg was eaten in a hurry and with little enthusiasm and after packing his bag, he vacated the room and left the hotel via a metal spiral staircase which was used primarily as an emergency exit. He was anxious not to be seen and it was still early enough for most people still to be in their rooms.

Harold was relieved that everything was going according to plan. It had been a good idea not to use his proper name when he'd booked into the hotel the night before. He climbed into his car and was soon driving towards the airport. It would be as if he had never been here in the first place, he thought as he patted the pocket which contained the letter and the birth certificate. The Epton Hall fortune will be mine, all mine, he told himself and eagerly savoured this delicious thought.

* * * * * *

Chapter Twelve

Katie opened her eyes and immediately panicked. She couldn't see anything and felt confused. Where was she and why was it so dark? She heard what she thought was the sound of a car driving away at speed, its wheels squealing on the pitted tarmac. She staggered painfully to her feet. Her head ached and she put her fingers tentatively up to the side of her head just above her temple. Her fingers felt sticky…with blood? Her legs began to shake uncontrollably and she sat down again.

Gradually she remembered what had happened. Of course, she had fallen and banged her head. Panic raced through her. How long had she been unconscious? Perhaps she ought to see a doctor…

Realisation then hit her!

The letter. Harold would have taken it and perhaps it was his car that she had heard leaving just now. Katie felt for the switch on one of the lamps on the desk and pressed it. There was a loud click, but nothing else. There must have been a power cut she decided. The possibility then dawned on her that once Harold Hapsworth-Cole had the letter and the certificate he'd turned off the electricity before leaving the house.

She tried hard not to panic, but it was exceptionally dark and raining heavily outside and she could hear it hitting the window. She knew that she had to get out of this dreadful attic. She felt dizzy, disorientated and frightened as she peered into the blackness. In desperation and with her legs feeling shaky, she tried to make her way to the door, but her progress was hampered by all the rubbish which was still scattered around the floor.

Fear took hold of Katie's senses when she couldn't find the door, but after taking a really deep breath and with her fingers pressed against the wall she was able to move along until she could feel the door frame. Her heart was thumping wildly when she had the handle finally in her grasp.

She turned it. Nothing happened. It was locked.

'Oh my god, no,' she cried out. A sinking feeling turned her stomach to jelly. She fumbled around for the light switch beside the door and pressed the switch down, but again nothing happened. Her suspicions had been confirmed: that awful man had turned the main power off and there was nothing that she could do about it. She rattled the door and called out, 'Hello, is anyone there? Help me please? Help…help…'

She did this several times until she realised the utter futility of calling out. Her situation was hopeless. She knew perfectly well that there wouldn't be anyone to hear her. It was Friday evening and Nancy wouldn't be back until Monday morning at the earliest. What was she to do? She had no heat, no light, or food and water.

She knew that she was trapped.

'If I had my mobile I wouldn't be in this mess,' she cried out. 'Oh why am I so disorganised at the moment.' Katie usually carried it around with her but her mind had been so preoccupied by Simon and the work here at the Hall that she had forgotten to do anything about getting a replacement. Feeling sick and miserable she found her way back to the chair. Her spirits were now at their lowest ebb and she sat down and cried.

After a while she was able to think more rationally about her predicament. How on earth did she get herself into such a mess in the first place? After all, none of this had anything to do with her. 'I should have let that awful man just take the letter and none of this would have happened,' she cried out in sheer frustration. But then anyone capable of doing what he'd done to her was surely capable of doing anything, she concluded. He didn't deserve to profit from his actions.

Katie then remembered the small torch that Nancy had given her and that she'd left it on the table. With shaking hands, she found it and switched it on but only a faint glimmer tried its best to penetrate the darkness. She realised that the batteries were running down and before the torch failed altogether, she needed to confirm that the letter had indeed been taken. A frantic search amongst the books and papers confirmed her fears: the letter containing the birth certificate was no longer there.

'Now what am I going to do?' she asked herself with renewed frustration. There was just enough light from the little torch to enable her to see the face of her watch. She was relieved to see that she hadn't been unconscious for long. But it had been long enough for Harold Hapsworth-Cole to steal the letter and make sure that she wasn't able to follow him or summon any kind of assistance.

With the help of the fading torchlight and still feeling sick, she searched for something with which she could force the door open. She soon realised that there was nothing in the attic that was strong enough to open the solid oak door. Her mouth felt dry after her exertion, but she knew that she shouldn't think about being thirsty. There was certainly no drink of any kind in this creepy old attic. What could she do now? Nothing she decided, except sit tight and hope that Brenda or Brian would eventually miss her.

It was only Katie's level-headedness and strength of character that prevented her from going to pieces. She tried every way possible to try to forget that she was trapped. But much to her annoyance she started thinking about Simon. Several days had now elapsed since he had told her that he was going to marry Sally. The first two or three days had been sheer hell, but now she was thinking of him less and less. She could hardly have gone on loving someone who had treated her so badly. Perhaps that meant that she'd never really loved him anyway, but had been in love with an ideal?

Her thoughts then turned to Stuart Wells. She'd had a wonderful weekend with Helen and meeting Stuart had been a high spot. She wondered what he was doing and whether he thought about her. When I get out of here I'll phone Helen and get his number, she decided. It would be good to see him again.

As the time went by she felt lonelier and lonelier. She had a bad headache and felt really cold. She jumped at every little noise thinking that Harold had returned, but eventually after what must have been a couple of hours of sitting bolt upright in the old wooden chair, she fell into an uncomfortable and fitful sleep.

Katie was woken by a shaft of sunlight which had filtered through the small window and it now shone directly into her eyes. She could hear the sound of birds twittering somewhere close to the window. She stood up carefully and had to rub her limbs hard to ease the stiffness she felt throughout her body. Katie stretched her arms out and as she did so, the injury to her head began to ache again. She looked at her watch. It was just before 8 o'clock on Saturday morning and at last she could see everything. She searched through the papers on the desk again just in case she'd missed the letter in the dark. But deep down she knew it was a wasted exercise. She sighed. She had promised Brian that she would look after it but in the event, there was nothing she could have done. And Harold had stolen the letter and the birth certificate and would probably have destroyed it by now. It would be her word against his and he could just sit tight in Malta and the estate would be his.

A small glimmer of hope came into Katie's mind. Perhaps Brian would wonder why she hadn't taken the letter round last night? Her shoulders then sagged. He's bound to think that I'll be bringing it in on Monday, because the solicitors' offices were always closed on Saturdays.

A terrible thirst now gripped her. Like before she tried not to think about it, but the more she tried the worse it became. She searched through her handbag and right at the bottom she found the partly eaten packet of boiled sweets that she had bought on the train at the weekend and a couple of aspirin tablets. After sucking one of the sweets, she managed to swallow the tablets. Next she laid all the remaining sweets out on the desk and counted them. Katie calculated that she would have enough if she ate one every two hours, assuming of course that she had to wait until Monday morning to be rescued. She also knew that she had to find herself somewhere more comfortable to rest. She certainly couldn't envisage spending another night sitting bolt upright in that dreadful chair.

Katie looked around the room. She saw the old Admiral's blow tube on the wall. Perhaps Nancy had come to work this morning she thought, sudden hope rising within her? She went over to the tube, picked it up and blew hard. A large amount of dust exploded in her face making her cough and choke. Oh if only she had some water!

She pictured herself walking through a desert desperately looking for a drop of water to assuage her terrible thirst. In her mind's eye, she could see an oasis shimmering in the heat just ahead of her but as she walked towards it, it just seemed to disappear along with all her hopes. She let the vision fade – she was still trapped and completely alone and although it was only about half an hour since eating one of her sweets, she took another one from her dwindling supply.

Katie found an old and battered chaise longue in the darkest part of the attic. It was hidden underneath some old carpets. She replaced some of the old horsehair stuffing which was trailing on the floor and closed the torn fabric with a safety pin that she found in a little pot. She managed to drag it nearer to the desk and the window. She also found some old musty-smelling, but clean blankets in an old laundry basket and shaking them to dislodge any resident spiders or other creepy-crawlies, she managed to make up a reasonably comfortable bed for herself.

All this activity soon tired her and she struggled to lie down on her make-shift bed with all her energy spent.

She woke about two hours later and sucked a sweet and the feeling of terrible dryness in her mouth eased slightly. The sun was still shining so at least a certain amount of warmth was coming in via the window, but she was afraid that the room was going to be really cold when the sun went down later in the day. Because she had nothing better to do and using one of the blankets as a shawl, she began to browse through some of the remaining books on the bottom shelf of the bookcase. At least I've nearly finished them, she told herself with some relief, but I certainly didn't expect to have to finish them under these conditions.

One book in particular held her interest. It was an old volume containing prints of various paintings by artists of the Impressionist era. Katie had always been fascinated by the colours and subjects chosen by artists such as Monet, Renoir and their contemporaries and she settled down to while away some time. The pages were thick and so she was surprised and delighted to find another letter and an envelope, tucked in between the pages. She couldn't believe it. Excitement and adrenaline began to flow through her. She picked them up. The envelope was already addressed to 'Miss Amy Butler' at an address in Vancouver, Canada.

With trembling fingers, Katie carefully unfolded the letter, it was dated the 17th May, 1953 and she began to read it:

"My sweetest, darling Amy,
I cannot tell you how excited I was when I received your letter. My dearest, what I would not do to be with you right now and watch you holding our son in your arms. I try to picture and feel what that must be like, but I only end up feeling frustrated and sad.
Yes, my sweet, we will meet as often as we can, the thought of holding you in my arms sometime in the future sustains me and helps me through my life. Marjorie is a good, dear person and does not deserve me, but I do know that I cannot do anything that will hurt her. The news of James's birth – our dear son – will always have to be a secret I am afraid. But as he grows older, I will write to him and perhaps he and I might even be friends. Tomorrow I intend to go to see my solicitor and make some provision for him in my will. It is with the deepest sadness and regret that I will not be with you to see him growing into the strong man that I believe he will turn out to be. With my stature and your beauty, your wonderful character and outlook on life, he cannot fail.
I am enclosing a cheque made out to you, which I would like you to spend on him. Please buy something that you think he will be able to keep as a reminder of my love for you both."

Katie stopped reading the letter and picked up the envelope. She looked inside. It was empty, Gerald obviously hadn't had time to write the cheque. She continued to read the letter:

"I too lie awake at night, pretending that I am beside you and often curse the size of the ocean that separates us. It won't be forever, I assure you.
My darling I..."

Katie turned the page over, but there was nothing more. She searched through the book to see if there was another page, but she couldn't find one. The letter finished there. It was as if Gerald Hapsworth-Cole had been afraid that his words would be discovered and had hastily placed the letter in a convenient book. He had probably hidden Amy's letter at the same time. Thank goodness he hadn't hidden them together, she thought. She sat staring into space for a few moments, her imagination now running riot. Her thoughts were all tumbling over one another in order to be aired. This letter probably meant that Amy Butler never received a reply to her letter informing Gerald of the birth of their son. She wouldn't have known about Gerald's and the two boys' disappearance either. The poor woman probably waited and wondered why he hadn't written to her. Perhaps she was no longer alive? And supposing James, never having known his father and remembering the anguish that his mother must have suffered, now couldn't bear to be reminded of his father? Oh how cruel this world could be sometimes.

Katie placed the letter back inside the envelope and put it safely in her handbag. At least Harold Hapsworth-Cole hadn't been able to get his grubby hands on this one, she thought with some satisfaction. An alarming thought then passed through her mind. Supposing he came back sometime this weekend and tried to take this letter away from her too? She shivered at the prospect, but eventually dismissed the idea, thinking that he was probably safely back in Malta by now. But just to be on the safe side, she placed her handbag containing the letter underneath the cushion that she was using as a pillow.

Throughout the day, Katie found that she couldn't help thinking about what had happened to Amy and her son James. After all, she had little else to do after she had finished cataloguing the remainder of the books and had ascertained that there were no more hidden letters. Perhaps this second letter would be enough proof of his existence and that they could then trace him? That way, Harold wouldn't be able to lay his hands on the whole estate and after everything he'd done, he certainly didn't deserve to.

She eventually settled down on the chaise longue and sucked one of her sweets. Eventually she closed her eyes. She felt hungry, thirsty, exhausted and frightened too, but stoically refused to let herself get in a panic. She knew that she had no alternative but to sit it out and hope that the time would pass quickly for her.

※ ※ ※ ※ ※ ※

Chapter Thirteen

On Saturday morning, the phone rang in Lilac Cottage. Brenda Bellingham answered it, yawning sleepily.

'Hello,' a man's voice enquired. 'Can I speak to Katie Nicholson please?'

'Yes, of course dear. Hold on one moment. I'll see if she's up.' She went to put the phone down and then said, 'Did you try her mobile by any chance?'

'Yes, but there was no answer – it just went to voicemail, I'm afraid.'

'She's been in a bit of a state lately, it probably needs charging. Hold on one moment and I'll see if she's up.'

'Thank you.'

Brenda walked upstairs and knocked on Katie's door. There was no reply. She knocked again, but there was still no answer. She hurried downstairs and picked up the receiver. 'I'm sorry but I can't seem to wake her at the moment, she probably had a late night. Perhaps I can take a message?'

'Yes please, if you wouldn't mind? My name is Stuart Wells and we met in Cornwall recently. Would you tell her that I'm sorry to have missed her and I will ring again later, please.'

Brenda couldn't help noticing the disappointment in his voice. 'Of course I will,' she said.

'Thank you, bye.'

Brenda frowned as she climbed the stairs. Perhaps I'd better go in and make sure she's OK. She usually lets me know if she isn't coming home, she thought suddenly feeling anxious. She hesitated before using her spare key to open the door to Katie's flat. She hated the idea of prying on anyone and as she walked in, she discovered that Katie's bed had not been slept in.

Brenda began to feel even more worried as the day wore on and Katie didn't phone or return home and eventually she couldn't stand the tension any longer and phoned Brian at his home. He wasn't there, so she tried the shop.

He seemed a long while answering and she almost gave up. At last she heard his voice. 'Hello, Good Book Shop here, can I help you?'

'Brian, it's me, Brenda.' Her anxiety showed in her voice.

'Hello my love. What's wrong, you sound a little tense?'

'I'm…I'm rather concerned about Katie: she didn't come home last night.'

'Oh, that's alright, no need to worry I had a call from a boyfriend of hers last night. He said he was taking her to the cinema in Brighton. She probably decided to stay down there. She'll be fine.'

'Who was the call from?'

'Let me think. Yes, it was that boyfriend of hers, you know, Simon Brand.'

'Simon Brand' Brenda repeated. 'Are you sure, Brian?'

'Yes, of course.' He paused. 'Yes, I'm positive that's what he said his name was.'

'But Simon Brand was the boyfriend who let her down so badly a couple of weeks ago. He simply, to use the vernacular,"dumped her" and has gone to live with her friend, Sally. Katie told me that the girl was pregnant and that they were going to get married soon.'

'Really, he seemed nice enough.'

'Oh Brian,' she said in exasperation. 'Don't you remember? I told you about it last week. I hardly think that he would be taking her to the cinema,' she replied sceptically.

'I'm sorry Brenda, but I've been so busy, that I clean forgot. Must be going senile in my old age, but yes on reflection, it does seem a little odd.'

'Odd Brian, that's putting it mildly! Katie has been terribly upset about the whole thing. She told me that she never ever wanted to see him again.'

'Now you've got me worried,' he said, letting an anxious tone creep into his voice. 'I thought it was bit funny at the time? The man said that Katie wouldn't be bringing me a letter that I was waiting for until Monday morning and it is an extremely important one.' He paused. 'I wonder…'

'What Brian?'

'Brenda, I'll tell you all about it later. I want you to meet me at Epton Hall as soon as you can, please.'

'Yes of course, Brian. But why?'

'I'll explain when we get there. I do hope that I'm wrong though. See you in a few minutes.' The phone went dead.

Brenda looked down at the phone. 'The man has been reading too many of his own books,' she exclaimed. She hurriedly prepared to meet him at The Hall.

Stuart Wells tried Katie's number again, but there was still no reply. With growing frustration, he hung on a little longer. He eventually accepted the fact that she wasn't answering it and replaced the receiver with a sigh. 'Damn, I wonder where she is?' he said quietly to himself. He glanced at his watch – it was now 6.30 pm on Saturday evening.

Stuart realised that he had absolutely no idea how Katie spent her spare time. He only knew that she'd been dreadfully unhappy during her stay in Penzance. This Simon character had treated her abominably and he could feel his anger rising. The bastard…he must have been crazy to have done such a thing to Katie of all people and with her best friend too. He picked up a brightly coloured cushion from the floor and threw it angrily on to a nearby chair. She was really getting under his skin and he just couldn't stop thinking about her. He had never felt this way about any girl before. Perhaps he should be grateful to Simon Brand? After all Katie was now a free agent.

Stuart walked through into his small bathroom and looked at himself in the mirror. He was 27 years old and just over six feet tall, with a good physique. His broad shoulders and narrow hips and waist, were the result of many games of squash and tennis. He ran his fingers through his mass of dark curly hair. Girls had always found him attractive. He had a straight nose and a strong jaw line, which he now rubbed gingerly. He badly needed a shave.

With his electric razor skimming over the surface of his skin, he continued to think about Katie. Meeting her had made him aware of the passing of time. What had he done with his life up to now? He'd had a good time hadn't he? But now, he knew that there was more to life than just having a good time and even his mother and father had recently started to utter little innuendos about his lack of a regular girlfriend. His two brothers had already been through the same metaphorical hoop, so why should he be any different? He couldn't blame his parents of course, they wanted to see him settled that was all.

Until now, he had always managed to change the subject. But was it such a bad idea? His studies were now more or less complete and he had a good job, so perhaps he should be thinking about the future. Katie was such a special person, kind-hearted, gentle and intelligent. Her knowledge of books and history especially, impressed him. She was incredibly enthusiastic about what had gone on in the past and was an incurable romantic. Stuart found himself smiling.

History had never really interested him when he was at school: mathematics had been his main passion in life, but Katie's delight in all things old was contagious. He had begun to look at everything in a different light. During the short time spent together in Penzance, they'd discovered a mutual love of music and poetry. Now that he was living in Lewes, he was looking forward to taking her to the Opera at Glyndebourne: there was so much he wanted to share with her.

Whilst he had been studying for his accountancy examinations, Stuart had found little time to go out socialising. He had taken one or two girls out, but none of them had really set his soul on fire. They had all been cardboard cut-outs of one another – all basically the same and interested only in make-up, clothes and binge drinking in pubs.

After a hot shower, Stuart walked back into his living room. He looked around the room, it was in such a mess. He picked up his supper things and took them out into the kitchen. A letter from his mother stared up at him from the table. He knew that he ought to ring his parents and arrange to go over to see them. He felt guilty that he hadn't had time to speak to them since his move from Cornwall and they were probably waiting for news. He looked around the room. Would he ever have the time to get it straight? He had moved in two days earlier and the floor was still cluttered with boxes of all shapes and sizes. But since his arrival at the flat, there had been only one thing on his mind and that was to contact Katie. He was longing to hear the sound of her voice once more. Whenever he thought about her, he pictured her large blue eyes and her gentle smile.

Stuart realised that he had fallen head over heels in love with her.

He resisted the temptation of ringing her number again. One of his colleagues had invited him to meet a few friends in the pub just around the corner from his flat. He knew that he ought to go and at least get to know a few people.

Minutes later, and ignoring all the untidiness surrounding him, Stuart threw his brown leather jacket nonchalantly over his shoulder, picked up his car keys from the coffee table and strode out of the door.

* * * * * *

Chapter Fourteen

Brenda arrived at Epton Hall before Brian. She parked her car and walked towards the house. The heavy clouds of the afternoon had been blown away and it was a clear, cold night. She looked upwards. She could just make out the vague outline of the ramparts way above her head and they gave the house a mysterious aura. Everywhere was in complete darkness and she shivered as a chill wind blew some of last autumn's leaves around her feet, creating a rustling sound. The added sound of a twig snapping in a nearby bush made her jump and sent her scurrying up the old stone steps.

It was then that she noticed that the old oak door was open. What on earth was going on, she wondered? Perhaps the house has been burgled? And what about Katie, surely she's not still here? So what was Brian on about then? Brenda heard the noise of an approaching car and soon afterwards, headlights pierced the darkness as it swept around the corner. She was relieved to see that it was Brian.

He hurriedly climbed out of his car and raced over to her. 'Hello Brenda love. Are you OK?'

'Yeees,' she answered slowly. 'I've been here for a few minutes and I find it all a bit creepy here to tell you the truth.'

'I'm sorry to keep you waiting in the dark, only I had a phone call and with Katie missing, I thought that I ought to stop and answer it. But it was only a customer wanting to know if I had a spare copy of the latest Dan Brown novel.' Brian's expression was grim.

'Well now that you're here, I want to know what all this is

about. You've made me imagine all kinds of ghastly things. When I arrived just now I found that someone had left the front door wide open, but I didn't dare go inside and I also didn't see any sign of Katie's bicycle.'

'Well that's a good sign then,' he said. 'But even so, I'm glad you didn't go in on your own.'

Brenda began to feel really worried when she saw how agitated Brian was. 'Do you think we ought to call the police?'

'No, not yet. I think we'd better just have a look around before we call them. There may be some quite ordinary explanation for all this.'

'I hope you're right.'

'In any case, we must tell the executors about it. There's far too much valuable stuff lying around. I can't understand why this house hasn't been burgled before.'

'And you think that perhaps it has been burgled now? Oh Brian.'

'Come on, we'd better get inside.'

Brenda had never been inside Epton Hall before and she shivered as they entered the large hallway. 'Ooh, it's so cold in here. Now then Brian, please tell me what's been going on. Ever since your phone call, I've been frantic with worry about Katie. Do you think that this has anything to do with Simon Brand?'

'I'm not sure,' Brian replied shaking his head. 'When you reminded me earlier that Katie and Simon Brand had split up recently, I realised that the man I had spoken to wasn't quite what he seemed. I went over in my mind what he had said.' He tugged absent-mindedly at his beard. 'He was tense and hesitant and wasn't cocky enough I suppose and it was then that I had this inkling that Katie could be in some sort of trouble.'

'So you think that she might still be in the house?' Brenda said looking warily around her. 'But remember Brian, her bicycle isn't here.' Nevertheless, she felt the first cold stirrings of real fear creeping up her spine. 'I do hope that you're wrong, though'

'So do I. I won't rest until I've had the chance of searching the house from top to bottom,' Brian said sternly. 'Before we start, we'd better turn some lights on.' He found the nearest light switch and pushed it downwards. Nothing happened. 'That's funny, this light doesn't work.' He found his way round the wall in the dark until he found another switch and pressed it down. 'This one doesn't work either. The power's off for some reason and I don't know where the main power switch is.'

'Perhaps we should look for it?'

'No, we haven't got time. I've got two good torches in the car. I'll go and get them.'

Brenda shivered again. 'Don't be long, will you?'

A few moments later, he came racing back into the hall.

'Come on,' he said handing her a torch. 'We'll search the attic first.' He turned and rushed off with an anxious look on his face.

Brenda followed him, but Brian was more nimble on his feet than her and at one time she almost lost contact with him. She quickened her pace and as she turned a corner, she could just see a light up ahead and the sound of footsteps climbing yet more stairs.

'Wait for me Brian,' she called out as he hurried along yet another corridor feeling out of breath and sick with worry. Supposing something awful had happened to Katie. Brenda's heart missed a beat: she'd been unable to have any children of her own and she now had a motherly affection for her. Finally, they reached the attic door. Brian turned the handle. It was locked from the outside, but the key was in the lock. He turned it and opened the door. A floorboard gave a loud creak as they walked across the threshold. He shone his torch around, but it was so cluttered and dark, that it was difficult to see anything clearly.

'Shhh,' Brian said holding his finger to his mouth. 'I heard a noise.'

'Yes, so did I,' Brenda whispered, hardly daring to breathe. Sure enough in the silence that followed, they heard the sound of heavy breathing. She shone her torch in the direction of the noise.

There was another cough and a moan. Brenda walked towards the window where small fingers of moonlight enabled her to make out a vague shape wrapped in blankets and lying on what looked like an old chaise longue.

'Quickly Brian, over here,' she whispered as she knelt down beside the makeshift bed. She angled her torch in such a way that she could see who it was, but without waking and scaring them. She lifted a corner of the old blanket. 'Brian, it's Katie.'

'Oh Brenda, thank god she's still alive; I was beginning to feel that...'

'But she's hurt, look.' Brenda felt shaken and relieved all in one go and tears began to fall down her face.

Brian swept the beam of his torch around Katie's head. 'My god, so she is. There's a deep cut and some really nasty bruising here just above her temple. What on earth has been going on in here?'

'Perhaps someone broke into the house and disturbed Katie while she was working up here,' Brenda said, her breath coming in short bursts.

'Yes, and if I know Katie, she probably tried to stop them and got hurt in the process. The bastard obviously hit her, locked the door, turned off the electricity to the house and then ran off. If I catch whoever has done this to her, I'll...' he hissed angrily. A worried enquiring look from Brenda made him calm down rapidly. 'Yes...well...I'll see if I can wake her,' he whispered gently shaking Katie's shoulder.

She woke suddenly and cried out in fear. 'Who's that? Go away, please go away.' She put her hands in front of her face.

'Katie, it's Brian and me,' Brenda said. 'You're quite safe

now,' she said placing her hand reassuringly on her arm. In an instant, Katie's face crumpled and she burst into tears. 'Oh thank you, both of you. I thought that it was that awful man again. What's the time?'

Brenda was quite surprised that she wanted to know the time. She shone the torch beam on to her wristwatch. 'It's nearly 7 o'clock on Saturday evening, love. And what awful man? Was it a burglar?'

'No, it definitely wasn't a burglar. It was Gerald Hapsworth-Cole's nephew, Harold.'

'Harold Hapsworth-Cole!?' Brenda and Brian chorused.

'Yes, he came here unannounced yesterday,' Katie replied with some vehemence.

'And he did this to you?'

'Well not exactly, but he caused it. Brian, when I was downstairs in the study, Harold overheard our conversation about the letter I'd found. He appeared from nowhere and introduced himself. He seemed quite reasonable and I came back up here, to carry on with the books. He followed me and demanded to have the letter and in trying to stop him, I tripped and fell. I...I must have been unconscious for a few minutes, because when I came to, he'd taken the letter and gone. And I was trapped here without any...' She began to tremble and then burst into tears again.

'Come on, you're safe now. Here, have this jacket. Brrr, it feels really cold up here.' Brenda said as Katie struggled to get up. 'And do lie there for a while, you're obviously in no fit state to move.' Brenda placed her hand on Katie's forehead. 'And you're feeling a little hot love, are you sure that you're OK?'

'Yes, I'm sure I'm over the worst now. I've been asleep, I...I was exhausted.'

I'm not surprised,' Brenda said.

A look of thunder had crossed over Brian's usually friendly

features. 'Look, we mustn't take any chances. Brenda is right and you must stay put for the moment. What on earth was the man thinking of? He must have been crazy.'

'Yes, I think perhaps he was. Do you think I could have a drink?'

'What on earth are we thinking about, you must be really thirsty and hungry. Look I'll go straight downstairs and get you a drink and then I'll phone the doctor. I'm responsible for you being here in the first place, remember?'

'But I don't need a doctor. But I do need a drink.'

Brenda started to rummage in her large, capacious handbag. 'Look will this do? It's only a small carton of blackcurrant juice and it's been in my bag for nearly a week, but...'

'Oh Brenda, you're an angel, thank you.' She took it and drank every drop.

'You're a good girl scout, Brenda,' Brian said with a wry smile. 'And I am going to call the doctor, despite what you say. It's better to be safe than sorry.'

'Yes, I suppose it is,' Katie replied wearily.

Once Brian was downstairs, he began to search for the main power switch. The old house had many little nooks and crannies, but he eventually found it and restored the power to the house. He scratched his head. How on earth did Harold find this switch so quickly? It must have been pure luck, he concluded. He then phoned the local health centre to see if the doctor on duty would come out to see Katie. The receptionist said that he was out on another call, but that she would try to contact him. Next, he tried Nancy Brown's number to tell her what had happened, but she was out too. He left a message with her husband asking her to come round to the house as soon as possible.

Even though he was relieved that Katie had been found, he felt his anger rising again, but he knew that he had to keep his emotions under control. He was quite sure that Hapsworth-Cole was probably well away from the house by now, but for his own peace of mind, decided to look around the house, just to make sure.

In the meantime, Katie had to force herself to lie on her makeshift bed. She felt that if she had to spend any longer in this room, she would scream.

'It's no use, Brenda. I can't stay up here any longer. If I don't have something to eat soon…I'll…'

Katie love, I'm so sorry. For a moment I'd quite forgotten just how long you've been stuck up here, you must be starving. Do you think that you feel strong enough to come downstairs now?'

'Yes, I'm quite sure I do. And in any case, I'm dying to go to the em…loo…!'

'Oh you poor thing. How on earth did you manage, you know, being in the attic all that time, I mean?'

Katie giggled. 'I managed to find an old Victorian "po", you know, one of those antique ones with a rude painting on the bottom. The Victorians were quite odd, weren't they?'

'Yes, but they were remarkably innovative too. Some of their engineering skills wouldn't go amiss nowadays. I remember writing an article about their prowess some years' ago. Come on then, let's go downstairs.'

Katie was soon comfortably installed in Nancy's small sitting room next to the kitchen. This little room was always so neat, tidy and homely and a million miles away from the cold, dark and creepy attic upstairs. Brenda soon produced a cup of tea and within minutes Katie was beginning to feel better. Soon afterwards, Brian entered the room, closely followed by a middle-aged man carrying a case.

He sounded a little breathless and sighed deeply. 'Everything's fine and I'm pretty sure that the house is empty and a lot of the rooms are locked in any case,' he said. 'I was worried in case Hapsworth-Cole was still here. Anyway Katie, this is Dr. Castle and I've told him what happened to you.'

Dr. Castle examined her thoroughly before finally folding up his stethoscope and placing it neatly back in his case.

'Well Katie, apart from your head injury, everything seems OK. Under the circumstances, I feel that you have been quite lucky. Should your headache continue or worsen, take a couple of painkillers and try to take it easy. Come and see me again in a day or two in any case, just to be quite sure. And I'll leave you some sleeping tablets in case you have difficulty sleeping.'

'Thank you, Dr. Castle.'

He stood up. 'Right I must be off to see my next patient – it's been a busy night. Goodbye and do take care.' He was about to leave when he suddenly stopped. 'Ah yes, and Mr. Ainsley, I think under the circumstances, we must tell the police about this, as a matter of urgency.'

'I totally agree with you doctor. The next thing on my list is to go round to see Sergeant Stone, our local police officer and explain everything that has happened, and perhaps we can get to the bottom of all this,' Brian said nodding his head fiercely.

After the doctor had left, Brenda made another pot of tea and handed Katie a plate of chocolate biscuits. 'These are not hugely nutritious, but Nancy doesn't seem to keep a lot of food here.'

'Thank you Brenda. Quite honestly, I could eat anything right now. I've been feeling sick with hunger.' Brian and Brenda sat silently while she elaborated on the details that she had given them up in the attic. She relived his frighteningly cold words and how she had tripped over the carpet in an effort to get at the letter before Harold did. Katie paused and glanced at Brian. 'Nancy told me that there was some mental instability in the Hapsworth-Cole family and the way that Harold treated me, I wouldn't be surprised if he is seriously mentally ill himself.'

Brian looked fit to burst. 'The man's an evil bastard. For all he knew, you could have been seriously injured or even worse.'

'Brian,' Brenda pleaded, placing a placatory hand on his arm.

'Well, he certainly doesn't have any scruples, that's for sure,' he grumbled.

Whilst Brian was talking, Katie had been rummaging in her handbag. 'But listen, I had to do something to help pass the time and whilst I was looking through the last pile of books, I...I found another letter,' she said revealing it with a triumphant flourish.

'Another one!' Brenda exclaimed. 'Who is this one from?'

'Gerald Hapsworth-Cole's reply to Amy Butler's letter and it was unfinished, but he had already written the envelope, so we have an address now too. It seems as if he had been worried that her letter and his reply would be discovered, so he must have panicked and hid them in different books. It's just as well he did under the circumstances,' she said smiling broadly.

Brenda took the letter and with Brian looking eagerly over her shoulder, she began to read it. She immediately realised its significance. 'This probably means that nobody ever found out about their affair, or about the child. Poor Amy Butler must have believed that he'd completely deserted her when she didn't receive a reply.'

'Yes I agree. I had lots of time to think about it all, stuck up in the attic for so many hours. I couldn't imagine that Amy wouldn't have written again, when she didn't receive a reply from him, after all she was very much in love with him. What if a letter arrived here addressed to Gerald after his disappearance, Marjorie could have opened it, couldn't she?'

'Well, yes I suppose so, but...,' Brenda replied thoughtfully.

Just at that moment, Nancy Brown walked into her sitting room. She looked extremely upset.

'No you're wrong,' she said quietly. They all looked up at her in surprise. 'I'm sorry but I...I couldn't help listening to the last part of your conversation.'

'Hello Nancy. Glad you could come,' Brian said. 'You say that we are wrong about the letters? How do you know?'

She took a deep breath. 'I don't know what's been going on, but you were right in one respect. Some letters did come and I took them.' She looked shamefaced. 'You see I knew about Mr. Gerald's affair with that Canadian woman. I overheard him speaking on the telephone one day about her going back to Canada. I was quite young and impressionable at the time you understand. I was in my teens and this was my first job.' She shook her head sadly, 'I adored Mrs. Hapsworth-Cole and I just couldn't let her read...them letters.' She stopped speaking suddenly, when she glanced at Katie, who was sitting in her favourite armchair and wrapped in an old blanket. 'Oh my goodness gracious me Katie, what on earth has been happening to you?'

Brian told her and she slumped in a nearby chair looking shocked. Finally he said 'Hapsworth-Cole took the letter and the birth certificate and locked Katie in the attic. So you see why we asked you to come round here tonight, Nancy?'

'Yes, I do. Oh Katie m'dear, what a dreadful thing to have happened. I'm so sorry that I wasn't here to help you. The solicitors promised me faithfully that Mr. Harold would telephone me before he came here. Well I never did!' Brenda handed her a cup of tea. 'Thanks,' she said looking even more hot and flustered. 'Now where was I? Oh yes, I was talking about them letters. I didn't want to see Mrs. Hapsworth-Cole hurt any more. The disappearance of her whole family was bad enough, but at the time I didn't think that she could have handled any more bad news.' She looked around at each one of them. 'What would you have done?'

'The same probably, Nancy, but do go on,' Brenda said.

'So you see, soon after Mr. Gerald's disappearance, a letter arrived for him with a Vancouver postmark. I sort of put two and two together, and...' Nancy's voice weakened to a whisper, '...and I took the letter home with me.' She paused. 'There was another three letters after the first one, you know and I kept all of them. Then they just stopped coming. Did I do wrong do you think, keeping them? I've often wondered what happened to the young lady involved. And you must understand, I didn't ever read them and I've kept it all to meself all these years. And even after Mrs. Hapsworth-Cole's death, I still didn't want anyone to pore over the details of their private lives. It just didn't seem right somehow.'

'No of course you didn't do anything wrong,' Brian reassured her. 'You only did what you considered was right at that time. You were protecting Mrs. Hapsworth-Cole from a lot more heartache.'

'I've often thought about Mr. Gerald and them two lovely boys and what could have happened to them. At the time the police were following several leads, but they never uncovered any evidence. I only know that the official line at the time was that they went out in their boat and it sank.' Nancy put her hands out in a gesture of hopelessness. 'You see the boat was usually kept in Chichester harbour and it disappeared too.'

'Ah,' Brian said gently stroking his beard. 'That sounds like the most logical conclusion.'

'I've still got the letters as I explained just now. I hid them in a box in one of my cupboards at home. I didn't have the heart to throw them away, Mr. Ainsley.'

'On the face of it, it's a good job you didn't.'
'Why what do you mean?'
'There's something that you didn't know.'
'Yes?'
'Amy Butler returned to Canada to have Gerald's...baby.'
Nancy went pale. 'A baby! Oh...oh my goodness me. I...I

see what you mean, Mr. Ainsley. Oh deary me.' She was silent for a moment. 'Was it a girl or a boy?'

'According to the letters Katie found in the attic, it was a boy. Amy Butler called him James.'

'A boy! Thank goodness Mrs. Hapsworth-Cole never knew. It would have broken her heart.' Nancy looked bewildered. 'Why, he must be fifty odd by now – well I'm blowed. What's gonna happen now for goodness sake?'

'I don't really know. We can only assume that Hapsworth-Cole will destroy the first letter Katie found, along with the birth certificate. The letters you have and the second one that she found, will all have to be examined to see if they're genuine I suppose. I think perhaps nowadays, illegitimate children can inherit, but don't quote me on that one. I'm not so sure what the law was in 1953 though: they weren't so broad-minded about such things then.'

'Yes, it was an unmentionable subject then,' Brenda added with a wan smile.

'Just think, those letters have been up in that old attic all those years,' Nancy said, shaking her head sadly. 'If I'd done my job properly...'

'Now come on Nancy? You can't go blaming yourself,' Katie said, reaching for her hand.

'Now then, I think we must get young Katie home,' Brian said suddenly standing up. 'She's beginning to look a little jaded.'

'Yes please. You can have too much excitement in one weekend. I can't wait to have a proper meal, and a relaxing bath, before crashing out in my own bed. Oh and by the way, did anyone happen to see my bicycle? I left it outside by the steps.'

'Katie, it wasn't there when we arrived,' Brenda replied. 'Harold must have put it somewhere when he left the house.'

'Right, we'll look for it later, but in the meantime, Brenda will drive you home and I'll go round to see Sergeant Scott at his home. I'm sure that he'll be interested in what's been going on here. Nancy, would you like a lift home?'

'No thanks, Mr. Ainsley. My husband is sitting outside in the car.'

Once they were back at Lilac Cottage, Brenda cooked a light meal while Katie had a much needed bath. For once, Katie had time to breathe and as she wallowed in the deliciously perfumed water, she tried not to think about the last couple of days and luxuriated in the soothing water. But once she was in bed, despite feeling desperately tired, she couldn't sleep. Everything was going round and round in her mind. She recalled the frightening and now alarmingly prophetic dream that she'd experienced during her long journey to Penzance the week before. When she added this to the horrible and terrifying events of this weekend, it all seemed to assume enormous proportions in her mind. She closed her eyes tightly and tried to shut it all out. She shivered and her exhausted mind made her temporarily forget where she was…

Katie found herself back in the attic. Harold was moving towards her, his hand outstretched and his eyes blazing with madness. She tried to pull herself away from his terrifying gaze, but every time she moved, invisible fingers held her like a vice. She cowered away from him, her heart thumping wildly. She screamed. But no sound came…

She opened her eyes and sighed with relief. Once again he was just a figment of her exhausted imagination. She hoped never to have to see that awful man's face ever again. The doctor had insisted on giving her some sleeping tablets, and she'd resisted the temptation of taking any. But with her mind in active and emotional turmoil, she swallowed one.

* * * * *

Chapter Fifteen

After Brian left Epton Hall, he drove straight round to Sergeant Scott's house which was on the other side of Anston. He had been a friend of Alan's for several years now and had often spent the odd evening in the local pub with him. They were unfortunately widowed at the same time and had a lot in common including their outlook on life.

Alan's neat little cottage was tucked away behind a stand of tall trees. Brian parked his car in the small lay-by and walked up the narrow pathway. The skies had clouded over again and it had started to rain, so he pulled up the collar of his jacket. He heard the piercingly sharp bark of a vixen as she scrambled around in the bushes somewhere to his right. The screech of an owl made him jump, as it flew like a ghostly apparition just above his head and headed for the trees. He rang the doorbell.

Alan Scott opened the door. He was still in the process of buttoning up his shirt, as he'd been preparing for an early night.

'Hello Brian, what a surprise. Do come in man, or you'll get soaking wet.' The gentle rain had now become a torrent.

'Yes, er…thank you.'

'Now then, what can I do for you? Is it personal or official?'

'Official, I'm afraid, Alan…I'm sorry that it's so late, but it is important.'

'Of course. Please don't worry and have you brought me that book I ordered last week?'

'No, I haven't, I'm sorry. I think that it's coming in with my next order. I'll give you a ring when it arrives.'

'Good. Come through into the office.' He beckoned Brian

into a small room off the hallway. It was untidy: a curious mixture of office furniture, including a computer console, papers and other personal items. An old, but obviously favourite armchair had been positioned beside the fireplace and a pair of slippers sat warming in front of the open coal fire. 'Do sit down, Brian.'

'Thank you.'

'Right then, fire away.' Alan Scott was about 45, bald and slightly rotund. The police uniform that he usually wore didn't detract at all from the fact that most people were glad to turn to him for advice. He was the type of person to whom friends and even strangers would often tell their innermost secrets. This had proved to be quite an advantage to him over the years in his dealing with criminals and victims alike.

Brian explained his reasons for calling in great detail and Alan's jovial expression gradually changed to one of concern.

'Absconded with the letter did he? Right, I'll see what we can do. Have you any idea where he went after leaving Miss Nicholson in the attic?'

'I'm sorry Alan, I've no idea.'

'Hmm,' he said glancing at his notepad. 'That's a pity.' His forehead creased in concentration. 'Now then, looking at it from Hapsworth-Cole's point of view, where would you have gone?'

'Straight back to Malta, I suppose.'

'Yes, precisely, and he's had a good start too.' He stood up. 'Right then, I'm off duty at the moment, but this is sufficiently important for me to let my superiors in Epton know about it. I'll ring you tomorrow if we manage to find out where he is.' He stood up and shook Brian by the hand.

'Thanks Alan, I'd be most grateful if you would. And I must apologise again for coming round so late, but I thought we ought to get things moving.'

'I couldn't agree more Brian. Well, I'll say goodnight and I promise that I will keep in touch.' Alan Scott showed him to the door.

***

Penny Humberston had just arrived back home after an exhausting weekend meeting with two of her partners. She had been with Messrs. Sharpe, Holyoak and Masters, Solicitors, for over ten years now and she enjoyed her work immensely. The company had several quite thorny problems on its books at the moment and she had been working at full stretch for some time. She slumped into her armchair and closed her eyes. She lived alone by choice: she enjoyed her own company and the fact that she could do exactly as she liked, when she liked. Her television stood like an enormous unseeing eye in the corner of her living room and she switched it on with the aid of the remote control. It was news time, which was about the only programme she ever had time to watch. The newscaster looked gloomy as he read the latest news bulletin. There were more bombs and several people killed in Iraq and yet another British soldier had died in Afghanistan. Penny sighed deeply and clicked it off again. She walked slowly into her kitchen, kicked off her shoes and slipped her feet into some ancient but comfortable slippers.

Kitson, Penny's white fluffy Persian cat, greeted her by curling and wrapping himself around her legs. He looked up at her, mewing and purring alternately and eagerly awaiting his supper.

'You're a typical male,' she said bending down and stroking his soft fur. 'The way to your heart is definitely through your stomach.' She pressed the switch on her kettle to the "ON" position and started to prepare his supper. The cat's mewing became more and more insistent and she placed the dish in front of him to keep him quiet. She heard the phone ringing in the hall and looked up at her kitchen clock. It was nearly half past ten, so who would be calling her at this time of night, she wondered? She stifled a yawn as she picked the receiver up.

'Hello.'

'Hi Penny, Brain Ainsley here. Look, I'm sorry to disturb you so late, but we've got a bit of a problem regarding Epton Hall. If you remember, we're cataloguing the library.'

'Brian,' she replied feeling sleepy, slightly aggrieved and every bit of her 39 years. 'I've had a hell of a hard day and I don't usually work late on a Saturday, so…' She pushed her long hair back behind her ears – the fact that it kept falling into her eyes, was beginning to annoy her. 'Can't it wait?'

'I don't know, but wait until you hear what's happened, I'm sure you'll agree with me.'

'Try me. I'm warning you, it had better be good.' She then realised that she must have sounded a little churlish. 'Look Brian I'm sorry to be so grumpy, but I'm really tired. What's the problem?'

Brian cleared his throat. 'I honestly don't know where to begin, so much has happened.'

'Try the beginning,' she said with a hint of sarcasm.

'Well here goes. My young assistant Katie Nicholson has been closeted at The Hall for several days now. On Friday afternoon she had almost finished, when she found a letter…'

Penny listened with mounting apprehension to what Brian had to tell her. Finally she said, 'But that's incredible Brian. Harold Hapsworth-Cole is bound to have destroyed them both by now. You've contacted the police, you say? Any help coming from that quarter?'

'Well Alan Scott was a bit pessimistic about the chances of Harold still being in the country. Poor Katie opened up a real can of worms, bless her.'

'Yes, she certainly did. Is she OK?'

'I think so, but she is suffering from slight concussion and is a bit shaken of course.'

'It must have been an awful experience for her. I hope she realises that she could have him for assault?' Penny said taking a sip from the cup of tea she'd made about ten minutes earlier.

'Well, as far as I can make out, the injury was only indirectly caused by Hapsworth-Cole – apparently he didn't touch her. Katie said that she accidentally tripped and fell on to the edge of the desk and knocked herself out. He merely took advantage of the situation and absconded with the letter and more importantly, the birth certificate...'

'Which strictly didn't belong to him,' Penny added with a frown. 'He must be a callous bastard. He had no idea how long Katie would have to stay trapped in that attic and unless he has some kind of medical knowledge, he would have had no idea of the extent of her injuries. We could get him on that point alone.'

'Yes, that's true.'

'And thank goodness she found the other letter.'

'Oh yes, before I forget. In 1953, Nancy Brown apparently waylaid a few more letters, each written by Amy Butler AFTER the disappearance of Gerald Hapsworth-Cole and his two sons. She told us about them this evening, luckily she still has them.'

'It gets better and better, Brian. All the letters will have to be looked at carefully of course.' She paused. 'I think that Thomas Broadbent, of Broadbent and Crombie in Epton, will probably be acting for Harold Hapsworth-Cole. Did either Gerald or Marjorie Hapsworth-Cole leave a will?'

'Apparently not. Why?'

'Because once Harold found out about Gerald's illegitimate child, it became essential from his point of view that nobody else found out about it. That's why he took the letter of course. Mm...listen...this is pure conjecture, mind.'

'Yes?' The phone crackled and fizzed and Penny pulled the

receiver away from her ear. 'Are you still there?' Brian enquired.

'Yes. It sounds as if there are gremlins on the line. I'm trying to get inside Harold's mind for a moment. If he'd been thinking straight, he would have thought of some way of silencing Katie for good. Once he had started down that road of course, he would then have had to have silenced everyone else involved too. But, if his mind was deranged and it didn't occur to him...?'

'My god, Penny. I thought that Katie had been lucky not to have been seriously hurt, but this...'

'But on the other hand, I suppose he might have thought that once he'd taken the letter and destroyed it, it would have been her word against his? Do you get my drift?'

'And he must then have completely forgotten or discounted, the fact that Katie had told me about the letter,' Brian said thoughtfully.

At this juncture, Penny had to force herself to concentrate, because she was feeling really tired. 'Can you imagine how upset Harold must have been to discover that Gerald had an illegitimate son? It could have been the catalyst which pushed him over the edge. Was there a Vancouver address with the second letter?'

'Yes.'

'Well with any luck, Amy Butter might still be alive and hopefully still living there. If her son, James still has the original birth certificate, we'll be in business. Keep all your fingers crossed Brian.'

'They already are, Penny,' he said dryly. 'I would hate to think that a sleaze-ball like Harold Hapsworth-Cole could benefit by inheriting the whole estate.'

'Well, if we can prove that the baby in Vancouver is a direct descendant of Gerald's then he could under current law, inherit even though he is illegitimate.'

'Hapsworth-Cole certainly doesn't deserve to inherit

anything. Marjorie apparently hated her brother-in-law Stanley, because he didn't contact her at all after Gerald's and the boys' disappearance. According to Nancy Brown, her employer swore that she would never forgive either of them. Isn't it strange then, that she didn't make a will either?'

'You'd be surprised how many people forget, or deliberately refuse to make a will. But it's probable that she was so eaten up by the loss of her family that it didn't occur to her,' Penny replied thoughtfully. 'Well there's nothing much we can do until tomorrow morning and then we can get things moving. But you can rest assured that I will be thinking about it until then. Thank you for telling me.' She sighed deeply. 'Wow, Brian.'

'Wow indeed, Penny.'

'Look after this second letter won't you?'

'Don't you worry I'll stick to it like glue. Once again, I apologise for ringing so late.'

'Oh, that's alright, I wasn't in bed or anything,' she said frantically stifling another yawn.

'Good. Talk to you tomorrow, then. Bye.'

After Penny had turned off her mobile phone, she stared at the pad of paper on her hall table, and all thoughts of sleep simply disappeared. She'd been taking note of everything that Brian had told her. Most of the time, her work was routine and often tedious, but this…this was intrigue at its very best and she longed to find out what had happened all those years ago, and how it would affect the remaining members of the Hapsworth-Cole family.

She couldn't wait to get started.

* * * * * *

PART II

All that we see or seem
Is but a dream within a dream
(Edgar Allan Poe – 1809-1849)

Chapter Sixteen

Vancouver, Canada

James Butler walked out of the building carrying a few personal belongings underneath his arm. He was shaken, bewildered and still reeling from the impact of his boss, Andy Carstairs' words. He stopped, turned round and looked back at the tall building where he had spent so much of his time. It soared upwards and dominated the Vancouver skyline.

It was a miserable, dull day and as he stood there a misty blanket of rain began to fall. I've spent years in that building working my fingers to the bone and where has it all got me, he thought bitterly?

His friend Andy had started up the company about twenty years' earlier. At that time there had been a real need for computers, videos and all the associated accoutrements of a high-tech business. Everyone had jumped on the bandwagon and millions of dollars had been made. Now the world was an entirely different place: there were different needs, different attitudes and many more companies vying for the same business. He knew that Andy hadn't any choice but to let him go. Of course James wasn't the only one, because in all over 20 people would, like him, walk out of that building to find themselves unemployed and in some cases, unemployable.

James had been aware for some time that redundancies could be on the horizon, but felt sure that his 'special' relationship with Andy, would have made him immune. So, it had come as quite a shock when he had called him into his office earlier that morning.

'Please sit down, James,' he'd said pleasantly. 'How are Sarah and the kids?'

'They're fine, thanks.' James' heart thumped wildly.

'Well, I won't beat about the bush. I'm afraid that the end of year figures are much worse than I'd feared. Very much worse,' he repeated with heavy emphasis. He shook his hand sadly. 'You probably know what I'm getting at?'

'Yes, Andy...I...I know that the company is not doing very well.'

'That's an understatement. I've been told that the only way the company can keep its head above water...,' he leant forward as if to drive home his words, 'and I'm talking almost drowning here, is to offload some of the workforce. I'm sorry but your whole department and Ted Bolton's, is gonna have to go. I'm afraid that it won't end there either,' he said sadly looking down at his feet. James looked at the man who was supposed to be his friend. Could it be that he was embarrassed?

Andy Carstairs continued. 'It's a sad fact that we can no longer have the luxury of carrying low profit making departments. I shall be really sorry to see you go, after all you've been with me right from the start.' He rose from his seat and walked round to the other side of his desk and sat down on the edge. 'James, if there was any other way, you know that I would...'

'Andy,' James interrupted him, 'I've known for some time that this might happen, but it still comes as a shock to learn that my expertise is no longer required.' His pride prevented him from saying anything more detrimental. He wasn't about to beg! 'Have you spoken to your father?' He knew that Andy's father was a wealthy man and that he had provided some of the capital which had enabled him to set the company up in the first place.

'No, I haven't and I'm not going to either. He helped me out last year, although nobody knew that of course, because I managed to keep the wraps on it. He told me in no uncertain terms that he would not do it again. He's a powerful man James and he doesn't have a lot of patience with people who don't succeed.'

'I understand. Well that's it.' He stood up with a nonchalance that he wasn't feeling. 'When would you like me to leave?' Andy didn't answer, but looked down at his feet again. 'Right, I'll clear my desk then. May I wish you the best of luck in the future?' he said, trying to put on a brave face.

Andy stood up and a look of relief spread over his face. 'Thanks, James. It's good of you to take it so well. I hope that we can meet sometime under better and different circumstances. Stop by at Accounts, there's an envelope waiting for you. Well, that's it, I'm afraid. Give my regards to Sarah…er…goodbye and good luck.'

They shook hands and James walked quickly out of the office.

He walked back to his car in the pouring rain, his mind in complete confusion, unlocked the door and climbed in. He was wet through. He sat for some time wondering how he was going to tell Sarah that he no longer had a job. He reached into the glove compartment and picked up a pack of cigarettes and a mauve plastic disposable cigarette lighter. He had meant to throw them away. He shook the packet – there were two cigarettes inside. He had given up smoking about a month earlier, in order to save money. The first few days had been difficult, but he had persevered. After two weeks he'd begun to feel a lot healthier and this had helped him in his resolve. But now, what was left for him? He quickly took a cigarette from the pack and almost without thinking, lit it. He sucked the smoke deeply into his lungs: it felt so good. The smoke swirled around him, getting into his eyes and then they began to water. But was it just due to the smoke, he asked himself? What was happening to him? 'I'll tell you what's happening feller, you're nearly 56 years old and on the scrap heap,' he shouted.

He twisted his long slim legs into a more comfortable position and once more drew the smoke into his lungs. He could feel it there, insinuating itself in the recesses of his being. 'Hell, I don't want to start smoking again, dammit,' he shouted again. He stubbed it out.

For several minutes he remained motionless, his eyes peering into space. What was he going to do? He rubbed his fingers through his thick hair. A strange moaning sound came from his throat and he buried his head in his hands. How would Sarah react? Would she now regard him as a failure?

'Hell, I am a failure,' he whispered.

He realised that he now couldn't look after his home, his wife or his two kids properly. Perhaps she would leave him and take them with her? How can I tell them? Teenagers could be quite cruel at times and having their father out of work was definitely not good for the image! James knew that he was being unfair, because he really had no idea how they would react. They were two such lovely kids. Michael was 12 and John, now almost a man at 15, and he knew that he would be a great disappointment to them. His thoughts were now totally focused on the fear of his family and friends discovering his secret. He was out of work. He said the words over and over in his mind. What was he gonna do? The thought that he might actually find another job, didn't even enter his head.

He cast his mind back to his childhood. His poor mother had been beautiful and sad and constantly pining for the man who was his father. Unhappily, she had died from cancer about five years ago. Hardly a day went by when he didn't mourn her loss. When he was quite young, he had been told by his grandmother that his father was English and that he had deserted his mother, but nothing more. He had often looked at her and wondered how anyone could have been so unkind to her.

His complete ignorance of part of his family's background eventually became an obsession with him. He had grown up feeling bitter about the fact that he didn't have a father, which in the end made his mother's life even harder to bear. He shrugged his shoulders. The irony of it was, that if Sarah left him, his children would soon get used to it: one parent families were almost the norm now.

James remembered the time that he had first met Sarah. He thought that she was the prettiest girl he had ever seen, with her short, dark, curly hair and her sparkling brown eyes. It wasn't long before he had asked her to marry him and she had accepted, making him the happiest man in the world. It didn't seem to matter to him any more that he didn't have a father, all he wanted was to make Sarah happy. It had taken them several years to start a family and they had almost given up hope, when Sarah became pregnant with John and then later, Michael came along. He certainly couldn't have been a better father to his two boys and always lavished much love and affection on them: on reflection, perhaps too much. He had managed to shelter them from everything and money had never been a problem. He had always bought them anything they'd wanted. And now, what was left for him? He was a proud man. He didn't want to be a disappointment to his wife and family.

'Hell, what am I gonna say to them?' he wailed. His mind worked rapidly. 'I just can't tell them. That's it, I just won't tell em.' The more he thought about it, the more depressed and morose he became. Now he no longer had a job, he had somehow to find the money to pay the mortgage on their house and the payments on their two cars. He knew for a fact that the balance at the bank was not as high as he would have liked it to be. Last year, Andy had reduced everybody's salaries including his own and James hadn't told Sarah about it.

With a heavy heart, James started up his car. Without looking behind him, he moved away from the parking lot and drove towards the main highway. He felt the need to get away from Vancouver. He needed to clear his head. He couldn't go home yet.

It was mid-morning and the highway was busy and James stayed in the second lane. His mind was in complete and utter turmoil and he wasn't thinking straight. He noticed a signpost to a motel off to the right and moved quickly over to the inside lane. He would spend some time there. Because he had so much on his mind, he forgot to signal. He also failed to see a small truck which was coming up behind him on the inside lane and by the time he'd noticed the movement beside him, it was too late. Neither driver had time to panic or take evasive action.

They collided.

There was a horrible scrunching and tearing sound as metal connected with metal. James' car being the lighter of the two was tipped over and continued to turn several times, before finally coming to rest in a culvert at the side of the highway. Everything was still, except for the noise made by the spinning of one of the car's wheels. The heavy stench of spilled gasoline filled the air. He was in pain...intense pain. He only knew that he had to get out of the car. Danger...fire. He tried to move...more pain... His head fell backwards and...total blackness enveloped him.

Sarah Butler was a happily married woman. She loved her husband James and their two children passionately. He'd gone off to work that morning with his usual cheery wave and then she proceeded to try to coerce Michael and John into getting ready for school. She could hear sounds of frantic activity upstairs as they fought over something or other.

She looked around their neat and comfortable home with complete satisfaction. James had always been a good provider and a wonderful father. He idolised his family always putting their feelings before his own. She had often considered his behaviour to be rather at odds with the way he had been brought up. His early life had been a lonely one and lonely people often lead lonely lives. But not James: he seemed to overcompensate for his lack of previous happiness and to him, his family was everything.

After she had waved the children off to school on the bus, Sarah did all her chores and made one or two phone calls to some friends, inviting them over to supper the following weekend. She drove the car out of the large double garage attached to their home and drove off to the nearest shopping mall. Once there, she filled her shopping trolley to the brim and drove home again feeling truly satisfied with her life. It was early spring and all the birds were singing and the buds on the trees were swelling before burgeoning into new life. She was happy and everything seemed wonderful, so she was totally unprepared for news of the disaster which had just hit her family.

Sarah placed her key into the lock of the Georgian style front door, when she heard the phone ringing. She rushed indoors and grabbed hold of the phone.

'Hi,' she answered breathlessly.

'Can I speak to Mrs. Sarah Butler please?'

'Yes, speaking.'

'Mrs. Butler, this is the Casualty Department at the General Hospital. I...I'm afraid that your husband has been involved in an accident on the highway and...'

At that moment, the only thing Sarah could think about, was that it couldn't have been James, because he'd said that he would be in the office all day. 'Mrs. Butler, did you hear what I said, I said that your husband...'

'Yes, yes...I heard you. Are you sure that it is my husband, only...?'

'Yes, Mrs. Butler, we've had a positive identification. Your husband is...'

'Is he alright...what happened, please tell me?' she interrupted. A feeling of dread enveloped her.

'Your husband is in the Emergency Room: he is conscious, but I'm afraid that he has quite extensive and serious injuries. The doctors are monitoring his condition closely. I assume that you'll be coming in to see him?'

'Yes...yes, of course. I'll come in right away,' she mumbled feeling shocked and bewildered. 'Thank you.'

Sarah placed the phone back on the hall table and stood for some moments desperately trying to collect her scrambled thoughts. She tried not to panic, but...what was she to do? James was lying in hospital badly injured, supposing he was to die? Her heart thumped in her chest. She felt sick and close to hysteria until she remembered that the boys' school was closing at lunchtime and immediately rang her friend Babs, who agreed to pick them up for her.

Sarah drove to the hospital in a daze. She felt confused and had to ask the girl at reception twice for directions to the Emergency Room. She stopped short when she eventually walked into the room and saw James looking so battered and frail. She cried inwardly. He was hooked up to a monitor and there were bandages and tubes everywhere. His light brown curly hair was bloodstained and matted and his eyes were closed.

'Oh James,' she said softly trying not to cry out loud. Her heartbeat quickened. She felt impotent and fearful. 'James honey, it's me, Sarah. My love, what on earth happened?' She couldn't think of anything else to say at that moment. He opened his eyes at the sound of her voice.

'Hi Honey,' he croaked. He closed his eyes again.

'James, they...they said that you were on the highway. Where were you going?' James' closed eyes began to brim with tears and he turned his head away. Sarah noticed the look on his face before he turned away from her: he had the drained, sad look of a beaten man. 'James tell me please? Why were you on the highway?' It seemed important for her to know.

'I'm afraid that I...,' he said weakly. He opened his mouth to speak again when a young doctor walked into the room. He wore a white coat and had a stethoscope swinging untidily from his pocket.

'Mrs. Butler?'

'Yes.'

'Hi, my name's Harrison Worthy. I'm sorry to interrupt you, but I'd like to talk to you outside for a moment if you wouldn't mind?' He put out his arm, beckoning her to leave the room with him.

'Sure... of course.' She turned to James. 'Honey, I won't be long,' she said kissing him on the cheek. His eyes followed her as she left the room.

Outside, two armchairs and a small table had been set aside for visitors and Sarah sat down on one of them with a worried frown upon her face. The doctor's whole demeanour expressed deep concern.

'We've had a chance to examine your husband and assess the problems. He has a couple of broken ribs, one of which has slightly punctured his lung, hence all the tubes. In addition, there are a number of contusions and lacerations, none of which are too serious. But I have to tell you that he has injured his back quite severely and at the present time, he has lost all feelings in his legs and feet.'

'Oh my god, no...' Sarah felt stunned.

'I'm afraid that it's still too early to tell whether there will be any permanent damage. He also suffered a blow to the head causing slight concussion.'

'But will he...?'

'Mrs. Butler,' he said interrupting her, 'until the swelling around his spinal cord goes down, it is impossible for us to say whether he will ever walk again. The signs are not good. There's something else.' He shifted his position in his chair and looked straight at her. 'His mental state is not good. He seems to have something on his mind. When he regained consciousness after the accident, he spoke incoherently, but we did manage to understand some of his words. It would appear that he was told this morning that he had been made redundant. Did you know about this?'

'Why no,' Sarah said feeling even more bewildered. 'I'm sure that can't be right. His boss, Andy Carstairs has been a close friend of ours for years.'

'I'm sorry to have to discuss such a personal matter with you, Mrs. Butler, but it could have been a contributory factor to his accident this morning.'

'Gee, I can see that. I had absolutely no idea. He usually discusses his job openly with me. Although now I come to think about, he hasn't mentioned it lately.' Tears began to form in the corners of her eyes. 'Perhaps he knew and didn't dare say anything?'

'Well, that's as may be. Fortunately, the driver of the truck that he hit wasn't hurt. He said that your husband changed lanes without signalling and without looking to see if there was anyone coming up behind him on the inside lane.'

'But he's always such a careful driver. I don't understand.' Sarah shook her head in confusion. She could hardly believe what she was hearing: everything seemed to be going from bad to worse.

The doctor in a moment of compassion placed his arm around her shoulders. 'Now Mrs. Butler, you mustn't worry too much. Your husband's injuries, although serious, are not life threatening. He will recover, but there remains the spinal injury which is giving us the most concern and we are doing everything we can. Would you like to go back and sit with him?'

'Yes please, I would.'

On her return, she found that James had fallen into a deep sleep and she sat next to his bed, gently holding his hand for about two hours. A nurse eventually persuaded her to go home. Sarah kissed him lightly on the cheek and quietly left the room.

As she drove back to their home silent tears cascaded down her face. Her nerves were completely shot to pieces and her beautiful morning had been turned into a nightmare. How on earth was she going to break the news to the boys? What if he never regained the use of his legs? Poor James, how would he cope? Indeed, how would any of us cope? But we will, she told herself, we will.

Sarah was instantly filled with determination and courage – James would be able to cope, because he would have the love of his family behind him.

* * * * * *

Chapter Seventeen

Katie

Katie felt much more like her old self when she woke up on Monday morning. She yawned, stretched herself and snuggled back down under the duvet again. It was wonderful to feel normal again.

Her feelings of calm were short-lived however: she couldn't suppress thoughts of her dreadful ordeal for long. There were so many unanswered questions buzzing through her head. What on earth had possessed Harold Hapsworth-Cole to act the way he'd done? What had motivated him? She knew the answer only too well – it was money and greed. But not only that, she remembered the evil light in his eyes. Nancy had intimated that there had been some mental problems in the Hapsworth-Cole family in the past. Perhaps Harold had inherited the problem. Katie would never be able to forget the hours that she'd been forced to spend trapped in that lonely old attic, feeling cold, hungry and frightened and the thought of ever having to set foot in that dreadful place again appalled her.

Now she was safely at home, she realised how precarious her position had really been. Harold could have killed her. Thank goodness that fact hadn't occurred to her whilst she was trapped in the attic, she thought. It would have made her enforced stay there even more difficult to bear. She shook her head, almost disbelieving that such a thing could ever have happened to her.

She heard the phone ringing downstairs in the hall. A few moments later, there was a light knock on her bedroom door and the sound of Brenda's anxious voice.

'Are you OK, Katie?'

'Yes Brenda, I am,' she called out. 'Hold on a minute.' She got up slowly and placed her feet into the slippers that she kept by the bed and yawned sleepily as she opened the door. Brenda stood on the threshold with a tray in her hand.

'Hello, Katie love. I thought I'd just look in to see how you were feeling and to bring you a cup of tea,' she said putting the tray on the bedside table.

'Thank you Brenda, I'm feeling much better this morning, although my head still aches and I'm a little stiff, but bearing in mind what could have happened, I feel I got off quite lightly really.'

'Good. I'm so relieved. Brian and I were terribly worried about you. When I think what that dreadful man could have done to you, it makes my blood run cold.' Brenda stopped speaking for a moment and looked carefully at her. 'Still, you're alright now. Shall I pull the curtains open? It's such a lovely day.'

'Yes please.' Katie couldn't help smiling. Brenda was bustling around like a mother hen.

'You must take it easy and try not to worry about anything,' she said, at last sitting down on the edge of the bed. 'I've just spoken to Brian. Apparently the police are now trying to trace Harold. He also said that Penny Humberston is going to examine the letter and the ones held by Nancy Brown. After that she'll contact a firm of solicitors in Vancouver to see if they can trace Amy Butler, or her son. Then we'll just have to sit back and see what develops.' Brenda sighed. Katie thought that she looked tired, almost as if she hadn't slept properly.

'It's quite exciting in a strange kind of way, isn't it?' she said. 'The Hapsworth-Cole family certainly seem to have been a strange lot. Look at Harold for example. No normal person would have done something like that. And I can't help feeling sorry for Amy Butler,' Katie confessed as she climbed back into the warmth of her bed. 'All those years went by without her knowing what had happened to Gerald and what about her son?'

'Well, I would imagine that he grew up feeling embittered by it all,' Brenda said with a deep sigh.

'Yes, poor woman. I wonder if she ever found happiness with someone else. And can you imagine what it would have been like for Marjorie, losing both her children and her husband? What a mess.'

'So perhaps it was just as well that she never found out about Gerald's affair with Amy.'

'Oh Brenda, I'm afraid that I can only picture both women sitting all alone and pining for him. I wonder if he really deserved such devotion. He obviously had some kind of charisma. I had a lot of time to think about it when I was locked in the attic.'

'Come on drink your tea up love, otherwise it'll get cold. I'm sure we'll find that Amy Butler went on to live quite a normal life, so don't you worry your head about it any more. And we know how poor Mrs. Hapsworth-Cole coped, don't we?'

'Yes, by buying hundreds of books, which she never read,' Katie replied.

'Which was just as well under the circumstances, don't you think?' The phone downstairs began to ring again and Brenda got up from the bed. 'My, we are popular this morning. I'll pop downstairs and see who it is. Won't be long.' When she returned, she wore a quizzical smile on her face.

'Who was it?'

'It's er...a young man called Stuart Wells. He sounds rather nice. Quite gorgeous in fact. Do you want to speak to him?'

'Stuart...? Yes...yes of course. I met him whilst I was in Penzance. He's a newly qualified accountant and has probably moved to Lewes by now. I think that he promised my cousin

Helen, that he would keep an eye on me, but I'm not supposed to know about that of course,' she said with a giggle.

They both walked downstairs together and Katie picked up the phone.

'Hello.' Her heart began to race as she spoke.

'Katie, how are you? It's Stuart...Stuart Wells, remember me?'

'Of course, I remember you.'

'I'm now living in a flat in Lewes and I was wondering how you were.'

'I'm fine, thank you.'

'And are you still working in that creepy old house?'

'No, I'm glad to say that I finished all the books this weekend, thank goodness.' A cold shiver ran down her spine at the mere thought of it.

'Are you sure that you're OK, Katie,' Stuart said with concern in his voice. 'You don't really sound it. I've tried to get you several times over the last couple of days, both on this phone and your mobile.' He paused. 'I hope that you don't mind, but I managed to get your number from Helen.'

'No, of course I don't mind. I'm glad you did, Stuart,' she hesitated. 'I've had a really bad weekend actually, but I'm OK now.'

'Is there anything I can do?'

'No, I'm fine really I am.'

'One of the reasons I had for phoning you, was to ask if you were doing anything today? Remember we talked about Brighton? I was wondering if you would care to show me the sights.'

'Yes, I'd love to. I could do with getting away from Anston for a few hours, as long as it's not too energetic, but I'll tell you about it when I see you.'

'If you're sure that you'll be OK. We could have lunch in a pub somewhere?'

'That sounds great.'

'Good, that's settled then,' he said happily. 'We can stroll around The Lanes. I've heard that they are something special. I'll pick you up at about 11.30 this morning, if that's alright with you.'

'Yes, see you then, bye.'

'Er...before I go, what's the best way to get to Anston, I'm afraid that I don't know my way around yet?'

Katie spent the next few moments telling him the best route to take. Finally she said, 'I'll see you at 11.30 then Stuart, bye.'

Throughout her conversation with him, Brenda had been mouthing all sorts of things to her and nodding her head wildly. Stuart had quite a loud voice on the phone and she had more or less heard everything.

'I'm so glad that you said you would go, despite what I said earlier about taking it easy today,' she said. 'It's just what you need, something to take your mind off things. But don't do anything too energetic will you, you've had a tough time over the last few days?'

'Don't worry, I know my limits.'

'What is he like then?'

'Stuart, he's just a friend Brenda, just a friend.' Katie laughed and looked meaningfully at her. 'He's 27, just under six feet tall with dark curly hair and amazingly brown eyes. Is that enough?'

'It's enough for now. Anyway I must get on and you must get ready to meet your "friend"' she answered with heavy emphasis.

Katie spent ages trying on clothes before finally making up her mind what to wear. She was really looking forward to seeing Stuart again. She remembered the happy time they had shared in Penzance. That time now stood out in her memory like an oasis in a desert. It had been an emotional high spot in the midst of her unhappiness.

She examined her face carefully in the mirror. She looked

tired. The cut near her temple was not quite so angry-looking now, but the bruising showed up quite vividly and she tried to cover it up with make-up. But she eventually gave up because it was still shining through. She hoped that he wouldn't ask too many questions about it. Finally, she pulled up the zip on her bootleg jeans and looked at herself again, turning slightly this way and that and holding her hand over her flat stomach. She tucked her blue denim shirt in and bent down to tie up the laces of her trainers. She stood up straight and felt a stab of pain in her head. I must take Brenda's advice and not overdo things, she told herself. She glanced at her watch: it was nearly twenty past eleven. Finally, she picked up a bottle of Miss Dior and sprayed it behind her ears. The delicious aroma spread delicately around her.

Stuart arrived a few minutes early. He parked his car in the lane opposite the white barred gate and walked up the twisted pathway to Lilac Cottage. It was edged on both sides by a profusion of primroses, polyanthus, grape hyacinths and various members of the daffodil family and they all tumbled haphazardly on to the grey flinty flagstones. He stood nervously on the doorstep for a moment, trying to compose himself.

Hell, he thought, why on earth am I feeling so nervous? I've been looking forward to this moment for days. Finally he cleared his throat, ran his fingers through his hair and grabbed hold of the ornate bell pull. He pulled it downwards twice. He could hear the sound echoing in the hallway inside the cottage and the sound of a dog barking.

Katie opened the door immediately. Was she waiting at the bottom of the stairs for me, he wondered?

'Hi Katie,' he said with a broadening smile.

'Hello Stuart,' she replied. There was an embarrassing silence between them as they stood on the doorstep looking at one another. Katie at last took the initiative. 'Why don't you come inside for a moment and meet Brenda before we go? She's been dying to meet you.'

With the ice now broken, he took the first step of what would prove to be many, into Lilac Cottage.

On their arrival in Brighton, they had to drive around for a while trying to find somewhere to park, but they eventually found a space on the top floor of a multi-storey car park. Katie and Stuart were both feeling quite hungry by this time and made straight for The Lanes. The narrow streets and alleyways were a Mecca for thousands of people at all times of the year. They enjoyed looking at all the antiques, fine art displays and clothes in the quaint bow-shaped shop windows, before making their way to one of Katie's favourite restaurants.

It was tucked well away from the milling crowds of happy, sauntering tourists and despite the fact that she'd been to this restaurant with Simon in the past, she was determined to enjoy herself and forget about the "traitor" who used to be her friend. The menu was quite extensive, but Katie still didn't feel like eating a heavy meal. Instead she chose a light, creamy taggliatelli dish with a side salad. The fresh sea air had given Stuart an appetite and he soon tucked into an entrecote steak, boiled potatoes and a huge mound of vegetables.

Throughout the meal, it became apparent that Stuart could hardly wait to hear what had happened to Katie at the weekend. He was extremely attentive and asked her several times how she was feeling, but somehow she always managed to change the subject. She knew that she was being obtuse, but she didn't wish to burden him with her problems. They chatted on a lighter level and gradually she began to feel more relaxed. She looked at the young man sitting opposite her and her heart gave a little lurch. Could it be that she was falling for him? No, she told herself, not so soon after Simon. He looked at her, smiled, reached across the table and grasped her hand firmly.

'Katie, I know that it's none of my business, but when I called this morning, you seemed to be a little on edge for some reason. Something obviously happened to you at the weekend and I would have to be an insensitive dolt, not to notice the cuts and bruises on your forehead. I wish you would trust me enough to share it with me? Perhaps I could help?' He looked so earnest sitting there, that Katie knew that she had to tell him everything, right down to the fact that she was terrified at the thought of ever going into Epton Hall again.

'Wild horses wouldn't be able to make me cross that particular threshold again, Stuart, and I can't understand what motivated Harold Hapsworth-Cole into behaving the way he did.'

Stuart was furious. 'What an absolute bastard,' he said, his face turning puce with anger. 'Perhaps I could…'

'There's nothing you can do Stuart. Harold has probably returned to Malta by now and I'm feeling so much better, honestly. It is all in the hands of the police and the solicitors now.'

'But Katie, the thought of him leaving you lying injured on the floor for the whole weekend without light, food, water or heat for that matter, makes my blood boil. He wasn't to know that you would be rescued the following day. He sounds like a madman.' Stuart took a deep breath and then calmed down. 'Have the police heard anything yet?'

'I…I don't know.'

'Well, let's hope that they find him soon. Are you feeling OK?'

'Yes I'm fine and I'm enjoying myself too. You've no idea what it was like being shut up in that dreadful attic. It makes me shiver just to think about it and it's obvious that Harold

Hapsworth-Cole wasn't thinking about what he was doing.'

'I'm not sure that I would agree with you. I think that creep knew exactly what he was doing and it sounds as if he's a cold, calculating and dangerous man.'

'Well, I hope I never have to meet him again.'

'So do I,' Stuart said vehemently. 'Anyway, let's change the subject shall we?'

'It might be a good idea, before I start becoming too maudlin.'

'Katie?'

'Yes?'

'I have been wondering if you would like to come and meet my parents next weekend?'

'Your parents!'

'Yes. They live near Newbury in Berkshire. With my change of job and moving from Penzance, I haven't had a chance to see them for several weeks and I'd like to show you off.'

Katie felt surprised and flattered by his suggestion. 'Why yes, but won't they think that it's funny meeting me out of the blue like that? After all, we hardly know one another and you certainly couldn't have spoken to them about me.'

'I think I know you quite well and that's why I want you to meet them, at least for a couple of hours. After that I want you all to myself.' A devilish grin spread across his face and she giggled: the wine seemed to have gone to her head.

Soon afterwards, Stuart settled the bill and they walked out of the tiny restaurant hand in hand, a new intimacy having developed between them. They strolled along the promenade enjoying the spring sunshine and ended up at the end of the pier without treading on the cracks between the long wooden floor boards. Katie watched Stuart as he whooshed down the helter-skelter, finally falling in a heap on the rugs at the bottom and laughing fit to burst. Later they found their way on to the stony beach, scattering seagulls that were busily fighting over a dead fish lying amongst the stones. The huge birds flew noisily into the air as they approached, protesting vehemently with their harsh whining, raucous voices.

Time seemed to stand still as they stood at the edge of the water watching the waves come sweeping in and pounding on to the shore. Each wave quickly spent its energy climbing the steeply shelving beach, only to retreat back into the ocean again, making a curious sloughing noise as it dislodged small stones and other debris in its wake. Stuart turned to her suddenly and without hesitating, took her into his arms.

'Katie, I care for you so much you know. I've hardly been able to think straight since I met you in Cornwall. All I know is that I want to look after you from now onwards. I can't bear the thought of anything nasty ever happening to you again.' He looked down at her and tilted her face up to his. To her surprise, he kissed her lightly on the lips. A question began to take form in her mind, but before she could say anything, Stuart interrupted her. 'Come on let's walk back to the car park. You're beginning to look a little pale and I don't want you to overdo things after your ordeal.'

Katie felt confused. Did he mean what he'd just said to her, or had it been said on the spur of the moment? What were her feelings for him? She could still feel his arms around her and the pressure of his lips upon hers. Could she trust another man after the cruel and callous way Simon had treated her? She continued to speculate about the future, wondering whether Stuart would be a continuing part of it. She had really enjoyed herself today: he was good company, easy going and confident.

By the time they reached the car, she was feeling exhausted. It was early evening and they drove back to Anston and Lilac Cottage, both now feeling happy and comfortable with one another. Katie knew that her feelings for Stuart were deepening, but curiously enough they were nothing like the feelings that she'd had for Simon. Perhaps that meant that she had never really loved him?

She looked up into his gorgeous eyes. She could almost read his thoughts and felt sure that he had a deep and heartfelt understanding of what she had been through. Katie now needed to take stock of her life and try to regain her equilibrium. She also knew that Stuart would be there for her no matter what happened. Perhaps the future was not so bleak after all.

* * * * * *

Chapter Eighteen

Vancouver

James Butler slept for long periods of the day after his horrific accident. Sarah sat by his bedside willing him to get better, but even during his wakeful periods there was little communication between them. He would neither talk about the accident, nor the reason for his apparent mental confusion – the fact that he might have lost his job. His eyes would glaze over if she even as much as mentioned it. He did however, tell her with monotonous regularity that he had no feeling in his legs and this knowledge depressed her more each day.

Because of this, Sarah began to accept the inevitability of having a wheelchair bound husband. She couldn't help viewing the future with dread and deep foreboding. She knew that even supposing the doctor hadn't been right about James being made redundant, if he was confined to a wheelchair for the rest of his life, he would probably lose his current job anyway. She decided to give Andy Carstairs a ring to tell him about James' accident and to ask him to either confirm or deny that James no longer had a job.

Fortunately her friend Babs kindly offered to take the two boys under her wing during the day allowing Sarah to spend more time with James. She tried to cheer him up by telling him what the boys had been doing during the day or where she'd been. She repeated whole conversations that she'd had with friends, hoping that at least some of what she was saying would bring him out of his deep depression and help him to come to terms with his problems. But even though some of his physical injuries were healing, he continued to close his mind to her and his surroundings.

One morning, about two weeks after James had been admitted to the hospital, Sarah woke from an exceptionally fitful night's sleep, which had been peppered by confused dreams. One dream in particular alarmed her. She had been forced to endure a hazy existence in which every other person was in a wheelchair, including her children. She seemed to be the only able-bodied person around and had to run around in circles looking after everyone. She stayed in her bed for a few minutes feeling deeply disturbed. The dream had been so vivid and even though she knew that her emotions must have been at a low ebb for her subconscious to have behaved in such a way, she immediately went in search of the boys, just to reassure herself that they were OK.

Sarah found them in Michael's bedroom having a fight over a pillow. 'That's mine,' she heard her elder son complaining, '...and you know it is.'

'Oh no it's not, it's mine,' Michael replied in a whining voice.

'I tell you it's mine. Look I even put my name in the corner, so there.'

She smiled, they were obviously fighting fit! Even so, her dream had really frightened her, she was only too well aware of the heavy responsibilities which were now being heaped onto her slender shoulders. It was vital that she didn't allow herself to lose touch with reality.

After having a quick shower, she went down to the kitchen to have some coffee. She caught sight of her reflection in a mirror. My oh my, I look a mess this morning, she told herself. Just look at my hair: I'll have to find some time to get to the salon, but when? Even her eyes lacked lustre and the little lines underneath seemed to be more deeply etched than before. Sarah sighed deeply and then turned away from the mirror which appeared to be telling her that too much water had flowed under her particular bridge.

She was about to put the kettle on – she desperately needed a cup of coffee – when she heard a dull thud outside the front door and a noisy whistle: the morning's mail had arrived. The boys had heard it too and she could hear them stamping and shouting as they tried to race one another down the stairs. Michael and John always battled it out to see who could pick up the mail first.

John had obviously won, because a few moments later he burst into the kitchen holding a bundle above his head. A rather disgruntled Michael followed behind him scowling venomously.

'You never let me pick them up,' he grumbled. 'It wouldn't hurt you to let me get there first once in a while, would it?'

'I can't wait for you to get there, you're like a slow old tortoise,' John replied taunting him.

'Come on you two, stop it,' Sarah said with growing impatience. 'I can't put up with your constant arguing. What does it matter who picks up the mail first? Can I have it please, John?' Being the taller of the two boys, he was still busy waving the bundle above Michael's head, so he couldn't reach it.

'Not only are you like a tortoise, but you're also a midget as well.'

'Well, if I'm a midget then you're an overgrown louse,' was Michael's quick riposte.

Something snapped inside Sarah's head. 'John if you don't give those letters to me now, I'll tell your father how rude you've both been. He won't put up with your nonsense.' Realising what she had said, she sat down at the kitchen table and immediately burst into tears. She felt exhausted by it all. The two boys looked at one another, well aware that they had overstepped the mark.

John put his arms gently around his mother's shoulders. 'I'm sorry Mom, we didn't really mean anything.' He placed the letters in front of her on the table.

'I'm sorry too, John. I shouldn't have lost my temper, but with your father in hospital and the thought of him never ever being able to walk again, well I...'

'Mom, we do understand, don't we Michael?' he said gently nudging his younger brother into action. Michael stood there like the typical 12 year old he was, looking as if he was sorry, but secretly longing to be anywhere else but in the kitchen.

'Gee yes. Sorry Mom,' he hurriedly replied, 'and give Pops our love when you see him today.' He raced out the door and she could hear him running up the stairs. John soon followed him.

Sarah made her coffee and sat for a while slowly sipping the hot, calming liquid. She was becoming more and more worried about the boys. All this tension and upset was having a detrimental effect on both of them. John was old enough to understand what she was going through, but she was not quite sure about Michael. He was a little immature for his age and she knew that they had spoiled him a little. Her mind turned to the letters lying in front of her. Most of them were bills; they always arrived on time, she thought. Two others caught her eye. One was from the Canadian Automobile Association and the other, an airmail letter from England, and it was addressed to 'Mr. James Hapsworth-Cole Butler'. She frowned. James hadn't used his double-barrelled name in years. In fact he had felt embarrassed by it! She examined the envelope and held it up to the light, but without opening it she could gain no knowledge of its content. Despite being consumed with curiosity about who the letter was from, she placed both letters in her handbag.

After breakfast, she waved goodbye to the boys as they went off to school and walked upstairs into her bedroom. It was a feminine room. James had always given her a free rein with the décor in the house and the room reflected her personality: it was her domain and the place where she did all her private thinking. She walked over to her dressing table which was painted white with gold edgings and her toes dug into the luxuriously thick pile of the pale mushroom coloured carpet. Once again, she looked at her reflection in the long mirror and looked away in disgust. The two small table lamps placed either side of the mirror, gave everything a rosy glow. But even this did little to improve the way that she thought she looked.

Half an hour later, she climbed into her car and was soon on the way to the hospital. She parked the car in the parking lot adjacent to the hospital buildings and walked through the doors into the large reception area. She was about to walk into the ward, when a young nurse came hurrying towards her smiling broadly.

'Mrs. Butler,' she said. 'We've some good news for you. Your husband seems to have regained some feeling in his feet and legs. He's really quite upbeat this morning.'

Sarah's heart thumped wildly in her chest. Any lingering memories about the boys' arguments instantly evaporated. 'That's wonderful news, thank you.' Hot prickly tears began to form in the corners of her eyes as she entered the ward and approached her husband's bedside. He was wide wake and smiling for a change. She noticed that his cheeks were now tinged with pink and his eyes looked altogether brighter and clearer.

'Sarah honey, you'll never guess,' he said happily. 'I've gained a little feeling in my feet and legs. I can't believe it.'

'Oh James…' She sat down and grabbed hold of his hand.

'You've really no idea how awful it's been not knowing whether I would ever walk again. The specialist says that it's still early days of course, but I just know everything is going to be OK from now on.'

'Oh honey, I…I don't know what to say,' and as she'd done earlier that morning, she burst into tears.

'Come on Sarah, it's a moment for celebration not tears, isn't it?'

Sarah remembered the letters in her handbag and the last

thing she wanted to do was to spoil James' good mood. He'd been through a traumatic time, both physically and mentally and his mind seemed to have blotted out most of what had happened both before and after the accident. Even though she felt as if she was treading on hot coals, she knew that she had to let him read them. 'By the way, some letters came for you this morning,' she said trying to regain her equilibrium. 'This one is from the Insurance Company and...' James' face rapidly turned pale and grim. 'What's the matter?' she asked anxiously. 'Are you in any pain only you've gone quite pale.'

'No it's just that...' He looked away.

'What?'

'Oh...it's...it's nothing.'

'Please tell me, honey?' He remained silent. 'James, please don't shut me out? I can't bear it.'

'I've been made redundant. I'm finished but...'

'James honey, I already know that you've been made redundant. I phoned Andy Carstairs to tell him about your accident and he told me. It's not the end of the world you know.'

'But honey can't you see? I'm completely down the can, on the scrap heap or whatever else you'd like to call it. I didn't want you to know, but...I was running away from my responsibilities when the accident happened. I'm so sorry, it was cowardly of me. I couldn't think of a way of telling you.'

'But James, my darling, I...'

'Please let me finish, let me get it all off my chest, or I'll blow something. You see I thought that you might leave me and take the kids with you...'

'Leave you! James how could you think anything like that? The doctor told me that when you came round after the accident, you were mumbling something about being made redundant. So please don't worry, I was prepared for it to be true. Andy was actually very sorry to hear about what happened and sends his best wishes to you.'

'I see.' James turned away, as if he was trying to get away from her pleading eyes. 'What am I gonna tell the boys, they'll be so ashamed of me?'

Sarah's heart sank. Poor James, he must feel that all his hard work over the years had all come to nothing. 'It's not the end of the world is it? You'll be able to walk again and you'll find another job. I could even find one myself now that the boys are getting older.' She squeezed his hand hard, trying desperately to quell yet more tears, which were once more threatening to break through, like a huge dam holding back a flood. She tried to sound upbeat. 'You've often spoken about trying something new. Well now's our chance. When we were up in Kelowna last year, you said that it would be nice to run a holiday chalet centre there. Just think of all those cute little log cabins in that clearing amongst the pine trees? And remember the snow-capped mountains in the distance? We were in seventh heaven then, weren't we?' She looked at him. 'Well, weren't we?'

'Yes, but…I don't think you realise how little money we now have. After all the bills and the mortgage and the…'

'James don't. Surely, you'll be given a golden handshake from the company?'

'No, Sarah. The company simply can't afford it. Andy has paid me up to the end of the month that's all,' he said gloomily. He slipped back on to his pillow, his earlier happy and buoyant mood having dissipated.

'Honey, don't fret. We'll think of something. All you've got to do now, is concentrate on getting fit and well again.'

His reply was bitter, tense and distant. 'Yes, we'll sit back and try to think of something, shall we?'

Sarah felt a little angry with her husband. 'Now you're being defeatist and it's not like you,' she said with a sharpness, which she soon regretted. James looked as if he had just been stung. 'Well, if you're not going to open the letter from the Insurance Company, perhaps you should open this one?' She gave him the other letter. 'It's from England.' He glanced at it with disinterested eyes. 'Aren't you even going to open it? You never know it could be news of a long lost relative offering you lots of money,' she joked trying desperately to lighten the heavy atmosphere which seemed to hover over both their heads.

James stared at the envelope. 'Fat chance of that,' he replied. 'Hmm, Hapsworth-Cole Butler: I haven't used that name for years.' He put it down on the duvet in front of him.

'Aren't you even going to open it? It could be important.'

'Huh, important to whom? If it's anything to do with my precious English ancestry, I don't want to know about it.' He closed his eyes.

'Would you like me to open it for you?' she suggested.

He opened one eye and reached for the letter. 'OK, you win. I'll open the darned thing.' He withdrew the letter from the envelope and began to read it and his eyes opened wide. 'Hey, what's this?'

'What is it? What does it say?'

'I've only read the first page, but I...I can't believe it. Here you read it – see what you can make of it?' He handed the letter to her. It was from a firm of solicitors by the name of Messrs Sharpe, Holyoak and Masters of Anston in Sussex, England. It read:

"*Dear Mr. Hapsworth-Cole Butler,*

Re: Epton Hall - Mrs. Marjorie Hapsworth-Cole – Deceased

We are acting under the instructions of Mr. Brian Ainsley and Miss Katie Nicholson regarding the above.

> *Mrs. Marjorie Hapsworth-Cole died intestate, on the 10th February 2009.*
> *Mrs. Hapsworth-Cole was the widow of Mr. Gerald Hapsworth-Cole, who is believed to have died in May 1953, along with the two children of that marriage. Extensive and exhaustive searches at the time, failed to find any evidence as to their fate, and it was generally assumed at the time, that there was a boating accident in the Solent but their bodies were never found. As far as we can ascertain, there are no surviving relatives on the maternal side, but Mr. Gerald Hapsworth-Cole had a brother Stanley (now deceased) and his son, Harold, who is believed to be the only heir and would under normal circumstances, stand to inherit the Epton Hall Estate and any money or investments thereto.*
> *Since that time, certain letters have come to light. We have had the opportunity of examining the said letters and we feel that you could be a direct descendant of the family. Before we go any further, we feel that it is necessary for you to know what happened to the English branch of the Hapsworth-Cole family from the date of your birth."*

Sarah stopped reading the letter. 'James, is this what I think it is?' She handed it back to her husband, who turned the page and carried on reading, his eyes growing round with excitement. The letter went on to describe everything that had happened up until Marjorie Hapsworth-Cole's death.

> *"Whilst sorting through Mrs. Hapsworth-Cole's extensive library after her death, Katie Nicholson, a young librarian, discovered a letter dated 3rd May 1953 addressed to Mr. Gerald Hapsworth-Cole. The letter was from a Mrs. Amy Butler of Vancouver, Canada, informing him of the birth of her illegitimate child – a son born on the 23rd April 1953. The*

envelope also contained a signed copy of the original birth certificate pertaining to that child, naming Gerald as the natural father. This child was given the names of James Gerald Hapsworth-Cole Butler."*

'I don't believe this…I.'
'Here, let me see?'
'No shhh a minute.'

"Unfortunately, Gerald's nephew Harold, although living in Malta, turned up at the house unannounced. He later stole the letter and the certificate and locked Miss Nicholson in the attic. The police are investigating this incident. Another unfinished letter addressed to Mrs. Amy Butler and dated the 17th May 1953 was subsequently discovered, a copy of which is enclosed for your information."

James turned to the letter addressed to his mother, Amy. His eyes misted over with tears as he read his father's words. His shoulders slumped when he realised the implications of what had happened all those years ago. Without saying anything, he handed the letter to Sarah. She read it, and a look of wonderment gradually spread over her tense features. He turned to the main letter again.

*"We understand from your solicitors, (who incidentally will be writing to you under separate cover) that Mrs Amy Butler is also now deceased. We now need confirmation that you are in fact the illegitimate son of the said Gerald Hapsworth-Cole and if possible, we need to see a copy of your birth certificate in order for your claim to the Epton Hall Estate – should you wish so to do – to be considered. If you do not have the said certificate in your possession, we would suggest that you take immediate steps to obtain a certified copy, otherwise it could adversely affect your claim. We should add for your information that the value of the

whole estate amounts to a considerable sum of money.

We would therefore appreciate an early reply, so that we can put in a claim on your behalf, to the family solicitors, Messrs. Broadbent and Crombie of Epton, Sussex, England and bring the question of the inheritance of the said estate, to a speedy conclusion.

Should you require any further information, please do not hesitate to contact us.

Yours sincerely,
Ms. Penelope Humberston."

After they had both finished reading the letters, neither of them could speak for a few moments, whilst they struggled to try to understand what it actually meant to them.

'Sarah, I can't quite take this in.'

'No, neither can I, James.'

'I can't believe that this is happening to us. The letter said that the estate amounts to a considerable fortune. I wonder what this place…er…Epton Hall, or whatever it is called, is like?'

'Yes. Epton Hall: it sounds rather grand to me.'

'Yeah. I'd always known my father's name, but Mother never ever spoke about him. I didn't know if he was rich or poor and to be perfectly honest, I couldn't have cared less anyhow. She was always under the impression that he wasn't interested in the fact that he had a son living in Canada and had just cut us both out of his life completely. I find it incredible that these letters have been hidden inside a couple of books.' He looked down at the words written by his father so many years before and his eyes too, filled with tears.

Sarah placed her hand on her husband's arm in order to console him. 'Despite everything that has happened in the last few days, your father would've been proud of you, James.'

'What, proud of someone who's out of work, do you mean?' he scoffed.

'Yes, and he'd have been proud of his two wonderful grandchildren too. And…,' she continued, playfully moving her fingers up and down his arm, 'we do have your birth certificate to prove that you are Gerald Hapsworth-Cole's son, don't we?'

'If my memory serves me right, it's in that old carved wooden box that used to belong to Mom. I put it in the basement soon after she died and I've not needed to look at it since. As you know, I hated the name Hapsworth-Cole and that's why I dropped it. If I had known the real reason why he hadn't contacted her, I'd have been proud to use his name.'

'It sounds as if your new-found cousin, Harold, could be a bit of a problem though.'

'Yes, bearing in mind what he did to the girl who found the letters,' James added, 'but we'll work something out.'

Sarah gave a huge sigh of relief and kissed him lightly on the cheek just as a senior nurse walked into the ward. 'I think that's enough excitement for the moment Mr. Butler, it's time for your rest.'

'In that case honey, I'll be off home. I'll come in and see you again tomorrow, OK? And, we'll have to give some thought about what sort of a reply we'll be sending to England. Do you want me to contact our solicitors?'

'Yes, please, if you wouldn't mind. Do you know, Sarah, this could prove to be the most important time of our lives.' She kissed him goodbye and he blew her a kiss as she left the room. The last thing she noticed was his face: it was transformed into a picture of happiness. What an up and down day it had been, she thought. But she was quite sure that James was going to be able to walk again and everything would be wonderful. She walked away from the hospital with a renewed spring in her step.

* * * * * *

Chapter Nineteen

Penny Humberston's Secretary, Karen Bentley, staggered into her office armed with several files, packages and letters which she had picked up from reception. She was out of breath after walking up two flights of stairs and dumped them all unceremoniously onto her desk.

Karen, a slim and elegant woman in her early forties, was an excellent Legal Secretary and had been with the company for nearly twenty years, the last five of which had been spent working for Penny Humberston. She enjoyed her work and treated all the little problems that each new day brought with cheerfulness and fortitude. With a practised eye she quickly scanned through the mound of files and unopened letters on her desk and set about opening a scary number of emails. Most of the morning's correspondence related to existing local cases, some containing clients' cheques, a few unsolicited advertising magazines and pamphlets and a couple of letters requesting money for worthy causes. She placed them all to one side.

The last letter in the pile was from Vancouver in Canada and was marked "CONFIDENTIAL". It was the one for which Penny had been eagerly waiting.

The small village of Anston and the larger town of Epton, were quiet country areas in which nothing much ever seemed to happen. When the scandal over the past affairs of the Hapsworth-Cole family suddenly became common knowledge and public property, as a direct result of an article in the Epton Gazette, rumour and counter-rumour became rife. People from all walks of life took great delight in speculating about what had happened all those years before. There was nothing quite like a good piece of juicy gossip to chat about over coffee or a pint in the local pub.

Since her death, Marjorie Hapsworth-Cole's past life and that of her family were again being placed under a microscope. Every single scrap of new information no matter how small was eagerly pounced upon and then exaggerated beyond recognition. The staff who worked in the offices of Messrs. Sharpe, Holyoak and Masters, were neither immune from, nor disinterested in, the subject. The offices had begun to hum as various members of staff became totally engrossed in all the unfolding events and dramas. Fact or fiction was passed around and, just like the ancient game of Chinese whispers, invariably came back vastly altered and muddied.

Karen had become increasingly annoyed at all the tittle-tattle and speculation which was going on around her. Added to which, the latest scandal to hit the local headlines about the imprisonment of a local librarian's assistant at Epton Hall, was also discussed endlessly. With her astute and enquiring mind and with many years of legal work behind her, she was really only interested in the actual facts of the case. She picked up the letter from Canada and walked towards Penny's door. She knocked twice.

'Come in,' a curt voice answered. She entered waving the letter in the air. She found Penny sitting at her desk looking weary and swamped with piles of files and paper. She looked harassed and her face was red with anger. 'I thought that computers were supposed to alleviate some of the paperwork. Huh!' she mumbled. 'Sorry, don't mind me. Good morning and what other problems do we have on this bright sunny morning?' she enquired sarcastically raising her neatly shaped eyebrows. Karen cringed. She noticed the signs: her boss was in a prickly mood. It was in fact pouring with rain outside. Penny continued: 'I've just had the dubious pleasure of speaking to Mr. Brampton. You know, the man who was complaining about his bill. I tried to tell him that all our charges are standard, but I'm afraid that he won't be mollified.' She sighed.

'Good morning Penny,' Karen said, at last managing to get a word in. 'This letter should cheer you up a bit. It has just arrived from Vancouver.' She placed it on the desk in front of her.

'Good. Thank you, Karen. I'm sorry to be so tetchy, but I didn't sleep at all well last night.' She flexed her shoulders wearily. 'It's tension I suppose.'

'Well I must say that you do look a little tired. Would you like some coffee now?'

'Oh, yes please.'

'Right, I'll go and put the kettle on.'

'No wait a minute, I'll read this first. Let's hope that it's good news for a change. We could certainly use some.' She opened the letter and began to read it and as she did so, her forehead creased with concentration and a smile spread across her face. 'Wonderful,' she said, waving the letter around. 'It's from the Butlers' solicitors. You'll be pleased to hear that James Butler still has his birth certificate. Well, that definitely puts the cat amongst the pigeons as far as Harold Hapsworth-Cole is concerned, doesn't it?'

'Yes…yes, what else does it say?'

'Hold on a minute, I haven't finished it yet.' She continued to read. 'Oh no, how awful. Apparently, James Butler recently had a serious road accident and the car was a complete write-off. It would seem that he is lucky to be alive. They say that he had been worried about being made redundant. Karen…supposing that he'd died? It doesn't bear thinking about.'

'Does it say how he is now?' Karen asked. 'It's as if the Hapsworth-Cole family is under some sort of curse – it's been one tragedy after another.'

'Mmmm, it certainly seems that way. Look…it says here, that he's still in hospital.'

'The poor man. Your letter couldn't have arrived at a better time for him though, could it?'

'That's for sure.' Penny stood up. 'Right, we'll have to get things in motion this end now. By the way, the police still haven't had much luck in tracing Harold. He seems to have gone to ground somewhere in Malta.'

'Why do the words "rat in a hole" spring to mind?' Penny glared at her. 'Sorry. But I wonder how hard the police have actually been searching for him: although he will have to surface sometime if he has any hope of ever owning the estate, surely?'

'Of course he will surface, but it's what he plans to do, that bothers me. I think I'd better phone Mr. Broadbent, in Epton and then let Brian and Katie know. They were both worrying about it, along with a few other people I could name.'

'I wouldn't call all the people around here worried exactly,' Karen said pulling a face. 'I would call some of them downright nosy. Some people have actually asked me if I knew any of the grisly and intimate details about the family. Do you know, someone told me the other day, that Gerald Hapsworth-Cole committed suicide because he was worried about money? How on earth would they know that, after all, it happened fifty odd years ago? There's so much adverse speculation flying around, that I despair about people sometimes. I blame the media for stirring everything up. Anyway, I'd better get off my soapbox and put the kettle on. Afterwards, I'll ring Katie Nicholson, shall I?'

'Yes please, if you wouldn't mind. Have you had time to look at the emails yet?'

'Some of them, and there are quite a few.'

'Why am I not surprised, Karen?'

Karen chuckled as she walked from the room.

Katie was standing on the top rung of a stepladder, busily stacking some of the shelves with new books that had arrived from the wholesalers, when she heard the phone ringing. Brian was out all morning attending a meeting, so she hurriedly climbed back down to ground level, nearly falling over in her haste. She rushed through into the back office and grabbed hold of the phone.

'The Good Book Shop here. Katie Nicholson speaking. Can I help you?'

'Hello Katie, it's Penny Humberston. How are you feeling? Have all your bumps and bruises healed now?'

'Yes thank you, I'm fine.'

'I thought that you'd like to know that I've had a reply from the Butlers' solicitors in Vancouver.'

Katie listened eagerly to what Penny had to say and her heart sank when she heard about James' car accident. 'Thanks for letting me know. I'd hate the thought of Harold getting his hands on the whole estate.'

'So would I. Anyway, I'll keep you posted. Perhaps you could tell Brian for me.'

'Yes of course I will. Bye.'

Since being confined in the attic and the dramatic discovery of the letters, Katie had felt the need to learn as much as she could about the Hapsworth-Cole family. She was mortified when she'd learned that Amy had died some time ago without knowing that Gerald hadn't deserted her. And now her son James, had been involved in a car accident. Did anything ever go right for this family, she wondered? Events could have taken an entirely different course had Amy known that he had died so soon after their son's birth. Katie also couldn't help wondering what would have happened if Nancy Brown hadn't intercepted Amy's letters. She shrugged her shoulder. It was no use speculating about what might have been, that was all now in the past.

An idea began to form in Katie's mind. Somehow, fate had

decreed that her life should become intertwined with this unknown family in Canada. She felt that she wanted to meet them and explain her part in the dramatic events of the past few weeks. She could afford to go to Vancouver. The money she had received from the sale of her parents' home was still sitting in the building society and earning interest. She could visit her Aunt Beatrice at the same time. Katie had not had a chance of seeing her since she'd moved to Vancouver after her mother's funeral. She decided to talk to Stuart about it.

That evening the weather was fine and calm. Stuart and Katie were having a quiet drink in Epton's oldest public house, The Dog and Pheasant. It was a charming old building and typical of many in the area. On the outside, the front was painted white and interspersed with blackened oak beams. These had been put in place haphazardly, thereby forming curiously odd angles: there were no straight lines anywhere. In front of all the windows, the owners had placed window boxes and hanging baskets, and a profusion of spring flowers and greenery tumbled downwards, creating a waterfall of vibrant colour.

Inside, the ceilings were low and misshapen and the soot-blackened beams appeared to dominate the rooms. A slight smoke haze from the log fire hung suspended from the ceiling, waiting for a breeze to come through the door to disperse it. There were several small round tables dotted throughout the crowded lounge-bar, each surrounded by chairs and stools, and groaning under the weight of beer bottles and glasses. Most of the seats were occupied.

Stuart and Katie sat closely together on a long wooden straight-backed bench seat, which ran under the heavily draped leaded-light windows. Stuart had his arm around her shoulders and was gazing intently into her eyes.

'Katie. Katie, do say something? You've been quiet for ages. Is anything wrong?'

'I'm sorry, Stuart,' she replied, suddenly becoming aware that he'd been speaking to her. 'What did you say?'

'I asked if there was anything wrong. You were miles away. Please share your thoughts with me?'

Katie looked at him. She was growing really fond of him: no, it was more than that, she told herself, she now realised that she loved him. She loved everything about him. She loved the way he looked and dressed, his warmth, his tenderness and his air of calm assurance. Yes, she decided, life without him would be almost unthinkable. It didn't seem to matter that they hadn't known one another long, their lives together had just sort of clicked and she sensed that he felt the same way about her. Why else would he have taken her to see his parents at the weekend?

'Katie?'

She put her hand on his and smiled. 'I was just thinking about last weekend. I really enjoyed our visit to your parents' home you know. They're really nice and made me feel so welcome. Your father has a wonderful sense of humour, hasn't he?'

'Yes and mother sometimes gets a little exasperated with him. He likes to tell jokes over dinner.'

'So I noticed,' Katie said, trying not to laugh.

'Now that you've met my parents, I'll have to introduce you to the rest of the tribe.'

'Goodness, how many of you are there?'

'Two brothers: Mark is an accountant like me, he's married and lives in Yorkshire and David is still at University in Durham.'

'I'd love to meet them. You haven't spoken about them before. I've often wondered what it would have been like to have a sister or a brother, being an only child can be quite…'

'What?'

'Well it can be quite lonely sometimes, especially since my parents died, I had nobody to turn to.'

'Oh my poor love. I haven't spoken about them because I have been too busy adoring you.' He grabbed hold of her hand.

'Stuart?'

'Yes.'

'Would you come to Vancouver in Canada, with me?'

'What did you say?' he said looking somewhat puzzled.

'I asked you if you would come to Vancouver with me?'

'Vancouver?'

'Yes. Will you come with me, please?'

'I don't know. When were you thinking of going? And what is more to the point, why?'

'I was thinking of going next week.'

'Next week!' he exclaimed. 'Katie, it's a bit short notice, isn't it? Are you impulsive, or what?'

'Yes, I suppose I am, but…'

'You still haven't told me why you want to go.' Stuart looked perplexed.

Katie was almost willing him to agree. She didn't really want to go all that way on her own. 'I had a call from Penny Humberston, a solicitor friend of Brian's. She has been trying to trace the Butler family in Vancouver. Well, she's succeeded and James Butler does still have his birth certificate.'

'Oh I see now. But why should you want to…?'

'But Stuart, there's another problem.'

'Problem?'

'James Butler was told that he'd been made redundant and was then involved in a car accident. He is in hospital with serious back and leg injuries and it's quite possible that he will never walk properly again. Please say you'll come with me,' she pleaded. 'I know that it is short notice, but would it be possible for you to have a couple of days off work? Please?'

'Katie darling, I find it hard to refuse you anything. Yes, I will try, but remember that I haven't been working for the company very long and they might not take too kindly to me wanting time off so soon,' he said doubtfully. 'But I will definitely ask them. OK?'

'Yes thank you Stuart.' She heaved a sigh of relief.

'The thing that puzzles me, is why you feel the need to go over there to see him?'

'I feel that I would like to see the whole thing through. After all I was the one who found the letter which will probably help to change all their lives: he has a wife and two teenage children by the way and I would love to meet them. I also have an aunt living there and I haven't seen her since my mother died. I thought that I could visit her at the same time. What do you think?'

'Look Katie, I promise that I will ask the senior partner first thing in the morning. Failing that, we could fly over there on Friday and come back on Monday, how does that sound?'

'It sounds wonderful. Thank you Stuart.'

'That way, I'd only need to have a couple of days off. We'll have to cope with the dreaded jet lag of course, but I suppose it will be worth it if it stops you from moping.' On an impulse, he put his arms around her and kissed her.

'Hmmm,' was Katie's reply. He kissed her again and she pushed him away gently. 'Stuart, not here, people are staring.'

'Why not? They're probably only jealous,' he replied and tried to kiss her again, but she laughed and skilfully turned her head.

'How about another drink?' she said, grabbing hold of her empty glass. 'I'm dreadfully thirsty this evening.'

'That's right, change the subject why don't you,' he whispered, trying to sound petulant but failing miserably. 'I now have to fight my way to the bar to get you a drink, when all I really want to do is take you home and then...' Stuart rose from his chair and disappeared into the crowd of people who were clamouring for attention around the bar.

Katie felt contented and happy. She loved the cheerful banter and camaraderie that existed between them. She could hardly believe that she had found someone who was so perfectly attuned to her psyche – it was almost too good to be true. He returned a few minutes later with a drink in each hand and a packet of crisps clenched between his teeth.

'There you are,' he said. 'Enjoy.' She giggled: it was ages since she had enjoyed herself quite so much.

The old Grandfather clock in the corner of the lounge-bar struck ten o'clock just as they'd finished their drinks and they made their way slowly back to the car, chatting incessantly about their plans for the following weekend. They had only driven about half a mile along a quiet narrow lane when an ominous explosion occurred. Everything seemed to go haywire and the car snaked across the road.

'Hold on tight love, I think we've blown a tyre.' Somehow, Stuart managed to steer them out of trouble and they ended up on a narrow grass verge, their nerves completely shattered. It had been a close thing.

'Katie, I'm so sorry. Are you OK?'

'Yes, thank goodness.'

'Shit…I'm sorry Katie, I didn't mean to swear. But I've suddenly remembered that the spare is flat too. I've been so busy with the new job and finding somewhere to live, I completely forgot to have it repaired. Now what do we do?' As if on cue, the heavens suddenly opened and they could hear the heavy rain beginning to bounce loudly on the car's roof.

'Quick Stuart, close the sunroof,' Katie called out. Large drops of water were dripping through the opening.

'Oh hell. Once things start to go wrong, they usually do so with a vengeance.' Stuart reached up and closed the roof, shutting out the rain and as far as he was concerned, the world. They sat in silence for a few moments listening to the sound of the rain spattering on the roof. 'Katie,' he said placing his arm around her shoulders, 'I suppose I could turn this to my advantage.'

'Yes, I suppose you could,' she replied giving him a coquettish sideways glance.

With that, he drew her towards him and kissed her fully on the lips and she found herself kissing him back with a passion which surprised her. She had never felt this way with Simon…

'I love you Katie. I love you so much that I can't even begin to envisage a life without you.' He kissed her neck and her hair and the warmth of his body so close to hers, caused her emotions to flow through her like a river. She could smell the faint tang of his aftershave, as it mingled with the natural smell of his skin and her senses began to reel…

'Stuart, I…' He stifled her astonished reply with another kiss. When they came up for air, she pulled away from him.

'Yes?' he said, with a look of expectancy on his face.

'Stuart, I…I love you too.' She giggled at the sound of her voice: it sounded husky with emotion, but the moment of extreme intimacy between them was suddenly broken. She stared through the windscreen as rivulets of water cascaded erratically downwards. 'Stuart when we first met in the pub in Penzance, did you ever think that we would become…?'

'What friends do you mean?'

'Yes…well, you know.'

Stuart smiled. 'I thought that you were the most beautiful and gorgeous creature that I'd ever seen and I was determined to get to know you better.'

'And now that you have?'

'Do you really have to ask that question, Katie?'

'No, I suppose not.'

He peered out through the window. 'Come on my girl, we'll have to get you home somehow. I think that the rain has almost stopped, so how far away from Lilac Cottage are we?'

'About a mile I should think.'

'Well we can walk it, can't we? I've got a torch in here somewhere.' He rummaged about in the glove compartment. 'Voila!' he said in triumph, I'll lock the car up – I'm sure that it will be OK here overnight and I'll arrange for the local garage to pick it up in the morning. Do you think Brenda would mind if I stayed the night at the cottage? By the time we get there, it'll be too late for me to get back to Lewes tonight.'

'I'm sure she won't mind. Look the moon has just come out. We can have a romantic walk home in the moonlight,' she said as she climbed out of the car.

It took them over an hour to walk the distance between the car and Lilac Cottage, after all they were not in any great hurry. Even the weather was now being kind to them and most of the clouds had been blown away by an enervating breeze. They stood outside the cottage for some time with Stuart's arms wrapped around Katie, because neither of them wanted the evening to end.

Stuart looked up at the moon. 'I'm suddenly very grateful to the moon up there. I can see your beautiful face in all its glory and I meant every word I said in the car, Katie.' She gave a little chuckle and before she could reply, he placed both hands around her face and kissed her gently on the lips and then almost immediately, kissed her again. Her insides felt as if they were slowly melting and she felt herself responding to him. Warning bells began to sound in her head and with some reluctance, she pulled away from him.

'Stuart. It's getting quite cold, so perhaps we ought to go inside.'

'But why? I was just beginning to…'

'I know and that is why we must go inside.'

'But Katie…when?'

She understood the question. 'Soon,' she said her eyes

twinkling happily. 'But not out here...' Katie had noticed that Brian's car was still parked in the lane. Perhaps they had spent the evening together too, she wondered as she turned the key in the lock. They stepped into the warmth of Lilac Cottage and Brenda immediately came out of her sitting room to greet them.

'Oh there you are. I was beginning to get a little worried about you, but I can see that you're in good hands,' she said flashing a knowing, beaming smile in Stuart's direction.

'We spent the evening in the pub,' Katie said happily. 'On the way home, we had a puncture so we had to walk.' Brian was standing in the doorway and she turned towards him. 'Brian, I'd like you to meet Stuart. You remember I told you about him the other day?'

'Why yes, of course, hello Stuart. I'm really pleased to meet you.' He took hold of Stuart's hand and shook it warmly. 'After all the scrapes young Katie's been getting into lately, I'm pleased to see that she has at last got someone to look after her.' He looked meaningfully in her direction and she scowled at him.

Stuart cleared his throat. 'Yes, Katie told me about her recent problems at Epton Hall.' He turned to Brenda. 'As Katie was saying just now, one of my car's tyres has burst and believe it or not, my spare needs repairing too. We had to leave the car about a mile away, so perhaps I could phone for a garage to pick it up in the morning? It's a good job that it's Saturday tomorrow isn't it? I was wondering...'

'What Stuart really wants to know,' Katie said quickly interrupting him, 'is, would you have any objections to him spending the night here, because it's too late for him to get back to Lewes tonight?'

'Of course you can. I do have a small spare room, but I'm afraid that it's full up with rubbish at the moment, but I could quickly clear some space for you...'

'Oh there's no need for you to go to any trouble, I can crash out on the floor in Katie's room.'

'Yes Brenda, Stuart can easily stay in my room,' Katie reiterated. 'There's plenty of room on the floor,' she said with added meaning.

Brian coughed suddenly and Brenda looked flustered and a little embarrassed. 'Well then now that everyone is nicely sorted out and you are safe and sound, Katie, I think that it is high time I went home to my bed,' he said yawning sleepily. 'Thank you for the coffee Brenda. I'll see you tomorrow perhaps?'

'Yes of course Brian dear and thank you for coming round and I'm sorry to be such a nuisance, but since Katie's spell in the attic I tend to think like a mother hen. Don't worry I'll get over it.'

'Goodnight then Brenda my love.' He gave her a quick kiss on the cheek and walked out of the door, leaving her looking flustered again.

'Goodnight Brian.' She closed the door and turned towards Stuart and Katie. 'Well I er…well I think it's time for my bed too. I'll…I'll see you both in the morning then. Hope you both sleep well.'

After Brenda had gone upstairs, Katie nudged Stuart, whispering playfully. 'I'm pretty sure that those two have spent the whole evening together. I've never known Brenda to be at a loss for words before. Wouldn't it be good if…?'

Stuart shook his head and smiled. 'I don't think that was the only reason why Brenda was so flustered, do you?' He didn't wait for Katie to answer, but wrapped his arms around her and kissed her. 'I did hear something about a bed upstairs: do you think that we could…?'

'Yes Stuart, I think we could.'

******

Chapter Twenty

Stuart had little difficulty in persuading the Senior Partner to let him have two days off and Katie immediately made plans for the long journey to Vancouver. But, despite careful planning for the trip, all their preparations proved to be rushed. Stuart had to spend another night at Lilac Cottage because of the early start and an air of excited expectancy hung over them.

Brian had offered to take them to the airport and Brenda sounded worried that they wouldn't be ready. 'Katie are you nearly ready, only it's six o'clock?' Brenda called out anxiously from downstairs. 'Brian will be here in about ten minutes.'

'Yes, we're almost there,' Katie replied. 'I'm having difficulty closing my case.'

'From the number of things you're taking, anyone would think that you were going for a fortnight, instead of a few days,' Stuart pointed out, whilst trying not to laugh. 'Look at the size of my case compared to yours.'

'Well, I like to be prepared for everything.'

'So I see.'

'Do come on you two,' they heard Brenda call out yet again. A few minutes later they raced downstairs and quickly gulped down a cup of tea, just as Brian arrived.

'Well, are we all fit?' he said rubbing his hands together.

'Yes,' they chorused.

'Come on then. I'm sorry to rush you, but I've just heard on the radio that there's a traffic jam on the M25.'

'Do take care both of you, won't you?' Brenda said, 'and come home safely.'

'We will,' Katie said giving Brenda a hug before climbing into the car beside Stuart.

Brenda stood at the little white gate and waved goodbye to them. Albert sat obediently by her side wagging his tail and looking up at his mistress. She waited until the car had finally disappeared around the corner, before walking back inside Lilac Cottage. Later she took Albert for his usual walk and busied herself doing various household tasks for the rest of the morning. She felt relieved that Katie now had another boyfriend. Stuart was ideal for her. She had arrived at Lilac Cottage with so much emotional baggage, Brenda remembered. Why the poor girl had been nearly frantic with grief over the loss of her parents and for her own part, she had been determined to make her life as happy as possible. She had never been able to have children and she now regarded Katie as being part of her family.

She cast her mind back to the time when Simon Brand had been on the scene. Katie had seemed to be happy in his company and had already started making plans for her future with him. But it was not to be. She stopped vacuuming the sitting room carpet, when she remembered the look on Katie's tear-stained face that night. Simon had walked out of her life, without thinking of the effect it would have on her. Life could be so cruel sometimes and the poor girl certainly hadn't deserved such treatment.

Brenda eventually finished the housework and walked out into the kitchen. Her thoughts now turned to Brian. He's such a dear considerate, sweet man. He's good company and fun to be with and we even like the same music and books and we both enjoy walking. She sighed. Could it be that I'm falling for him, at my age? And supposing he feels the same way? She looked at her reflection in a small mirror: I'm not really a great catch, am I? Look at me with my greying wiry hair and the wrinkles that are deep as trenches around my eyes. Brenda sighed again. The idea of getting married again frightened her, but she knew that if Brian asked her, the answer would have to be "yes please". But he won't ask me of course, you're just being a silly old – well middle-aged – woman, she told herself. The phone suddenly rang beside her, making her jump. It was Brian.

'Hi Brenda love, it's me.'

'Hello me,' Brenda joked. 'Did they get off OK?'

'Well, I didn't hang around, but all the flights seemed to be mostly on time. Do you know, I can't help feeling a little apprehensive about the whole trip?'

'What do you mean, Brian?'

'Oh nothing...nothing,' he blustered. 'Well, you know Katie...'

'You do think that she's doing the right thing, don't you?'

'Of course they are. Don't forget that she has Stuart to look after her. By the way, are you doing anything tonight?' he said changing the subject. 'Only I was wondering if you would have dinner with me. We could go to that Italian Restaurant in Epton. What do you say?'

'Well, I was supposed to be giving a talk on Journalism to members of the Epton Evening Institute, and I must admit that I hadn't had the time to prepare for it properly. So I was quite relieved when the Secretary phoned to cancel it. So yes, I'd be delighted to have dinner with you. What time?'

'Does that mean that I'm second best?' he suddenly quipped.

'Not at all, Brian love. I know where I would rather be.'

'Splendid. I'll pick you up at 7.30 p.m. if that's OK.'

'Yes. I'll see you later then, bye.'

Later that night, after having spent an enjoyable evening with Brenda, Brian drove home to his house deep in thought. He put his car into the garage, walked slowly towards his front door and stood for a moment on the doorstep. He looked up at the windows: there were no lights anywhere and he sighed. He unlocked the door and walked in to the dark unwelcoming hall and fumbled for the light switch. For the first time since Louise's death, he felt the need for some warmth and female companionship. Up until now he had been quite content to come home to an empty house, but now... He had enjoyed himself immensely. Brenda was such a warm, sympathetic person. He entered his small tidy kitchen and made himself a drink of hot chocolate and sat down at the well-scrubbed old table which Louise had cared for so well over the years. Quietly and methodically, Brian contemplated his life.

He remembered how happy he and Louise had been, right from when they were first married. He had qualified as an architect about eighteen months prior to their wedding and had managed to secure a good job in the City. There was no shortage of money, they had a beautiful home and were able to travel extensively. Unfortunately, Louise found out quite early on in their marriage, that she would never be able to have a child. They worried about this for some time, but gradually managed to come to terms with it. They learned to live their lives to the full in other ways. Skiing was their passion and they would often just drop everything and go off to France or Switzerland to enjoy the snow. They were happy times, he reflected.

Brian smiled when he recalled all the fun they'd had as supporters of their local Repertory Company too. Louise had even appeared on the stage once or twice...a wave of nostalgia, immediately followed by melancholy swept over him as he remembered her singing voice. It had been a sweet sound and clear as a bell. He drained the last drop from his cup and walked over to the sink. He washed it and left it on the draining board and stood for some time staring out of the kitchen window. He couldn't see anything of course because it was dark, but his mind was too busy to notice. Louise had always been happy, supportive and fun to be with – a bit like Brenda, he thought as he tugged absent-mindedly at his beard.

There came a time when she complained of feeling unwell and, after first visiting her G.P. and undergoing exhaustive tests, she was given the shattering news that she was suffering from Multiple Sclerosis. He could still remember her words, as she'd walked towards him in the hospital waiting room.

'Brian,' she'd whispered. 'You are not to worry, darling, but I have Multiple Sclerosis. Mr. Clarke has told me all about the disease and we have to be patient and let it take its course.' At the time, she had sounded so brave that it had seemed to him that it was not the dreadful thing he had feared, but eventually he had learned that she was just putting on a brave face. Gradually, her health deteriorated and eventually she died, leaving Brian bereft, unhappy and lonely. For a while he became a mere shadow of his previous self and lost interest in himself and his surroundings. He couldn't concentrate on his work or his life any more and the amount of work he was offered decreased and feeling completely disillusioned with life, he resigned from the company and his career.

Brian had always had a great love of literature and books were a part of his life. When an elderly uncle, who owned a book shop in Anston, suddenly collapsed and died, he thought that he would try to run it. He was delighted later, when he learned that his uncle had left it to him in his will anyway. So he moved his belongings and his life, down to Anston.

He could hardly believe that Louise had been gone for such a long time and his mind turned to thoughts of Brenda again. She was good for his ego. She flattered him making him feel a much younger man than he really was. She was gentle, kind and felt deeply about many of the things that concerned him. She had even taken young Katie under her wing and for that he was enormously grateful.

Pangs of guilt filled his mind. Would Louise be worried and upset that his thoughts about Brenda had appeared more and more frequently in his mind? He locked up, turned off all the lights and walked slowly upstairs. When he was ready for bed he picked up her photograph which was mounted in a highly polished silver frame and holding pride of place on the small table next to his bed. Her image smiled sweetly up at him and he slowly told her about his growing fondness for Brenda. One of the last things she had ever said to him before she'd died was that she wanted him to be happy. He now knew exactly what he was going to do.

* * * * * *

Chapter Twenty-One

Valetta, Malta

Harold Hapsworth-Cole sat miserably in his small, cramped and sordid second floor apartment. It overlooked one of the narrow car-infested streets in Valetta, the capital of Malta. He was feeling intensely irritable. Since returning from England a couple of weeks' earlier, he had moved out of his comfortable rooms in Sliema, believing that the police would be interested in locating him. The temperature outside was rising daily and he was sweating profusely. I'll never get used to this climate he thought as he surveyed his present living conditions and it wasn't even the hottest season in Malta yet.

The room was poorly furnished and dominated by a large double bed, which took up most of the available living space. An old, scratched wardrobe groaned under the weight of a couple of battered leather suitcases containing books and papers relating to his now defunct boating company: it also contained the history of his whole life. The wardrobe door swung lazily to and fro, the catch having been broken aeons ago.

On the other side of the room and just beyond the narrow, curtain-less windows, was an equally old and dilapidated, dressing table. It was untidy and piled high with papers and other odds and ends that he hadn't yet found a place for and probably never would. Directly under the small window, stood a circular metal table and two chairs, only one of which was usable, the other one having only three legs. A small electric fan to one side of the table, whirred and droned noisily, but it had little or no effect on the stuffy oppressiveness of the room. The room smelled of decay and extreme age and several flies buzzed around his head, each vying for position. He groaned, feeling that if he had to spend another day hiding in this old and badly furnished hovel, he would go mad. He knew that he would have to do something soon, because the constant noise coming up from street level seemed to give him a permanent headache.

He couldn't sleep either. Even when he did manage to doze, his subconscious mind seemed to be peppered and populated by demons. Recently his nightmares had become so bad that he found himself incapable of separating his intensely upsetting dream state, from reality. In fact he was now almost too afraid to go to sleep. Instead he stretched out on top of the bed going over and over in his mind, the details of the letter he'd stolen from that stupid girl in the attic at Epton Hall.

Since returning from England, he had read and reread the letter, but for some reason he hadn't destroyed it. Instead he had placed it in a small metal box which he now kept hidden underneath his bed. He remembered every word that Amy Butler had written. Night after night, he would lie on his bed trying to picture this unknown woman who, through her actions all those years ago, now threatened his future existence and happiness.

How he hated her.

In Harold's mixed up mind, his uncle Gerald had been an equal partner in the crimes she had committed. He hated him too, with a fervour that grew in intensity every time he allowed his mind to dwell on it. He was glad that both Marjorie and Gerald were now dead. He had been a traitor to his wife, and to the whole family. He was damned if his uncle's fancy woman and her brat would ever lay their hands on what should rightly belong to him. The evidence of the illegitimate Hapsworth-Cole child's existence now lay on the floor beneath him, and nobody else should ever know about it. The letter and the birth certificate were now safe from anyone's prying eyes, especially those of that meddling girl Katie Nicholson. But yet again, Harold's mind was confusing him. He had the peculiar feeling that he'd left something undone, but he couldn't work out what it was and frustration was added to his catalogue of problems.

A loud noise from down below in the street aroused him from his misery. It was the sound of a car backfiring and he instantly identified its owner. The smell of the exhaust wafted upwards and in through the open window and made him cough. His eyes widened and lit up expectantly: his friend Marco had just arrived in his old ramshackle car. Perhaps there was a letter for him, he thought.

His fear of being discovered had compelled him to confide in his old friend a few days' earlier. He'd told Marco everything that had transpired, including the fact that if Harold played his cards right, he could expect to inherit a large amount of money and Marco's eyes had widened with avarice. He was poor, middle-aged and out of work now that the boating company had ceased to exist. Harold was quite sure that Marco had little or no hope of ever improving the standard of his life and had cunningly waved a Maltese ten pound note under his nose. It hadn't taken him long to agree to keep Harold's whereabouts a secret.

There was a sharp knock on the door. He stood up, stretched and opened the door. Marco held a letter in his hand and eagerly handed it to him.

'Zis came for you, Harold.' His heavily accented voice was deep and croaky.

'Thanks. Do come in for a minute.'

'I thank you.' Marco sat down heavily on the one serviceable chair, took out his handkerchief and mopped his brow. He was a large man and the chair creaked ominously. 'You are fine here, yes?'

Marco had been responsible for finding him this small apartment and Harold didn't wish to appear ungrateful. 'Yes,' he replied, 'it suits my purposes. Would you like a drink?'

'Yes, pliz I would. It is warm today, yes?'

'Yes every day more so. Now Marco, if anyone phones or asks where I am, you don't know, do you understand? And as soon as any other letters arrive, I want to see them straight away.' Harold put his hand in his pocket, pulled out another note and handed it to him.

He stayed for about ten minutes and after he'd gone, Harold opened the letter. It was from his solicitor, Thomas Broadbent in Epton and his eyes narrowed as he read his words. Mr. Broadbent criticised Harold for failing to tell him about the letter he'd taken from the house and the fact that he had left Katie Nicholson lying injured in the attic. He urged him to return to England immediately and face any charges that could be laid against him and that nothing would be gained by hiding away from his problems.

Harold's eyes blazed with anger and his heart began to pound and without reading further, he crunched the letter up and threw it across the room. If his solicitor could find his old address, then so could... Nobody must ever find out about it – I must destroy the letter right now, he told himself. It was starting to assume enormous proportions in his mind and seemed to be taking precedence over everything else. He rose swiftly from his bed, reached underneath its dusty depths for the metal box and withdrew the envelope from its hiding place. He picked up his cigarette lighter, flicked it on and held the flame underneath the envelope. It began to flare immediately and in a panic he threw it onto a dirty dinner plate on the table. He watched it burn until only ash remained.

He laughed. It was a deep, throaty frightening sound. 'I'm safe now and nobody will ever know...'

This frantic burst of energy exhausted him and he once more flopped down on the bed. In the corner of his eye he could see Mr. Broadbent's letter lying on the floor. He knew that he should at least read the whole letter: 'Why?' a little voice in his mind insisted. 'You've just said that you were safe now. Burn this letter too,' the voice whined. He curled himself into a foetal position - it always seemed to help him when his mind was troubled. He thought about his parents. He had disliked his father intensely, but his mother on the other hand, had been the one to whom he had always turned in times of trouble. Why couldn't he turn to her now? I should be able to, he thought, but she had died years ago and her death had left him feeling bitter and bereft.

Several minutes went by before he plucked up enough courage to retrieve the letter. With surprising gentleness, he smoothed the crumpled pages and turned to the second page.

The words hit him like a hammer blow between the eyes. His eyes blazed with abject hatred as he read it.

Katie Nicholson had found another letter hidden in a book in the attic, but this one was from Gerald and addressed to Amy Butler. Even though the letter had been unfinished and never sent, Mr. Broadbent told him that his cousin, James Butler, had been traced and had recently been badly injured in a car accident and was at present in hospital. He also said he was married with two children. Several minutes passed by before his mind could concentrate on the letter, but he forced himself to read on. Mr. Broadbent also said that Amy Butler had died some years ago and that he was being given the opportunity of examining the second letter.

Harold was overcome by a blind rage. 'It can't be true.' Every muscle, nerve and sinew in his body appeared to constrict and knot together and he pounded his pillow again and again in acute frustration. So, he thought, even though Gerald's fancy piece was now dead, she still had the ability to harm him. What was he to do? Unfortunately, his fury prevented him from thinking coherently which finally left him feeling weak and disturbed.

He slept for about half an hour. The sound of a car's horn woke him and for a few seconds he felt disorientated. Then he remembered the contents of the letter and his heart missed a beat. He rose unsteadily and retrieved it. What did Mr. Precious-bloody-Broadbent know about justice? Only he, Harold Hapsworth-Cole would be able to see that justice would be done now.

'But how?' a voice enquired.

With venom now in his very soul, he threw the letter on to his bed. 'I don't know,' he shouted as he continued to walk round and round his cramped room. Yet again that stupid prying girl, Katie Nicholson, was proving to be an irritating thorn in his side. She was always poking her nose in where it wasn't needed. His mounting hysteria made his whole body shake as he pictured her prying into his affairs. With shaking hands he picked the letter up yet again. He knew that he must now finish reading it, just in case it held any more incriminating evidence.

Mr. Broadbent explained in great depth, all the various points of law as they related to a possible claim from the Butlers. Harold found it impossible to concentrate on all this legal jargon. The only thing which now concerned him was that these people in Canada who were trying to usurp the family fortune, did not succeed. The more he thought about them, the more bitter and morose he became. He looked around his shabby, dirty room. All he saw was the peeling plaster and the huge ever-widening cracks that had opened up like yawning chasms between the walls and the dirty ceiling. Cockroaches and other unspeakable creatures used this route to come into his room to spy on him as they scuttled around.

He gazed at the cracks. They seemed to move and reassemble

themselves into strange patterns, which in turn reminded him of the demons that peppered his dreams. Even as he watched, a small lizard emerged from its hiding place. It moved its reptilian head from side to side before finally disappearing through another crack in the wall. This only briefly brought him back to reality.

Dark clouds began to form into a circle above his head and seemed to position themselves just to one side of the fly-infested, dirty lampshade. These clouds grew denser by the minute and his mind began to reel from this onslaught. His now completely uncoordinated thoughts enveloped him in waves...waves which came crashing over him like a sea of terror. His shaking hands grabbed hold of the duvet cover as he fought to gain even slight control over his emotions. He had in a short space of time become totally obsessed by the thought of owning Epton Hall. His eyes moved in jerky avaricious spasms as he thought of the money which should rightly belong to him. 'Nobody else will have it,' he shouted. His eyes misted over as he imagined living like a lord in that great big house. He remembered the paintings on the wall and the expensive ornaments which were dotted around the house. And the books, there must have been hundreds of them and several could be first editions, after all, his aunt had never done things by halves. Just think about it, he told himself, I will no longer have to worry about where the next penny was coming from.

When his father, Stanley had died, he had received several thousands of pounds from his estate, but now that his business had gone, so had the rest of his money.

He tugged at the dark beard which he had allowed to grow over the past weeks and plotted his revenge. A fierce battle now raged within him. The little voice in his head crowed insistently, 'You won't get any of that money, will you Harold...it doesn't belong to you, does it? This fancy woman of your uncle's and his bastard son will get it all, won't they Harold?' By this time, he'd quite forgotten that Amy Butler was now dead and in his confused state, she was still a threat to his future happiness.

'No, no, they won't,' he screamed. 'I will not let them have my money – it's mine, all mine.'

His breath came in short sharp bursts and he desperately needed some fresh air. He stumbled out of the door and into the small lobby. Like his room, it was oppressively hot and airless and it too, stank of age and decay – a peculiarly obnoxious mixture of neglect, dampness and stale cooking smells. He glanced at the drooping potted palm which his immediate neighbour seemed to have forgotten about, but it didn't concern him. On a scale of one to ten, a neglected plant rated low on the list of things he had to worry about. The cracks in the wall were even wider out here in the lobby. It seemed as if hundreds of eyes were watching him as he climbed the few steps which led upwards and out on to the flat white roof. He felt relieved when he set foot outside.

This relief was short-lived however. The strong Mediterranean sunshine hurt his eyes and exacerbated his headache. He searched frantically in his pocket for his sunglasses until he realised that he had left them in his room somewhere. He cursed loudly.

One of his neighbours, an elderly and lined Maltese woman, dressed completely in black, was busy hanging out her washing. He took no notice of her, but leant against the low, narrow ledge which ran around the perimeter of the flat roof. He watched while three stray cats searched and scrabbled for food in the courtyard below. Theirs was a perilous existence something akin to his own, he thought. He kicked the ledge, thereby dislodging a sizeable piece of ancient white-painted concrete: it clattered down into the courtyard below, scattering the terrified cats in all directions.

He had seen the old woman a few times in the last week and each time he'd completely ignored her. He didn't want or need human involvement. He was being eaten up by his fanatical longing for the family fortune. She turned round to him, smiled and said 'Good afternoon,' in halting English. He didn't bother to answer, but the look he gave her seemed to terrify the poor woman. She took one look at his face and scooted off in the direction of the stairs like a frightened rabbit, her speed belying her years.

Later that night, Harold lay on top of his bed sweltering in the heat with his bedclothes drenched in perspiration. His mind tortured him relentlessly.

A small whining voice was unremitting in its advice. 'You'll never be able to lay your hands on that money, unless you do something about it, will you Harold?'

Yet another voice niggled away at him. 'But you can't because you are worthless, aren't you? You don't deserve the money, but Amy Butler and her son do. You'll have to get rid of them…all of them…'

Harold sat up in bed when a clear image entered his thoughts. He pictured Amy and her son, two faceless individuals, gloating over enormous piles of money…his money. His mind cleared momentarily. He remembered then, that Amy Butler was dead and that James Butler now had a wife and two children. Now there were even more people after his money. He would have to stop any of them from ever getting hold of his money.

Harold decided there and then, that he would go to Vancouver. He would find these so-called imposters and be rid of them once and for all. His frighteningly cold laugh seemed to come from nowhere as he greedily consumed and welcomed the images his mind projected.

The following day he appeared to be quite normal again. He made his way to Luqa Airport and booked himself on to the next available flight to England. He found the whole process easy: he welcomed the fact that despite fears about terrorism, and the fact that he now sported a dark beard, nobody approached him. Once he had landed at Gatwick Airport, he tried to book a seat on a plane going to Canada. He soon found that there were no seats available. He eventually managed to book a seat on a flight from Heathrow and feeling strangely calm, he caught an express coach to London's main airport.

The journey seemed interminable. There were several hold-ups on the M25 Motorway due to accidents and the sheer volume of traffic. It never used to be like this, he told himself shaking his head, and nothing ever stayed the same. Even his mother had left him all alone, hadn't she? The now familiar melancholy swept over him and by the time he had arrived at Heathrow Airport, he felt exhausted and in the blackest of moods. But still nobody challenged him. Fortunately he didn't have too long to wait for his flight, because his coach had been so late.

Once he had settled down in his seat on the plane, he relished the thought of the excitement to come. He felt that he couldn't wait to meet his illegitimate cousin and his trollop of a wife. Oh what a surprise they had in store!

The aircraft was not that full and his seat was in the middle of a block of three near the window. He noticed a young couple walking down the aisle and they soon found their seats and sat down just two rows in front of him. He stared idly at them: the girl had her head slightly turned towards the young man sitting next to her. She was laughing. Harold studied her profile. She was a pretty girl and…and yet…her face looked vaguely familiar. Where had he seen her before? His brow wrinkled in deep and troubled concentration.

His heart slammed into his ribs.

His whole body jolted, as fury enveloped him. Now he

remembered where he had seen her. How could he possibly have forgotten the look on her face when she had realised that he was going to take the letter from her? It was that little bitch Katie Nicholson. What on earth was she doing on this flight? Then he understood. She was on her way to visit his cousin, James. Silent fury enveloped him and he stared at the back of her head. Yet again she was interfering with his life. Why did she always appear to be one step ahead of him all the time? Harold realised the importance of changing his seat, after all, he didn't want her to recognise him. There were several seats in the back of the aircraft which were unoccupied and he found one well away from her prying eyes.

The voices in his mind began again, only this time they were less decipherable. He felt that his mind would burst with the pressure that seemed to be building up inside his head, but in desperation, he clung to one coherent thought. If Katie Nicholson upsets my plans again, she will wish that she'd never been born. Harold's mind was returning him to the shadowy, frightening world of demons and nightmares…he was once again slipping away from normality and reality…

* * * * * *

Chapter Twenty-Two

Once Katie and Stuart had checked in and their luggage had finally disappeared from view on the moving ramp, they had time to wander around the terminal before their flight was called. Katie had flown to several destinations in Europe with her parents when she was younger, but the long haul terminal always fascinated her. The departures board illuminated the names of dozens of far off countries throughout the world: exotic sounding places that she had always wanted to visit like Bali, Sri Lanka, St. Lucia, Hawaii… and Katie tried to picture what it would be like…

A far distant, white sandy beach on a beautifully warm exotic island, where waves rippled gently on to the sand and tall palm trees swayed to the sound of gentle music beckoned her…there was a pretty little hut under the palms with a low white picket fence and…

'Here, Katie,' Stuart said taking hold of her hand. 'There's a bar over there and it doesn't look too crowded. Would you like a drink? We've got time.'

Katie sighed. Her mind was still in her daydream and it seemed reluctant to be pulled away. *The music was intoxicating and the hut seemed to be pulling her…*

'Katie, come back from wherever you are, please.'

'I'm sorry Stuart, I was miles away. What did you say?'

'I was asking you if you wanted to have a drink. We've got time and there's a bar over there that doesn't seem too crowded.'

'Yes, that sounds like a great idea,' she replied. 'Even though I can hardly wait to get under way, I can't help feeling a little bit scared. It's a long way.'

'Come on then. You grab that table over there and I'll get the drinks.'

The drink assuaged Katie's thirst, but not her worries. Why oh why, can't I be one of those people who take everything in their stride, she asked herself? I have to examine every feeling, every thought. These feelings of inadequacy were soon forgotten however, as they made their way through Passport Control and with their papers safely put away in their cabin bags, they were ready for the long journey to Vancouver.

Once they were on the aircraft, they quickly found their seats and began to settle down. Stuart squeezed Katie's hand as if to reassure her as the Jumbo Jet was cleared for take-off. The sound of the huge engines grew louder and more urgent, until it finally started to move forward eager to free itself from the constraints of the ground and, just like a huge bird, it gained the freedom of the skies.

The passenger cabin became a hive of activity once the illuminated "SEAT BELT" sign had been switched off. All the cabin crew were almost falling over one another in an effort to help everyone and there was a general hubbub of excited conversation. A girl wearing a smart British Airways uniform handed both of them a drink.

'Here's to a wonderful trip,' Stuart said trying to clink his plastic glass against hers.

'Yes, cheers.' Inside, Katie felt strangely uneasy. She closed her eyes, but it didn't help, her heart was beating so rapidly.

Like a bolt of lightning, the image of Harold Hapsworth-Cole's face appeared before her. She could feel his eyes boring painfully into hers. They seemed like red-hot coals which were trying to penetrate deeply inside her brain. She had the terrifying feeling that he was somewhere near and that he was trying to transfer some of his thoughts into her mind. No, no, go away, please go away? She tried to fight this overwhelming feeling of sheer hatred which was engulfing her and then, just as quickly as it had arrived, it disappeared leaving her feeling weak and helpless. She found herself shaking with bewilderment and fear and her heart was thumping so loudly, that she was convinced that Stuart would be able to hear it. She took a large gulp of her drink and nearly choked on it.

Stuart took hold of her hand. 'Katie are you OK? You look so pale. Would you like another drink or a glass of water perhaps?' Without waiting for her reply, he lifted up his arm to try to attract one of the crew's attention.

'No Stuart please don't make a fuss. I felt strange for a moment, that's all.'

'Well, if you're sure you're OK?'

'Yes, of course. It was nothing really.'

'It didn't seem like nothing to me, Katie,' Stuart replied, concern written all over his handsome face. 'Come on, tell me what's wrong?'

She shivered. 'I really worry about myself sometimes. I'm quite receptive to atmosphere and I've always had an overactive imagination. I used to get into trouble with my parents when I was younger. I was always daydreaming and imagining things.'

'I'm sure that most people daydream at some time in their lives, Katie. I know I did, and especially now since I met you…' he said smiling down at her. 'Now come on I insist that you tell me what this is all about. Something's not right that's for sure and it's not good to brood is it?'

Tears sprang into her eyes and she grabbed his hand and held on to it fast; she knew that she was close to panic. 'Stuart, it was horrible, really horrible. It was as if that dreadful man, Harold Hapsworth-Cole was here in this aircraft. I could see him with my eyes closed. His…his face was full of hate and it seemed to get right inside me somehow. It…'

'Here, Katie my love, please calm down? All that is in the

past and my guess is, he's sheltering somewhere in Malta right now and regretting what he did to you. It's bound to have an effect on you for a while. I'm no expert, but you were put in a potentially serious situation when he locked you in that attic. He couldn't have been sure that you were not seriously injured. It's not surprising that you are still experiencing flashbacks about it.'

'Yes, it's happened two or three times since then. Do you think that's what it is, a flashback? But he seemed so real...so close to me.'

'I'm sure it is my love. Nowadays everyone seems to believe in counselling after an accident or the kind of trauma that you've been through. If it keeps happening, perhaps you should go and see someone about it. Look here's the drinks trolley again. Come on, do have another one, it'll make you feel a lot better?'

'OK, you win.'

'And now you must forget all about it. We're on our way to meet the Butlers and your aunt and uncle and that's all you must worry about. Right?' He leant over and his lips just brushed hers and her heart melted.

The rest of the long flight turned out to be tiring and Katie found it difficult to relax, despite Stuart's reassuring words. She was really relieved once they'd landed. The travel agents had booked them into a good hotel which was quite close to the hospital and when they walked out of the airport buildings, a car was waiting for them.

The reception lounge of their hotel was ultra-modern and areas were laid out with low and sumptuously comfortable settees and armchairs. Towards one end, was an atrium containing dozens of exotic potted plants and palm trees of different shapes and sizes. She looked longingly at the trees and her mind began to return her to that desert island again.

'Mmm. This is lovely Stuart. It seems so peaceful here.'

'Come on love. There's a queue at the reception desk. Hurry up or we'll be here for ages.'

Having booked in, they took an express lift up to the 25th floor and after walking along what seemed like miles of corridors they found their room. Stuart inserted the plastic key card into the slot, it clicked and he opened the door.

'Clever things aren't they, but unfortunately you can't use them to get money out of the bank!' he said quickly pocketing the card. Katie giggled and walked into the room.

'Wow. It's not bad is it?' she said looking around with pleasure. It was modern and a bit stereotyped, but there were a few little touches of individuality. A small, glass topped circular coffee table contained an arrangement of spring flowers and a bowl of fresh fruit. She opened the built-in small refrigerator. 'Look we can get ourselves quietly sozzled without ever leaving the room!'

'And you'd have to pay the earth for that privilege,' Stuart reminded her.

She giggled again and for the first time since they had landed, she felt relaxed and flopped down on to the bed. 'This bed is comfortable too!' she said languorously patting the space beside her. When Stuart didn't respond, she stood up and joined him in front of the patio doors.

'We'll have the rest of our lives to sample comfortable beds, Katie darling,' he said putting his arms gently around her shoulders. 'Look there's a verandah and a couple of chairs. Let's go outside and see the view.'

They stood outside together for several minutes holding hands and drinking in the view and the atmosphere: there seemed to be magic in the air and Katie couldn't remember ever feeling so safe before. She looked up at Stuart and tightened her grip on his hand. 'I think that I will always remember this moment, my darling,' she said.

'So will I.' He put both his arms around her waist and pulled her towards him. 'And that is why…'

'What.' She held her breath.

'I feel that this is the perfect moment, to ask you to marry me, Katie. Will you, please?'

Tears of pleasure began to cascade down her face. 'Oh yes, Stuart of course I will marry you. We know that we both love one another and this seems to be the perfect time and the perfect place to celebrate our engagement.' Katie was overjoyed. Over the last few years since her parents had died, she had sometimes felt so lonely, but now…

'So why are you crying then?'

'Because I'm so happy.'

Stuart laughed. She placed both hands on to the balcony rail and looked at the view spread out before them and he stood behind with his arms around her waist. Laying her head comfortably against his chest she sighed. 'Do you know, I've often wondered why people cry when they're happy? Now I know.'

Stuart laughed again, turned her round and kissed her passionately. 'There, that's sealed it.'

The sound of a phone ringing inside spoiled the moment and Stuart swore lightly under his breath. 'Shall we answer it, or ignore it?' he said, his voice deepening with rising emotion.

'Stuart we must answer it. It could be important.' She pulled away from him and walked back into the room. She picked up the white handset. 'Hello, Katie Nicholson speaking.'

'Katie, it's Brenda.' She cupped her hand over the mouth piece. 'It's Brenda,' she whispered.

'Hello, are you still there?' Brenda's voice sounded a little breathless. 'I thought I'd give you a ring to make sure you arrived safely. Is everything OK?'

'Yes Brenda, everything is just fine. About five minutes ago,

Stuart asked me to marry him and I said "yes".'

'Katie that's wonderful. I knew that he was the right one for you. Hold on a moment, dear.' Katie could hear the sound of whispering and laughter in the background and then the sound of a male voice shouting, 'Goodo!' 'Did you hear that? Brian couldn't be more delighted and I must admit that it's the best thing I've heard for a long time too. Congratulations to you both. Take care both of you and I hope that everything turns out as you want it to. See you soon. Bye.'

Stuart wiped yet another tear gently from her cheek. 'Well, now that all the excitement is over, we have some phone calls to make.'

'Yes,' Katie answered, still deep in thought.

'Penny for them?'

'What?'

'Your thoughts.'

'That could be dangerous with you standing beside me and in any case my thoughts are worth much more than a penny.' She looked up at him. 'Do you know, it's such a short time since I was feeling so miserable about my life and now I've got you, everything is perfect.'

'Yes, life can be funny sometimes.'

'Funny?'

'Yes. There was I carefully minding my own business and living in Cornwall with not a care in the world, and then you come along and turn my life completely and utterly upside down and inside out. So much so, that I don't know what I'm doing half of the time: you have a devastating effect on me you know.'

'Do I?' she said. 'I wonder why?' She started to giggle and Stuart silenced her by placing his lips lovingly over hers.

'Let's just see how comfortable this bed actually is,' he said guiding her towards it.

Katie felt as if she was on fire, and the touch of his hands sent a frisson of desire throughout her whole body and she knew that

Stuart felt the same way. This feeling was urgent and real and not one of her daydreams which would disappear in an instant. All external influences were forgotten as they were swallowed up by love, passion and the hoped for determination to be as one. And this time, there were no interruptions.

Before going down to the hotel's dining room that evening, Katie phoned her aunt and uncle to let them know that she was in Vancouver. They were surprised and delighted to hear from her and suggested that they should meet at a restaurant in the city.

When Katie tried the Butler's number, there was no reply. She felt disappointed as she replaced the receiver and sat down on the bed for a moment, gathering her thoughts. Her sadness didn't last long because she felt deliriously happy. A short while ago, she had entered the shower with Stuart feeling shy and apprehensive and she felt a warm glow when she remembered his gentle touch. It had felt like every pleasant sensation she had ever known. In all her wildest dreams she had never imagined that it could have been like this.

Her life was now completely different. She was in love with the most marvellous man, she had a job that she really enjoyed, despite the frightening time that she'd spent in the attic and she had a lovely home. Even money was not a problem for her. Of course Katie knew that she would eventually have to tell Stuart about the large amount of money that she had deposited in her building society account and although she hated the thought of keeping it from him, she didn't quite know how to broach the subject. Apart from this, everything was perfect and seeing the happy faces of the Butler family would complete the picture for her.

Quite inexplicably and without any warning, a cloud seemed to hover over her plans. Would the Butlers consider her to be nosy, she wondered? Indeed, was she being nosy by coming here? A worried frown appeared on her forehead. Surely by wanting to visit them, she was being just as bad as the people who had passed juicy pieces of gossip around Anston over the last couple of weeks? She bit her lower lip. What were her motives for coming here, she asked herself? Were they genuine, or was she being overindulgent? Was she merely a voyeur? Katie felt horrified at the thought. Before she had time to think any more about it, Stuart came out of the bathroom wearing one of the large white hotel towels, toga-fashion round his broad shoulders.

'I've asked the dining room to put a bottle of champagne on ice for us.' He stopped short when he saw her sitting on the edge of the bed looking so forlorn. 'What's wrong Katie? I hope that you're not having second thoughts about...?'

'No Stuart, of course I'm not.'

'What's wrong then?'

'Stuart. I came over here on a whim, didn't I?'

'Well yes, you did really I suppose, but...'

'Why didn't you try to stop me, then?'

'You had a determined look in your eyes that night, so who was I to try to stop you?' He sat down on the bed beside her.

'I wish you had. Now that it's close to actually meeting the Butlers, I'm frightened that they will misconstrue my motives. Stuart, supposing they resent my visit? Supposing they think that I am interfering, or being nosy, or...?'

'Katie. Stop it, please.' He put his arm around her. 'You mustn't think like that.'

'But they might think that I'm after some sort of reward for finding the letters?'

'I'm quite sure that they will think nothing of the sort. Do stop worrying. You're in Vancouver to visit them and that's just what you're going to do. Honestly love, the fact that you are sitting here worrying yourself silly about it, means that your motives are only good ones, believe me.'

'Are you sure?'

'Yes. Now hurry up and finish getting ready. I don't want the future Mrs. Stuart Wells to look unhappy and weepy if we are supposed to be celebrating our engagement, do I? Come on. Tomorrow morning, we'll ring the hospital and make an appointment to see James. If you like I'll even speak to his wife and clear the way for you.'

'Thank you, Stuart. I know you're right. I have to go through with it.'

'You quite frightened me just now,' he said with a worried frown. 'When I saw you sitting on the bed and looking so miserable, I thought you were having second thoughts about us. Now then,' he said standing up, 'I must finish getting dressed as I can't go downstairs looking like this.' His towel had gradually begun to slip downwards whilst he'd been speaking and now a suspicion of a smile was creeping across Katie's face.

'I'll have to get ready too, before anything else starts to delay us,' she said looking up at him, her eyes sparkling with unspoken and added meaning.

The next morning, Stuart was as good as his word and soon after breakfast, he phoned the Butler's home. He waited anxiously for someone to answer.

Eventually a young-sounding voice said, 'Hi. Who is it?'

'Can I speak to Mrs. Butler please? My name is Stuart Wells and we have just come over here from England.'

'Where did you say?'

'England.'

'Wow! Hold on one moment please.' Stuart heard a few scuffling noises, then a voice shouting loudly, 'Mom, there's someone on the phone for you. Says he's come all the way from England...'

* * * * * *

Chapter Twenty-Three

Sarah Butler replaced the receiver with a sigh. Over the past couple of weeks, her family's whole world had been fractured and turned inside out. Firstly, the shock of James' accident and the news that he might never be able to walk again and secondly, the probable reason for the car crash – the news that James had been made redundant. Why, she wondered? Up to now, Andy Carstairs had been a good friend of theirs. The two families had even shared a couple of vacations together. Now he'd turned his back on James altogether and had taken his job away from him. This must have been a contributory factor to the accident she thought, after all James was a good driver.

Deep in her heart she was convinced that she could never quite forgive Andy for what he'd done. It was obvious that loyalty to his friends didn't figure too highly in his life. For several years, James had worked hard to help build up the company and his only reward was to be placed on the scrap heap, and despite being an open and caring person, she could now feel nothing but bitterness towards the man.

Sarah walked back into her bright and cheerful kitchen, sat down at the table and picked up her coffee. She sipped it and pulled a face. Because of the phone call it had grown cold and she walked over to the sink and poured it way. She watched it revolving in a miniature vortex until it finally disappeared out of sight. If only all our problems would disappear so quickly, she thought shaking her head.

Her thoughts then turned back to her telephone conversation with Stuart Wells. She was sure that James would be delighted to meet the girl who'd found the letters, if for no other reason than to thank her. Sarah knew only too well that their lives had been hanging on the brink of catastrophe before the arrival of the letter from England. The news it contained had enabled James to awaken from the deep depression into which he had plunged after the accident. The knowledge that he might have a legitimate claim to the Epton Hall fortune in England, had given him a renewed interest in life and not only that, the animosity and bitterness that he'd always felt towards his unknown father had now completely gone. She remembered that soon after reading the letter, James had spoken to her in great depth about his early life and had told her things about his mother that he'd never spoken of before.

'If only mother was still alive,' he'd said sadly. 'Father's letter would have brought some lightness back into her solitary life.'

'Yes,' she had replied with a rueful smile. 'At least she'd have known that he hadn't deserted her.'

'I can picture the way her face would light up with happiness when I did well at school and then college. She was always there for me and when I come to think about it, she really didn't have much to smile about during those long, lonely years. Why, she never as much as looked at another man even though she had many admirers. My grandparents and her friends tried to persuade her to go out and enjoy herself more, but she never did. I couldn't understand her loyalty to my father. I used to hate anyone even mentioning him and I soon learned to close my mind to the fact that he had ever existed. That's what makes it all so tragic.'

James had gone on to speak in depth about his hopes and fears for the future, irrespective of whether they were successful in their claim to inherit the estate. Finally he'd looked at her with tears in his eyes.

'I'm so grateful to Katie Nicholson for finding those letters.

If she hadn't found them, they could so easily have been destroyed or lost forever.' Sarah remembered the look of sadness which had crossed his features as he had said these words. 'And as for my so called cousin, Harold, what on earth was he thinking about when he stole that letter and left Katie Nicholson lying injured in the attic. He must have been deranged, after all she could have died in that room, think about that?'

Since that day, James' spirits had lifted considerably. He was determined to walk again and with Sarah urging him on, every day seemed to bring an improvement. He would always work just a little harder than the physiotherapist recommended, so anxious was he to try to get back to some semblance of normality.

Now, Katie Nicholson had actually flown over from England to meet us. How strange she thought? But was it so strange? She tried to imagine what it would have been like to have been trapped in an attic for two days. It must have been a terrifyingly traumatic experience for her. In similar circumstances, perhaps she herself would have been eager to meet the family involved?

Sarah looked up at the clock on the wall, it was 9.30 a.m. She was due at the hospital in half an hour. The Orthopaedic Consultant wished to speak to both of them about the results of James' recent tests. She picked up her handbag and walked out of the kitchen. She stopped at the foot of the stairs and listened to the argument she could hear raging upstairs. John was shouting.

'Michael, I thought I told you not to come into my room again. It's a "no-go" area, do you understand? Everything in it is mine and taboo to you – so stay out if you know what's good for you.' Sarah shook her head. Their elder son could be quite pompous at times.

'Huh,' she heard Michael's belligerent reply. 'I don't want your stupid, smelly things anyhow. So there!' She heard a door being slammed and he came charging downstairs like a thing possessed. He was out of breath, red-faced and angry as he stood on the bottom step. 'Mom, John slammed the door in my face for no reason. What are you gonna do about it?'

'Michael, I really haven't got time to listen to your infantile, petty fights. Just keep out of John's room please. You know what he's like.'

'Yes Mom,' he said looking deflated. He looked upwards and pulled a face in the general direction of his brother's bedroom. Sarah couldn't resist a smile.

'Now then, do you think that you two can stop arguing long enough for you to tell John that I'm going to the hospital? I have an early appointment with the consultant this morning and I'm hoping for some good news this time. Your father really does seem to have been making good progress recently.'

'Yes Mom, I promise.' His earnest freckled young face beamed up at her and her heart melted.

'Are you quite sure that you'll be OK on your own? Bertha next door said that she will be in all day, if there's a problem. And I'll have my cell phone switched on too.'

'Gee Mom, of course we'll be fine.'

'And you will behave won't you?'

'Yes,' he replied mechanically, shifting his feet from side to side.

'Good. I'll be back at about midday. Bye honey.'

James had been transferred to the Orthopaedic wing of the hospital a few days' earlier, so that he could have much needed intensive physiotherapy treatment. Sarah parked the car with a watchful eye on the time and walked straight up to the unit. She found that Dr. Kingsley was already waiting for her. He was a short balding man with slightly hunched shoulders and was deep in conversation with her husband as she approached.

'Ah Mrs. Butler,' he said affably. 'It's good to see you.'

James was sitting in his wheelchair and looking quite cheerful. Sarah bent over and kissed him warmly on the forehead. 'Hello darling, how are you this morning? Have you had the results of the tests?'

Dr. Kingsley interrupted her. 'Well Mrs. Butler, now that you're here, I can put you both out of your misery. Why don't you sit down?' He cleared his throat and looked at them over the top of his glasses. 'As you know, we've been monitoring James' progress over the last few days and...'

'But will he...?'

'Mrs. Butler, trying to predict the outcome of such cases can be very difficult.' He turned to James. 'What we do know James, is that you've made slow, but good progress and all the indications are there. That doesn't mean of course, that you will ever walk perfectly, but we are optimistic about your chances.' A brief look of hope flared in James' eyes. 'You'll quite possibly have a limp, because apart from the spinal injuries, those to your leg muscles were severe, but all the pointers lead us to believe that providing you keep up with the strict exercise regime we've worked out for you and obey it to the letter, the muscles will gradually strengthen and...'

'Oh James honey, that's wonderful news.' Sarah flung her arms around his neck and he laughingly tried to extricate himself.

'Can I get a word in now, please? Dr. Kingsley feels that I can probably come home in a few days. Personally I can't wait.'

'You and me both,' Sarah answered happily. 'The boys are on vacation from school at the moment and they're beginning to run riot. Quite frankly,' she whispered in his ear, 'I'm really missing having you around.'

Dr. Kingsley stood up. 'Is there anything either of you wish to ask me? If not, then I must be going. You must be patient you know, these things cannot be rushed. I'll call in to see you in two days' time. Do take care!'

After he'd gone, a feeling of intense relief engulfed Sarah. 'James, I don't know what to say. It's the most wonderful news and the boys will be thrilled to bits to have you home.'

'It's not going to be easy, Sarah. I won't be able to drive for a long time and I'll have to keep coming back here for these physiotherapy sessions. But I just know things will improve. Come here you beautiful creature and give your old man a kiss?' He took her in his arms and for the first time in weeks, kissed her fully on the lips.

A young nurse walked into the room and saw them in a tight embrace. She turned on her heels and walked straight back out again with a broad smile on her face.

'Mmmm…that was wonderful. You've no idea how I have longed for this,' Sarah said grabbing hold of James' hand and looking into his eyes. 'I can't wait to get you home.'

'I know what you mean. It's been tough on all of us. I used to lie here wishing that I'd died in that accident. I didn't feel that life was worth living any more.'

'James, how can you say a thing like that? You've got your whole family around you and we all love you.'

'I'm sorry, but that's the way I was feeling at the time – I wasn't thinking straight and I must apologise to all of you. I couldn't visualise a life sitting in a wheelchair and I didn't know how I was going to tell the boys that I no longer had a job. I'm sorry but I'd known for some time that my job was on the line. If only…'

'James honey, the boys are good kids. They know about your job and they understand what you've been going through. Besides, you mustn't worry about it any more. Your first priority is to get back on your feet and then we can sort out all the other things. You being able to walk again, is the most important thing for all of us.' Sarah paused. 'I think it's a blessing sometimes that we don't know what lies around each corner, don't you?'

'Gee honey you've never said a truer word.' He leant over and kissed her again. 'Thank you, Sarah. Thank you for putting up with me over the past few weeks. I know that it hasn't been easy for you. I love you so much.'

Her heart thumped loudly in her chest – she felt like a school girl who'd fallen in love for the first time. 'And I love you too, James,' she said. 'And even if we hadn't heard about your father, I'd have stood by you no matter what. We'd have coped somehow.'

'Yes, I believe we would. Now tell me what's been happening at home?'

'Well, I did have a strange phone call this morning.'

'Oh yes, who from?'

'A man called Stuart Wells.'

'Stuart Wells? Do we know a Stuart Wells?'

'No listen. He's Katie Nicholson's boyfriend. He told me more about what happened: he kinda filled in all the blanks.'

'Yes. Go on.'

'Apparently, Katie Nicholson has followed the case quite closely since her ordeal and felt the need to come over and meet us.' Sarah looked at her husband, trying to gauge his reaction. 'They're both in Vancouver now, and waiting for you to agree to meet her.'

'They've come thousands of miles to get here, of course we must see her. After all, if it wasn't for Katie, we wouldn't have known about my father, the estate, or anything. She's been our salvation,' he said sounding dramatic.

'I said that if you agreed, they could come round to see you this evening. Will that be OK?'

'Sure thing.'

'He said that Katie is worried that you might not understand her reasons for wanting to meet you.'

'I should say that the boot was on the other foot, Sarah. It's us who should want to meet her, to thank her for all that she's done. We should also apologise for all that she went through on our behalf.' His face clouded over. 'I know that Harold is supposed to be my cousin, but if I ever lay my hands on that creep, I swear I'll…'

'Well, let's hope that we don't,' she said feeling anxious all of a sudden. 'I've got their hotel phone number, so I'll give them a ring and tell them to come at about 8 o'clock this evening.'

'Good. I'm looking forward to meeting her and her fiancé. Now then, where was I…?' He drew her closer…

❊ ❊ ❊ ❊ ❊ ❊

Chapter Twenty-Four

During the flight to Vancouver, Harold had existed in a haze of hatred, but in his more lucid moments he'd plotted his revenge. He ate very little food – he was far too much on edge to eat – but drank plenty of water in between short periods of disturbed sleep. The last thing he needed was to be recognised by the Nicholson girl, so he sat huddled in his seat near the window with his baseball cap pulled down low over his eyes.

Once the plane had landed, he pretended to be asleep until he was quite sure that the Nicholson girl had left the aircraft. He purposefully took several minutes to gather his personal possessions together, before walking down the aisle towards the exit.

An attractive female crew member smiled at him. 'I hope that you enjoyed your flight with us sir?'

'Yes...yes, I did thank you,' he mumbled and walked on.

It took him some time to clear Customs. An over-zealous official insisted on examining every little nook and cranny in his bag and to make matters worse, his passport was given the fullest scrutiny. He even had to go through the indignity of having his iris scanned. Any minute now, he thought, they'll be arresting me on some pretext or other, and then what will I do? His heart beat quickened, but to his intense relief nothing was said and he was allowed through. Perspiration was trickling down his face as he walked away feeling physically sick. For god's sake calm down, he told himself, it was obvious that they knew nothing about what had happened in England.

Harold had calculated that as he didn't intend to stay long in

Vancouver, he could afford to hire a small car for the duration of his stay. But by the time he'd found the hire car desk and queued for about twenty minutes, his temper was almost reaching boiling point. When it came to his turn, he somehow managed to fill in an application form without making the girl behind the desk suspect that he was teetering dangerously on the brink of hysteria.

'Can I have a look at your passport please, Sir.' He hadn't thought that he would be needing it again and had placed it in a safe place in his bag. He scrabbled about in amongst his papers and eventually found it and handed it to her. Nobody seems to trust anyone now, he grumbled to himself.

She scrutinised it carefully and smiled up at him. 'Everything seems to be in order sir. You will find your car waiting for you in Bay 29. Have a nice day.'

Whilst he had been waiting in the queue, he'd seen the address of a cheap hostel and had picked up a map of the area. He found the car easy to drive and a lot better than some of the old cars he'd had in Malta. The fact that he had to drive on the other side of the road foxed him for a while, but he soon found the hostel. It was just like many others that he'd used in his youth, and fortunately, he was able to book into a single room. It was tiny and there was just room for a narrow single bed and a cupboard with hanging space and a couple of drawers, but it was clean and would suit his purpose well. The first thing he did was to lie on the bed. It was a little lumpy but otherwise quite comfortable. He laughed quietly to himself, anything was better than the sordid apartment he'd had to endure in Malta. At least there were no cracks in the walls and no little eyes to stare at him.

Now that he had a comfortable base, he knew that he had to concentrate on his plans. They were quite sketchy, but they involved finding a gun and if he couldn't buy one, he would have to try to obtain one by some other means. So far, so good, he thought. The ease with which this part of his plan was working had helped him to regain some of his composure. It's all going to be a doddle, he told himself.

He felt hungry. It was now many hours since he'd eaten anything substantial. He left the hostel and found a small but sleazy diner. It was crowded and there was a general murmur of conversation. People looked up at him as he passed by their tables, but otherwise showed little interest in him. After looking furtively around, Harold sat down at an empty table and pushed the dirty crockery to one side with obvious distaste. It was some minutes before a young woman came over. She seemed sullen and disinterested in her work and held her pad and pen defensively. Harold watched as the gum she was chewing passed from one side of her mouth to the other.

'Yeah. What'yer want huh?'

'I'll have a hamburger and a black coffee please.'

'Ketchup?'

'I beg your pardon, what did you say?'

The girl yawned. 'Hey mister. What are you on? I asked ya if you wanted some tomato ketchup. Yes or no?'

Harold glowered at her. Just for a fleeting moment the girl's eyes became guarded and unsure, but it didn't last for long. 'Yes,' he replied in his most plummy English accent, 'I think that I would like some tomato ketchup.'

'Gonna be ten minutes,' she said contemptuously and continuing to chew her gum.

'That's fine, but just make sure that it doesn't take longer than ten minutes,' he replied. She glowered at him and walked away. When his food and coffee eventually arrived, he ate it with little enthusiasm as the bar smelt of stale food and unwashed bodies and it made him feel sick.

There was a hint of rain in the air as he walked through the grimy glass doors and out into the narrow street, found the car and made his way back to the hostel. As he entered the old building, he was immediately struck by its emptiness: all or most of the residents seemed to be out. Now was his chance to search for the gun he so desperately needed. This was North America and he felt sure that this hostel was just the place where he could find one. He walked along several dark and gloomy corridors, and looked into various rooms and soon his obsession with his task gave him the confidence he needed to actually go and search through drawers and cupboards to see what he could find.

He was rummaging through a particularly untidy room, when he heard the sound of someone returning to one of the rooms down the corridor. He hid behind the door, hardly daring to breathe and hoping that he wouldn't be discovered. The man, who was obviously drunk, soon left again and Harold could hear him coughing and swearing loudly as he staggered back along the corridor and then less and less as he negotiated the narrow and winding staircase. Harold took a long deep breath and continued his search. He was past caring about other peoples' possessions by this time and regarded everything he touched and examined with complete indifference. But he was methodical. Everything that he moved, he replaced in its original position.

Harold was quite sure that Lady Luck was smiling down upon him, when he opened a drawer in a room on the first floor. 'There you are, my beauty,' he said licking his lips: an ex-Army revolver was tucked tightly in one corner. 'And some ammunition too, how convenient,' he said, a sadistic smile spreading over his features. He picked the gun up and holding it up to eye level, he looked along the length of the barrel to see if the sight was true. It was. And before making sure that the firing mechanism was functioning properly, he checked to see if it was loaded. It wasn't.

He pulled the trigger. It clicked. The sound echoed in the

confines of the small room. Good, he thought, it's in good working order, well oiled and ready for use. He placed it and some ammunition into his pocket, closed the drawer and walked out of the room.

That night he lay on his bed in the small, stuffy room and stared upwards at the ceiling. He didn't notice the lumps in the mattress and the feel of the coarse grey blanket on which he was lying. He didn't see the newly painted ceiling or smell the antiseptic on the freshly washed floor, but instead he saw pictures. Just as in a film, images continually reeled through his mind. Harold's whole being was being focused on one important act.

He wanted to be rid of his so-called cousin, James Butler.

He had to have a meticulously worked out plan. He knew that he couldn't afford to make any mistakes and he savoured the images he was seeing, until a worrying thought crossed his mind. Hospitals were busy places. The layout too, could be a problem, and also one on which he had little or no influence. He could feel the revolver in his jacket pocket and it was digging into his ribs: a stark reminder of his task. But what if he was unable for some reason to use it? Harold's brow creased with concentration and he massaged and methodically tugged at his now luxuriant dark beard. He suddenly shouted and laughed out loud. 'Yes, of course. That's exactly what I will do.'

That night he tossed and turned for what seemed like hours, but he must have slept because he woke at about six in the morning. He spent the next couple of hours working out the finer details of his plan, until he knew that he couldn't do any more. Harold drooled with delight and emitted little bursts of uncontrolled laughter. Plans…plans, he said over and over in his mind. That is where other people go wrong. They only have a Plan 'A' , whereas I have a Plan 'B' and if I am very clever, I might even think of a Plan 'C'! As he savoured thoughts of killing James Butler, another little worm of doubt and worry began to gnaw on the edges of his consciousness. What about the Nicholson girl? Would she once again interfere with his plans, he asked himself? His thoughts were growing bolder. 'If she does, I'll have to get rid of her too,' he said out loud. He felt invincible, all-powerful and strong. 'Nothing and nobody can stop me now.'

Harold began to sweat. The room was too hot. He felt the large radiator on the wall beside him and it almost burned his hand so he got up from his bed and turned on the large fan above his head. This cooled him down, but the constant whirring noise started to annoy him and something seemed to be moving at the edge of his field of vision. A large fly swooped down upon him and the whining sound of its wings increased the vibrations within his head. He hated flies. He hit out at it so savagely that the impact stopped it in its tracks and it fell to the floor.

He stared at the dead fly for some time. It had a calming effect on him as his respiration gradually returned to something approaching normal and his heart rhythm became more regular. He sighed in exasperation. He had to keep a clear head and be one step ahead of anyone who might try to threaten his plans. He decided to wait until the evening before making his way to the hospital.

He left the hostel at 7.30 p.m. and walked to the parking lot. He felt quite calm as he climbed into the car, put the key into the ignition and turned it.

Nothing happened.

He tried again and still nothing happened. He couldn't believe that his nearly new hire car should have let him down at the time of his greatest need. Renewed anger burned within him. He snatched at the keys, climbed out of the car and slammed the door so hard that the car rocked crazily from side to side. He stormed off in the blackest of moods.

Harold's only chance of getting to the hospital now, was to go by bus. He didn't have enough cash on him to call a cab. He remembered that there was a bus stop outside the hostel and he made his way back there. It began to rain and as he waited he began to feel cold, so he pulled up the collar of his jacket in an effort to keep himself warm and dry. He cursed the hire car company and the weather. He looked at his watch and cursed the bus company too – it was late. Several other people were standing huddled under umbrellas and looking as miserable as he felt. Things were starting to go wrong and his hands began to shake and not wishing to draw too much attention to himself, he placed them in his pocket. I have to stay calm, he told himself.

A young woman joined him at the bus stop. She smiled at him. 'Not really the weather for standing around,' she said, trying to make conversation.

'No, it certainly isn't,' he said forcing himself to answer.

'Do you have far to go?'

'No, not far.' Damn the woman, he thought. Why do people always want to talk?

'This bus is always late.' The woman shook her head.

Several minutes later, the bus appeared around the corner. Feeling grateful that he didn't have to say any more to her, he climbed in and walked to the end of the bus, it was less crowded there. It seemed to take forever to get to the hospital, but eventually it pulled up outside. It had stopped raining, but all the street lamps wore a misty glow rather like a curtain, as the temperature dropped further. His fellow passengers hurried off in different directions to their homes and their humdrum lives. He followed some of them with his eyes and his hatred burned insidiously within him.

He pulled his baseball cap further over his forehead and stood outside the hospital for several moments. He felt the revolver in his pocket: its presence there, gave him the courage and the impetus he needed for the task ahead.

He turned, took a deep breath and walked up the stone steps which lead into the hospital and onwards towards his destiny.

* * * * * *

Chapter Twenty-Five

Having arranged to meet her aunt and uncle for tea on Saturday afternoon, Katie and Stuart spent the morning sightseeing. They wandered hand in hand around the beautiful Queen Elizabeth Park and admired the magnificent Vancouver skyline. It had been raining earlier in the day, but now the sun shone brilliantly, making the omnipresent snow-capped mountains in the distance, sparkle and shimmer. It was a magical scene and Katie began to feel quite intoxicated by it all.

A river wound its gentle way through the park and they stopped for a while on a small bridge and side by side and with Stuart's arm around her shoulders, they stared down into the water. It was a peaceful interlude in their short stay in the city.

'Stuart?'

'Yes, my love?'

'Now that we're engaged, I suppose that we ought to give some thought to when we will actually get married?'

'I've been thinking the same thing myself. I can't wait.'

Katie looked up at him. 'There's nothing stopping us from getting married in a few weeks, is there?'

'No, not a thing,' he said with a chuckle that seemed to reverberate throughout his whole body.

'And we could live in Anston. What do you think?'

'I don't care where I live as long as I'm with you. As far as I'm concerned we could live in a tent or even a cave and I'd still be happy.' He smiled wickedly. 'I could play the caveman and drag you about by your long and silken hair. Oh "Kate, the prettiest Kate in Christendom: Kate of Kate-Hall, my super-dainty

Kate…" Then how does it go? Ah yes… "Kiss me Kate, we will be married o'Sunday," ' Stuart continued, laughing happily.

'Yes, something like that. I also did The Taming of the Shrew at school you know.'

Stuart was now in full flow. "Thy husband is thy lord, thy life, thy keeper…thy…"

'Stuart, do be serious for a moment. Wouldn't it be wonderful if we could find somewhere like Lilac Cottage?' She sighed.

'Oh Katie that would be wonderful, but I'm not sure we could afford it straight away. We've got the wedding and everything else to think of.'

'But…but that's not…'

'As you know I've been studying for years and the old bank balance has had a bit of a battering. With the price of homes being so expensive nowadays, we'd need a sizeable deposit, wouldn't we, and even supposing we could even get a mortgage?'

'Yes, but that's not a problem.'

'What do you mean?' Stuart's brow furrowed.

'I am an only child, Stuart. Think about it. I told you that both my parents had died. We had a house near Brighton which I managed to sell and what with their savings, it all amounted to…'

'Come on, out with it. I didn't know that I was going to marry an heiress.'

'Well, the money I had left over after the sale of the house is in a building society and gathering interest and my latest statement said…'

'Katie, why didn't you tell me this before?' Stuart looked stunned. 'I'm not sure that…'

'Look Stuart, I have…quite a lot of money,' she replied biting her lip, worried now that Stuart didn't seem to be reacting the way she thought he would.

'How much, Katie?'

'Just over £300,000.' Stuart spluttered. 'I'm sorry, I was going to tell you, but I didn't quite know how.'

There was a long and painful silence. Stuart gazed downwards at the swiftly flowing river as it disappeared under the bridge. He kicked out at a small stone and sent it spinning into the water. Her heart started to thump loudly. 'Katie,' he finally said.

'Yes.'

'Katie, I'm not at all sure that I will like being a kept man! You see I have this rather old-fashioned notion about being the main bread winner.'

'But it won't be like that, will it? Once we're married, you can pay the mortgage if we need one and my money can look after everyday expenses. We'll be able to buy some really decent furniture, but in any case, we'll share everything won't we? It will enable us to have a fantastic start together.'

Stuart was silent again. He looked really miserable when he finally turned to her. 'Do you know,' he said, 'the night before we left to come here, I was lying in bed worrying about what I had to offer you, if you agreed to marry me.'

'And I was scared stiff of telling you about the money.'

Stuart's expression hardened. 'Come on,' he said swiftly changing the subject. 'We've got other places to see.'

He was definitely not happy now, Katie told herself miserably. But she was glad that it was now all out in the open. He would have found out about it sooner or later anyway. Of course, she hadn't expected him to be over the moon, but she was a little disappointed that his reaction had been so negative. She didn't want the fact that she had some money of her own to drive a wedge between them. They were still in that tender area of getting to know one another. Katie felt that one of the most important things that they needed to know was to discover each other's sensitivities. She now knew that money was one of them.

Despite this setback, she could hardly believe her good fortune. Stuart was the single most important person in her world and she sometimes had to almost pinch herself just to make sure that she wasn't dreaming. She felt unbelievably happy and contented. Simon Brand had done her an enormous favour by preferring her friend Sally to her. She knew that despite all the good times they'd spent together, her feelings for Simon were nothing like the love she now felt for Stuart. Her first waking thoughts were always dominated by him.

They stopped at a flower stall and Katie bought two bouquets of flowers: one for James Butler in hospital and the other for her Aunt Beatrice. Stuart still appeared to be a little withdrawn and this worried her, but she tried to put it to the back of her mind. She had arranged to meet her aunt and uncle in a restaurant in the centre of the city and as they made their way there, she experienced a feeling of growing excitement.

They were shown into a bright, beautifully decorated room with elegant Grecian columns separating the different dining areas and the use of oleander and other tropical plants gave everything an air of exotic peacefulness. The Head Waiter showed them to a table tucked away in a quiet corner behind a potted palm tree. Her aunt and uncle were already there.

Aunt Beatrice, an elegant woman in her mid-fifties, looked radiant as she rose from her chair and walked towards them. 'Katie honey,' she said with real pleasure on her face, 'it's wonderful to see you again.'

'Hi Aunt Beatrice, how are you? You're certainly looking well.'

'I am very well, thank you. Look Katie, none of that old 'aunt' business if you don't mind. It makes me feel quite ancient.' Beatrice put her hands on her shoulders and looked at her. 'You're looking great my girl,' she said kissing her on both sides of her cheek before turning her attention to Stuart. 'And this has to be Stuart. I'm so pleased to meet you, Katie told me a lot about you yesterday.'

'Only good things I hope,' he replied.

'But of course.'

Katie gave an embarrassed laugh. 'I'm sorry, with all the excitement of seeing you again, I completely forgot to introduce you. 'Beatrice meet Stuart, Stuart meet Beatrice. There.'

'Anyway, come over here and see David, he's been longing to see you both.'

Their time spent together proved to be both sad and happy – there was so much to talk about – and when the time came for them to say goodbye, Katie felt a momentary pang of sadness. Her aunt was so much like her mother and she couldn't help noticing the tears which had gathered in her eyes as they prepared to leave.

David, a tall man with short white hair and pale blue eyes, placed his arm protectively around his wife's slight shoulders. Katie could tell by the way he looked at his wife, that he understood the reasons for her tears: she missed her sister dearly and Katie was now her only relative in England. 'Be sure to come and visit us again and stay longer next time. We have plenty of room to put you up,' he told them as they said their final goodbyes. 'Your mother always said that she would come over to see us, but sadly she never made it.'

'Yes honey, do come and spend some time with us. You're all we've got now, you know,' Beatrice said squeezing her hand hard. 'Goodbye my dear and do take care.'

Katie felt depressed when at last they walked away from the restaurant. Not only had Stuart's unwillingness to accept the fact that she had plenty of money upset her, but the memories of her mother's funeral, suddenly came flooding back.

Stuart glanced at her as he drove their hired car through the streets of Vancouver. He placed his hand tenderly over hers, giving it a gentle squeeze.

'Katie love, are you OK?'

'Yes, I'm fine thank you,' she said staring miserably into space. 'No, I'm not fine. Oh, I'm sorry to be such a drag Stuart, but I was remembering the last time that I'd seen them both. It was at my mother's funeral.'

'I'm sorry, I should have realised. I've been a little preoccupied I'm afraid. I quite forget sometimes that unlike me, you don't have a large family around you.'

Katie was now really hurting inside. 'The passing of time is strange, isn't it? You don't see someone for a long time and then you meet again and it's as if you'd seen them only yesterday. The memory of that dreadful time when both my parents died so soon after one another and I had to sell the house, is still…is still so vivid in my mind.'

'I'm quite sure that your aunt felt the same way. She seemed rather subdued when we left.'

'Yes. That's what started me off.'

'Never mind, you must try and put it all behind you and remember the other reason that we're here.'

'Yes…yes of course, as if I could forget.' Katie couldn't believe that she was at last going to meet James Butler and his family.

That evening, Stuart drove her to the hospital. During the journey, she tried to work out what she expected from her visit. Since finding the letters, she had wondered what James looked like and whether he was anything like his father. She had seen many photographs of Gerald at Epton Hall. He had been an upright, handsome and aristocratic-looking man with lots of thick, tousled-looking fair hair. Perhaps his nose had been a little on the large side, but this had only made him seem more attractive somehow. Katie had decided that it was little wonder poor Amy Butler had fallen so deeply and desperately in love with him.

She'd had plenty of time to look at albums crammed full of family photographs during her enforced stay in the attic and Nancy had been eager to show her the various portraits of Gerald, Marjorie and those two dear little boys, which were dotted around the house. She remembered that they had all looked so happy. Life could be so cruel at times she reflected.

Whilst looking at these photographs, she'd tried hard to imagine him and Amy being together, knowing that their illicit love affair was doomed. Amy must have been much the stronger of the two. It would have needed a tremendous amount of courage to walk away from the man she loved and even harder to keep going once she was back home in Canada. Amy must have lived in hope of seeing him again and showing off her son. Katie could imagine her waiting every day for the postman to arrive, only to find that yet again, there was no letter from England. She must have been bitterly disappointed. I wonder how long it took her to realise that there would never be another letter, she thought sadly. It was probably years before she could come to terms with it, because she had never married.

In the event what had she got out of her years of sacrifice and devotion? Nothing, except a lifetime of misery and heartfelt rejection: in essence, two families' lives had been shattered in one dreadful, stormy afternoon.

It was 7.30 that evening, when Stuart dropped Katie at the bottom of the long flight of steps which lead up to the main door of the General Hospital. They had decided that she should see James Butler on her own. The main reception area was still busy, despite the fact that it was evening. She stopped at the reception desk to ask her way to the Orthopaedic Unit and was told that it was on the second floor. She climbed into a crowded elevator and was soon whisked upwards. Once the lift had stopped, Katie had to fight her way through several people before she could get out and just in front of the elevator she saw a notice which read

"ORTHOPAEDIC UNIT", followed by a big red arrow. She finally turned a corner and was immediately confronted by two see-through plastic doors which didn't quite meet in the middle. She pushed her way through. The doors made a funny plastic swishing sound as they closed untidily behind her. She had arrived. It was her big moment and her pulse began to race.

She bit her lower lip apprehensively as she approached the nursing station. A young nurse was sitting behind a desk and concentrating on a computer screen. Katie waited for a few seconds and then cleared her throat.

'Excuse me.'

'Oh, sorry. Can I help you?'

'Yes please. I'm here to see Mr. James Butler.'

'Why yes. He's in the third room down on the right hand side. You can't miss it. Is he expecting you?'

'Yes.'

'Good. There's no one else with him at present, so I'm sure he'll be pleased to see you.'

'Thank you.'

'You're welcome,' the nurse said turning once again to her computer.

Katie found the room and stood outside. She lifted her hand to knock on the door and hesitated. She was suddenly caught in a blind panic. Why was she here? What was she going to say? The door stood like an impenetrable barrier between her and the man she believed that she wanted to see: the impetus which had driven her for so long had failed her at the last hurdle.

A nurse was walking along the corridor towards James' room and noticed Katie standing there. 'Can I help you?' she enquired.

'No...no thank you.' She paused. 'Yes, I'm sorry, perhaps you can. I'm just trying to pluck up enough courage to go in,' she replied.

'He won't bite you know, he's a really nice guy. It's such a pity that he has had so many hard knocks. Are you a relative of his?'

'No.'

Realisation sprang into the girl's eyes. 'I know you're from England aren't you? Let me see, you must be...'

'Katie Nicholson,' she nodded. 'I arrived here yesterday.'

'I spent some time in England you know. Lovely place and I just loved London, but it didn't stop raining the whole time I was there. A bit like today really.'

'Yes, it can get like that sometimes,' she answered politely.

'Well, are you going in or not?'

'Yes, but...'

'Look, I'll go in and tell him that you're here, shall I?' The nurse knocked on the door and walked straight in. Katie could just hear what she was saying. 'James, I have a young lady outside who says that she's come all the way from England to see you and then stands in front of the door too frightened to come in.'

'Ah, that'll be Katie. Would you send her in please?'

'Sure thing.' She poked her head back round the door. 'Come on in, everything's OK.'

'Thank you,' Katie answered with a nervous smile. Her heart was thumping like a drum as she walked into the room. It was a large airy cheerful room with bright yellow curtains and modern furniture, and every available surface seemed to be covered with cards, plants and flowers. The flowers that she had purchased in the park that morning, seemed almost one bunch too many. She walked over to where James was sitting and held them out to him.

'Hello,' she said. Katie could feel her knees shaking. 'I'm Katie Nicholson and...I bought these for you.'

'Hi Katie. It's good to meet you and thank you,' he said. His voice was deep, but it had a soft, velvety quality which put her immediately at ease. She was surprised to see that he wasn't much like Gerald Hapsworth-Cole at all, apart from his hair which was thick, tousled and wayward. His features were altogether smaller than his father's, but there was something familiar about his eyes. Yes she thought, she'd seen the same look in some of the portraits on the wall at the old house. There was definitely a family resemblance there.

James Butler sat awkwardly in his wheelchair, almost as if it wasn't large enough for him. He was slim and had long legs and Katie guessed that he was well over six feet tall. He had an engaging smile and his eyes regarded her with amusement and friendliness. She liked him on the spot. He placed the flowers on the table beside him and without any warning, took hold of both her hands, clasping them firmly.

'Do you know I really can't thank you enough for what you've done for me and my family? We will be forever in your debt.'

Katie was quite taken aback by this outburst. 'Well…it…it was nothing really. I learned a lot about your family whilst I was at the old house and especially after I'd found the letters and I just felt that I had to come over to see you. I have an aunt living in Vancouver and I took the opportunity of visiting her at the same time.'

James turned to the nurse who was just about to walk out of the room with the flowers in her hand. 'Do you know, Sally, Katie has been responsible for bringing me back to life?'

'Yes, I realised that she's the one that you've been talking about.'

'The very one.' By this time, Katie was feeling even more embarrassed.

'Katie, after his wife, Sarah, you are the tops in the popularity stakes, you know,' Sally said. 'He's talked about nothing else over the past few days. Now I must go and put these flowers in water. Enjoy yourselves.' She hurried from the room.

'Please sit down Katie, after all we've a lot to talk about,' James said pointing towards a chair by the bed. 'Now then, you must tell me all about yourself and how you just happened to be in the attic of that old house and how you found the letters. I'm familiar with most of the story of course, but you know what lawyer-speak is like – all facts and no filling. You've no idea how odd it feels to have such a large portion of your family history, as one big blank.'

'Well it all started with the death of Gerald's wife, Marjorie...' James listened intently while Katie was speaking and occasionally asked the odd question. Finally she said, '...and that's it and why I felt that I had to come over here to see you and explain my part in it all.'

'Thank you Katie, I'm really glad you came. I feel a lot happier about it all now.'

The door opened and a well-dressed woman of about forty-five entered. She was small, petite and with attractively shaped brown eyes and short dark hair which curled delicately around her face. 'Sarah darling,' James said, 'I'd like you to meet Katie Nicholson.' He tried to stand up but without success and a look of acute annoyance crossed his face. He was obviously frustrated with his condition, she thought sadly and hadn't yet come to terms with the fact that he wasn't mobile.

'Hi Katie. I'm really pleased to meet you,' Sarah said walking over to her and grabbing hold of her hand.

'Hello, Mrs. Butler.'

'Oh please call me Sarah.'

'I was just telling your husband about my part in what happened and how I felt that I just couldn't get on with my life until I'd met you. I hope you can understand my reasons for coming all this way? To be perfectly honest with you, once I'd arrived in Vancouver, I began to have second thoughts about it.'

'I don't see why Katie. We quite understand don't we James?'

'Gee of course we do, so please don't worry any more about it, Katie.'

'It's our pleasure.' Sarah looked at James as she spoke. 'You see, after James' accident, everything seemed to go haywire for a while – nothing seemed normal any more. Then quite out of the blue, the lawyer's letter arrived from England and our whole lives were turned upside down again. This time however, fate seemed to be smiling on us.' It soon became apparent to Katie that they were still very much in love with one another. The warm atmosphere which existed between them, washed over her like a warm, welcoming blanket. She felt completely at ease with both of them.

'We had some really good news yesterday, too,' James said. 'The specialist said that he can see no real reason now, why I shouldn't walk again. This means that I won't be confined to this awful chair for the rest of my life.' He reached out for Sarah's hand and they both looked deeply into one another's eyes. Sarah then turned to her.

'Well Katie, it's been wonderful meeting you. I only popped in to bring James some clean clothes and to meet you, so if you'll excuse me, I'll get back home to see how the boys are doing. If you get time before you return to England, perhaps you and Stuart would like to call at the house and say hello. I'm sure the boys will be delighted to meet you. Once again, thank you for all that you've done. I'll leave you two to chat for a little longer. Bye.' She kissed James on the forehead and left the room.

A silence developed between them. Katie couldn't think of anything interesting to say and fidgeted slightly. She glanced idly around the room. It was comfortably furnished and the large picture window gave a panoramic view of the city. She could see hundreds of lights twinkling in the distance as the city carried on its life below her.

Her eyes finally rested on a wooden bookcase. It was full of books. Books definitely seem to follow me around, she decided and seeing them all neatly stacked, made her remember the photographs that she'd brought to show James. One photograph was of his father which must have been taken when he was about thirty. He was standing in front of the ornately carved fountain in the garden with Epton Hall rearing up behind him. The other one had been taken on board his boat. He had his head thrown back as if he was laughing and had his arms wrapped around his young sons' shoulders.

Katie was just reaching into her handbag to find them, when once again she had an overwhelming feeling of fear, or was it another premonition she wondered? Just like before and without any warning, Harold Hapsworth-Cole's evil face came into her mind and his dark eyes leered menacingly at her. They were cold and calculating, just like hard steel. She shivered.

'Katie, I'm sorry,' James said, his face registering concern. 'Are you feeling cold? Perhaps I can get that window closed.'

'No, no James, thank you. I was just remembering something that's all.' She found the envelope containing the photos and handed them to him. 'I thought that you might like to see these.'

James took the envelope and stared at it for a moment. 'Are these what I think they are?' His hands shook.

'Yes, there are two photos of your father and…'

'Wow! Gee thanks.' He opened the envelope slowly almost as if he was reluctant to view the contents. A look of sorrow passed over his features as he looked at the likeness of his father for the very first time. 'My god, looking at these, gives me a funny feeling you know. I wish I could have met him and…is this Epton Hall? Wow! I'd no idea it was so big: it must cost a fortune to maintain.'

'Yes. There's quite a lot that needs doing to it. The gardens and the estate are huge.'

'I can't imagine what it must feel like to live in a place like that.' He then turned his attention to the other photograph. 'Was this their boat?'

'Yes, I think so. It was called "The Sea Witch".'

James continued to stare at the photographs for some time. 'Do you know Katie, I find it hard to look at this photograph of my father and my two half-brothers, knowing that they could all be lying somewhere at the bottom of the Solent. Is that what it's called?'

'Yes, it's a stretch of water between the mainland and the Isle of Wight.'

'Yes, well it makes me feel kinda sad. I've been reading some of the family history and my father, and indeed my grandfather, was in the Royal Navy, and it's ironic that I have an inbuilt resistance to being on water of any kind.'

Katie could only imagine what thoughts would be going through James' mind at that moment. She was so glad that she had come to Vancouver: if nothing else, her visit had enabled him to see what his father had looked like. Her heart went out to him.

* * * * * *

Chapter Twenty-Six

Harold Hapsworth-Cole entered the hospital and looked around him. He had no idea in which part of the hospital James Butler was being treated. He took off his baseball cap and placed it in one of his pockets. His hair was hanging down over his forehead in wet untidy strands and he rubbed his hands through it in an effort to make himself look more presentable. He certainly didn't wish to draw too much attention to himself. His clothes felt and smelt damp and his sodden shoes left imprints of moisture wherever he stood. He spotted a sign which read 'MEN'S ROOM', and he walked towards this temporary haven. There were far too many people around for his liking and he was quite convinced that they were all staring at him.

Fortunately the room was empty and he spent a few moments gathering his thoughts. He combed his hair and splashed his face with cold water and looked at his reflection in the mirror. He looked dreadful. The continual battles which now raged within him had made him look tired. He had dark circles underneath his eyes and his eyelids were red and puffy. The intense strain was beginning to take its toll and his neck and shoulder muscles ached too. It was only hatred and the knowledge that his quarry was nearby, that was keeping him going.

Harold's emotions were going up and down like a yo-yo. One moment he was feeling as high as a kite and on the verge of hysteria and the next, he was in a trough of such deep depression, that he felt impotent and unable to extricate himself. It was like trying to claw his way up a slippery, vertical tunnel.

Paper Dreams

He could clearly see a bright and beckoning light above, which appeared to be forever pulling him upwards.

But each time he made a little progress, he always seemed to fall back again. Meanwhile, that elusive light grew further and further away from him.

He flexed his shoulders muscles several times until he felt calmer and walked back into the main reception area. The glare of the lights, the incessant noise from so many people and especially the pattern on the carpet, made him feel sick. The carpet seemed to move in waves in front of him, making his head ache. Or was it the cloying smell of hospitals which had always had an effect on him, he wondered? He was now quite unable to separate these differing feelings. This sickness like bile began to creep upwards. He knew that he had to leave this huge, cavernous room as soon as possible.

A girl was sitting behind a long curved desk surrounded by telephones and a computer screen and was in animated conversation with someone. Her chair was slowly swinging from side to side and he walked over and stood in front of her. She ignored him and he could feel his ire rising. He closed his eyes and took in several deep breaths, letting his shoulders rise slightly each time, until he felt a little more in control.

The girl's voice suddenly enquired. 'I'm sorry to have kept you waiting, sir. As you can see, we are busy this evening. How can I help you?'

'I want some information, please.' Inside his head a little voice was saying to him "Keep calm Harold, keep calm," and even though perspiration was starting to trickle down his face, he managed to say in his most impeccable English, 'I've actually come to visit a friend, but unfortunately I've forgotten which unit he is in. Do you think you could possibly look it up for me? Thank you.' Harold had an overwhelming and perverse feeling of power over this young girl. Inside he was seething, but outwardly, he was able to portray a picture of complete normality. These fools will not get the better of me, he told himself. He felt nothing but contempt for these people who set themselves up in authority over him.

'Why certainly sir,' the girl added affably. 'Can I have the patient's name please?'

'James Hapsworth-Cole.'

The girl smiled at him. He was fascinated by her teeth: he had the curious impression of tombstones standing in a perfect row. Why was his mind continuing to play tricks on him, when all he needed was to remain in control? He shook his head and the vision disappeared. She turned towards the screen. 'Hold on just one moment please.' The machine buzzed obediently as her long-nailed fingers flew across the keyboard. 'There's a Mr. James Butler here, but no mention of a Hapsworth-Cole. Are you sure that you have the right name?'

'Yes…yes…I'm sorry, it's Butler. Hapsworth-Cole is another family name which he doesn't always use,' he replied, quickly realising his mistake. Within a few seconds, the information he needed was displayed on the screen.

'Yes sir, he's in the Orthopaedic Unit, Room number 3.' She spent the next few moments telling him how to get there.

'Thank you,' he replied.

'You're welcome.'

Harold's mind was put on hold as he made his way up to the unit. He climbed up the stairs like an automaton with its deadly aim programmed into its brain. He felt out of breath when he reached the second floor and stood for a moment to recover before walking through some clear plastic doors. He noted that the nursing station desk was empty. Good, he thought. He walked down the corridor and stood outside door number 3. Adrenaline now began to course throughout his excited body and his pulse accelerated perceptibly. Harold was now deliciously close to the object of his hatred. He looked around, making quite sure that he was alone and then placed his ear against the door.

He heard voices. Hell and damnation, James had a visitor. He bent down to listen again.

He froze.

His rapidly beating heart lurched and stumbled. He could hear the sound of a woman's voice and…it was an English voice. No, it couldn't be, he told himself. His head began to buzz and he shook it from side to side in disbelief. Even though the sound was muffled, he knew that it was Katie Nicholson. He could clearly hear her saying, '…I was just remembering something, that's all…'

Harold couldn't believe his ears. That meddling bitch was one step ahead of him yet again! His breath now came in short, sharp bursts: he felt light-headed and could hear the buzzing sound in his head gradually getting louder. He placed his hands over his ears in an effort to stop it, but it was no use. He stood away from the door feeling almost blind with fury and stumbled back along the corridor, his hands clutching at the walls for support. He found a door which was partly ajar, and was relieved to find that it was empty. He walked in, closed the door behind him and leant against it until his breathing and heartbeat had returned to something approaching normal.

Once he was feeling calmer, he looked around. It was a small room rather like a kitchen with cupboards all around the periphery. There was a large, deep stainless steel sink unit with some shelves above it containing kidney bowls, bed pans and rolls of paper. One by one, Harold opened the cupboards, but nothing really interested him until his eyes alighted upon a box of syringes in individual sterile packs and with trembling hands he opened the box and withdrew one.

Harold grinned. A plan began to form in his mind as he

looked at the syringe. Why hadn't he thought of something like this before? It could be the easiest way to dispatch this person who was stealing his fortune: his hatred for his cousin was total now. His eyes moved from side to side as he considered all of his options. The syringe had to be Plan A, and the gun that was omnipresent in his pocket, would be there as Plan B. He pictured pressing the plunger and smiled, his first aid training in Malta was now coming in very handy.

'Pure air, dear boy, pure air,' he whispered as he imagined plunging the needle into his cousin's arm. His hand shook slightly. He needed it to be ready in an instant and he drooled as he tore off the sterile protective wrapping, thus revealing the instrument which was going to ensure the death of his cousin. He looked at it once more, before placing it gingerly in his pocket.

There were still parts of Harold's brain which remained sufficiently normal for him to think logically. Only the jerky movements of his eyes would have betrayed him. He knew that he had to kill James Butler, but if Katie Nicholson was still in the room, this would present a much bigger problem. Not only that, but he had to carry out his task now, because he would not have another chance. He noticed a white coat that was hanging on a hook and couldn't believe his luck. They were all handing it to him on a plate.

Harold knew that he had to get the Nicholson girl out of his cousin's room for a while and another plan began to form in his mind.

He walked out of the anteroom, leaving the white coat where it was for the moment and made his way downstairs to the main reception area. Yes, there on one side of the vast area, was a bank of about five telephone booths. He'd noticed them earlier and what was even more convenient, was a notice on the wall beside the booths giving the phone numbers of the various units in the hospital. He made a mental note of the Orthopaedic Unit's number and walked towards the only booth which wasn't occupied.

Now, of course, he needed someone to be behind the desk at the Nursing Station. With shaking hands and heart aflutter, he dialled the number and without thinking, crossed his fingers. It rang for some time and he was on the point of replacing the receiver, when he heard a voice.

'Hello. Orthopaedics. Nurse Allen speaking.'

Harold forced his voice to sound much deeper than usual and even affected a credible Canadian accent. 'Hi, reception here. We have a telephone call to one of the booths for a Miss Katie Nicholson. I believe that she's visiting a patient...er...James Butler. The caller said that it was urgent.'

'Thank you, I'll go and tell her.'

Harold replaced the receiver and hurried back up to the Unit. He was just turning a corner when he saw Katie Nicholson hurrying along the corridor with a worried look on her face. Fortunately for him, he was close to the anteroom and he slipped inside and stood behind the door. He hurriedly donned the white coat and transferred the gun and the syringe from his pocket and into the coat. It actually wasn't a bad fit and could have been made for him. He left the relative safety of the room and made his way to the Nursing Station. He heaved a sigh of relief...the desk was now unmanned again and he walked stealthily along the corridor to room number 3.

James Butler was sitting in his chair. 'Hi there,' he said as Harold entered.

'Hi,' he replied. Harold couldn't help noticing that James was holding a book entitled "English Country Houses", and its significance was not lost on him. His anger heightened and he fought to control himself. 'I'm s...sorry,' he stammered, 'b...but the blood sample we took wasn't tested properly due to some mix up in the Haematology Department. I'm afraid that we will need some more blood. Would you mind rolling up your sleeve for me please?'

James grimaced slightly and then looked puzzled. He watched as Harold took the syringe out of his pocket and his face registered concern. 'Hold on a minute fella, I haven't had any blood taken recently.'

'Oh, whenever,' Harold retorted. 'In any case, perhaps you could just roll up your sleeve for me er…Mr.Hapsworth-Cole?' His anxiety allowed the hatred he was feeling for his cousin to creep into his voice and this alerted James.

'I'm not sure that I…' Harold grabbed his arm viciously and he began to struggle. 'Hey just a minute, you must have the wrong patient.' James then looked strangely at Harold. 'How the hell did you know about the name Hapsworth-Cole?' Fear showed in his eyes. 'Who are you and what are you trying to give me?'

'Nothing but pure air, dear cousin…nothing but pure air.'

'Cousin…what the hell…get off me you idiot.' Harold quickly realised that he was losing control of the situation.

'Damn you…' he cried with spittle flying from his mouth. 'Damn you.'

'Cut that out,' James cried, his voice beginning to crack.

They struggled, but Harold was too strong for James in his weakened state. 'I won't let you have my money…I won't…I won't,' he cried out. Despite his confusion he realised that his cousin wasn't going to die without a struggle. In sheer desperation he hit him. It was a truly vicious blow to the side of the head and it momentarily stunned James. Harold picked up the large spare pillow which was lying at the foot of the bed. There was no stopping him now: this was what he'd travelled thousands of miles to do. He forced it down on to James' face and pressed it down with surprising force.

He felt ecstatic.

He would soon be rid of this man for ever. He couldn't think of anything else and only had one aim in view and that was to finish what he'd started. Why hadn't he thought about using a pillow in the first place, he wondered? It was so easy. He laughed.

Suddenly the whispering voices inside his head returned with a vengeance. This made him relax the pressure on the pillow and James began to struggle again.

"Push harder," the voices demanded. "Harder Harold, push it harder." A lone voice seemed to say, "Harold you're stupid and worthless. You will still not get the money..."

Harold ignored them. 'I will...I will...I will,' he repeated his eyes flashing maniacally. He felt triumphant as his victim's movements gradually became weaker.

* * * * * *

Chapter Twenty-Seven

Katie ran down the last few steps, wondering who could be calling her. Perhaps it was Stuart? Was he in some sort of trouble? Her heart thudded in her chest. She turned into the main reception area and raced towards the bank of phone booths she could see directly in front of her. She stopped short when she discovered that each one was occupied. That's odd, she thought. She looked round to see if there were any other phones, but it soon became apparent that they were the only ones available for the public to use.

Katie frowned and walked over to the reception desk. 'Excuse me, I was told that there was a telephone call for me. My name is Katie Nicholson and the nurse said that it was urgent.'

'A phone call? No, I don't think…' the girl looked puzzled. 'I'm sorry but I've no knowledge of any such call. Was it from one of the public booths?'

'Yes, that's what I was told, but I'm afraid that they're all occupied.'

'Well, in that case, I can't help you. They must have hung up.'

'But…'

'Look, I'm really busy. We're dealing with an emergency right now. There's a huge fire on the other side of the city and there could be several casualties. Please excuse me.'

Katie felt flummoxed. There was either a call for her, or there wasn't. What on earth was going on, she wondered?

When Harold Hapsworth-Cole's face loomed up before her yet again, something seemed to click inside her brain. She will never know how or why she came to the conclusion that she did.

Could it be...? she thought. 'Oh my god no... James,' she cried. With mounting panic, Katie turned and ran towards the elevators. An elderly couple were passing by and she quickly skidded past them. They stopped and stared at her, with their eyes full of hostility. The old woman grabbed hold of her husband's arm, sniffed audibly and then they hurried on their way.

Fortunately one of the elevators was waiting on the ground floor. Once inside, she pressed the ASCEND button. Nothing happened. She pressed it again. Still nothing happened. Several people piled in through the partially opened doors. Katie pressed the button again and the doors closed and the elevator started to rise. Much to her frustration, it stopped at the next floor to let some passengers out. Come on she pleaded silently like a prayer and why didn't I walk up? Katie couldn't exactly put her fears into words, but deep inside something was telling her that all was not well with James.

When the doors eventually opened, she raced out and ran along the corridor towards the unit. She fought her way through the plastic doors and collided with a young man who was pushing a trolley piled high with clean sheets and towels. Several of them fell to the ground.

'Hey you!' he yelled. 'Why don't you look where you're going?'

Katie called out, 'Sorry, it's an emergency,' over her shoulder and ran on. The corridors were deserted. Where was everyone? As she approached James's room, she could hear strange noises and fear took hold of her. As she raced breathlessly in through the door, she saw a man in a white coat leaning over James as he sat in his chair. To her horror, she saw that he was holding a pillow in both hands...and seemed to be pressing it downwards...

'No,' she shrieked. 'What the hell do you think you're doing?' Panic enveloped her and without stopping to worry about her own safety, she rushed over and tried to pull the pillow out of the man's hands and away from James' face. The man turned and pushed her away savagely.

In a split second and with a sinking heart Katie recognised him. 'It's you,' she spluttered. 'Oh my god...stop it,' she pleaded.

Harold Hapsworth-Cole's face was contorted with hatred and fury.

Again Katie attempted to wrest the pillow from his grasp but it was useless as he was far too strong for her. He pushed her away again.

'Get out of my life, you...stupid, interfering, bitch.' Harold sneered menacingly at her.

'Please don't...killing him is not going to solve anything. Please...' At that moment Katie knew that mere words were useless. 'Help, help me someone?' she cried out in desperation, hoping that someone might hear her. 'Help me please?'

Katie's shouting finally seemed to get through to Harold's befuddled brain. He bellowed like an enraged rogue elephant and with eyes blazing madly, he turned to face her and dropped the pillow on to the floor.

In the meantime, James began to make small whimpering noises, but Katie, now being confronted with danger herself could not go to his aid, instead she called out to him. 'James, it's Katie, are you OK?' James' breath was now coming out in enormous painful-sounding bursts and there was no reply.

'You can't help him now, nobody can,' Harold said with the bloodlust still smouldering in his eyes and he once again turned his attention back to the object of his hatred.

'Mr. Hapsworth-Cole,' she foolishly found herself saying. 'Why don't we just sit down and discuss everything quietly and calmly?' Her voice sounded strained and distant, almost as if it didn't belong to her.

Harold reacted violently to her words.

'No,' he roared.

Katie could see the area around his temples pulsating rhythmically and the veins in his neck stood out like steel cords. Spittle had formed in the corners of his mouth and Katie had never felt so terrified of anything or anybody before. He continued to stare at her and his loathing swept over her like a huge black storm cloud: he was an animal trying to mesmerise its prey.

The hypodermic syringe which Harold had attempted to use on James earlier had fallen to the floor during their struggle. He stooped down to retrieve it. Katie tried to move, but he grabbed hold of her making any escape impossible. His fingers felt like a vice as he gripped her painfully by the arm and she tried hitting and kicking out at him, but it was useless. Madness had made him incredibly strong. He pushed up the material of her sleeve in order to expose a suitable vein…it was then that the full horror of her situation hit her. She glanced quickly over to where James was sitting sprawled like a broken doll in his chair. His chest was heaving desperately trying to allow enough air in to his lungs to keep him alive. Harold smiled down at her: he was actually enjoying this moment as he held the syringe over her arm.

'No you can't…you can't do this,' she sobbed hysterically. 'This is madness.'

Harold mouthed an obscenity and hit her hard around the face and she fell heavily to the floor. He immediately pinned her down with the weight of his body and at the same time held the syringe aloft once more. 'Keep still,' he said. 'This won't hurt a bit.' Then he began to laugh in short, disturbed, phobic bursts. Katie knew that any resistance would be useless and she looked at the door hoping against hope that someone would come. Surely somebody must have heard all the noise. She opened her mouth to scream, but he placed his other hand over her face and instantly smothering her cries. Katie felt that she was choking.

'Oh no you don't my little lady-friend. Please be quiet as I find all this noise quite upsetting.' Harold's face had twisted into an amused grimace. 'You need to know why I'm doing this, yes? Well, I'll tell you. It's truly amazing that we keep bumping into one another like this. You really are persistent...you with your interfering ways. If you hadn't found those bloody letters, I would have become the new owner of Epton Hall. Because of you, I stand to lose everything that I have ever dreamed of. I should have killed you the first time we met – that was very remiss of me.'

Katie looked up at his dreadfully contorted face and instinctively knew that she could expect no mercy from this man. Her eyes widened with terror as Harold continued speaking.

'And because of you, I cannot let my cousin live.'

Katie struggled and he gave another chilling laugh. He was really enjoying himself now. He was playing with her, just like a cat played with a mouse, before the final bite!

Harold was no longer civilised...he belonged to the primeval jungle and only wanted to kill. She could feel his hot, foul breath falling over her in waves. Nothing could save her now and she closed her eyes.

The door swung open and Stuart rushed into the room. For a split second, he looked mystified by what was going on.

'Katie...what on earth?'

Harold turned round and relaxed his hold on her. 'More of you...more of you,' he roared and his eyes glazed in confusion. 'Who are you? Are you after my money too?'

Katie opened her eyes and tried to get up. She felt sick with fear.

'Stuart. It's Harold Hapsworth-Cole. He was...'

'Harold, but...keep still, Katie. Don't do or say anything,' he warned.

'But Stuart, he was trying to kill James,' Katie shouted. As soon as the words had left her mouth, she regretted them. Harold reacted instantly to her outburst and he hit out at her sending her flying across the room. She curled herself up into a ball, sobbing hysterically. Her world was crumbling around her.

Harold's body was filled with adrenaline now, and his brain was functioning like an automaton. His eyes lit up with sadistic pleasure as he quickly reached into his pocket and withdrew the revolver...

...and the dreadful sound of the safety catch being removed stunned them into silence.

Stuart stared at the gun and without thinking about the consequences, he rushed at Harold. 'Why, you evil bastard.' But Harold was ready for him and stuck out his foot, sending Stuart sprawling across the floor. With surprising speed, Harold raced over to him and before he could recover his balance, kicked him sadistically and stamped down hard on his back, pinning him to the ground. Harold smiled once again and pointed the gun at the side of Stuart's head.

'This will teach you not to interfere with my plans. I'll take great pleasure in killing all three of you.' His hands were shaking as he waved the gun at each one of them in turn. 'All of you,' he repeated, his voice filled with malevolence. 'How could you take my Uncle Gerald's side in all this? He was a fornicator, an adulterer and as for his bastard son, well...'

His eyes turned towards his cousin. For a moment, confusion kept Harold rooted to the spot, as James began to stir. He groaned loudly and Katie cast a terrified look in his direction.

'Killing us is not going to solve anything,' Stuart interjected, trying to shift himself into a more comfortable position.

'Silence,' Harold roared, once more shoving the revolver

against Stuart's head and making him wince and cry out. Even from her foetal position on the floor, Katie could see and hear what was going on and she screamed loudly.

Suddenly, Nurse Allen rushed into the room, followed by two burly male nurses. Their appearance caused Harold to turn round enabling Stuart to scramble untidily to his feet. 'Be careful, he has a gun,' he warned.

Harold bellowed with rage. 'I warned you…you interfering imbecile. I'll take great…'

Meanwhile, one of the male nurses walked slowly towards him. 'Can I have that gun sir, before someone gets hurt?'

'No…keep away.' Harold was cornered and from the look of panic on his contorted features, he was uncertain what to do next. The other male nurse made a movement towards him, but it was too late, Harold noticed this from the corner of his eye and leapt towards him. They struggled violently as each of them tried to gain supremacy. Even though the nurse was the taller and heavier of the two, Harold was wrapped in his madness and exceptionally strong.

Meanwhile, Stuart raced to Katie's side and they clung to one another as they heard the terrifying and muffled sound of the gun going off. Katie closed her eyes, placed her hands over her ears, waited and prayed…

* * * * * *

Chapter Twenty-Eight

Harold finally fell to the floor leaving the male nurse lying in the middle of the room looking completely dazed and shocked after their fight for supremacy.

It was as if time had stood still and it was several moments before anyone moved. Nurse Allen was the first to react and she raced to the phone beside James' bed.

'Hello,' she said with real urgency in her voice. 'Get the crash team up to the Orthopaedic Unit, room 3, at once please. Someone has been shot, a patient needs urgent medical attention and three people have been injured. Please hurry.'

Nurse Allen then turned her attention to James and started to help him.

Katie's heart felt as if it would burst, when eventually Stuart struggled over towards the two men on the floor with a look of utter disbelief on his face. He looked pale and anguished and suddenly the enormity of what had just happened seemed to take over his body and he started to shake. Katie uttered a cry of relief and rushed sobbing to his side. She couldn't believe what had just happened and she couldn't believe either that they were now all safe. How could the thought of money turn a man like Harold into this...this pathetic creature who was now lying in a pool of blood that was gradually spreading across the floor?

They stood side by side looking down at the two injured men. Stuart looked at Katie and put his arms around her, completely cosseting her. 'My darling Katie, are you alright?'

'Yes...yes I am, but what about you?' Stuart was holding the left side of his ribcage and a bruise was rapidly spreading across his cheekbone.

'I'm alive, you're alive, James is alive. Our wounds will heal my darling, but I'm not sure about our memories. What an awful thing to have happened. Has this all been worthwhile, do you think?' he said looking down at Harold, whose face was deathly pale.

Katie shivered violently. 'I can't bear it, Stuart.' She turned away and walked towards James' bed. His lips were blue and his breath was still coming out in short, sharp bursts. Nurse Allen and the other male nurse, had helped him to get back into his bed and were busy fixing an oxygen mask to his face. Katie was aware that she ought to try to explain what had been happening. 'I...I found that man over there trying to suffocate James. His name is Harold Hapsworth-Cole and he's James' cousin.'

'His cousin?' was Nurse Allen's incredulous reply.

'Yes. It's a long story, I'm afraid. Is James going to be OK?'

'Yes, I'm sure he will be, but we'll have to get one of the doctors to have a proper look at him. All I can say is, it's a good job you came in when you did.' James moaned and opened his eyes. He looked around in shocked confusion and attempted to lift his head from the pillow.

'Don't try to worry yourself about anything at the moment James, we'll explain everything when you're a little stronger,' Nurse Allen crooned as she placed her hand on his forehead.

'But...'

'No buts.' James settled back on his pillow and closed his eyes.

While all this was going on, another male nurse was administering first aid to Harold. He was lying at a peculiarly crumpled angle on the floor and blood was still flowing from a nasty wound in his chest where the bullet had entered. He was still alive, although his breathing was shallow and each time he took a breath he let out a strange cry like a wounded animal.

A few moments later the emergency team arrived and Harold was taken downstairs to the Emergency Room. His three near-victims heaved a collective sigh of relief and looked at one another in dazed wonderment at still being alive.

Katie and Stuart then explained to the assembled medical team exactly what had occurred and throughout this time, James looked pale and shaken. He had a nasty bruise on the side of his head and his cheekbone was badly swollen and already showing the signs of severe bruising. His eyes were red-rimmed and puffy and mirrored the trauma and strain that he'd been under.

One of the hospital's doctors was soon at the scene and proceeded to examine each of them in turn.

'Mr. Butler, do you feel well enough to tell me what happened?' he asked sympathetically. James tried to answer him, but because of the severe bruising he had sustained during the attack, he found it difficult to speak. 'Well never mind, we'll talk later. I have to say that you're extremely lucky to be alive.' He stood up, folded his stethoscope and placed it in his pocket. 'A few more seconds and well…' Only James' eyes betrayed the fact that this particular piece of information had sunk in.

The doctor then turned his attention to Katie. She felt dreadful and couldn't seem to stop shaking and her head ached dreadfully. She sat in a chair feeling sick and completely bewildered. Had all this been her fault, she asked herself? If she hadn't found the letters, none of this would have happened. Her memory tried to shrink from it all, but she was still haunted by Harold's face as he had loomed above her with the syringe in his terrifying, but strangely smooth, hands.

'Well young lady, you look as though you've been in the wars too. I'd like to take a look at the side of your face first if you wouldn't mind?' He went on to examine her thoroughly. Afterwards he frowned and sat down on the edge of the bed.

'There's some quite recent scarring on your temple. Have you been involved in an accident recently?' Katie found herself having to recount and relive the trauma that she'd experienced whilst being trapped in the attic in Epton Hall. He shook his head in disbelief. 'I think that we have three very lucky people here, Nurse Allen,' he said as she began to tidy James' bed.

'Yes Doctor, you can say that again. And what Mr. Harvey is going to say about all of this, I can't even begin to imagine.' She turned to Katie. 'He's the big white chief, you know!'

Whilst they were speaking, Stuart had been walking up and down agitatedly with a worried look on his face. Katie looked at him with concern. 'Are you alright Stuart?'

'I…I think so…but I just can't seem to…'

'Sit down man,' the doctor said interrupting him, '…before you fall down.' Stuart did as he was told. The doctor examined him. 'Hmm, I think that we'll send you down to have some X-rays and perhaps an MRI scan: I'm not too happy about those ribs either. You say that Hapsworth-Cole kicked you?'

'Yes, he also stamped on my back, amongst other things,' Stuart replied bitterly.

'Right, don't make any sudden moves. I'll organise it with the X-ray unit straightaway and also get someone to bring you all a cup of tea: tea works wonders at times like this.' He smiled at them and left the room.

After all the hubbub had died down the three of them sat quietly for a while. Stuart was the first one to break the silence.

'My god, I can't quite believe this, can you?'

'No Stuart, I can't,' and without any warning, she burst into tears. 'I'm sorry. I can't stop thinking about it. I can still see him…I…'

'It's alright now Katie,' Stuart said trying to gather her into his arms. He winced. 'Thank goodness I came back when I did.'

'It was dreadful. You see I had a message saying that someone was on the phone down in reception. I raced downstairs but there was no telephone call. It was all so strange.'

'Then what did you do?'

'Well,' she sobbed, her words tumbling out in a rush. 'As I stood in the reception area wondering what was going on, I had what can only now be described as some sort of premonition – I've had them before you see and I've always been a bit of a dreamer – and I sensed that James might be in some sort of danger. I had another image of Harold's face in my mind...I put two and two together and realised that I had been tricked. He wanted to kill James and I was in the way. Without stopping to think I raced back upstairs. I found Harold trying to suffocate James with one of his pillows. I can remember calling out, but nobody came. I tried to stop him...it was horrible. Then he tried to kill me...he...he was going to use a hypodermic syringe on me. He said that he should have killed me the first time we'd met and I...I was petrified. I couldn't go to help James because I couldn't move...and...and if you hadn't come to pick me up earlier than we'd planned, I...I would have...' Katie finally took a deep shuddering breath. 'Then he started on you and I...I thought that he was going to kill you and I thought that I was going to lose you and...and...' Her shoulders began to heave.

Stuart did his best to try to console her, but his injury was hampering him. 'I'd had enough of walking about in the rain, so I thought I'd come up and introduce myself. When I saw what he was about to do to you, I just saw red. I didn't seem to care what happened to me, I only knew that I had to stop him.' He took out his handkerchief and tried to dry her tears. 'It's all over now Katie my love, don't distress yourself any more.'

'I feel as if all this has been my fault,' she added sniffing miserably. 'Trouble seems to have followed me around since I found those letters.' As soon as the words had left her mouth, she realised that she'd been a little insensitive. 'I'm so sorry

James,' she said, 'I didn't mean anything by that remark, it's just that...'

'I...I quite understand Katie, don't worry. The last few weeks have been traumatic for all of us. Now I...I'm even more indebted to you.' James' voice was weak and hesitant and he closed his eyes.

Nurse Allen came into the room carrying a tray. She looked carefully at each one of them in turn. 'Gee, we're all looking dreadfully sorry for ourselves, aren't we? But I'm sure that these cups of tea will help to calm you down.' She placed the tray down on to the table at the foot of James' bed and handed each of them a steaming cup. Katie sipped hers almost immediately and couldn't help pulling a face: the tea had sugar in it.

'By the way, Mr. Hapsworth-Cole is undergoing surgery at the moment. I've spoken to one of the theatre nurses and apparently the bullet did a lot of damage on the way in and actually bruised his heart. He's lost a tremendous amount of blood and it'll be touch and go whether he survives or not.' The young nurse's revelations created another stunned silence. 'And...I feel that I...I mean we, the staff, have to apologise to you all. We're sorry that we didn't come to your aid sooner. We were having an unofficial meeting.'

'An unofficial meeting?' Stuart said, his voice full of incredulity.

'Yes, over pay as a matter of fact. It only took about ten minutes. But, bearing in mind what happened, I think that we could all be in trouble right up to our little necks. Heads will definitely roll.' She held her hands out, palms uppermost and looked upwards. 'That's why we didn't hear anything. The two rooms either side of this one, are empty and the walls are well insulated.'

'I wondered why someone didn't respond to all the noise.' Katie replied.

'Unlike the rest of the hospital, we're not too busy at the moment. We honestly thought that it would be OK.'

'Sally,' James said. 'You really must not reproach yourselves. I cannot complain about any of the treatment I've had in this hospital, up 'til now.'

'Thank you James,' she said sheepishly. 'Would you like me to give your wife a ring?'

'Oh my…I should have let her know. I'd have thought about it myself, but right now I'm finding it a little difficult to concentrate.'

Nurse Allen interjected. 'Before I forget, Mr. Harvey would like to speak to all of you. I know that you've already told the medical team, but would you mind going through it all over again for him?'

'Well, we'll have to explain everything sooner or later won't we? But at least now it's still fresh in our minds,' Stuart added looking tenderly at Katie. 'Are you feeling strong enough?'

'Yes, of course,' she replied. A little colour was at last beginning to appear in her cheeks. She looked anxiously at Stuart. 'But what about you, he attacked you as well?'

'I'm fine, really I am.'

'Well if you're both sure, I'll tell Mr. Harvey that you're willing to talk to him.' She was about to leave the room when she remembered something. 'I'm sorry Stuart, I forgot to tell you that the doctor has arranged for you to have an X-ray and a scan in about ten minutes' time. So I'll take you down now. At least you will get it out of the way.'

After persuading Stuart to get in a wheelchair, Nurse Allen pushed him out through the door. Katie looked around her. James had fallen into a deep sleep and everything seemed strangely quiet and peaceful. Nobody coming into this room would ever have guessed that a drama of such magnitude had recently taken place. The pillow which Harold had used to try to suffocate James, had been taken away. The syringe which could have killed both of them, now lay in a kidney-shaped stainless steel dish on the table beside the bed and had been placed inside a securely tied plastic bag and the revolver...was nowhere to be seen. She shuddered when she remembered the sound it had made as it went off and all the telltale signs of blood had been completely removed from the floor. There would have to be some kind of an inquest on what had happened here today she supposed, and it would all have to be used as evidence.

She stooped to pick up one of James' books which had fallen unnoticed onto the floor. It was the one he was reading when she first came into the room. Books were so much a part of her life now and she was fascinated by people's choice of reading material. James' choice was easy to understand, it was all about English Country Houses. How different his life and the lives of his family would be now. He had lost his job and had little money saved for a rainy day. But now, a new world would be opening up for him and his family. They would have all the money they could ever have dreamed about. But try as she may, she couldn't quite see James living happily in Epton Hall along with all those dark, dusty rooms and that dreadful attic... Thinking about the attic made Katie feel strange again and she shivered violently and didn't hear Stuart as he came back into the room.

'Are you cold?' Stuart whispered gently in her ear and making her jump. 'If so, I think I have a way of warming you up.'

'Oh Stuart, I was miles away. I was back at Epton Hall and it made me feel quite odd for a moment.'

'I see that poor James is asleep. It's all been a tremendous ordeal for him.'

'It's been an ordeal for everyone. I was going over everything in my mind. Harold could so easily have killed all of us. And...and supposing he dies, what then?'

'You mustn't worry. We have witnesses to prove what actually happened, so try not to think too hard about it, my love.' He leant over and kissed her gently on the forehead.

'How did the X-ray and scan go?'

'They're looking at the results now, so it probably won't be too long before we know anything. I personally don't think that I have broken any ribs, but it's best to be on the safe side.' He grimaced as he changed position in his chair. 'Oh yes, and remind me not to have an MRI scan again, please: not a nice experience.'

The door opened and a man of about 55 entered the room. He projected an immediate aura of authority. He was of medium height and build and had his white hair cropped short. He wore a light grey expensive-looking suit and a pair of light brown Gucchi shoes. Overall he looked immaculate, right down to his gold rimmed spectacles.

Arthur George Harvey was a senior member of the staff and his main duty was to investigate anything which could potentially harm the hospital. He was an expert in calming troubled waters and was well known for taking his responsibilities seriously. Above all, he was not a man to be crossed.

'Good evening,' he said, his face betraying a hint of a smile. 'My name is Arthur Harvey and I hope that it's not too late for us to have a little chat? I've been briefed about what happened here this evening of course.' Katie looked at him: he was trying to make an effort to be conciliatory, she thought. 'The more I think about it, the harder it is to understand how such a thing could have gone on right under our very noses.' His manner became sickeningly obsequious as he continued. 'I can only say how sorry we feel, here at this hospital that such a dreadful thing could have happened. There has been a serious breach of security and the nursing station should never have been left unattended.

I believe that pressure of work and temporary staff shortages are partly to blame. But I can assure you that everything that can be done will be done to get to the bottom of it all. Will you please accept our sincerest apologies?'

His opening speech concluded, he cleared his throat, pulled up a chair and sat down.

By this time, James had woken up and was listening intently. Arthur Harvey took off his glasses and began to twirl them around as he spoke. 'I need to know exactly what occurred here tonight. I will have to make out a detailed report this evening so that the police and the hospital management can see it first thing tomorrow morning.' He looked at them all expectantly.

Yet again, Katie and Stuart had to recount their stories and Mr. Harvey made notes on a pad of paper underlining various points that he felt were important or relevant. When they had finished he was silent for a few moments. 'Thank you for being so candid. The police have already been here and have been given an outline of what happened here this evening. They decided that you had been through enough tonight, but they do wish to interview everyone involved tomorrow morning at nine o'clock. I'm sorry that you'll have to go through it all again, but we do have to get to the bottom of it and that way we can make darned sure that this kind of thing cannot ever happen again.' He said the last few words slowly. 'Have you anything else to add?' They all shook their heads. 'Well then, it only remains for me to officially check you all over – purely for my report you understand.'

He looked gravely worried as he examined each of them in turn. 'I know this has all been a great shock to you and believe me heads will roll. Security will have to be tightened and I'll set up an immediate Inquiry. Patients and indeed visitors must not and cannot be put at risk in this fashion,' he retorted vehemently. He turned to Stuart.

'Mr Wells, I have looked at your chest X-ray and the scan. It would appear that there are a couple of hairline cracks on two of your ribs, and some severe bruising, but otherwise everything seems to be OK. You must be extremely careful for a while.' He then turned to Katie.

'Miss Nicholson, bearing in mind that you have had another blow to your head this evening, and the fact that you may have been suffering from concussion after your previous injury, we feel that you should also have a scan this evening, just to be on the safe side you understand. I will arrange for it to be done in the next hour.'

Stuart's words just now about having the scan came rushing back to her. 'Oh, do you think that's necessary, only I...feel OK, really I do.'

'Yes, I do think that it is necessary, Miss Nicholson,' he said firmly.

'If everything proves to be OK,' Stuart interjected, 'can we return to our hotel this evening?'

Arthur Harvey shook his head. 'No, I would like both of you to stay here for the night just to be on the safe side. We can't be too careful in these cases. The nurse at the nursing station will be able to tell you where to find the rooms set aside for just such an emergency.' He looked down at the various notes that he'd made with a worried frown. 'I'll see you all in the morning,' he said walking towards the door. 'Oh, by the way, the reception area is now full of members of the Press, but we'll make quite sure that they don't disturb you in any way. Goodnight.'

Katie and Stuart were preparing to leave to find their rooms, when Sarah Butler arrived, looking deeply shocked and pale. 'James, honey,' she said rushing breathlessly over to his bed. 'Are you OK?' She looked around the room. 'I just can't believe what you've all been going through.' Tears filled her eyes as she lifted his hand and held it to her cheek. 'I went to a late night shopping mall and I met Betty Simpson, so we stopped for a chat over a cup of coffee. Nurse Allen told me what's been happening.' She shook her head in disbelief.

Kate and Stuart stayed and chatted for about an hour. It was generally agreed that their brush with death had been a little too close for comfort. Sarah sat by James' bedside hardly daring to take her eyes off him.

'Honey, are you sure that you're feeling OK now?'

'Yes Sarah. I'm still a bit sore, but I'll live.'

'Who'd have thought that your newly-found cousin would have done a thing like that? He must be a desperately disturbed and unhappy man.'

'You can say that again.'

'What shall I tell the boys?'

'Tell them everything of course.'

'But...'

James shook his head. 'No honey, just tell them how it is, but play it down a little. If I know anything about the media, it'll be common knowledge soon enough and I'd like them to hear the correct version.'

'Yes of course, I suppose you're right. When I came into the hospital earlier, the Press were there in force and it was becoming difficult to move anywhere.'

During their conversation, Katie had risen from her chair and had walked over to the window. She sighed deeply. 'Vancouver looks wonderful at night. I'd love to come back here again under less traumatic circumstances. Wouldn't you, Stuart?'

'Yes, my love, I would.' He turned round to speak to Sarah and James. 'Well, I don't know about you, but I've had too much excitement for one day. I'm absolutely bushed and everything is aching. I think that we'd better leave you two in peace and make our way to our room. What do you think Katie?'

'Yes, it's been quite a day and one I would not wish to repeat.

Apart from meeting you two of course,' she said with a wan smile. 'Goodnight both of you and I'm sure, like Mr. Harvey said, we'll all feel better in the morning.'

* * * * * *

Chapter Twenty-Nine

At 8.45 a.m. the following morning, Katie and Stuart were shown into a small room on the ground floor. James was already there sitting in his wheelchair. He was smiling and seemed quite cheerful despite his ordeal.

'Hi you two. How are you both this morning?' His voice was still sounding weak and he had dark circles underneath his eyes, which belied his false *bonhomie*. This brought home the reality of the near catastrophic happenings of the night before.

'We're bruised and tired, but relieved to be alive.' Katie walked towards James and placed her hand on his arm. 'I've just had the results of the scan I had last night. Everything seems to be fine, thank goodness: a lot of bruising, but nothing serious. But what about you?'

'Wow, how do I feel?' He looked heavenward. 'I feel tired but generally a lot better than yesterday and…tremendously relieved. I kept thinking about Harold and how bitter he must have felt about my mother and me. I just can't imagine having those kinds of feelings.' His voice faltered. 'Sorry, but my throat still feels as if it has been rubbed with sandpaper and I'm still a little wheezy.'

'Do you still want to talk?' Katie's concern for James was obvious.

'Gee of course, I wanna get it all off my chest. I've never been what you might call wealthy, but we've always been able to live well. But to even think about killing someone just for money is beyond me.'

Katie shook her head sadly. 'Yes, I know exactly what you mean.'

Suddenly, the interconnecting door between the two rooms opened and a uniformed officer walked in.

'Mr. Butler, do you think that you could come in first and tell us exactly what happened last night?'

'Yes of course. Well, here we go again,' he said winking at them as his wheelchair was manoeuvred through the door. It was immediately closed behind him.

When it came to Katie's turn, she gave her answers to the best of her ability, but in the cold light of day she felt that it had all happened to someone else, not her. It was all part of a bad dream, from which she hoped she would eventually awaken. The only thing that she was really sure about, was that every bone in her body seemed to be aching.

Stuart, in his turn, stood up gingerly, gave her a nervous smile and followed the police officer into the interview room. Katie watched him until the door was closed behind him. He was such a lovely man: he was loyal to a fault and she knew that he would always be there for her, unlike Simon Brand, and that they would face any problems which came their way together.

After the police had gone, they all went back up to James' room to join Sarah, who had arrived back at the hospital quite early. He was in reasonably good spirits and even managed to joke about one of the police officers, whose habit of standing to attention whilst twitching his nose like a rabbit had amused them all.

'Do you know I'm quite convinced that he didn't know he was doing it?' he said, suddenly twitching his nose. They all laughed and any tension which had remained after the ordeal of speaking to the police quickly disappeared. But before their laughter had a chance to die down, Nurse Allen walked into the room. She wore a serious expression on her usually happy and friendly face.

'Good morning everyone. I'm afraid that I've some

disturbing news for you. Harold Hapsworth-Cole died about fifteen minutes ago. The doctor treating him said that he had a massive post-operative embolism and there was nothing anyone could have done to save him.'

There was a stunned silence.

Katie was the first to speak. 'I can't believe it. I...I've been carrying the image of that awful man's face around in my mind ever since he locked me in the attic.' She experienced a tremendous surge of relief. It was like a curtain being opened and enabling the sun to shine upon her again. But it was also tinged with sorrow to think that someone like Harold had been so completely obsessed by greed and had lost his life because of it.

'The thought of all that money must have driven him totally insane,' Nurse Allen said quietly, 'nobody in their right mind would have done what he did.'

Sarah glanced tenderly in her husband's direction. 'I've came so close to losing you twice, honey. Thank heavens you're OK. I told the boys and they were really quite grown-up about it, but I suspect that they'll embellish it once they go back to school. They're coming in to see you this afternoon.'

'Thanks honey.' James sighed deeply. 'I can't believe that he's dead. I...'

Katie could see which way the conversation was going and said, 'Would you like us all to leave you in peace so that you can discuss things in private?'

'Of course not, no,' they both chorused.

Sarah then turned to her husband. 'You do realise don't you, that there's probably nothing to stop you from becoming the new owner of the Epton Hall Estate now?'

'Yes, Sarah honey, that thought had crossed my mind too. I can't help thinking and wishing that if Harold had been normal, we could have shared it: there was plenty enough to go round, and I had more or less made up my mind to write to him suggesting some sort of shared ownership. I'm quite sure that under normal circumstances, we could have come to some mutual agreement, but now, it's all ended in disaster.' He shook his head sadly. 'What a waste – just one more tragedy to add to the list. That branch of the family must have been truly cursed. When I get out of here, we'll have to hold a family conference to decide where we go from here.' He grabbed Sarah's hand and squeezed it so hard, that she winced. 'Sarah, I feel that we are the lucky ones, we have been given 'an out', so to speak. I feel that I should tell you right now that I'm happy living in Canada and if Epton Hall doesn't come up to scratch, I have no intention of dragging my family over to England.' His love for his wife, shone through in the smile that he gave her.

Sarah was quite overcome and tears began to roll down her face. 'Thank you, James. I really appreciate what you've just said.'

He turned his attention to Katie. 'I can't thank you enough for everything that you've done for us. The fact that you came close to being killed twice because of all this, leaves me for ever in your debt and yours too, Stuart. I hope that doesn't sound too formal, only I just don't seem to be able to find the appropriate words right now.' He looked away, almost choking with emotion.

'Well, it has certainly been an experience,' Katie replied.

'And it's something that we'll both be able to relate to our grandchildren in the far distant future perhaps?' Stuart said cutting in. He placed his arms protectively around Katie's shoulders. 'I think that you should both know, that two days ago Katie promised to become my wife. She probably hasn't had the time to tell you about it yet.'

'Well, I have been otherwise engaged you know,' she said with a twinkle in her eyes.

'Congratulations, both of you,' Sarah said grasping them both warmly by the hand.

'Yes, congratulations: at least some good has come out of your visit to our city,' James said.

Stuart looked at his watch and stood up. 'And now, I'm afraid that with all the excitement, we've almost forgotten that we have a plane to catch tomorrow morning, so we'll have to be going. Fortunately, the police have given us the all-clear to return home and will keep us informed if anything else develops, as they feel that it's all cut and dried. Do you think that you'll be fit enough to come over to England soon?'

'Yes, I suppose we ought to at least have a look at the estate,' James replied. 'I've never been to the U.K., but Sarah has.'

Sarah smiled. 'I have relatives living near London and I haven't seen them for years. How exciting!'

'Anyway, do let us know when you're coming over and we'll make all the arrangements regarding hotels etc., and we could even pick you up at the airport if you like, couldn't we Katie?'

'Yes, of course.'

Sarah rose from her chair. 'Thank you that would be wonderful. James and I have a lot of thinking to do, but you may be quite sure that we'll keep in touch and let you know what we decide to do. Once again, thank you for everything, and I can't tell you how grateful we are.'

Whilst this was all going on, Sally had been busying herself around James' room. She turned to Katie and Stuart.

'You say that you're returning to the U.K. tomorrow?'

'Yes,' Stuart replied.

'In that case, I feel that you should be examined by the doctor just to make sure you are fit to travel. I'll make arrangements for you, shall I?'

'Yes, of course, if you feel that it is necessary. Thank you Sally,' Stuart said. 'And Katie my love, we really must go back to the hotel, so we will say our goodbyes. I must say that despite everything that's happened, it really has been a pleasure meeting you both.'

Katie bent down and kissed James on the forehead. 'Goodbye James. We seem to have been through so much together in such a short space of time, and it would be wonderful to keep in touch with you, wouldn't it Stuart.'

'Absolutely, wouldn't have it any other way,' he said proudly wrapping his arms around Katie's shoulders.

'Right, that's a date then,' James said. 'You will excuse me if I don't get up, but I'm making you a promise that the next time you see me, I'll be standing and walking unaided.'

'We'll drink to that,' Stuart answered enthusiastically.

After making their final goodbyes, Katie and Stuart walked quickly from the room.

* * * * * *

Chapter Thirty

The 747 touched down smoothly at Heathrow and after taxiing down the runway, turned off towards the parking bays. Katie felt exhausted, and filled with a tremendous feeling of relief to be back home in England. She now felt safe. What a strange weekend it had turned out to be. Stuart had asked her to marry him and she had accepted. She'd been reunited with her aunt and uncle and she'd met James Butler and his family. They should both have been feeling on top of the world, but instead, because of Harold Hapsworth-Cole, they were feeling totally bewildered and bruised in both mind and body. Would they ever be able to come to terms with what had happened, she wondered?

She looked out of the small porthole beside her. She saw a man wearing large headphones and brandishing a large lollipop-shaped board. The sun was shining and life was going on around her as if nothing untoward had ever happened. Eventually the aircraft stopped moving. There was a mechanical clunk as the portable walkway was attached and the SEAT BELT sign was switched off. Suddenly everyone was standing up and retrieving their belongings.

Stuart turned towards her. His face showed some of the pain and strain that he'd been under. He held his hand over his ribs as he stood up and winced slightly.

'Well, Katie, we made it, didn't we?'

'Yes,' she sighed, 'we did.'

'Come on then. I feel the need to be back home and what I wouldn't give for a steaming hot mug of real English tea made with real English milk right now,' he said longingly.

'Mmm...me too. I can hardly believe that we're home. I've had enough excitement over the last few weeks to last me a lifetime. All I want to do is get back to normal.'

After walking through customs, they passed through some double doors and into the arrivals lounge. Brian and Brenda were waiting for them. Katie could see their happy, smiling faces amongst the throng of people milling around the barrier. Stuart steered their luggage trolley wearily over to where they were standing.

Unrestrained tears began to stream down Katie's face as she tried to put her arms around both of them at once.

'Hello. You've no idea how good it is to be back home.'

'What's all this, Katie?' Brian said looking surprised at her reaction. 'Why the tears? You've only been away for a few days.' He then saw the cuts and bruises on the side of her forehead. 'You haven't had another accident, have you?'

'Well,' she answered, 'not exactly.' They hadn't had time to let Brenda and Brian know about what had happened and they were obviously feeling concerned.

'What does 'not exactly' mean?' Brenda wanted to know. 'Everything went well over there, didn't it?' The young couple exchanged glances.

'No, it obviously didn't,' Brian concluded. 'I'd have thought that you'd be happy, after all it isn't every day that you get engaged to be married.'

Katie was about to answer him, when Brenda interrupted.

'Brian, do leave them for a minute. They've had a long and tiring journey and neither of them seem all that well, in fact they both look dreadful.'

'Yes we have had a tiring journey,' Stuart said, 'and it's not the only thing that we've had. Do you think we could get to the car and then we can explain everything to you on the way home?

The weekend turned out to be a bit like the Curate's egg – only good in parts: in fact, if I'm honest, it turned out to be a disaster.'

Brenda and Brian looked at one another in alarm.

'A disaster eh?' Brian sighed and hurriedly took hold of the luggage trolley. 'Come on, the car is this way.'

'I just can't believe it,' Brian said after listening intently to what Stuart had just told them. 'Do you mean to say that he actually tried to kill all of you?' He looked fit to explode which immediately alarmed Brenda.

'Brian, watch what you're doing: you nearly missed that red light,' she chided.

'I'm sorry, but it sounds like something out of a Hammer House of Horror movie.'

'Yes, that's precisely what I mean and he very nearly succeeded too.'

'Words fail me.'

The full implications of what might have been, suddenly dawned on Brenda. 'My goodness, you poor things,' she said in obvious anguish. 'I...I can't imagine what you've both been through. And there was I thinking that you were enjoying yourselves over there. What a dreadful man.'

'And now he's dead,' Brian said with some vehemence.

'He was completely out of his mind,' Stuart went on to explain. 'He'd become totally obsessed with the idea of owning Epton Hall and the estate over many years. And once James Butler appeared on the scene, well you can imagine how he felt when he realised that he might not be the one to inherit it all.'

'And because you were there at that time, his plan to kill James Butler failed. Well thank goodness all your injuries are not too serious.' Brian stroked his beard thoughtfully.

'So what happens to the Butlers now?' Brenda asked.

'Well, their lives have been completely turned upside down.

There will be a lot of legal points to be covered regarding James' claim to the estate and....' Stuart twisted in his seat and winced.

'Are you in much pain, Stuart? I have some aspirin in my bag.' Katie was aching quite a bit herself, but at least she didn't have any cracked ribs.

'No thank you my love. The doctor said that it would take a little while before it all knits together. I've just got to be careful that's all.'

'In the litigious society in which we now live, is there a chance that you could sue the hospital for negligence? It sounds pretty horrific when someone is screaming for help and all the staff are at an unofficial meeting,' Brian asked.

'Presumably the male nurse who was quite badly injured in the scuffle could sue the hospital, but personally, I'm just grateful that we are now back home and relatively unscathed. What do you think Katie love?'

'I agree with you. I just want to try to get back to normal as soon as possible. We'll probably hear eventually if any action is going to be taken anyway and the person most affected by this is James. The specialist and James' physiotherapist both said that there is a possibility that he might be able to walk again.'

'And if he does and he recovers sufficiently well for him to travel, they will come over to look at the house,' Stuart continued. 'They will then be in a position to decide what they're going to do in the future.'

'I can't help thinking that they will probably sell Epton Hall and continue living in Vancouver, Stuart,' Katie interjected. 'I can't see either of them wanting to move here.'

Stuart looked thoughtful. 'Yes, I'm inclined to agree, and he still has the problem of the car accident and whether the lorry driver will wish to press charges as well.'

'How awful for them both – on top of everything else I mean,' Brenda said. She looked at Katie, who was sitting in her seat with her eyes closed. 'You've both had quite a time of it.'

'Yes,' Katie said, opening her eyes. 'I'm all for the quiet life from now onwards. But I must say that despite everything, James and his wife Sarah are two really lovely people. I'm so glad that we were there for them. It's ironic, because James was actually thinking of contacting Harold to ask him if he would consider sharing the estate. Just think, none of this need ever have happened.'

'But don't forget that Harold was mentally unstable,' Stuart reiterated.

'And therefore not really responsible for his actions, poor man,' Brenda added.

'Well that's as may be,' Brian said. 'I hope that there wasn't a problem regarding the actual shooting, was there Stuart?'

'No. Fortunately it all happened in front of staff witnesses. The police questioned us separately and seemed entirely satisfied with each account of what had occurred, so we were allowed to come home. There will have to be an inquiry of course, but I think it will be pretty straightforward under the circumstances.'

They were just approaching the outskirts of Anston, when Brenda broke a rather long silence.

'Now listen both of you. We have some news too, don't we Brian?'

'Yes, we most certainly do.'

'Come on then, out with it?' Katie said, looking at their excited faces and wondering what they were going to say.

'I hope that you don't think that we're stealing your thunder or anything, but we...Brian and I, are getting married next Saturday morning. The ceremony will be held in the Register Office in Epton at 11.30 a.m. and we expect you both to be there. What do you think of that, then?' Brenda said with a broad smile on her face.

'Brenda, that's fantastic news,' Katie said. She couldn't

believe what she was hearing. Brenda and Brian were getting married and…she had waited for so long for this to happen. 'Oh…oh, I'm so pleased for you both, and of course we'll be there. You just try to keep us away,' Katie said as tears sprang into her eyes. 'And we don't mind one little bit, do we Stuart.'

'Of course not. Congratulations both of you. But I'm afraid our wedding will have to wait for a while until we can get ourselves organised. I want to save up a little money so that we can at least afford a decent honeymoon. And we've got to find somewhere to live.'

Katie looked at Stuart sharply. 'But you said that you didn't mind about my money. You…'

'I know what I said Katie,' Stuart replied rather too brusquely. 'But I've been thinking about it and call it stubborn pride if you like, I feel that I can't rely totally on your money.'

'It's really not a big issue, Stuart,' Katie said quietly. 'As I said before, it will help us…we could…'

'Did you have to bring that up again?'

'But you started it just now.'

'Katie, I don't want to talk about it. We're both tired and it is not a good time to be arguing like this.'

Brian and Brenda looked at one another in alarm.

'But…'

'Katie!' Stuart gave her a warning look.

'Look you two,' Brenda said looking slightly embarrassed. 'I feel guilty about talking to you about our plans before you are actually home, but you were so excited about your engagement, that I thought you would like to know about our plans. I'm sorry if…'

Brian interrupted her. 'There shouldn't be a problem about finding somewhere to live, because Brenda and I are now living in my house, so…that means Lilac Cottage is empty.'

'Yes, and I will be selling it in due course. You could both live there until you both make up your minds, couldn't you? You could even consider buying it!'

'We'd be more than interested Brenda, wouldn't we Stuart?'

Stuart remained rather tight-lipped as he replied, 'Well, we can certainly think about it.'

'Good. We'll discuss it further after the wedding,' Brenda said busily opening her handbag and pretending to sort out its contents.

'Thank you Brenda,' Katie said. She turned to look at Stuart but his expression seemed to be set in stone and her heart sank.

* * * * * *

Chapter Thirty-One

Over the next couple of days Katie tried unsuccessfully to put the weekend's horror behind her and in bed at night she tossed and turned wondering whether she would ever be able to forget what happened, especially the sound of the gun going off. It had been exceptionally loud and had reverberated around the room.

She was uneasy too about Stuart's reaction to the fact that she had more money than he did. He'd returned to his flat in Lewes for a few days, saying that he had a lot of unpacking to do and she missed him dreadfully. He had phoned her only once since then and she couldn't help remembering that he'd been unusually quiet when they'd said goodbye. Up until then, Katie had felt confident about his feelings for her. The last thing she wanted was that her money should become an issue between them. It wasn't as if she had a vast fortune, like the Hapsworth-Cole estate, was it? How could she get Stuart to see that it wasn't a threat to their future happiness? She knew that she couldn't ask Brenda for advice, because she was far too involved with her wedding plans, so how was she going to get around Stuart's stubborn, manly pride?

In the end, she decided to phone Helen in Penzance.

Katie was in an agony of suspense as she waited for her cousin to answer the telephone. She tried to work out what to say as she waited, but her thoughts were becoming so jumbled that when Helen finally answered, her words tumbled out of her mouth in a rush.

'Katie darling, hold on a moment. Just what are you trying to say? You've been across to Canada haven't you? What on earth happened out there?'

'Oh Helen, you've no idea how awful it's been,' she replied suddenly feeling deflated.

'You mumbled something about that awful man Harold, wasn't he the nephew of the owner of the estate where you were working?'

'Yes, he was and now he's dead.'

'He's dead?'

'Helen, have you got a few moments while I explain everything?'

'But of course, how could I not Katie darling. You sound so upset.' Katie took a deep breath and told her cousin everything. 'Wow,' Helen exclaimed. 'You don't do things by halves do you? I mean, how on earth could someone like you, get involved in such a thing? It makes my life here in Penzance sound positively staid.'

'Yes, it must seem like that to you. But at the moment staid would seem an extremely desirable position to be in right now and...'

'And? Come on my girl, I know there's more, so share it with me. A problem shared and all that.'

'Well...I...'

'Katie.'

'Helen, whilst we were in Vancouver, Stuart asked me to marry him and I accepted. It seemed like the most natural and marvellous thing in the world, but...'

'But what? Don't keep me in suspense. You two were made for one another that's obvious.'

Katie felt reluctant to air her problems even if it was with her cousin. It wasn't as if she was ashamed of anything, it was just that she knew that Helen had known Stuart far longer than she had. A little voice inside her told her that because of her long friendship with Stuart, she had to be the one to talk to about it. 'Stuart is unable to accept the fact that I have more money than he has. He kept going on about how we would have to wait to get married, so that he could save up enough money for our honeymoon and a home and…'

'Katie that's a man thing. Call it stubborn pride. He'll get over it.'

'But he went back to Lewes two day's ago and he's only phoned me once since then and he's not answering his phone when I ring him. I've left several messages. What am I going to do, Helen?'

'Nothing.'

'Nothing! Helen, I can't just sit here and do nothing!'

'You can. Stuart will be back at his flat and missing you, thinking about the money and feeling a bit of a fool. You mark my words in a couple of days he will have forgotten all about it.' Helen had quite a forthright nature and really believed in her ability to sum up various situations and this had stood her in good stead throughout her life. 'I wouldn't mind betting that by the weekend, he will have almost forgotten about it.'

'Oh, I hope you're right. How are things with you? Here's me moaning and groaning and I haven't even asked you how you are.'

'Me? I'm fine.' She gave a throaty chuckle. 'Actually, I'm more than fine Katie, I've got a new man and he's gorgeous. He's a farmer, comes from Penzance and paints in his spare time.'

'Helen, I'm so pleased for you. Forgive me for asking, but do farmers actually have any spare time?'

'This one does and he's also quite well off financially. His name is Andrew and apparently he has just inherited his father's quite substantial farm and that's how he finds…'

'…the time to paint,' they both chorused. Once their laughter had died down, Helen became more serious. 'Look Katie, don't make this money situation of yours worse, just give him time, he'll come round you'll see. So, can I go out and buy a new hat for the wedding then?'

'We haven't set a date yet, but you can be sure that your name will be on the top of the invitation list.'

'Good. Well that's all cleared up then,' Helen said briskly as though she'd cleared up the whole of the world's problems. 'Give me a ring and let me know how things turn out.'

'Of course I will. And Helen, thank you for listening.'

'Think nothing of it. See you soon love, bye.'

To help keep her mind off her problems, Katie became engrossed in helping Brian and Brenda with their wedding preparations. They didn't want it to be a large affair, but they had invited about forty people to the ceremony and to the small reception which was to be held afterwards at Brian's house.

On the Thursday after their return to England, Katie went to the offices of Messrs. Sharpe, Holyoak and Masters. She had a ten o'clock appointment with Penny Humberston.

Karen looked up and smiled as she entered the office.

'Hello Katie,' she said warmly. 'I've been told all about your trip to Canada. How are you now?'

'I'm well thank you,' she said glancing up at the ornate antique clock on the wall of the oak-panelled office. It was 9.45 a.m. 'I'm, sorry, I am a little early.'

'That's fine, Penny is having one of her quieter mornings – you must appreciate that they don't happen very often in this job, so we enjoy them all the more when they come. I'll see if she's ready to see you.'

Karen picked up a folder marked 'CONFIDENTIAL – Hapsworth-Cole/Epton Hall Estate' and rose from her chair. 'Won't be a minute.' She knocked on Penny's door and walked in. 'Penny, Katie Nicholson is here. Would you like to see her now?'

'Yes of course. Would you show her in please?'

Penny stood up as Katie entered the room. 'Hello Katie,

please sit down.' She gestured towards the seat in front of her desk. Before doing so, Katie had to remove a pile of papers on the chair and she placed them on a small table beside her. 'Oh, I'm sorry. There never seems to be enough room for anything here. Now then, are you feeling any better? Brian told me how dreadful you both looked when you got home.'

'Yes I am, thank you, although it was quite an ordeal actually.'

'I hope you don't mind, but I would like you to go over what occurred in Vancouver in greater detail. I've already had one or two telephone conversations with the Butlers' Lawyers, but I'm anxious to hear your side of the story.' Penny stretched her long legs underneath her desk and prepared herself to listen to what Katie had to say.

When she'd finished, Katie looked down into her lap with her hands clasped firmly together. 'As you can see, despite everything that's happened, we're both still alive and relatively unscathed, thank goodness.'

'Apart from a good deal of mental anguish perhaps?'

'Yes, that as well.'

Penny remained silent for a moment. 'Mmmm,' and eventually said, 'Who would have thought that Harold Hapsworth-Cole would have done such a thing? We know from Mr. Broadbent that there has been some evidence of mental instability in the past, but I'm quite sure that violence on this scale had never occurred before.'

She sat upright in her chair. 'Mr. Broadbent told me that after Harold's father Stanley, died, he asked the firm to check that he would be the next in line to inherit Epton Hall once Marjorie eventually died. He was able to confirm this, with the knowledge they had at the time of course. So Harold had quite a long time to glory in it. What he didn't realise was that he was in a no win situation once the letters had been found and even if he had managed to kill James Butler, the estate could conceivably have passed to his children.'

Katie shrugged her shoulders. 'It's all been such a waste hasn't it?'

'I'm afraid so. Anyway, I must say that I'm pleased to see you both back all in one piece. I wasn't sure about the advisability of you going to Canada in the first place, but Brian said that you were determined to go, so…'

'Well, as it turned out, it was a good job we did. Between us, we were able to prevent Harold from killing James.'

'And you very nearly got yourself killed in the process and as a result, there are quite strong grounds for suing the hospital for negligence, and that is the main thing that I wanted to talk to you about.'

'Penny, both Stuart and I agree that nothing would be served by suing the hospital, unless of course someone else does, but from our point of view, we would like to try to forget it all.'

'Well if that's how you feel. The main thing is that you're both safe. Now then,' Penny paused whilst she opened the Epton Hall file. 'There doesn't appear to be any further impediment to James' claim on the estate, although there are a lot of finer details to be looked into. I think we will soon be able to bring this whole sorry saga to a satisfactory conclusion.'

'It can't come soon enough for me.'

Penny stood up and reached across her desk to shake Katie by the hand. 'Thank you for coming in and I hope that it hasn't opened up too many painful memories for you. I'll keep you informed about everything that happens from now. I'll see you at the wedding on Saturday then.'

'Yes of course. I'm so pleased for them both.'

'It's wonderful to hear some good news for a change, isn't it? I understand that you and Stuart have recently become engaged too?'

'Yes, we have. We hope to get married in a few weeks' time.'

'Congratulations to you both and once again, thank you for your help. I must get on. Goodbye.'

As the day of the wedding approached, Brian seemed to become more and more worried that their carefully planned day wouldn't go smoothly. He nearly drove Brenda mad by checking everything several times. Consequently, Katie had to spend more time than usual at the book shop, but at least it kept her mind occupied and prevented her from brooding too much. Even so, she felt desperately worried and unhappy about the situation and whether Stuart would actually come to the wedding.

Saturday turned out to be one of those beautifully warm summer days when not one single cloud would dare to spoil the brilliant blue of the sky. But inside, Katie's stomach was churning and she was in an agonised frenzy. Stuart was late. In fact, she sat down on her seat in the register office, with an empty chair beside her. Why wasn't he here? Was he actually coming and was their engagement now over?

Just as Brenda and Brian were set to walk down the centre of the beautifully decorated room set aside for weddings, Stuart raced in looking hot, bothered and a little sheepish. He sat down beside Katie and breathlessly whispered an apology. Katie's heart thumped wildly as he spoke.

'I'm sorry I'm so late, but my car broke down. Katie, how can you forgive me? I know I should have phoned, but I'm here now and we must put everything behind us. Can we please?'

'Yes, Stuart, we can.' She tucked her hand into his. 'We most certainly will, but can we talk about it later? The ceremony is about to begin.' His loving smile gave her the answer she needed.

Brenda looked radiant in a peach-coloured dress and jacket, finished off with a small pageboy hat and a veil of the same colour. Her outfit was quite unlike anything that Katie had ever seen her wearing before. She carried a spray of white carnations, interspersed with lily of the valley and stephanotis and finished off with a beautifully tied blue ribbon. Brian wore a light grey suit and a blue velvet bow tie and much to everyone's amazement, he'd even had his beard trimmed for the occasion. It was obvious from the way that they both repeated their vows together, that they were very much in love with another.

After all the photographs had been taken, everyone returned to Brian's house to enjoy the feast that had been prepared for them by a local firm of caterers. The tables looked resplendent with beautiful displays of delphiniums, rudbeckia and lady's mantle and also continued the theme of white carnations, lily of the valley and stephanotis in small pots on the tables. The food was laid out in the form of a buffet. Whole salmon had been poached and laid out on trays, surrounded by sliced tomatoes and garnished with cucumber, lemon and parsley. A man stood behind a table serving slices of turkey and ham and the guests helped themselves to an array of salads. To follow, there was a choice between a huge bowl of fruit salad, strawberries and cream and two different pavlovas and other seasonal fresh fruit.

Once all the champagne had been drunk and the speeches had been delivered, Brian and Brenda mingled with their guests, both smiling broadly and enjoying being the centre of attention, especially amongst all their "bookish" friends. The room was filled with the noise of excited and happy people. Katie sat with a few friends for a while but deep down, she only had one thing on her mind.

She went to find Stuart.

She found him talking to Brian. They had their heads together like a couple of school boys and they broke apart when Katie walked towards them. Brian offered her another glass of champagne which she gladly accepted. In fact, she even felt a little light-headed but she was in no mood to worry about it. 'Brian,' she said as lightly as she could, 'would you excuse us for a moment, we'll talk to you again later.'

'Yes, of course my love, for you anything,' Brian said. He was obviously enjoying his day and she didn't want to spoil things for him.

They managed to find a quiet corner, because they both felt the need to clear the air. 'Stuart, why didn't you phone me?' Katie whispered with a worried look on her face.

'I don't know. I...' he replied, looking crestfallen. They spoke for several minutes about general things and the fact that they had been through a terrible time together was not mentioned at all. Eventually, Katie plucked up enough courage to ask him again.

'I asked you why you didn't phone me, Stuart.'

'I know. It's just...'

'Look we can't talk now, Brenda is on her way over to see us. Do smile Stuart please.'

'Ah there you are,' Brenda said happily waving a champagne flute around as she spoke. 'I've been looking everywhere for you. Brian and I are about to go. I've left the address of our hotel in the top drawer of my dressing table. I only wish to hear from you if there is a real emergency mind,' she said with a sparkle in her eyes. 'Yes and by the way, please make Lilac Cottage your home together whilst we're away and oh yes, Albert is spending his holidays in the local kennels. Perhaps you could look in on him just to see that he's not pining or anything?' Brenda gave them both a big hug. 'Bye Katie love and please don't get into any more trouble whilst I'm away, will you?'

'I'll try not to, Brenda. And don't worry about Albert, he'll be fine,' she assured her.

Ten minutes later, Brian and Brenda were ready to leave and all the guests were assembled outside to see them off. Brenda walked over to Katie, gave her another hug and handed her the bouquet of flowers that she'd been carrying. 'I didn't want to throw them as they generally get bruised when people do that and they are so beautiful.' She whispered gently in her ear, 'besides which I only wanted you to have it. It's your turn next my love and I hope your day will be as happy as mine has been.'

'I'm sure it will be Brenda and thank you for everything.' Deep inside Katie wondered whether their wedding would ever be a reality because their argument over money was beginning to sour things between them. She looked at Stuart and wondered what he was thinking. She knew that she hadn't known him for long and his expression seemed to be one of quiet acceptance, but was this a mask covering his true feelings? Was he about to end their relationship just as Simon Brand had done?

She shuddered.

Stuart put his arm around her shoulders protectively. 'Are you OK Katie, only you look quite pale?'

'No Stuart, I'm fine. Look, Brian and Brenda are about to go.'

There was a lot of excited chatter and the sound of 'Goodbye' and 'Bon Voyage.' Then someone shouted, 'Don't do anything I wouldn't do Brian,' which was followed immediately by great guffaws of laughter. Soon the happy couple were climbing into the waiting car and were quickly whisked away to their honeymoon destination.

Once they were back inside Lilac Cottage, Katie busied herself in the kitchen. She prepared coffee in two china mugs and stirred the contents slowly, her forehead creased with worry. She had tried to speak to Stuart during the day, but he hadn't been at all forthcoming. It seemed to her that he was undergoing some inner torment and once again Katie thought about the evening when Simon had told her about his affair with her best friend. She steeled herself for what she thought was going to happen, as she was not at all convinced that everything was well between them. She walked back in to the small but cosy sitting room, put the tray on to the coffee table and sat down beside him. She grabbed hold of his hand.

'Stuart?' she asked softly. 'We need to talk.'

'Oh yes. What about?'

'I'm worried about us.'

'What do you mean, worried about us?' Katie didn't answer. 'Hello, is anybody there?' he said waving his hand in front of her face. 'What are you worrying about now?'

'Did you…did you enjoy the wedding?'

'Yes of course I did, although blokes don't enjoy these things quite as much as you women do.' He picked up his mug and sipped it slowly.

'Is everything alright…you know…between us?'

'Yes of course. Why so many questions?'

'It's just that…you don't seem very happy, that's all. You do want us to buy this house, don't you?'

'Another question, Katie?'

'Well?'

'Followed by another,' he said suddenly standing up and proceeding to pace around the room with a troubled expression on his face. 'You asked me about the house? Well to be perfectly honest with you, I'm not really sure.'

Katie's heart missed a beat. 'You're still not on about the money are you, because if you are…?'

'Hold on a minute Katie. You're being unfair,' he said angrily.

'I'm being unfair?'

'Yes, you didn't tell me about it, did you?' He turned his back on her.

'I didn't tell you because I thought that you might be upset.' Tears began to form in the corners of her eyes as a dark cloud of hostility hovered between them.

'Well then, you were right weren't you?'

'Stuart come on, don't let's argue about it. It's not worth it. I can't understand…'

'What, that I have no desire to be a kept man? You bet your sweet life I don't,' he retorted.

'Now you're being unfair,' Katie shouted.

Stuart walked away from her. 'I'm going to sleep in Brenda's spare room tonight because we have both got a lot of thinking to do. Goodnight.' He walked out of the room. Katie was left sitting on the sofa with her mouth wide open and immediately burst into tears: Brenda and Brian's happy day for her, was completely ruined.

Later, upstairs and alone in her bed, she couldn't sleep. Why did nothing ever seem to go right for her, she wondered? I seem to take two steps forward and then one step backwards all the time. How can I make Stuart see sense? A lot of couples have a really hard time when they first get married. That wouldn't happen to us, she thought miserably. Providing of course, that he now still wants to marry me or I him, come to that? Doubts crowded into her mind, which she desperately tried to brush away.

When she awoke next morning, she went downstairs and knocked on Stuart's bedroom door. There was no reply. She opened the door cautiously.

The room was empty.

Katie sat on the edge of the bed and cried. Once again her life had been turned upside down.

On Sunday afternoon the phone rang in Lilac Cottage. Katie raced downstairs to answer it. It was Stuart and he sounded subdued.

'Hi,' he said.

'Hi. What happened to you last night?'

'Katie, I'm so sorry. I couldn't sleep, so I drove back to the flat. I was pretty steamed up you know. I've er…I've had time to think about us.'

'And…' Katie's heart sank. This is it, this is the big heave-ho, just like Simon, she thought.

'I realise that I have behaved like a two year old. I love you Katie and I love Lilac Cottage too. If it makes you happy, I'll do anything.'

'Stuart, I was so worried when I found that the bedroom was empty this morning. I thought that you'd gone for good.'

'I'm really sorry. I can't believe how stupid I must have seemed to you. Can you forgive me?'

'Yes, of course I forgive you.'

'Katie, I promise that I will never ever do anything as immature as that again. Is that a deal?'

'What do you think? I love you too remember. But Stuart, I can understand how you feel, but what made you change your mind?'

'I…' he hesitated. 'I phoned my parents this morning and I told them about our engagement and they were really pleased. I…I also told my father about the money.'

'What did he say?'

'He laughed. In fact he told me not to be such a bloody fool of course. He said that money was extremely tight when they were first married and it put a tremendous strain on their relationship, so much so, that they nearly broke up because of it. He said that we were lucky.'

'Well we are, aren't we?'

'Yes, and I am only just beginning to realise how lucky.'

'So there are no regrets then?'

'None at all my love. I'm sorry. I was being incredibly petty, proud and stupid, especially after what we've both been through together. What must you have thought of me?'

'As I told you just now, I love you. I suppose arguing over something relatively trivial, is symptomatic of the strain that we've both been under. Stuart, I'm so relieved that we've been able to sort it out. I couldn't bear the thought of something like this coming between us.'

'Neither could I. Thank god I phoned my parents when I did. They made me see sense and they have actually invited us over to dinner next Saturday, ostensibly to quiz us about our wedding plans. Mum is already talking about a new outfit. Anyway, enough of all this: I'm putting the phone down now and I'll be with you in…no time at all my darling.'

'I'll look forward to that, but please drive carefully.'

'I will. Bye my sweet one.'

Half an hour later, Stuart and Katie stood together in the hallway of Lilac Cottage.

'I'm sorry, really I am. I don't…'

Katie didn't let him finish his sentence. She kissed him fully on the lips. 'That subject is taboo from now onwards, OK? Forgiveness all round?'

'Yes my darling, forgiveness all round. I must be the luckiest man alive.' He took her in his arms and kissed her passionately.

All Katie's doubts and fears evaporated. 'I've prepared lunch for us both,' she said breathlessly. 'Do you want it now, or…later?'

'I think that it had better be later, don't you?'

'Mmm…yes,' Katie replied softly. She started to climb the stairs, turned round to face him and slowly beckoned him upwards.

* * * * * *

Chapter Thirty-Two

Vancouver

James stared hard at Sarah. She was standing about six feet away from him and he tried to concentrate on her face. She was so beautiful and despite the fact that he was desperately trying to learn to walk again, the thing uppermost in his mind was how much he loved her. Sarah was his absolute ideal and he had to be close to her. He pushed down hard on the arms of his chair and with his hands taking his weight he managed to lift himself a few shaky inches from his chair. Come on, he told himself forcefully.

His legs felt all wobbly, but he could feel the muscles in the backs of his legs hardening slightly. All he needed now was one more supreme effort and he would be standing with his beloved Sarah. James' heart thumped wildly in his chest and the sinews in his arms stood out in relief as they took the strain. Pain shot through him, then he could feel the adrenaline flowing throughout his whole body…and excitement began to take over.

To his surprise, James found that he was standing unaided.

He continued to fix his eyes on Sarah's face. She was smiling at him…loving him, encouraging him. I'll do it this time dammit. He had never wanted to do anything so much in his life before. His whole world now depended upon whether he could now start to move his feet.

Right from an early age, he'd been a determined kind of guy. He'd been determined to make something of himself, despite the fact that he didn't have a father like all his friends. And because of that, he had always worked just that little bit harder at whatever he was asked to do, just so that his mother would feel proud of him. He had been determined to carve out a career for himself and to meet someone like Sarah. And he had been successful hadn't he? It hadn't been his fault that his friend's company had folded and he'd lost his job. But it had been his fault when he'd careered across the road and hit that darn truck...

For two long weeks, he'd worked hard at the exercise programme the physiotherapist had worked out for him. Today he actually felt stronger mentally and physically and concentrated first on one foot and then the other, testing his resolve. It now all felt so right. He focused on his right foot which had always been the stronger of the two. Keep calm, you must keep calm, he told himself. You can do it, you know you can.

Almost without any warning, his foot moved forward about an inch.

James felt an elation which he could never have described to anyone. After all, walking was an automatic thing, wasn't it? You learned how to do it when you were a child, so it was easy. You got up in the morning, you shaved, you showered, you mowed the lawn, or ran for a train. It was all taken for granted. He now knew that people in wheelchairs couldn't do that. They had to rely on other people; people who, in their ignorance, thought that if you were disabled you were somehow deaf or stupid and sometimes even both. His heart thumped even louder in his chest. Perspiration bubbled up on his forehead, as with sheer determination and grit he managed to move his other foot forward too. It wasn't exactly a step, but a curious sort of shuffling movement, but it was surely the start of something.

Standing a few yards away from him, Sarah was praying and willing him onwards – James could see it in her eyes. He'd tried hard several times in the last week, but each session had ended in bitter disappointment and failure. Now Sarah was here to watch him.

'Come on James,' she said. 'Keep going honey. You can do it, you know you can. You're nearly there.'

'Yes I can, can't I?' he said gritting his teeth. 'Phew this is exhausting.' He stopped for a moment to catch his breath. Again he lifted his right foot from the ground: it wavered and then moved forward again...and excitement raced through him. He swayed as his long weakened legs took the unaccustomed weight of his body and almost immediately he took another step forward. 'Sarah, I'm nearly there.' He let out a whoop of delight as his feet began to obey, albeit clumsily, his desperate will to walk again.

Sarah stepped nearer to him, holding out her arms. He had to reach her. He took a few more stumbling faltering steps...and...and suddenly they were standing together. They embraced as if for the very first time. 'Oh Sarah, I just knew that I could do it this time,' he sobbed. 'I'm sure it was because you were standing there. You gave me the confidence and impetus I so desperately needed to succeed,' he uttered breathlessly. He clung to her and took her face in his hands and kissed her. Their tears blended: it was the happiest day of James' life.

Gaby Johansson, his physiotherapist, was watching this drama as it unfolded in front of her. She stood up and clapped her hands.

'Well done, James. I knew that you were getting stronger, but even I didn't think that you could actually walk just yet. Well done.'

'I can't believe it either, Gaby.' His eyes filled with tears of joy.

'I'm quite sure that there'll be no looking back now. But that's enough effort for one day. Now, you must go home and rest and I'd like to see you again tomorrow, if that's OK? I know that you're not due to come here again for two days, but I want you to come in tomorrow, to see if your progress can be maintained. Make sure you do your exercises this evening mind.'

James had come to know Gaby quite well over the past few weeks and he gave her a look of pure affection. 'Thanks a lot – I know that I couldn't have done it without your help and encouragement. I don't know what else to say.'

'Just you make sure that your walking continues to improve and that'll be thanks enough for me. I'll see you at ten tomorrow morning.'

A week later, James was sitting in his favourite armchair reading a newspaper, when the phone rang in the hallway. He called out to Sarah. 'Honey the phone's ringing and I haven't got my cell phone with me.' There was silence. 'Sarah, can you hear me?' He soon realised that she was still out in the garden putting in some new plants, so she hadn't heard anything. The ringing stopped. A few moments later, it started again.

James was growing stronger every day. His leg muscles were beginning to respond to the demands that he now placed upon them. Could he reach the phone before it stopped ringing again, he asked himself? It was no great distance, just a few feet that was all. He grabbed hold of the walking stick which stood beside his chair and stood up. Carefully and deliberately he walked out of the sitting room and into the hallway. It seemed to take an age and yet the phone continued to ring. His heart was beating like a drum with the sudden exertion and unaccustomed exercise until finally he reached the hall table and grabbed hold of the phone.

'Hello,' he said breathlessly.

'Hi James, how are you?'

He quickly recognised the voice of his lawyer, Brad Dainton. 'I'm feeling really great as a matter of fact Brad, thanks. What can I do for you?'

'Well things have been moving quite quickly this end and I

thought that I oughta phone you to tell you about it. I was just about to ring off – I thought there was nobody at home.'

'Glad you didn't. So what's happening?'

'Well, the last papers that you signed have now gone over to England, so things should soon come to a head. How's the walking coming along?'

'I think the walking is coming along just fine.' James was still shaking from the effort of walking to the phone, but he wasn't going to admit his feeling of weakness even to a good friend like Brad. 'I actually walked from the living room into the hall to answer the phone.'

'Wow, there'll be no looking back now fella,' Brad replied, obviously delighted at his news. 'Look, I've had another letter from the Hapsworth-Cole's lawyers in England and everything seems to be going well. There are only one or two more ends to tie up and it will all be settled.'

'Thanks Brad. That's great news.'

Brad was silent for a few seconds. 'James. I know that you said that your walking was coming along just fine, but do you think that you'll be fit enough to travel over to England in a couple of weeks? It would be a good idea if you could go, because there are a few outstanding problems regarding the Estate that can only be settled by you being there, if you get my drift? By the way all the books in the house have now been valued'.

'Good. How much for?'

'James, are you ready for this?'

James' heart began to pound. This was turning into a good day he thought. 'I...I...think so Brad. Go on.'

'Now remember that this is in pounds sterling and not Canadian dollars.'

'Yep.'

'It's just a cool £150,000 and that's without the actual house and contents – you know the furniture, pictures, china etc. and all the land and property involved, including tenants' farm buildings and houses. You're looking at a fortune!'

'No kidding? Wow,' was James' surprised and delighted reply. 'You wait until I tell Sarah and the kids.'

'Knew you'd be pleased. Anyway what do you think about going across the pond to England? Do you think that you'll be fit enough?'

'Brad, I'll make myself fit enough. OK?'

'Fine, that's what I hoped you'd say. Oh yes, and there's one more thing. The driver of the truck that you collided with during the accident has apparently decided not to press charges. Your insurance covered all the damage to his truck and he regarded his injuries as being at most superficial. He felt that you'd been through enough. He also sent you his best wishes, which I must admit is quite a departure from the norm I can tell you. I wish all these sorts of cases could be concluded so amicably.'

'It's getting better and better, Brad, thank you.'

'It sure needed to. Anyhow I'll look forward to hearing from you then. Bye.'

Soon after James had replaced the phone on the table, Sarah walked into the hall. Her hair was untidy and she had a smudge of dirt on the end of her nose. There was a questioning look on her face, midway between concern and amazement. He thought that she'd never looked more beautiful.

'James honey, what are you doing out here?'

'What do you think I'm doing? I was answering the phone, didn't you hear it ringing?' He grinned at her smugly.

A look of wonderment passed over Sarah's features. 'No, I've been at the bottom of the garden sorting out the compost heap.' She continued to stare at him and then she began to bite her lower lip – something she always did when she was agitated or nervous. He could see that she was having great difficulty in remaining calm.

'I don't know where my cell phone is, so I walked out here to answer it.' By this time he was oozing confidence and even teasing her.

'You mean you walked out here on your own?'

'Yup.'

'Who...who was it?' she finally stuttered. Before he could answer her she ran over and hugged him. 'James, when you took those first tentative steps last week, I could hardly bear to hope that one day you'd be able to do such an everyday thing again. I'm so happy, I could cry,' she spluttered as tears cascaded down her face. 'And I can't wait to tell the boys, they'll be so excited.'

'No honey,' he replied suddenly looking stern.

'James, what do you mean? Of course we must tell them.'

'We won't tell them because...I mean to show them when they get back from school.'

'Yes, but you mustn't tire yourself so come and sit down again,' she said taking his arm.

'No,' he replied firmly. I want to walk by myself thanks.' With the aid of his stick, he walked slowly back to his chair. He felt exhausted and elated all at the same time. Once he was safely ensconced in his chair, he smiled and looked up at Sarah who was hovering over him, not quite able to take everything in. 'Sarah, now that my body has remembered how to walk, I can't possibly sit down here for long periods. I have to keep moving in order to build up the muscles in my legs. Besides which, we have to prepare for a long journey.'

'James, do stop being cryptic. What are you talking about?'

'Sarah, we are going across to England in two weeks' time.'

'We're what?'

'We're going to England.' James flicked at an imaginary speck on his trouser leg.

'But James...do you think that you'll be fit enough to travel all that way? I know that there must be a need for us to go over at some stage, but it seems an awfully long and tiring journey for someone in your condition.'

'Yup, I do. In fact I have to think it.'

'And what about the boys? Could we take them with us?'

'I hadn't really thought about that, but I don't think that they should miss any schooling as it's an important time for both of them.'

'I agree. But they'll be so disappointed if we do go, James.'

'Of course we'll go. In two weeks' time I'm convinced that my walking will have improved and I'm getting stronger each and every day. Don't underestimate the determination of your old man to get completely back to normal, well as near normal as possible.' He grabbed hold of her hand and squeezed it. 'What a day huh?'

'Yes honey, what a day!'

'And perhaps your sister would be prepared to look after the boys for us? Remember that she did offer to have them whilst I was in hospital.'

'So she did,' Sarah said with a relieved smile.

'And don't forget that we'll be able to take them over there on some other occasion, after all, money isn't going to be a problem for us in the future thanks to my dear father. Shall I ring Katie and Stuart and give them the good news?' He started to rise from his chair, but Sarah's hand pushed him down again.

'No James.'

'What do you mean, no?' he said feigning disappointment. 'Getting our own back, are we?'

'Of course I am. I want to do it, silly.' She laughed and ran out of the room.

James sighed. His mind drifted back over the last few months. Who would have thought that so much could have happened to him and his family: the loss of his job, the accident and the appalling prospect of never being able to walk again, but worst of all was the horrific time he'd shared in the hospital with Katie and Stuart. Whenever he thought about it, he went cold. Harold's death had been so unnecessary. It had been a nightmare from which he thought he would never wake. But fate, or his guardian angel had seen to it, and had decreed that his future and that of his family would now be assured. He would have to learn to put away his feelings of betrayal from his friend and former employer and his regret over his cousin Harold's insane jealousy, and instead look forward to a new and different life. He smiled and settled down in the comfort of his armchair knowing that if he really wanted to he could stand and walk. He listened to Sarah's excited voice as she spoke on the phone.

If only he had been allowed to meet and get to know his father, he thought shaking his head sadly. But it just wasn't meant to be. At least now he could think about him as a real and living person and not some faceless individual who'd had an affair with his mother and then deserted her. His father had been misguided certainly by having the affair in the first place, but both of them had tried to do the right thing by putting a large ocean between them and who was to say how difficult a decision that had been? Would he have had the courage to come to such a conclusion himself, he wondered? Somehow he doubted it.

James' mind turned to Katie and his cousin, Harold. They were the key figures in this drama. What if Katie had never found the letters and what if Harold hadn't been on the verge of madness? But, Katie did find them and everything that had happened since was all part of the great scheme of things.

Sarah walked back into the room her face full of smiles.

'Guess what, Katie and Stuart are getting married in three weeks' time and that will coincide with our visit. We've been invited to the wedding. Apparently a written invitation is on its way. I'm so pleased for them both and we must never forget how much they've been through on our behalf.'

'As if,' James replied with a rueful smile. 'And life for all of us is suddenly getting better and better, honey.'

* * * * * *

Chapter Thirty-Three

Katie stood excitedly in front of the Terminal 3 arrivals barrier at Heathrow Airport. James and Sarah's Air Canada flight had landed about thirty-five minutes earlier and a stream of weary travellers were pushing their trolleys through the swing doors and out into the arrivals lounge. She tried to read the labels on the luggage as people walked by to see if they were from the Vancouver flight, but they were all moving too quickly.

Suddenly, she thought she saw Sarah. She lifted her hand in an excited gesture, but it wasn't her. The girl turned round and waved to somebody else in the waiting crowd. Stuart looked down at her and smiled. 'It won't be long now I'm sure, unless of course there's a hold up in the baggage hall. Do you remember the way some of the cases managed to get caught up on the moving ramp and created a log jam when we came back home?'

'Yes, I do remember,' she said, pulling a face. She couldn't wait to see James and Sarah again. The dramas they had all shared had created an unbreakable bond between them.

'Look, there they are,' Stuart cried. 'I don't believe it, James is walking! Look Katie.'

'So he is. Sarah didn't say anything about it when she phoned. I just bet they wanted to surprise us.' Sarah was pushing a trolley with one hand and holding James' arm with the other. And he of course, was looking immensely pleased with himself and looked up when he saw Katie and Stuart waving frantically from behind the barrier and waved back.

Once all the hellos and embraces were over, they made their way slowly to the car park chattering excitedly as they went.

The journey back to Anston was a noisy one, as they all wanted to speak at once, mostly about James learning to walk again. He sat comfortably in the back of the car explaining how he had felt when he'd taken his first steps. Finally he said, '…and it was Sarah and the kids that helped me in the end – they were relying on me so much and you have no idea how far away Sarah seemed during those first tentative steps.' He looked lovingly in her direction as he described his feelings at that time.

'You see, it was not just the fact that I was moving my feet, it was as if I was joining the human race again. I know that this sounds melodramatic, but it's how I felt. Being in a wheelchair kinda makes you feel like a second-class citizen and people talk to you as if you're at best deaf, or at worst stupid and I was neither of those things.'

Sarah joined in. 'Katie, you've no idea how agonising it all was and yet at the same time, it was wonderful. I could see the pain and the joy on his face as he struggled to reach me. I thought that he was going to fall every time he took a step, but he didn't. I knew that I couldn't help him: he had to do it all by himself and he did, he did.'

'After that something seemed to click,' James interjected. 'It was as if my mind had suddenly remembered how to do it. I'll always walk with a limp, but anything is better than being stuck in a wheelchair, believe me.' James paused for a moment and looked out of the car window as all the English countryside sped by the car window. 'And now I'm here. I must say it all looks quite beautiful, but oh so small.' Everyone laughed.

'We're nearly there,' Katie said. 'We've booked you a room in a small hotel called the Black Fox. It's extremely 'olde-worldy', you know oak-beams, the works and the food is superb.'

'As we weren't sure when you wanted to go to see Epton Hall, we haven't arranged anything,' Stuart explained as he negotiated the sharp bend which lead into the Hotel's car park, '...but Penny Humberston did say that she could arrange for the housekeeper to show you around. Just let her know the day and time and she'll do the rest. Well, here we are. May we be the first to welcome you to Anston?'

'Thank you,' Sarah replied. 'It'll be nice to stop moving and to sample our first cup of real English tea.'

They all climbed out of the car and Sarah stood quite still and looked up at the old building, 'Why it's beautiful.' She wore a rapt expression on her face. 'That's a Wisteria isn't it? James look at the thickness of the branches, especially the lower ones. It must be very old.'

'Yes, I believe that it was planted over one hundred years ago,' Katie explained. 'Anyway come inside and we'll introduce you to the owners. Then I think we'd better leave you both to settle in. You must be exhausted after your long journey.'

'And I'd certainly like a nice long shower, or better still, a relaxing spell in the tub. Airline johns are not renowned for their size are they?' James quipped.

Sarah obviously had something on her mind and she hesitated before going inside. 'Katie, as you know Epton Hall so well, we were wondering whether you would like to help show us round?'

A cold shiver suddenly ran down Katie's spine. She remembered the last time she was in the house only too vividly. 'Sarah, I'm sorry but I'm not quite sure that...'

'Oh come on, please say that you will.'

'Well there are a lot of rooms that I didn't go into. It's such a rambling old place and I...'

'Katie, it'll be such an exciting time for James and me and, we'd like you to share it with us. Anyway, think about it and we'll talk later. Come on.' They all walked through the doorway and into the hotel and James somehow managed to get his walking stick tangled up in some greenery which was creeping across the floor from a large earthenware pot.

'Darned awkward thing this is. I think that I'll have to dispense with walking sticks quite soon.' The others glanced at one another and smiled. Once all the introductions and form filling had been completed, James and Sarah said goodbye and made their way up to their room.

Katie and Stuart drove back to Lilac Cottage in silence. Their earlier conversation about visiting Epton Hall had rekindled Katie's fears. Since the time she'd spent in the house, she had felt adamant that she would never set foot in it again, ever. Despite the fact that she knew Harold Hapsworth-Cole was dead, the thought of physically going there again filled her with abject horror. For the first time in weeks Harold's face and especially his eyes, began to frighten and trouble her.

Stuart parked the car in the lane and they walked arm in arm up the path and into the cottage. He flopped down on the settee and looked up at her questioningly.

'Come on love, tell me what's bothering you?'

'Sorry, what did you say Stuart? I was miles away.'

'Yes, I know you were.' He pulled her down on to the cushion beside him.

'It's just that...'

'What's up Katie? You were so happy earlier.'

'You will probably think that I'm being silly Stuart, but...but all that talk about visiting Epton Hall with Sarah and James, has made me remember all the bad things that happened there that's all. Sarah seemed quite adamant about me being with them when they look around the house.'

'And you don't want to go back there again, is that it?'

'Yes,' she replied in a small voice.

'I think that you should go with them, otherwise you will never get over it.'

'I know you're right, but you've no idea what it was like

being trapped in that house. It was awful. No it was more than awful, it is one of the most terrifying ordeals of my life, apart from what happened in Vancouver, and I never, I repeat never, want to go through anything like it again.'

'But darling, that's all in the past. Harold is dead.'

'You don't understand, Stuart. At the time I was convinced that I would never get out of that attic alive. I was petrified at the thought of him coming back and finishing what he had started and...'

'Katie don't,' Stuart said firmly. 'Stop torturing yourself, he died in a hospital room in Vancouver and there is no way that he can ever hurt you again.'

'I know that but...' she said biting her lower lip.

'To my mind you only have one alternative and that is to go back to the house and put all those ghosts to rest once and for all. We've both got much more important things to worry about, haven't we? Remember our important date in the Parish Church in a few days' time?'

Katie knew that she was being unreasonable, but she was extremely scared at the thought of seeing the house again, yet alone entering it. She looked at him and saw that his face was beginning to show the strain that he, like her, had been under.

'I'm sorry,' she whispered. 'Of course I'll go to Epton Hall with James and Sarah. I must go for both our sakes and Stuart,' she said with her fingers firmly crossed, 'would you come with me, please?'

'Of course I will. I was intending to come with you anyway.'

'Thank you Stuart. And...'

'What?'

'How could I possibly forget about our wedding day? I love you so much Stuart.'

'And I love you too.' He put his arms around her shoulders and kissed her gently.

'Well I'm glad all that is out of the way, so can we now change the subject?'

'Yes please.'

'It was lovely to see Sarah and James looking so happy and I can't get over how well he's walking now. His accident and his injuries were really serious and to my mind it is nothing short of miraculous that he's doing as well as he is.' He stopped speaking and stared deeply into Katie's eyes. 'We have known one another for how long, a couple of months?'

'Yes?'

'In that time, we seem to have gone through a lifetime of problems, but I'm promising you here and now, that once we're married, everything is going to be plain sailing and I'll let nothing get in the way of our happiness, do you hear?'

'Yes Stuart, I hear you.'

'By the way, have you heard from Helen? I was feeling a little worried when you didn't get a reply to the wedding invitation. It's just not like her to let things slide.'

'Yes, a reply came this morning. She'd forgotten to tell us that she was going up to the Lake District for a few days. She only got back two days ago.'

'And did she say who she went with?'

'Someone called Andrew Baker. Do you know him?'

'No. He's not one of the usual crowd.'

'I wonder if he'll be Mr. Right?'

'Why are you so interested in marrying everyone off, Katie? First Brian and Brenda and now Helen.' Stuart threw his head back and laughed.

'Don't laugh. It's because I want them to be as happy as I am.'

Once again Stuart took her in his arms and kissed her passionately this time. 'Mmm. I don't fancy going anywhere this evening, do you?' he said twisting a tendril of her long hair around his finger.

'No, neither do I,' she answered suppressing a yawn. I'm feeling really tired.'

'Would you like me to cook tonight for a change?' When she didn't answer, he looked down at her: she was already fast asleep. He smiled, 'we look like an old married couple already' and he closed his eyes too.

* * * * * *

Chapter Thirty-Four

Two days later, Sarah Butler drove through the old rusting gates that lead to Epton Hall, feeling strange and full of trepidation. The eagles standing sentry on the gate posts seemed almost menacing and she glanced at James who was looking through the car windows as they proceeded along the uneven drive. His face too, betrayed the mixed emotions that were charging around deeply inside both of them. What were they to expect from this visit? Would they fall in love with it, or would the sheer size of the place make them want to run straight back to Vancouver?

She didn't know the answer. But she did know that she had to give this old house a chance.

She looked at James again. I wonder what's going on in his mind right now. She tried to put herself in his place, but found it impossible. Her early life had been so different from his. She had adored both her parents, her sister and her two brothers and couldn't envisage a life without any of them.

James on the other hand, had led a solitary life, almost as if he was looking for something, or someone. Could it be that he'd now found it? She looked around her and shivered slightly. It was a grey, miserable showery day. In fact, it was much more reminiscent of mid-November than summer. Is the weather always like this, she wondered? The trees in the grounds all around them seemed to have been cut in half by the mist which gave everything a peculiarly gloomy appearance. Several startled rabbits scattered in different directions as they drove by and a deer with its ears laid flat, suddenly ran from behind a tree in front of her, making her brake violently.

James grabbed hold of the sides of his seat. 'Phew that was a close one, Sarah!'

'Sorry, honey. I didn't see that one coming. We're nearly there.' She manoeuvred the unfamiliar English car around several large potholes and suddenly Epton Hall loomed menacingly before them.

'This is it James. Oh my god – will you just look at that?'

'I'm looking, honey. Wow! It's even bigger than I thought. This house has been the cause of so much heartache and now…it all belongs to us kiddo. Aren't we the lucky ones?'

'I find it incredible to think that one old lady has lived here on her own for so many years.'

'Yup, it's a sobering thought isn't it?' He suddenly laughed. 'With all this mist around, you could almost imagine Count Dracula peering at you through one of the windows. Which one do you think it is?'

'Don't James, please,' Sarah said as she climbed out of the car and walked round to let her husband out. They stood together side by side, looking up at the old house. She shivered. 'It's so cold here and isn't it supposed to be summer?'

'Yup, but I'm reliably informed that it's not always like this.'

'I'm relieved to hear it.'

A moment later, a red Porsche came round the corner. 'Good, that must be Penny Humberston,' James said. 'And it looks like Stuart and Katie are following on behind.'

'Well here goes. This is what we have been waiting for, honey.'

James didn't appear to be listening at this point. 'Now that's what I call a nice car: I wouldn't mind one like that, would you? We could certainly afford one now and just think what the boys would say if we drove up in something like that…wow.'

'It's only a car, honey.' James gave her an old-fashioned look.

'Hello both of you,' Penny Humberston said, as she climbed

elegantly out of the car. 'It was good to meet you both yesterday in my office.' She looked up at the sky. 'I'm sorry about the weather. It would have been much nicer to have seen the house in the sunshine, but at least you're seeing it at its dismal worst. Welcome to Epton Hall. Nancy Brown is here and she'll be able to answer any queries that you may have.'

'Hi Penny. Is this place for real?' James exclaimed, giving a deep-throated laugh.

'What you see, is what you get,' Penny replied.

'It seems much bigger than it did in the photographs and it looks a lot older. Come on let's go inside.' James was obviously in a hurry to view his family's ancestral home.

Sarah hesitated. Surely he wouldn't ever consider living in a place like this, she thought. 'James?' she whispered.

'Yes, honey.'

'To be perfectly honest with you, I don't like it. I don't like it at all. In fact it's scaring me to death,' she continued, holding her hand over her mouth and frantically trying to hide her reaction from the others. No wonder Katie didn't want to come back, she thought.

'Shhh. Please don't say anything detrimental until we've had an opportunity of seeing the whole house, Sarah.'

'OK,' she answered sceptically. 'I'll give it a chance, but I must say here and now that I'm not one little bit impressed. I wouldn't swap our house for this for…for anything.'

By this time, Katie and Stuart had climbed out of their car and were standing uncertainly looking up at the house. 'Stuart, I can't do it. I can't just walk in there.'

Stuart placed his arm around her shoulders. 'Katie, you can and you will so come on,' he pleaded. 'Let's get it over and done with shall we?' he insisted and they walked over to join the others.

Nancy had left the door slightly ajar. With Sarah's help,

James walked slowly up the steps and into the huge entrance hall. They immediately looked upwards.

'Oh my golly-gosh, this place must cost a fortune to heat,' Sarah said pulling her jacket collar up a little. As she walked over to the stairway, the sound of her high-heeled shoes echoed eerily and she gave a little laugh. Suddenly she stopped. 'How quaint. James do come and look at this – I just can't believe it? It's a suit of armour. Do you think that it'll fit you?'

He walked slowly over to join her. 'No, I don't think so, it's much too small. I'll have to have a larger one made for me: this guy had short legs.' James was obviously enjoying himself.

Stuart was just as amazed as the others. 'Katie darling, I see what you mean about this house. It's enormous! How on earth they ever managed to keep this running, I really don't know.'

'Well I did tell you. I know that I exaggerate sometimes, but this is real. Anyway, while you're looking around down here, I'll go and find Nancy,' Katie said looking anxiously around her. 'She'll be in the kitchen I expect.' She disappeared down a dark corridor.

'Katie seems a little on edge,' Sarah said gently touching Stuart's arm.

'Yes, she does a bit. But I suppose it's hardly surprising when you remember what happened to her in this house and that's why I decided to come with her.'

'Oh my...' Sarah looked upset and turned to her husband. 'James, what have I done? I've made the poor girl come back to the place that she feared most. How insensitive I must have seemed? And I must say that I tend to agree with her. This house is weird.'

'It's not only weird, but it's also like a rabbit warren. I wouldn't be surprised if you didn't require a map to get from one side of the house to the other,' James said looking completely bemused. He turned round to speak to Penny. 'The contents of these wooden cases here look quite old. Are they worth anything?'

'Yes, apparently a man came down from Sotheby's last week to value them: the Executors are still waiting to hear from him. As you can appreciate, there's been so much to do. It took weeks for the books to be valued and there are dozens of pictures and portraits dotted around the house that still need valuing.'

'Gee honey, this is fantastic. I've seen places like this in films, mostly gothic horror films I might add, but I never dreamt that I'd ever end up owning one.' He chuckled away amiably. 'I wonder what the boys would think of it.'

'Yes, I wonder,' Sarah answered dryly. She felt quite sure that if they were here, they'd be running riot by now.

'There are more display cases in all the reception rooms, each containing some really fine porcelain,' Penny informed them. 'I just can't imagine why this place hasn't been burgled over the years. The local 'crims' would be kicking themselves if they knew what was in here. I suppose they thought that because Marjorie Hapsworth-Cole was a recluse, that she lived in squalor.'

'Yes, I was wondering what security precautions had been taken, now that the house is empty?'

'Well, since the executors discovered that there was so much of value here, they arranged for a security alarm system to be installed. The work has now been carried out and the police will be alerted automatically if there are any intruders. Come on I'll show you the library and the study.'

'Right, lead on MacDuff.' James said, eagerly waving his walking stick in the air with a flourish.

Penny strode off towards one of the huge old oak doors. 'This is the library which held most of the book collection.'

'Just look at this old door, honey,' James said as he limped into the huge room. 'It must be hundreds of years old.'

Katie couldn't wait to get to the relative safety of Nancy's kitchen. She'd slept badly and was feeling almost sick with fear and apprehension. Nancy always managed to make her feel calmer and she could hear the clatter of crockery as she entered the room. Nancy turned round quickly on hearing her steps.

'Katie m'dear, it's so good to see you again. And thank you so much for the invitation to your wedding. My hubby won't be coming of course, it's his arthritis you see. But I'll be delighted to come.' She looked a little flustered as she said, 'The invitation was so unexpected, thank you, and I'm really looking forward to meeting your fiancé, too.'

'Oh, I'd forgotten that you haven't met Stuart yet and Nancy, I feel that I know you so well now…and…and I don't have many relations, so that's why I want you to be there.'

'And I will be. I've even bought myself a new outfit and a hat,' she said with a girlish giggle. 'It's ages since I've been to a wedding – they're such lovely affairs. How are you feeling now? Miss Humberston told me all about what happened to you when you were in Canada. I could hardly believe it.'

'I can hardly believe it myself. Yes, I'm a lot better, now Nancy, thank you. It was all a bit of a shock.'

'You can say that again. I came over all peculiar when I realised what Master Harold could have done to you all. Who'd have thought it?' She shook her head, tut-tutting quietly to herself. 'I'll make you all a nice cup of tea before we look around upstairs. Do they drink tea in Canada?'

'Yes they do. That would be lovely Nancy thank you. You do still want me to come round the house too, don't you?'

'Well, if you wouldn't mind m'dear. You know them and I don't. It would be a big help.'

'Yes, I suppose you're right.'

'Look Katie,' Nancy interrupted. 'I think I know why you're

dragging your heels young lady, but not walking around the place with us isn't going to cure it. This is just a house, no matter what you may feel about it. I've worked 'ere for years and I've never ever felt uncomfortable, not for one moment I haven't. It's just old stones and mortar that's all it is, and…'

'Yes?'

'All the ghosts are friendly,' Nancy said suppressing a giggle.

A look of abject horror spread over Katie's face. 'What do you mean ghosts? Nobody ever said anything about ghosts. Please say that you're having me on, Nancy.'

'Oh years and years ago people made up stories about Epton Hall. After all, large old houses are all supposed to be haunted aren't they? But all I know is, I've never seen one.'

'Well that's a relief.'

'So, there's nothing really to stop you coming round the house with us, is there?'

'OK Nancy, you win.'

'Good.'

Nancy placed a beautifully embroidered tray cloth on to a tray, picked up a silver teapot and some blue and white bone china cups and saucers and arranged them neatly on top. She stared at them sadly. 'This was Mrs. Hapsworth-Coles' favourite tea service. Every afternoon she would have her tea and a few sandwiches – mostly cucumber I might add – in the drawing room. She did the same things, day after day, year after year and now…? Do you think that Mr. and Mrs. Butler will like the house?'

'I really don't know, Nancy.'

Nancy picked up the tray and walked to the door. 'And do you think that they'll actually come and live here?' She stopped and turned round. 'I must admit to feeling nervous meself dear, but for a totally different reason. It's giving me quite a funny feeling meeting Mr. and Mrs. Butler like this. He's Mr. Gerald's son and I haven't got used to that yet. Come on. We'd both better get on with it.' She walked quickly through the door.

They all went into the drawing room to drink their tea, and Katie sipped hers with little enthusiasm. If only I hadn't come, she thought. She looked around the room: it was large and square and had been the hub of the Hapsworth-Cole family's home. Several silver framed photographs of the children grinned happily at them as they sat in the old armchairs. Marjorie Hapsworth-Cole had spent many years sitting alone in this room, with only her memories for company. Katie shivered. She felt uncomfortable and couldn't wait to get the whole thing over and done with.

'Shall we look round the house now?' she said hopefully.

'Why yes of course,' James said, struggling to his feet. 'Nancy would you like to lead the way?'

It seemed to take for ever to walk around the rambling old building. Nancy gave them all a running commentary about each room and how it had fitted in with the Hapsworth-Cole family life over the years. It was generally agreed that they wouldn't look at all the rooms, especially those in the eastern wing of the house.

'They haven't been used for years,' she told them.

Every now and again, James had to stop for a rest: he just couldn't keep up with such a hectic pace. Nevertheless, his face wore a look of dogged determination, as though he didn't want to miss anything. Finally Nancy slowed down.

'Well m'dears, there's only the main attic room left now. Do you want to see it? There are a few more stairs to climb unfortunately Mr. Butler.'

'Do call me James, it's much easier. Of course I want to see the attic, Nancy. As far as I'm concerned, it's the most important room in the house.'

'James, are you quite certain that you want to go up there?'

Sarah asked, looking at him with concern. 'It's important that you don't overdo things.' His face looked pale and his eyes showed the signs of the fatigue which had plagued him since his accident and the trauma in the hospital.

'I'm OK Sarah. I can rest afterwards.' He turned round to speak to Katie. 'Perhaps you could show us where the letters were found? I don't have to tell you how much it means to me?'

'Well, I...I...' she stuttered. Her heart began to pound.

'If I say please, will you do it, for me? Please Katie.'

'Yes James, of course I'll show you.'

Nancy walked up the final flight of stairs which lead to the old oak door to the attic and the others followed closely behind. 'Please be careful as you come up, because the lighting isn't at all good up here I'm afraid and the carpet has seen better days too.'

Katie deliberately waited until the others had climbed the stairs, thereby delaying the moment that she most dreaded. She remembered the last time that she'd walked up these same stairs. Harold Hapsworth-Cole had been following her, hadn't he?

Stuart always seemed to be able to read what was going on in Katie's mind and waited at the bottom of the stairs with her. 'Well,' he said placing his arm around her waist. 'You've made it so far: there are only a few more stairs and you're there!'

'I've been dreading this bit.'

'One small step for mankind and...' Stuart said with a hint of devilment in his eyes.

'Stuart, please stop poking fun at me. You weren't here.'

'Sorry, I won't say another word.'

'Good,' she said and immediately started to climb the stairs. But for once her overactive imagination didn't conjure up anything: not even the cold steely and evil eyes of her hated protagonist. Harold was dead and the house now belonged to James and Sarah. Her heart started to beat like a drum as she neared the top and her legs seemed to be made of jelly. Suddenly, she found herself standing in front of the door and heard the familiar creaking floorboard and she realised that she felt…absolutely nothing.

Nancy had been right. It was only an old house and there was nothing to fear. All the ghosts, perceived or otherwise, had simply flown away.

Katie was left with an all-pervading feeling of sadness when she walked into the attic. This room epitomised the sorrow and despair that the Hapsworth-Cole family had suffered in this house over the years. Would James and Sarah knowing what had happened here in the past, ever be able to live here, she wondered? One look at Sarah's face gave her the answer.

She was staring blankly around the room and it was patently obvious that it didn't mean anything to her. In reality, this was just a dirty, musty-smelling room crammed full of old odds and ends of a bygone era. There was nothing here now that could link their present life in Vancouver to this sad old mouldering mansion.

James walked slowly over to the window and stood for a while looking out of the area of window cleaned by Katie during her imprisonment here. Katie wondered what was going through his mind. Did he really believe that his family could move into this house and carry on their lives here? Somehow she doubted it. Sarah went over to the window to join him and grabbed hold of his hand. Between them they looked out at the acres of woodland and farmland spread out before them.

'Sarah honey, this estate is simply beautiful. Look at it: it is English countryside at its best. Thousands of people have worked this land over the centuries to make it what it is today and it all belongs to us, but somehow I don't feel that it truly belongs to us. Do you?'

'No James, I don't,' Sarah replied in a whisper. Neither of them said anything else for several minutes. It was as if the other occupants of the room didn't exist.

Penny was the first to break the long silence. 'Well, that's it. You've seen the house now, but not the rest of the estate. That would take some time and I don't feel that you are yet fit enough to undertake this. What do you think? And the big question is, do you like the house enough to want to come and live here?'

James didn't answer Penny's question immediately, instead his brow creased with concentration as he looked around the attic again. He examined the bookcase where Katie had found the letters which had had such a profound affect upon their lives. He rocked the old horse and it creaked eerily in the silence of the room and he examined the blow tube questioningly. 'What is this?'

Nancy joined him. 'It used to be used a lot in days gone by. Now we have mobiles and telephones. It's a kind of speaking tube.'

'No kidding! How does it work?'

'Well you blow into it and it makes a sound downstairs in what used to be the servants' quarters, but is now my kitchen. They used to have similar things on ships. Your Navy-serving ancestors would have been very familiar with things like this.'

'Wow. Look honey.' Even Sarah was fascinated by it and they both giggled when after trying to blow into it, they both sneezed loudly.

Eventually, they both walked over to where the other three were standing. 'You asked me what I thought about the house, Penny,' James said. 'I know that we haven't yet looked at the gardens, the old stables and the estate in general, but...but I'm sorry, nothing would induce me to bring my family over here to live in this old house,' he said quietly. Sarah reached out and patted his arm.

'Well, if you're sure, we'll have to discuss what is to be done with it over the next few days.'

'Yes, Penny, I'm sure. We are both sure.'

'But wouldn't you like to go back to your hotel and think it all over. It's a really big decision for you to make.'

'That's it, and because it is such a big decision, I've decided that the answer has to be no. I know my father must have loved this place and perhaps once upon a time it was beautiful, but I'm afraid that it's not for us. I don't even have to ask Sarah for her views – I can see the answer written all over her face. I've already therefore made up my mind to sell Epton Hall and most of its contents.'

'Right,' Penny said looking rather disappointed. 'We will have to accelerate everything value-wise and see where we go from there.'

Katie looked over to where Nancy was standing and saw her face begin to crack as she sobbed, 'Oh my poor old lady and master Gerald and the boys, oohh.' Unrestrained tears ran down Nancy's face as she looked first at one of them and then the other. Katie raced over to her and tried to console her.

'Nancy, don't please. There's nothing you can do about it. James and Sarah have a life out in Vancouver, so please don't blame them.' She thought her heart would break when she saw how upset Nancy was.

'Oh, master James and you Sarah, I'm so sorry, but this whole house has been my life and I can't imagine a life without it,' she sobbed.

'I'm sorry too, Nancy, but it is the end of an era, or a saga if you like. The Hapsworth-Cole saga,' he said with a smile. 'Come on, dry your tears, but you never know there might eventually be another family here, who knows.'

'Yes, master James. You're right,' she sniffed.

James turned to Penny. 'There are of course, a few things that I'd like to keep for purely sentimental reasons, but the rest well,' he said shaking his head sadly. 'My one regret is that I never met my father. I'm sure that we'd have got on well, but it just wasn't meant to be. My poor mother, Amy, died with his name on her lips, you know. Even after all those years, she still loved him, so he must have been a really special fella. Are you coming down stairs now, Sarah honey? I'm beginning to feel rather tired.'

'Yes James. I've seen enough and thank you for not asking me to make this decision for you. It could only have come from you. Although I must say, that I was praying that you would come to the same conclusions I did.'

They walked out through the attic door and the others followed them in silence.

* * * * * *

Chapter Thirty-Five

A shaft of sunlight pierced Katie's eyelids. She opened her eyes slowly. The sun was shining brightly through the gap in the curtains. She yawned sleepily and then remembered that it was her Wedding Day.

Her long ivory satin wedding dress was hanging from a ledge on the top of the fitted wardrobe on one side of the bedroom. The sun also shone on the tiny satin bows which dotted the scalloped hem of the skirt. It picked out the small dainty buttons on the cuffs and the pearls which had been so painstakingly sewn on to the bodice. Mary Ashington, a local seamstress and a good friend of Brenda's, had spent many hours making it. Katie was delighted with the result.

On a small boudoir chair under the window, lay a short veil attached to a circlet of tiny white satin flowers, each interspersed with pearls and tiny pale green leaves: it was exquisite. Katie stared at it wistfully: if only her parents had been able to witness her marriage to Stuart today, she thought.

She tried to picture what it would have been like to have walked down the aisle with her hand coiled firmly and lovingly around her father's arm. He would have looked down at her with pride and love and told her that she was a beautiful bride. She pictured her mother sitting in the front pew of the church and wearing the blue hat that she'd worn to a friend's wedding some years before. She was smiling happily, but at the same time she was holding a little lace handkerchief up to her nose and…

Katie's eyes began to mist over with emotion and gradually allowed the picture to fade, she really couldn't have the luxury of dwelling on such sadness today of all days.

Brian was such a dear. Katie knew that she would feel proud to walk down the aisle on his arm and that she must put all morbid thoughts completely out of her mind. They were all lost paper dreams now and only the reality of the day remained.

The mobile phone on a small table next to the bed suddenly rang. She reached over and picked it up. It was Stuart.

'How are you Katie darling?' he said lovingly. 'I missed you so much last night.' He'd spent the night in the Dog and Pheasant, because she'd insisted that it would be bad luck for her to see him on the morning of their wedding day.

'I missed you too. Do you know that the sun is shining?'

'Yes, of course it is. I ordered it especially for you.'

'Stuart?'

'Yes?'

'Today is a new beginning for both of us, isn't it?'

'Yes, it is my darling.'

'And and I just know that the future is going to be wonderful for both of us.'

'No regrets?'

'None at all. How about you?'

'Ditto,' he replied. 'Look I must go now. I'll see you in the church and don't you dare be late: I'll be waiting for you.'

'I won't be late, I promise. Nothing is going to spoil this day for us, Stuart.'

Katie made a beautifully serene bride and everyone considered the ceremony to be a happy and moving experience. With the sound of the traditional Wedding March ringing in their ears, Stuart and his new wife Katie walked out of the church arm in arm, their faces radiant with happiness. They walked together as man and wife down the old worn steps of the church and stood as one, whilst the photographer went busily about his task of organising family and friends, to form a tableau around them.

When he'd finished, Katie picked out a face in the crowd. It was Helen and she had her arm closely entwined with that of a rather tall, quite good looking man of about forty-five, with short greying hair. He was looking down at her in obvious adoration. Katie smiled. Her gaze took her towards the happy, smiling faces of Brenda and Brian. They looked so good together, she thought.

Next to them stood Nancy and she actually looked a little lost, which wasn't surprising when Katie remembered how upset she'd been that day when James and Sarah had decided not to keep Epton Hall. She remembered the look on her face when James had told her about a generous sum of money which was to be put aside for her when the house was eventually sold. He had said that it in no way would compensate or make up for all her years of devoted service to the family, but it would in some way, make their decision not to live there, a little easier for her. Nancy was wearing a pale green straw hat and a green belted dress and she was holding a handkerchief up to her face. Dear, dear Nancy, Katie thought. I've only ever seen her wearing her pale blue nylon overall and she looks quite different. We must keep in touch.

Further along the line, she saw James and Sarah. James looked a little tired. It had been a gruelling and emotional time for him. He'd seen where his family had lived, loved and died. He'd come here to try to find answers, but only the questions still remained. They were due to fly back to Vancouver tomorrow. Katie knew that neither of them would ever have been happy living here in England, even though their financial future was now secure. But they had all sworn to keep in touch, because they'd been through far too much together, not to have done so.

A black limousine drew up outside the church and Stuart looked down at her. 'Well Catherine Angela Wells, the deed is done and now your carriage awaits you.' He gestured towards the waiting car with mock gallantry.

'Thank you husband mine,' she replied coquettishly, eagerly playing her part. She carefully lifted the long train which was attached to the back of her wedding dress and climbed into the car. She had difficulty fitting it all in, as it took up most of the back seat and she giggled hopelessly. Stuart had to climb in from the other side. He too laughed as he did battle with the material which was threatening to engulf him.

Once they were seated, the driver handed them a glass of champagne each. Stuart turned to Katie, with his glass held high. 'Here's to us my darling girl and to the rest of our lives together.'

'Yes, Stuart, my love. Here's to us.'

The car sped off towards the Dog and Pheasant, where the wedding breakfast was awaiting them.

The rest of their day went happily and smoothly and the time eventually came when they were due to leave.

Katie was standing in one of the upstairs rooms in the old hotel, which had been set aside for the wedding party and was carefully caressing her beautiful wedding dress. She hung it lovingly on a hook on the wall and examined her reflection in the full length mirror on the wardrobe. She now wore a pale blue dress made of silk that floated around her as she moved. It was fashionably short and showed off her slim and shapely legs. She picked up her cream coloured straw hat and placed it on her head. It had a broad rim and a pale blue ribbon that hung down the back.

'Well, what do you think?'

'You look absolutely beautiful, dear,' Brenda said as she looked at Katie's reflection in the full length mirror.

Katie turned round and on an impulse threw her arms around Brenda's neck. 'I don't know how to thank you for all you've done.'

'Katie darling, you must know that it's been the greatest pleasure of my life. I always wanted a daughter and to me, you're the next best thing and if you don't stop hugging me soon, you'll have me in floods of tears.'

The door burst open and Stuart rushed into the room. 'Are you ready, only the car's waiting outside for us?' He stared at her for a moment. 'You look so wonderful in that outfit.'

'She certainly does,' Brenda said nodding in agreement.

'Thanks for everything Brenda. You've been a real friend to both of us,' Stuart said, giving her a hug. She just stood there with tears in her eyes.

'Go on, off with you, before I turn into a blubbering heap. Brian will wonder what's happened to me.'

'I don't think that he'll be too surprised to find out where you've been Brenda,' Katie said.

A few minutes later, they stood together by the car saying their final goodbyes. Stuart's parents and Brenda were the last to come over.

Diana Wells embraced Katie and Stuart with tears in the corners of her eyes. 'I know you two are going to be happy together and please come and see us the minute you come home from your honeymoon. We've got lots to talk about haven't we?' she said warmly.

Stuart's father shook him by the hand, saying 'Good luck, son. You've got a lovely young wife, so make sure you look after her and remember what I said to you the other week.'

'Yes Dad, I will. We've sorted everything out in our minds and from my point of view, I couldn't be happier about it.'

'Good. You two have no money problems at the start of your life together and a lot of couples could never even dream of being so lucky. As I said before, your mother and I would have given our back teeth to have the kind of start you are having. So go off and enjoy yourselves.'

Katie could see that Brenda was itching to talk to them both. 'Do take care Katie dear,' she said. 'Have a wonderful time and

Brian and I will see you when you get back.' Unrestrained tears now fell silently down Brenda's face as Brian joined in.

'Goodbye "bonny Kate, the prettiest Kate in Christendom".'

'Brian!' Katie laughed. 'Have you been talking to Stuart?'

'No, honestly. Sorry, it's my bookish background, you see. I just like the name Kate, but I do like Katie as well. I know everything has been said, but I have to put in my two pennies worth, don't I. I wish you god speed and a life together full of happiness and sunshine. And I must say that looking at the two of you, my wishes can't fail to come true.' Brian's voice began to break as he put his arms around Katie in an enormous bear hug.

Brenda gave her a final hug, saying 'Goodbye my love.'

Before finally climbing into the car beside Stuart, Katie threw her bouquet to Helen, who caught it cleanly. 'Thank you Katie,' she said giving her a knowing look.

'Bye Helen, see you when we get back.'

The car moved off slowly. They both waved until they could no longer see the quaint little hotel and the eager, happy crowd of people who were standing in front of it. Their wedding day had been perfect and Katie felt deliriously happy. Stuart took her in his arms and kissed her. 'And then there were two,' he said with deep passion showing in his eyes.

Katie smiled.

They had both decided not to go back to Vancouver for their honeymoon, because it held far too many painful memories that only time could heal. Instead they had chosen somewhere peaceful: a place where they could while away their time together and try to forget everything that had happened.

They flew off together to a distant warm exotic island, where tiny waves rippled onto a light golden shore and tall palm trees swayed in a warm, sultry breeze. They sunbathed and dreamt together on the beach underneath an umbrella of coconut palm leaves, and gazed deeply into one another's eyes as brightly coloured birds called to each other as they flew overhead.

There was a little hut…and the sound of gentle music was wafting lazily towards them, as the sun gradually slipped further and further downwards and westwards, before finally disappearing gently into the sea…

✻ ✻ ✻ ✻ ✻ ✻

To all, to each, a fair goodnight,
And pleasing dreams, and slumbers light!
(Sir Walter Scott – 1771-1832)

THE EPILOGUE

The following article appeared in the Epton Herald a few months later:

"Epton Hall, a part-medieval mansion set in hundreds of acres of beautiful Sussex countryside, and situated midway between Anston and Epton, has been sold. The house was put up for sale on November 3rd by Private Treaty. The house remained empty following the death of Mrs. Marjorie Hapsworth-Cole, earlier this year. She was the widow of Captain Gerald Hapsworth-Cole who was believed to have died in a mysterious boating accident in 1953, along with his two young sons. Their bodies were never found.

The Hapsworth-Cole family and Epton Hall gained even more notoriety recently, when the ownership of the Estate was keenly contested by the remaining members of the family. Mr. James Hapsworth-Cole Butler, the only surviving relative, finally inherited the whole estate after the untimely death of his cousin, Harold. Mr. Butler has since returned to his home in Vancouver, Canada.

It has been disclosed that it will now be used as an hotel with conference and equestrian facilities. We understand that planning approval has been granted for renovation work to be carried out on the building and the estate in general. The actual work will commence some time in the New Year.

A local action group, calling themselves 'The Epton and Anston Preservation Society', recently criticised the new owners following the publication of the plans. Regarding this criticism, a spokesperson representing the consortium that has acquired these premises, has reiterated that Epton Hall will be renovated "...in complete harmony with the spirit of the house and the surrounding countryside".

We understand that the work is expected to take about two years to complete and will cost something in excess of £15 million."

* * * * * *